Woven in the Mist

Woven in the Mist

by

Carole Lehr Johnson

Published in Shreveport, Louisiana, by Ink Map Press
www.inkmappress.com

Cover Design by Victoria Davies (vikncharlie on Fiverr.com)
Interior Design by Morgan Tarpley Smith (morgantarpleysmith.com)
Map by Artist Monica Bruenjes (artistmonica.com)
Cover Photos courtesy of the author

Scripture quotations are from the King James Version of the Bible.

This is a work of fiction. Names, characters, places, and incidents either are the product of the author's imagination or are used fictitiously. Any resemblance to actual persons, living or dead, events, or locales is entirely coincidental.

ISBN 978-1-952928-36-9
ISBN 978-1-952928-37-6 (ebook)

Printed in the United States of America

To Morgan Tarpley Smith

*Thank you for following God's prompting to walk into my office nearly sixteen years ago. You have been more than a friend, writing partner, encourager, and publisher.
The list is long.*

And to Mellanie Book Randall

*Thank you for sharing your amazing daughter with me.
You raised her right!*

Books by Carole Lehr Johnson

NOVELS

Permelia Cottage

A Place in Time

The Burning Sands

Of the Past and Eternity

Woven in the Mist

NOVELLAS

Christmas at Permelia Cottage

SPECIAL COLLECTIONS

Seasons of the Past

N
W
E
S
Moray Firth
Hidden Glen
Freuchie Castle
Castle Deveron
River Ness
Loch Lomond
North Sea
Firth of Forth
Edinburgh

Chapter One

Castle Deveron
Aberdeenshire, Scotland
May 1710

What lay ahead would be for God to elect.

Lady Isabel Stewart's disclosure echoed in Muirie's mind and heart while she stood in the castle gardens, her birthday mere months away. The words gave Muirie pause and gratitude regarding her age of seven and ten. Many lasses wed years younger than herself, yet she had not been forced to do so—a kindness to someone in her position.

She shuddered. Time was, in truth, coming toward such an event. Given her status in the household, marriage was the sole prospect as she was not a member of the family and neither a servant.

Muirie shook away the doom-filled musings and returned

to the brightly hued, perfumed flowers before her. She snipped large purple blooms of a many-petaled rose and brought it to her nose to inhale the sweet scent. It resembled the flower woven into one of the embroidered panels hanging on the wall in Lady Stewart's parlor, a tapestry she had long admired.

The lady had promised to complete the story woven in thread once she removed the others from the chest. There were apparently many more, but because there was no room to hang them all in the small chamber, they were stored for safekeeping.

Muirie tucked the glorious flowers into her basket, continuing to gather more roses and other plants—colorful blooms and foliage alike. When she had collected enough to fill several vessels, she rose and walked past the stables to a bench facing the castle's entrance.

Taking stock of the cuttings, movement caught her attention, and she glanced to see Cormac Stewart amble from the stables. He straightened his shirt and ran a hand through his tousled, raven hair, a slight smirk on his bonny face. Although the way she perceived him was more in the way of a brother, he held a certain *je ne sais quoi* about him. The phrase was one she recently learned from the tutor Lord Stewart secured for her and Cormac. It rolled off the tongue pleasantly and described Cormac with accuracy.

A few moments later, Beathag, who was a servant at the castle, strolled in Cormac's wake, straightening her garments. Muirie's spirit waned in the shadow of their conduct. Many times she had warned them of their behavior. There would be consequences. No good could come of it.

Lord, please touch their hearts to repent of their actions.

She cared for both—Cormac as a brother and Beathag as a friend.

Cormac approached, his pleased countenance fading at her expression of censure. "I know, Muiriel Stewart, what travels through your head." He dropped to sit on the bench and slung an arm around her shoulders.

"Brother, ye are a torment to my patience. Ye know not what ye do—to yourself nor to Beathag. 'Tis not seemly." She shrugged off his arm. "Ye do her an injustice. The end result of your behavior is . . ." Her glare served as a warning. "More so that it is a sin before God."

His exasperated sigh brought her pain. "We desire a small measure of enjoyment in our baleful lives, sweet sister."

"Though I am not your sister by blood, I care for ye as a brother and want nothing but the best for ye. Please do not continue this dallying."

He burst into laughter. "Sister, ye are a mere few months my elder, yet ye speak as an old woman."

Muirie stood with force, the basket of flowers spilling at their feet. "Cormac Stewart, ye are a thoughtless brute." She knelt and snatched up the cuttings, tossing them into the basket, heart pricking with injury.

Cormac dropped to his knees and helped gather the flowers. "I am sorry, Muirie." He took her hand and kissed it. "Truly I am."

Muirie jerked from his grasp and stared into his dark eyes. "Each time I admonish ye about your misdeeds, ye utter the same thing. When shall ye learn?" She choked on a sob. "I fear for ye and Beathag." Her voice lowered, and she glanced over her shoulder, the rose-scented breeze soothing fragile emotions. She lowered her voice. "Mayhap Beathag becomes with child. Your parents shall not allow ye to marry her."

He swallowed hard. "Ye know it shall not occur, Muirie."

"How do ye know this?" She held his gaze, not releasing him, praying the reality of it would soak into his heart and soul. Instead, he rose and stalked away.

Muirie placed the remaining flowers in the basket and went in search of Beathag to see if she could instill some sense into her. She found her near the stone bakehouse.

"Ye must see the folly in your time spent with Cormac." Muirie's quiet voice held more power than if raised. She wanted Beathag to hear with her heart, not her ears. She held her friend by the shoulders, imploring her to listen, just as she had held Cormac's gaze.

Beathag did not waver, the firm set of her jaw holding fast, yet Muirie saw the affection of a friend in the depths of her eyes.

Muirie pulled Beathag behind the bakehouse where they could find privacy. A few sprinkles of rain dotted Beathag's dark shawl, yet she remained still under Muirie's grasp, unyielding.

"Muirie!" a woman's voice called, and she peered toward the corner of the bakehouse where the cook beckoned her. "My lady be seeking ye, mistress."

Muirie quickly hugged Beathag and whispered, "Ye are my dear friend. I wish ye to come to no harm. Please consider this."

Beathag nodded, eyes now shining with unshed tears.

Muirie dropped her hands, turned, and trotted toward the beckoning voice—and the summons of her kind guardian.

ଓଃ৪ଠ

"My dear, Lord and Lady Lamont are the best of friends. We must prepare and present a warm welcome."

Muirie stared at Lady Stewart as she relayed the news of impending guests, wondering why she was so nervous. Of a surety Cormac's schoolmates would not require as much attention as the lady directed.

Though she was still uncertain how Lady Stewart came to be her guardian, the woman had been like a mother to her, and she would not disappoint her.

"Aye, my lady. I shall do all ye instruct." She curtsied and departed to attend to her duties.

Muirie could not imagine why their visit was of such consequence, yet she would not fail her mistress.

Upon entering the kitchen, she cringed to find Cormac perched on the bench at the hefty worktable in the center of the large chamber watching Beathag work. Her friend wore a rough, flour-dusted apron over a grey dress, her slender work-worn hands deftly manipulating the dough into smooth loaves.

The yeasty smell met Muirie's senses with enough potency to elicit a growl from her stomach. So absorbed with caring for Lady Stewart's directions, she had forgotten to break her fast. Everyone's regard went to Muirie upon her entrance, Cormac's and Beathag's expressions holding a mixture of guilt and rebellion.

How they could carry on in the presence of others was an amazement. Should their actions reach Lord or Lady Stewart, there would be a high price to pay. The Stewart heir was to wed someone of consequence, not a lowly kitchen maid.

Muirie's conscience burned for thinking of Beathag in such a way, yet truth was truth. Her friend's position was not much better than her own. Her heart would not be allowed to choose.

"Muirie!" Cormac's sharp voice cut through her thoughts like the knife Mistress Picken used to slice meat at the opposite end of the table. "Ye look as if ye swallowed one of the caup snails ye pick off the herbs."

Beathag chuckled. "Ye have that look about ye, lass, afore ye tell Cormac and me to hide from one anither."

Her words brought a loud guffaw from Cormac, and Muirie's face flamed with indignation. "I only tell ye this for your own good."

Mistress Picken's lips pursed, revealing the cook was about to share wisdom.

Muirie forestalled the speech by speaking first. "I am unable to change the way I look when the two of ye vex me to tears. When ye are in the same chamber, all can see what ye are about. 'Tis written upon your faces." She looked at the cook for support and received a slight dip of her chin as approval.

Cormac and Beathag had the good graces to appear remorseful—if only for a moment.

"Beathag," Muirie whispered. "I do not want to see ye hurt. Ye can never wed Cormac."

The words had just released when Beathag's expression crumpled like bits of dough dropped to the floor. Wide eyes glistened, then closed, a tear traveling down her cheek to stain the front of her apron. "I ken." The murmur was meant for Muirie's ears alone.

Although Cormac likely did not hear the quiet words, he rose and stood shoulder-to-shoulder with the maid and glanced at Muirie. "Ye must stop your preaching!" He wrapped an arm around Beathag and brought his mouth to her ear, whispering words Muirie could not discern. The maid brushed away the tear and gave him a hesitant grin.

Heart hurting at the shared moment between them, Muirie longed for them to be happy, yet there could be no path to such joy.

A warm hand rested on her shoulder, and she turned to peer into the face of Mistress Picken. Silver-streaked red hair peeked from under her cap, throat bobbing on a swallow. She tugged Muirie from the couple and out the door into the yard.

"My dear, while I ken what ye be about telling them their fate should they not heed your warning, I cannot help suppose the time has come for ye to stop."

Muirie's jaw tensed, and she stared at the kindly woman. She opened her mouth to respond, but the cook lifted a palm.

"Say naught more. Let them do as they wish. Ye have preached to them enough. If they have not learnt anything thus far, they never shall." Mistress Picken patted her cheek. "Sometime 'tis best to leave things be. They shall lie in the bed they make. Ye are not responsible."

Muirie disagreed but nodded. Why did Mistress Picken not

understand she only wanted the best for them? They walked a dangerous path that could only lead to heartache—and as an orphan with no knowledge of her past, Muirie knew a fair share about heartache.

Chapter Two

Loch Lomond, Scotland
April 1603

Scents mingled and wafted toward Sorcha, kneading dough at the long table in the center of the chamber, the roiling in her stomach growing stronger. The babe had made his or her presence known much since the battle, giving a continued sense of dread as if an omen. Castle Falloch's kitchen bustled with morning activity as the cook and kitchen maids baked bannocks and stirred porridge in the iron pots suspended above the low fire.

She brushed aside the morbid notion, thankful for the protection of her brother-in-law and his kin. Security for their babe was to be found with Clan Gregor, and should the child be a lad, he would be nephew to the clan chief and in line to one day be chieftain.

The thought of being sheltered brought much comfort, and she soon found herself humming a tune that John favored, his warm smile on her mind.

Footfalls sounded in the passage to the kitchen—a man's steps. The door opened, and Evan MacDonald's tall form filled the space, his grey eyes seeking Sorcha.

He took several long strides and halted at the end of the table. "How are ye, lass?"

The mysterious set of his jaw took Sorcha aback. Uncertain why, she shuddered as if an icy wind had blown across the loch and into the chamber. She moved to stand in front of him and examined his eyes more intently.

"I am well, but ye do not appear so. Have ye brought news?"

His throat convulsed with a hard swallow. "Aye." He placed his hands upon her shoulders, his gaze holding hers with tenderness. "Aye," he repeated. "'Tis not an easy thing to share."

Her heart turned to the scene when she watched John die on that bitter February day. Could this telling hurt more? "*Evan.*"

"I have just come from the Gregor . . ." His jaw clenched for a moment before continuing. "The king issued a proscription against Clan Gregor."

Sorcha blinked, not comprehending what it meant, yet the look in Evan's gaze told it was most dire. She nodded slowly in silence, with no words to inquire.

Evan leaned closer until they were a handsbreadth apart.

"Sorcha, amongst other things, the unborn shall not take the MacGregor name, and those keeping the name shall be put to death. Nae more than four clansmen shall meet at a time, and bear no weapon, save an unpointed knife to cut their victuals. To kill a MacGregor is not a crime, yet something to be encouraged. MacGregors must take other surnames or risk the ire of anyone who sees fit to measure out judgement."

Clara gasped, and their gazes swung toward Evan's sister. She covered her mouth with both hands, tears forming in her blue eyes.

Evan gave a sad look, released Sorcha, and strode to his sister, gathering her into his arms, his head resting on hers. "Shush, sister. I shall take ye somewhere safe. Dinnae fash yourself."

He watched Sorcha over his sister's head and gave an imperceptible nod. She licked her lips and tried to offer a slight smile, feeling nothing but fear. The silence engulfing the chamber held only sniffles and soft sobs from the cook and maids.

A loud commotion broke their mournful quiet, and a lad from the stables burst into the kitchen, panting from his exertion. "Evan! Evan! Ye must come at once."

Evan released his sister and came to the lad. "What say ye, Marcus? What has ye in a hurry scurry?"

"Campbells, sir. They be carryin' halberschois, powaixes, twa-handit swordies, bowis and arrowis," he stopped to draw in a breath, "and with hagbutia and pistoletis."

Evan's eyebrows lifted. "Aye, are ye certain, lad? 'Tis a powerful load of weapons, to be sure." He slapped the lad's back good-naturedly, and Sorcha heard distress in his voice.

"Aye, sir. 'Tis truth."

Sorcha handed the boy a mug of small ale, staying beside Evan. "Marcus, have ye told anyone else?"

He gulped the drink and shook his head, sending drops of liquid into the air.

Evan led the boy to a bench at the long table and spoke to his sister. "Clara, feed the lad and keep him company while I see what is aboot." He sent Sorcha an encouraging smile and left.

Fear surging in her heart, Sorcha placed a protective palm on her stomach and watched Evan depart.

✂

The MacGregors kept the Campbells back, and they sent a lad through the secret passage to request aid from their allied clans, including the MacDonalds, holding them off until they arrived. Sorcha could not watch the terror filling the area surrounding the castle. Screams, clanging metal, and shouts of attack filled the hours.

A small silence hung. Rushing to the window, she peered into the inner bailey to find the MacGregor men talking in groups as the sudden sound of hoofbeats filled the space. Cries from outside the castle roared.

Evan stood tall and strong, his large-bow in his hand, the tip resting at his feet.

Their allies had arrived and suddenly the battle began, many of the MacGregor warriors leaving the castle to aid their saviors.

Clara came to stand beside her, their shoulders touching. Clara trembled, and Sorcha placed a comforting arm around her.

"All shall be well. The men must have us be strong, so we may care for the wounded."

"Aye." She felt Clara's shudder. "And for the dead."

Sorcha had no words, for she too knew that pain. Clara had lost her love—the man she was to wed—in a skirmish against the Colquhouns who were raiding their cattle.

The day ended with the invaders tucking tail and running, the MacGregor's triumphant. The allied clansmen entered the castle, the Gregor in the lead, not a single soul on their side had been lost. There were many wounds to see to, though none so bad as to lose their life.

Sorcha offered a prayer of thanksgiving to God for His providence.

☙❧

Sorcha welcomed the morning light into the small chamber to illuminate the cloth she deftly worked the needle through, missing the tambour frame John had built to form wall hangings upon. As a girl she had watched a tambourer work dreamlike images and longed to make such wonderful likenesses to hang upon the walls of the cottage she shared with her parents.

She followed her mother's teaching of embroidery. Though unlike the women in the village, she did not make flowers. Her work was of pastoral scenes of people and interactions such as the lambings, shearings, and farming—the goings on of everyday life.

A dream from her youth caused Sorcha to begin telling the story of their family through cloth and thread. She would capture one year of their lives within a small panel in hope to pass the pieces to her daughter along with the skill.

A tear dotted the crimson thread worked into the design. In the early days following the Battle of Glen Fruin in February, Sorcha had started a new panel chronicling the death of her husband. The tip of a finger traced the outline of the blood she stitched next to the body of John. More tears followed, and she brought the scene to her lips and kissed the image of the man she could no longer touch.

Gentle snow upon the battlefield gave the impression of quiet peace, the cries of the wounded and dying shattering the thought as John fell. Evan was at his back and swung to find him collapsing to the frozen earth. John's brother, the Gregor, caught the moment from across the glen and raced toward them, and others followed. They encircled John and Evan, their strong backs surrounding the pair.

Evan knelt beside his friend—his brother in arms—and Sorcha watched as their heads met. Although she could not see their lips moving, she knew they shared something that fateful day. The moment seemed to go on for a long time, and Evan wrapped John's long plaid around him and laid his head on the ground. He stood and roared an oath and broke into the fighting alongside the MacGregors and his kinsmen.

The last thing she remembered before her view gave way to darkness was the falling snow shifting into a finely woven mist like a veil upon the land.

The rustling of a woman's skirts brought her to the present, and she glanced up to find Clara standing over her.

"My dear friend, ye must not weary yourself over what cannot be changed." Clara smoothed Sorcha's hair and peered down at the empty cradle beside them. "Ye must be happy or else your babe mayhap be born afflicted when he comes in a few months' time."

Sorcha reached to caress the side of the cradle, nodding in response to the declaration. It was a truth, and watery eyes peered up to see Clara through a haze.

"Thank ye, Clara. I shall try." She smiled up at her friend, older by but a few years.

A gentle knock interrupted their commiseration, and Clara opened the door. Evan entered, hands clasped behind his back. He acknowledged Sorcha with a subtle nod and leaned toward his sister, softly murmuring something that Sorcha could not hear. The reddish streaks in his hair glimmered in the morning light.

Clara stepped back and allowed Evan to stand before Sorcha. "I shall return with food and drink for the two of ye."

Once Clara departed, Evan brought his hands around to reveal a bunch of dried heather. "I know 'tis not fresh, yet a bit of the scent is still noticeable."

Hesitantly, Sorcha accepted the offering and sniffed it. "Aye, 'tis. Thank ye."

Evan's gaze stayed on the flowers. "John did once tell me it was your favorite."

Taking a seat next to Sorcha, he dipped his chin, his voice just above a whisper. "I must ask ye something of a direct nature." He glanced over his shoulder before continuing.

"The king's proscription shall make the clan landless, and

we must flee or else take on different names. Should we not do this, they shall hunt us like animals in the forest. Ye have a bairn to think of, and I would that ye wed me. Ye shall be safe with the MacDonald name."

Sorcha blinked, lashes moistening. *Marry Evan?* She stared at this man her husband loved as a brother—*had* loved. Evan had shared the battlefield with John. Shoulder-to-shoulder they fought the Colquhouns until that evil clan, and the clans that aided them, cut her love down as if a red deer to feed their families.

Hatred fed the Colquhouns by way of the Earl of Argyle, the Justice-General of Scotland. Word had traveled across Scotland of his treachery. Now a powerful man, he had manipulated the king through falsities.

There was safety with the Gregor as he was brother to *her* John, yet she did not wish to burden him further with the care of her and the unborn bairn.

Sorcha sank deeper into the chair, staring at Evan, hands clasped tightly at her waist, the needlework now forgotten. How could he ask this? She and her child were MacGregors. Dare she shove away the name so blithely?

"What did ye say, lass?"

Had she spoken the words? Eyelids closed, she cleared her throat as if to speak—no words arose. All she could feel was deep, abiding sorrow. Sorrow for the loss of bairns, her beloved husband, and now their name. Sobbing engulfed her.

Evan knelt beside the chair. "I would not treat ye unkindly. Ye ken?"

He made no move to touch her, yet his hands gripped the

sides of the chair with such force his knuckles whitened. She peered into his eyes, only compassion filling their grey depths. She did not fear him. Yet could she wed him?

She placed a shaking hand on his. Their gazes held shared grief. In that moment she knew a goodly life mayhap be found for her and John's bairn. The nod was slight. He saw it, lips tilting on one side.

Rather than rising, he brought his lips to the back of her hand and whispered, "I shall not fail ye, lass."

In that moment, she knew he would give his life for them both if that time should come.

ᚳᚷᛋᚩ

Few days passed when a MacDonald lad appeared at the castle to pass on a missive containing the names of MacGregor men who were to be arrested and taken to Edinburgh for their part in the Battle of Glen Fruin.

It was Allaster, the Gregor, who brought the message to Sorcha. He stood over her seat by the fire, and with kind eyes, peered down at her.

"Och, lass. I would not have ye sorrowful. Ye have had enough of that of late. 'Tis just that the name of your cousin is upon the list of those they seek to arrest."

Sorcha pulled in a ragged breath. "Who, sir?"

"Iain MacFarlane."

She released a held breath as she pictured the tall, light-haired cousin of a near age to herself. Though fierce in battle, he was a kind soul and most protective of his kin.

"Why him?" The pain sliced through her. Would the hatred

and killing ever end? Lord, why could not men see they were alike and learn to care for one another as brothers and not enemies?

Allaster, so like John, his elder brother, a tall, broad-shouldered man. He lowered into the chair across from her and gripped his knees.

"Lass, ye are my sister by marriage, and I shall always have a care for ye and your bairn . . ." His voice trailed off into a miserable silence.

Sorcha leaned toward him and placed a trembling hand upon his. "Allaster, if ye have poor news to share, let it be said."

"Aye." He patted her hand, then leaned back into his chair. "Iain is one of many to be roused and taken to Edinburgh. The edict states many more shall follow in the coming months."

She sighed, her heart tearing yet again. "Evan did tell of the proscription. He said we must flee into the Highlands."

"Though Evan seeks your safety, I dinnae think it is as dire as all that the now. Yet I would rather ye go with him." His gaze dropped to her stomach. "Ye may carry the future clan chief, for I fear my days are numbered."

Sorcha gasped, hand flying to her throat. "Nae!"

"Aye, lass. If they come for Iain, who holds no authority, they shall come for me."

Sorcha's heart pounded, mind running from scene to scene with John and Evan at the center of the battle, then seeing Allaster upon the gallows with his powerful hands tied behind his back.

Chapter Three

1710

Muirie stumbled into the kitchen to find Mistress Picken removing a loaf of bread from the oven.

The woman looked up at Muirie's entrance. "What are ye doing up afore the sun rises?"

Muirie yawned. "I slept ill, troubled about Cormac and Beathag."

"There is a word I must have with ye." She shot a worried look and twitched her chin toward the stillroom.

Muirie followed, and once inside, the cook closed the door.

"I know I telt ye to stop fussing over Cormac and Beathag. I fear those two," her thumb gestured toward the door, "shall be in a peck of trouble if they continue on this path."

Muirie dropped to a low stool by the table where bottles lined up like soldiers ready for battle. She propped her elbows on the surface and cradled her chin in her palms. The heady scent of lavender welcomed and calmed her spirit as she focused on Mistress Picken's words.

"That lad haunts my kitchen more and more wearing those moon eyes always aimed at Beathag. He braisit her body, and she seems not to mind where they perch." The cook snorted a most unladylike sound and jammed her fists onto ample hips.

Muirie heaved a sigh. "I know. Yet what are we to do? I have spoken with them, and they seem unconcerned."

The cook patted Muirie's shoulder. "Nothin' to be done now. God shall see to them. I hoped ye to have some idea though. I know ye and Beathag are close." The older woman hung her head for a long moment.

"Sorry I am to burden ye. I am also sorry I chastised ye for preachin' to them." She gripped her hands together tightly at her waist. "Mayhap that is what they need to hear until they grow some sense. They appear to have gotten worse since I telt ye that."

Muirie's sorrow over her friends' behavior grew at the cook's new concerns. She patted the woman's clasped hands. "God shall see to them. We must keep praying."

Mistress Picken stepped to an herb-filled basket and gathered a variety of sprigs in her meaty hands.

Muirie did not rise to follow, but said, "I think I shall stay here and pray. Mayhap I may *grow* more answers about Beathag and Cormac's lack of sense."

The woman chuckled and returned to the kitchen.

If only Cormac were soon to return to school. Yet his friends' arrival within a fortnight, along with Lord and Lady Lamont, would mayhap keep Cormac too busy to pay much attention to Beathag.

Mayhap she could *arrange* things in such a way to keep them apart. She had some days to consider but chose to inquire of Mistress Picken if she had some thoughts on how to achieve this.

She returned to the kitchen, and a maid informed her that Mistress Picken had gone across the bailey to the bakehouse.

Once out of doors, Muirie blinked at the bright, rising sun and made quick steps across the wide yard, gravel crunching underfoot. Cormac leaned in the bakehouse doorway, a cluster of flowers clenched tightly in his fist. Slowing her steps, she tried to hear what was being said.

Mistress Picken's stern voice gave her pause. "Lad, ye must stop this. Beathag be down by the river collectin' grosers for me to prepare for our comin' guests."

Cormac's shoulders slumped, and he dipped his chin and spun around. What she saw near broke her heart. The disappointment scored his face and made her want to weep. He really cared for Beathag.

Their eyes met, and he halted, his darkening when he caught sight of her. "Do not reprimand me, Muirie. I care not to hear it." The flowers dropped to the ground, and his hard, quick steps ground them beneath his booted feet as he swept past.

He spat out over his shoulder, "I care not to hear your sermon this day, *sister*."

Muirie had never heard him speak so spitefully, and hot tears filled her eyes. She made to follow, yet a warm hand on her shoulder halted her progress.

"Nae, lass. He is hurtin'. Leave him be." The kindly woman steered Muirie into the bakehouse. "Come. Have a cup of tea with your auld friend."

Muirie smiled at the woman and the aged words she used, much like Grannam. "Never shall ye be old to me." She was thankful for those caring eyes and followed her to gain much-needed wisdom and peace.

◈

Muirie arranged the freshly cut flowers into vessels lined up on the counter of the stillroom. Beathag chattered endlessly about the upcoming visit of the lord and lady's guests as Muirie snipped stems and offered a word or two into the mix of her friend's nattering.

She knew there was no need to reprimand Beathag of the latest encounter with the lord's son. Mistress Picken was right. No amount of preaching could draw the two from their bond. None of her admonitions had helped thus far, so why continue?

The mention of the soon to arrive guests played on Muirie's mind. What would Cormac's friends be like? She hoped they were not of the dallying sort—like Cormac. She cringed to think of the castle's maids treated so carelessly. Although she believed Cormac's feelings for Beathag ran deeper. She sensed he truly cared for her—and she for him.

"Muirie? What ails ye?" Beathag held a small sack of oats against her hip as she stared narrow-eyed at Muirie.

"Nothing ails me. Why do ye ask?"

"In truth, it seems ye are far removed from this castle and in another place entirely."

Muirie peered through the thick-paned glass and across the yard toward the stables to see Cormac caring for his stallion. His strong build and dark hair reminded her of Beathag's attraction for him from an early age. Their mutual fascination had been strong for a long while. Who was she to fight such a thing? The powerful urge to protest railed. Their places in life would not allow them to forge an alliance. One did not rise above their station in such a way. It could only end in disaster for her friend.

She pasted on a smile. "I wondered about our guests."

Beathag cocked her head. "Aye. The lads that shall come to see Cormac?"

Muirie chuckled. "Is that all ye think of—lads?"

"One in particular." Waggling her eyebrows, she sauntered from the chamber carrying the sack.

Muirie returned to her chore and whispered, "Lord, please guide Cormac and Beathag to consider what they do and how Ye would have them live instead."

Mistress Picken's throaty voice made Muirie jerk, and she pricked her finger on a rose thorn.

"Child, 'tis a right proper prayer, and the Lord shall see fit to answer it in His timing." She huffed. "We may only hope." She snatched up one of the flower-filled containers and left Muirie to her musings.

Muirie turned back to her task. Her gaze found the window again, and she saw Cormac and Beathag stroll to the stables as if the entire world did not exist.

She fought the urge to follow and give them a preaching. The grip on her heart kept her in place, and deep sadness enveloped her. Why could she not let it go?

Mistress Picken's voice from the kitchen called, "Muirie, Lady Stewart asks for ye. Best be off."

Muirie snatched up the vase that was her ladyship's favorite and strode through the kitchen and toward the parlor. What need could she have at this hour? Her mind twirled with the possibilities, and her footsteps quickened along the corridor.

The door to the chamber was open, and she stepped in to find Lady Stewart and Grannam sitting near the fire, needles in hand.

She dipped a curtsy and placed the flowers on the table near the window.

"Those are lovely, my dear."

"Thank ye, Grannam. They are particularly strong-scented this season I am happy to say."

The old woman snorted. "All the better to toss upon the fire once they have dried—shall fill the chamber with their aroma whilst we warm ourselves."

Lady Stewart's eyes met Muirie's over her grandmother's head. "That is most thoughtful of ye, Muirie, to supply the castle with your arrangements."

"'Tis kind of ye, Lady Stewart."

"Come, sit." Lady Stewart waved a delicate hand toward a chair across from her.

Muirie sat demurely, hand folded upon her lap, curious what was to be discussed.

"Brace yourself, Muirie. My granddaughter cares to share a few words of warning about our guests." Grannam tittered. "About the young men who shall arrive." Her expression shone with mischief. "Handsome young lads, I assume."

Clattering in the hall brought Grannam's head up, eyes gazing at the ceiling. "Some of that dreaded tea again, I fear." Her words, meant for Muirie alone, gained Lady Stewart's attention, and she smiled good-naturedly.

"Aye, Grannam, tea *has* arrived."

After a brief knock, Beathag entered, her lively face aglow with some unknown secret. Muirie recognized the look.

Unable to share anything, Beathag departed, and Lady Stewart sipped tea while Grannam stared at her cup with disdain.

"Muirie, please add a touch of milk to my grandmother's drink, for it may make it more palatable. Let us see."

Grannam smirked, holding the cup toward Muirie. They watched as she stirred, then tasted the mixture. Her eyebrows peaked, lips pressing together.

"Does this mean the tea is more pleasant now?" Lady Stewart sent her an affectionate expression, then focused her attention on Muirie.

"My dear, I shall speak to ye about our guests." She held one hand, palm out, toward her grandmother, whose mouth opened to speak. "I shall have my say, Grannam. Muirie may be mature for her years and a most pious young woman, though I will share cautionary instructions."

The old woman closed her wrinkled mouth and huffed, returning to the tea.

Muirie's senses heightened, focused on Lady Stewart. "Aye, my lady."

Lady Stewart's light brown eyes hinted at something Muirie could not identify. She was the kindest of women, having cared for Muirie since infancy, more like a mother than a guardian. Her creamy, flawless skin revealed outward loveliness, her inward beauty shone even brighter.

The lady's clear, well-enunciated words flowed through Muirie like the sound of the Deveron's water gliding over the smooth stones toward the North Sea.

"My dear, please heed what I say." Lady Stewart placed her cup on the table beside them and leaned toward Muirie.

"I am most sorry, my lady."

"I know 'tis hard to hear such things, yet I must say them." She patted Muirie's hand and took hold of it for a moment. "There must be no room for misplay whilst we have guests."

Muirie's confusion grew, and she gulped her tea, working the courage to ask what she meant.

"Isabel, just tell the lass." Grannam sniffed and stretched her empty cup toward Muirie, pointing a crooked finger toward the teapot.

Muirie poured, wondering what was so dire that she should be made aware of.

"Very well." Lady Stewart drew in a shaky breath. "It gives me no pleasure to ask ye to be on your guard by the young men arriving soon. I am aware they are close friends of Cormac's, although one can never know their true character."

Lady Stewart presented her cup to be refilled, which Muirie did with slightly unsteady hands.

"'Tis not so ominous a thing to discuss, child. I merely want to warn ye of the possibilities." She took a sip, peering over the rim of the cup.

"Aye, my lady."

"Ach! Isabel, ye draggle so. Just tell the lass!"

Lady Stewart's brow wrinkled. "These young men have lived in Edinburgh, a very large city, for some years. They are more worldly than we."

A flush crept across Lady Stewart's cheeks, and Muirie hurt for her.

"Do not allow their sweet words, educated minds, or comeliness to sway ye."

Grannam burst into laughter, and Lady Stewart sent her a reprimanding glare. It did not affect her merriment.

"No, my lady." Muirie swallowed the lump in her throat with a gulp of tea. "I am somewhat acquainted with the ways of men." The lady's eyes widened, and Muirie quickly countered, her cheeks aflame, "No, not directly, of course."

Lady Stewart threw her a questioning glance, then looked down at her cup. "I understand. I am aware of my son's indiscretions."

Murie's gaze sought Grannam's, and they shared a knowing look.

"There is no need for the two of ye to act as if ye are not privy to his conduct. I love Cormac more than words may express. I wish him to have a care for his actions." She sniffled into her handkerchief and muttered, "I also have a care for

Beathag. She is a sweet girl, and I wish her no ill."

Not knowing how to respond, Muirie chose the path of the golden rule. "Beathag is an amiable young woman and a friend. I have tried to speak with them about their actions—to no avail."

A deep inhale and exhale sounded in the small chamber. "I am aware of your ministrations toward my son and am most appreciative. If only they would heed your *sermons*."

Muirie started at the comment.

"Do not fear. I have overhead his remarks of your quoting scripture to him—and to Beathag."

"Forgive me, my lady. It was not meant as censure, only as a warning of the consequences of their behavior."

Lady Stewart's head dipped. "Ye were correct in your assumptions. They do not appear to be aware of those outcomes." She heaved a sigh. "That is why I desired to speak about our guests. I would not have ye fall into the same trap as my son."

Muirie straightened. "*My lady?*"

"My dear, men can have an unexpected effect upon us. We tarry along in life and see others committing mistakes we think we are incapable of." She lifted her chin. "Then, of a sudden, a *certain* man appears and within an instant they are Dundee Cake before a starving woman."

Muirie's eyes widened, and she wondered if it was true of Beathag. Was Cormac her *Dundee Cake*?

Chapter Four

1603

Sorcha sorted through her possessions as much fussing occurred as the villagers and occupants of the castle packed what they could carry on horseback or in their arms. Carts would not survive the rugged highland hills. She wondered if she would.

Her weariness seemed constant, struggling to do the most mundane of chores. Evan eyed her curiously when they were in the same chamber. Now he aided her to choose what to bring. Upon his arrival, he asked Clara to go to their cottage and gather their things. With a puzzled glance over her shoulder, his sister did so without a word.

"Evan, ye do not have to help me. I have little I care to

take."

He cupped her hands in his and forced her to put down the babe's lovingly prepared clothing she had made over the past months.

"Lass, we must wed now, afore we depart. Allaster is at the kirk awaiting us. 'Tis to be a quiet, quick visit to the kirk. I am sorry." He dipped his head.

"Is Clara not to attend?" She wanted her dear friend there to bolster her courage.

"Aye, she shall."

"Ye just sent her—"

He gently squeezed her hands. "Allaster will find her."

It now made sense why he had sent her home. Their cottage was near the kirk, and Allaster would explain all to Clara.

Her stomach lurched. Now was the time. It was not as if she had little affection for Evan, for he was a good man. The best of men. John thought as much. A small voice spoke as if into her heart. *All shall be well. Trust Evan. Trust Me.*

Sorcha had heard God's voice before, and it bolstered her strength. She heard it the day John died, yet she did not understand how John's death could lead to anything of worth. Yet God knew all things afore they happened and how those happenings ended.

She inhaled deeply and met Evan's understanding gaze. "Aye. I am ready."

His expression shifted from one emotion to another, uncertain if she first saw sadness or joy.

They bundled her possessions into a small trunk, which he hoisted to his shoulder. Once they strapped it to a horse, they strode arm in arm to the kirk. They exchanged wedding vows with Allaster and Clara standing nearby.

Sorcha's tumbled emotions begged to be sorted, yet there was no time. They must flee.

೦೮೩೮೧

Sorcha cried when Allaster said he would not accompany them. They were warriors and needed to fight for their clan, or so he had said as Evan's countenance registered remorse that he could not stay. She thought to tell Evan to remain when he took her hand and gave it a reassuring squeeze.

Admission that she really did not want him to stay behind held her silent, and they departed as a long trail of bedraggled, landless vagabonds. The hints of warmth in spring had chosen not yet to come, and snow mingled with rain accompanied them to the north. The outcasts broke apart upon their arrival at the many forked trails that led to different clan holdings, each allies of the MacGregors.

This was Allaster's contrivance for them to part ways for the trails to confuse their pursuers. As for Sorcha and all those in Evan's keeping, they were bound for Stewart or Grant lands to the north and east, counting on their allied clans to shelter them.

Sorcha stumbled as they crossed a rocky burn, clutching at the walking stick Evan had fashioned for her. They divided the horses among the different groups, primarily for the purpose of conveying their belongings. The elderly or infirm sat among the possessions the garrons or shelties carried.

Adjusting herself on the curved, damp rock with her staff, a strong arm encircled her waist, and she abruptly moved, glancing up to see Evan's concerned gaze.

"I am well." She offered a small smile as Clara rushed to her side.

"'Tis nae bother, Evan. I shall keep beside her. I aided the widow Gibbs onto a horse behind poor auld Tomas. She weighs nae more than a stick, so the beast shall not notice."

Evan grimaced. "I fear I had not paid it much attention." Remorse shadowed his voice at having been unaware of the need.

"Dinnae fash yourself, brother. Ye are not the only braw man here. The full responsibility does not fall upon your shoulders alone."

Sorcha saw Clara glance ahead where Kester MacDonald stood a head taller than most. Kester, along with a few other men, led the group while others positioned at intervals along the trail, weapons at the ready.

Clara blushed, and Sorcha knew it was not because of the cooling afternoon. She had noticed the woman's bearing change when Kester was near. Yet she had never seen the man glance Clara's way.

The weight of Evan's arm still around her brought her thoughts to the present, and she allowed Clara to guide them across the burn, an icy splash hitting her foot now and then. The feel of his arm against her now rounding middle filled her with shame. Why, she could not say. Yet it should be John's.

"I am sorry to be such a bother to ye both. I grow tired more easily of late."

Sorcha took in Clara's sad smile and the sorrow in her gaze. She could not look at Evan, not wanting to see the grief she expected there. Sorrow for her John.

They stepped onto the banks of the rushing burn, walking much easier upon the path littered with a mix of pine needles and dried leaves from the winter months behind them.

Although April still held the chill of winter, the freshness of the air was restful.

Evan's low voice rumbled in understanding. "I ken the babe claims much of your strength. This shall pass."

Sorcha snickered. "Aye, Evan. It shall pass indeed."

She heard him sputter and could not help herself peering at him over her shoulder. His face reddened much as Clara's had earlier.

Clara chuckled. "Dear brother, she means because the bairn shall be born in God's time, and she shall not suffer from this affliction any longer."

He sputtered again, cleared his throat, and made quick steps to move ahead.

Sorcha and Clara shared a laugh and strode closer to one another. The indistinct murmur of voices surrounding them, a horse's whinny, and birds chattering overhead made it appear they were a group of merry travelers on their way to a friendly gathering rather than people of exile.

If only Sorcha's mind did not keep returning to the reason they fled.

CR⁂SO

By the time they settled for the night, Sorcha's aching body collapsed upon the crude pallet Clara made for them to share. The naturally cushioned spot under an ancient pine welcomed her. The crisp scent of the pines surrounding them almost lulled her to sleep before she had eaten.

Sorcha leaned against the trunk, her head resting upon its rough bark. Her eyelids sagged, and she could feel herself drift into that moment before blissful sleep arrived. Shuffling footsteps brought her groggy head up, and she noticed Evan crouching before her, extending a small fabric wrapped parcel and placing it on her lap.

"To fortify ye." He lifted one side of his lips into a boyish grin as he eased himself into a sitting position.

Sorcha unwrapped the offering. "Thank ye."

A shriveled apple lay inside, along with a hunk of dried venison. She bit into the apple, savoring it as if picked fresh from the tree. She sent him a warm smile.

Clara arrived, a small parcel tucked under her arm, two pewter cups full of fresh, icy water from the burn in her hands.

Had the burn not been so cold, Sorcha would have found a secluded spot and bathed. The long day's journey had been toilsome. Before she had been with child—with all her children—she was never tired unless after a full day's chores. Now it only took walking a bit, and it wore her to the ground.

Eating the venison tired her more, chewing endlessly to make it easy to swallow was more a chore than going hungry. The apple must suffice. She drank the water, wrapped the remaining meat in the fabric, and tucked it into the small pouch beside their makeshift bed.

"Thank ye both for your kind attentions." She struggled to

rise, and Evan was by her side before she moved more than a few inches. He helped her stand and peered a question at her, obviously fearful to ask why she did so.

Clara glanced at Sorcha with a knowing expression, rose, and looped her arm through Sorcha's, then looked at her brother. "We shall go for a brief walk by the burn." She lifted her brow and pursed her lips, giving Evan a tiny glare as if to say, '*No men allowed.*'

He either did not get the missive, or chose not to heed it, for he stood. "Aye, I shall go with ye."

"Nae, Evan." Clara's voice was tinged in warning.

"*Clara.*" He reached for his dirk and held it up. "I shall stay within shouting distance—my back to ye. I shall *not* let ye leave the encampment alone."

Clara froze, halting Sorcha's exit as well. She stared at her brother, and in an instant, her expression changed to one of understanding. "Aye, brother. I ken."

As did Sorcha. He wanted only to protect them, and she was grateful for it.

They walked abreast until they heard the rush of water, the whispering pines, and smelled the rich clean scent of something akin to lavender. Sorcha relaxed at the meeting of such a—the word *blessing* came to mind. This was God's creation, and He had made it for them. His children. Why had she not thought of Him in days? It shamed her to know she had forgotten to thank Him for their provision and protection.

 C&SO

Sorcha breathed in the cold, perfumed air, longing for a fire's warmth. Yet fear made them act with caution and light no fires in the night. Instead, they huddled together, shivering, close together with their kinsmen. Clara rested on the pine needles beside Sorcha with her hand cupping her cheek, her features serene in sleep.

Sorcha slept for a time, then something—she knew not what—awakened her, and she sat, leaning against the tall pine they sheltered beneath. A flutter of snowflakes floated before her, and she captured some in her mouth rather than rising and making the taxing journey to the burn.

Evan spoke in a hoarse whisper, and she started. "Ye cannot sleep, lass?"

Sorcha tilted her head to see him sitting against a nearby tree, dirk dangling from his hand. The half-moon gave just enough light to see his amused expression.

"Nae. I did for a bit, now I grow skittish." She heaved a sigh. "It seems the forest talks a great deal."

He gave a low chuckle. "Aye. 'Tis truth. It speaks much. The sound of the fox and the wild cat what hunts at night."

He chuckled again. "Dinnae fash yourself. They do not like the scent of man and shall stay afar."

She pointed at his weapon. "Then why do ye stay awake and wield that?"

His face darkened, and his grip tightened on the weapon. "Our enemy does hunt us like beasts."

Footsteps approached, and they swung their gazes to find Kester. He waited to speak until he loomed over them. "Evan, 'tis time for ye to rest." He lowered himself beside Evan and shoved him on the shoulder. "Be gone." His eyes traveled to where Clara slept, and they lingered.

Sorcha's heart leaped at his attention toward her sweet friend, and she rose just as Evan did.

Her gaze lifted to Evan. "I would like to drink from the burn."

He stared at her with a questioning air, and after a brief hesitation, he lifted his arm so she could take it.

The occasional snore and a few low murmurings mingled with the sounds of the forest as they made their way to the burn without a word between them.

Moonlight winked as they slowly strode, Evan's arm warm beneath Sorcha's hand. She liked the protective feel of it and reprimanded herself for the thought. John had been dead barely three months, and her thoughts should not be upon another man even if they were wed.

Evan halted their progress. "Are ye cold?"

"Nae . . . nae." Her gaze dipped to the floor of the woods, and she jerked when a rabbit darted in front of them.

He quickly put a shielding arm around her shoulder and rested his chin on her head. "'Tis naught to fear."

Her hard swallow hurt her throat, and she nodded. "I ken. The beast just startled me."

She had never heard Evan laugh so freely, and it gave her pause. "I am that glad to make ye so merry."

He shook his head slowly. "Oh, lass. Ye do make me joy glad." He froze. "I . . . 'tis that I have never heard a rabbit called a beast afore . . . 'tis all."

Sorcha held his gaze in the yellow-white moonlight, his grey eyes appearing like silver, searching hers.

The snap of a twig brought them around to see a dark figure skulking a great distance from their encampment. Evan grabbed Sorcha's arm and tugged her behind a grouping of underbrush, and they hunkered behind it. Sorcha trembled with fear and hung onto Evan's arm. His free hand sought his dirk and motioned for her to remain quiet.

She nodded, knelt, and broke free of him. The figure moved from their hiding place, and Evan whispered, "Stay here. I shall see where they go. Maybe it is an innocent traveler who means us nae harm. We are near the fork at Crianlarich, and mayhap they travel to one of the Highland trails as we intend."

Sorcha nodded again and settled herself to wait. He half rose and took tentative steps toward the visitor, careful not to step upon a twig and send out an alarm. She watched him disappear into the dark and out of the moon's rays.

Sorcha grasped the branch nearest her, steadying herself, as she breathed out a prayer. "Lord, please keep him from harm. I dare not lose another I care for."

Her lips parted, her own words surprising her. She did care for Evan MacDonald.

Chapter Five

1710

Muirie's heart raced with the announcement of Lord and Lady Stewart's guests. A guard alerted them of the party's approach coming from the east where the old Roman road led to their very door.

As children, Muirie and Cormac would play on the few remaining cobbles of the ancient path, wielding their wooden swords to rid Scotland of the Roman invaders. She smiled at the memory as she hurried along the passage leading to the castle's main gate.

The entourage was just entering when Muirie skirted behind Cormac. She poked him in the back, and his head snapped around, his gaze sharp.

He muttered over his shoulder, "Now ye shall meet my friends whom I have told ye much of."

"Aye, too much I fear."

His shoulders shook, careful not to allow his laughter to reach his parents.

Lord and Lady Stewart stepped forward in greeting before Lord and Lady Lamont, the women embracing and the men bowing deeply.

Lord Stewart motioned for Cormac, and he stepped from Muirie, greeting their guests. He craned his neck to peer behind them.

"Where are Gavin, Peader, and Reid?"

Muirie heard the distress in his voice and knew he had missed his friends since they parted from school, although he had not missed his lessons.

"Aye, Gavin and Peader are a few hours behind. Peader's horse threw a shoe, and Gavin insisted on remaining to aid him. They should be along shortly."

Although Muirie could not see Cormac's face, the subtle slump of his shoulders showed his disappointment. "And what of Reid?"

Lord Lamont heaved a sigh. "He shall be along in a few days. His father required his presence in Edinburgh a while longer to attend to business matters."

Cormac mumbled something Muirie could not hear and backed from the group. She moved from the shadows of the loggia and tapped him on the shoulder. He jerked and spun.

"What do ye want—" He averted his eyes. "—to preach me another sermon befitting John Knox?"

"No, Cormac. I am sorry your friends have not arrived." She kept her tone low and touched his arm. "I hope they are not too long delayed."

"Mayhap." He shrugged off her hand.

Footsteps shuffled behind them, and they brought their gazes to find Beathag carrying a basketful of linens to the washhouse.

Cormac's eyes brightened, and when the maid passed with a nod and a welcoming smile, Cormac stepped behind her retreating figure, following at a respectful distance.

Muirie made to grip his arm, and he sidestepped her, his voice a hoarse whisper. "Mind your own affairs, *sister*."

The words stung, and she fought back scalding tears, her gaze following Cormac before she strode toward the visitors.

"Muirie, please come and greet our friends." Lady Stewart's warm touch against her back brought her around.

She pasted on an amenable smile and curtsied. "Good day, Lord and Lady Lamont. 'Tis most wonderful to see ye again."

Lady Lamont took Muirie's hands in hers. "My dear, ye have grown into a beautiful young woman. I am quite amazed ye remember us. Ye were but a wee lass on our previous visit."

Muirie honestly liked Lady Lamont. Her manner exuded kindness, and her smile brimmed with sincerity. Standing several inches below Muirie's height, the regal woman appeared as if a fairy queen, pretty and delicate.

"Thank ye, my lady."

The woman waved a porcelain hand to beckon the girl standing behind them. "Come along, Elizabeth, ye are far from shy." She presented the young woman to Muirie and the others. "This is my daughter, Elizabeth."

Taller than her mother, Elizabeth stepped forward and tilted her chin up a notch, presenting a toothy smile. She curtsied and straightened to stand stiffly beside Lady Lamont.

Everyone greeted her in turn, the girl merely muttering a greeting, as if bored with her surroundings.

Lady Stewart cleared her throat, and the men excused themselves to go to the stables for Lord Stewart to show off his newest acquisition.

"Let us retire to my parlor for refreshment. Afterward, I am certain ye shall want a long rest before we dine this eve."

Lady Lamont took Lady Stewart's arm, and they walked ahead, leaving Muirie to escort Elizabeth. Muirie attempted cordiality, the girl lifting her short, upturned nose as if sniffing the cool air. She tossed her long, near-white blonde hair over a shoulder.

One more attempt at politeness and Muirie was done with the haughty miss.

"Was your journey enjoyable?" She sent the girl a smile, and a glare met her.

"Not in the least." Elizabeth's mouth puckered into an exaggerated pout. "Such a journey and all for nothing more than to visit *old friends*."

Muirie opened her mouth to reply, nothing coming forth. Of all the guests that arrived through the castle gates, this person was the rudest she had ever encountered.

They reached the parlor in silence and met Grannam.

"Cecilia, are ye not a sight!" Grannam rose and hugged Lady Lamont. "Ye are still as lovely as ever, my child."

"'Tis so very nice to lay eyes upon ye, Lady Euphemia." She kissed the old woman's cheek affectionately and presented her daughter. "This is Elizabeth. She would have been a babe since ye last saw her."

Grannam tilted her head and chewed on the corner of her lip. "Aye, pretty thing. Though she does not have your coloring."

Elizabeth stared at the woman with a frown. "'Tis because I take after my father's mother, madam."

"Pfft!" Grannam dropped onto her chair, keeping her gaze on the girl. "Ye have an outspoken daughter, Cecilia."

"I do beg your pardon." She took her daughter's arm and led her to a chair across the chamber, whispering something Muirie could not distinguish.

Lady Stewart took a seat next to her grandmother and motioned for Muirie to sit on the old woman's other side while Lady Lamont chose the place across from them.

An uncomfortable current hung in the chamber until Murie broke the quiet. "Grannam, would ye care to take a walk in the garden? The weather is fine."

One side of Grannam's mouth twisted into a cocky smile. "Ye know what the chill air does to my old bones, lass, not to mention my *complecion*." She patted her lined cheek. "'Tis why I appear so youthful."

Her teasing smile made Muirie swallow a chuckle. She glanced across the parlor.

"Let us have tea, Isabel." Grannam reached for Muirie's hand. "If I am to walk with ye I must have fortification, and the warmth shall ward off the chill of the day."

Elizabeth muttered under her breath, "I abhor tea."

"Well, my dear, that makes two of us." Grannam shot daggers at the girl. "Ye need not partake. My granddaughter adores it, and although it costs more than 'tis worth, I share it to please her."

Lady Stewart sent a generous smile to her guests, and Muirie admired her indulgence with the elder woman. The women had a strong bond, and though Grannam could be difficult, they mostly overlooked her moods.

Elizabeth smirked. When she noted Muirie watching her, her expression changed to one of disdain.

Muirie blinked, so startled at the clear disgust on the girl's face she missed the entrance of Mary, the kitchen maid, asking to speak to Lady Stewart. They stepped from the chamber, and upon their return, Mary placed a tray on the table near Lady Stewart, curtsied, and left.

Lady Stewart smiled at Muirie. "Will ye please serve? Beathag is occupied with meal preparations."

Muirie squirmed under the unmistakable disapproving glint in her eyes, donning a wavering smile. "Aye, my lady."

She feared for Beathag if Lady Stewart discovered her continued involvement with Cormac. Heaven help them if it was revealed to Lord Stewart.

Elizabeth's shrill, girlish voice sliced the air. "Was she speaking of the young maid Cormac followed through the loggia?" Her small, dainty fingers gripped the teacup she now sipped in exaggerated grace.

Lady Lamont coughed. "Elizabeth, do not be impolite."

"Mother, I was only curious." Dimples appeared on her

cheeks along with a condescending smile.

Lady Stewart drew in a ragged breath, and Muirie sensed her discomfort, the urge to protect too strong to ignore.

Muirie answered for her, "Aye, that was Cormac. Beathag is recovering from an illness, and he aided her to lift the heavy basket." She silently asked God for forgiveness for the lie.

Grannam sniggered, saying nothing.

"Aye." Lady Stewart agreed. "He is most helpful."

Muirie kept her thoughts to herself of *why* Cormac was so helpful to Beathag.

Grannam muttered to Muirie, her gaze on Elizabeth. "I think that lass's behavior is detestable."

Lady Stewart rose. "I am fair certain ye are weary and care to freshen yourselves and rest before we dine." She peered at her grandmother. "Ye as well, Grannam."

"I am not tired." She huffed. "Nor do I need to freshen myself. Muirie and I have a stroll to commence." The old woman stood with a force belying her age and reached out to take Muirie's arm. "Come, child."

Grannam and Muirie excused themselves until dinner, and stepping into the spring afternoon, Grannam leaned closer to Muirie. "Dinnae let Cormac and Beathag distress ye. What shall be shall be. 'Tis not your fault they act addle-pated."

Muirie's thoughts muddled over what to do to help her friends. She could not stand by and allow them to travel down a path that led to their destruction.

CB&ED

In Muirie's judgment, the evening meal had been anything

but pleasant. Elizabeth knew how to command the attention of everyone at table, and she sensed the men growing tired of the display of selfishness. The moment the meal concluded, the men excused themselves to Lord Stewart's library.

In a light, forced tone, Lady Stewart entreated the women to accompany her to the parlor where the men would join them later. Muirie desired to leave, claiming an ache in her head. She heaved a sigh, unwilling to disrespect Lady Stewart by doing so. She led Grannam to the chair nearest the hearth, knowing she favored the spot in the evening.

Beathag entered carrying a tray of tea, and Muirie's meal roiled in her stomach, her gaze flying to Elizabeth. She feared the girl would make trouble for Beathag in the presence of all in attendance.

A sudden revelation surfaced—she had eyes for Cormac. Mayhap that is why Lord and Lady Lamont brought her.

Without warning, the door swept open, and two men she did not recall entered.

A tall man of an age to herself with dark brown hair streaked with gold lagged behind a light-haired, medium built man wearing a wide smile.

The shorter of the two bowed. "Good eve to ye, ladies. We mean not to interrupt, only to seek the men who hold the port."

Grannam chuckled. "I do ken a man who knows his own mind, lad." She motioned to the chair nearest her own. "Come and entertain an old woman."

To everyone's surprise, the young man did as bid, wearing a sincere expression. "I shall do all to please ye, my lady." He bowed. "Madam, I am Peader, your servant." He quickly took the seat and gave her his full attention.

Elizabeth was the only one who did not laugh at the display.

The taller man bowed. "Gavin Lamont, ladies." His gaze traveled to Muirie, and her face heated. "As much as I enjoy your company, I would seek sustenance before retiring. Peader and I have had much distress in our journey's delay."

Lady Lamont rose. "My son, I am glad to see ye and Peader have come to no harm. I am certain Lady Stewart shall understand your needs."

Waving a dismissive hand in the air, Lady Stewart said, "Certainly. I shall send for someone to show ye to your chambers and have them send up a tray. We shall become acquainted on the morrow."

Lady Stewart turned to Grannam. "Peader, please excuse my grandmother." The look she shot the woman brooked no argument, and Muirie was surprised to see Grannam dip her chin with a mischievous smile.

Before the men slipped through the door, Muirie met Gavin's bemused look, which held not a hint of impropriety, and to her surprise, a sudden feeling of intrigue mixed with joy spread through her. What was it about him that made her feel thus?

⁂

Muirie sat at the kitchen table the next morning speaking with Mistress Picken, a small bannock in one hand. "Thank ye for the bite afore I break my fast."

"Ach, child. I know ye have the nerves when guests are

here. Ye are a lovely young lass and need not feel so.”

"I am not family and yet not a servant. What am I to do? I fit nowhere."

The cook's expression softened. "Ye fit anywhere, dearie."

Beathag burst into the chamber, face flushed and surprise clear when she saw Muirie. "Did ye come to check on me?"

Her tone was unusually harsh, and Muirie's shame surged. "No. I came to eat." Muirie stood and faced Beathag. "Ye have a suspicious mind, Beathag. I shall not explain my behavior to ye as 'tis unreproachable. Is yours?" Guilt slapped at her, remembering the lie she had told to protect her friend's reputation.

Without another word, Muirie spun around and rushed from the kitchen, bannock still in hand. One step into the passage she slammed into the strong chest of a man—Gavin.

He gripped her upper arms to steady her, amber eyes boring into hers.

"Please forgive me. I confess the aromas coming from the kitchen drew me like deer to water."

Muirie lost all words. There was something about him that unsettled her *and* drew her in, yet it did not feel akin to what she had heard of romance. Perhaps another emotion she could not define. She swallowed hard as they continued to stare at each other until he gently released her.

"Have our paths crossed before?" Gavin cocked his head, studying her. "Ye appear familiar."

The idea sprouted, and she wondered if that was why she grew so unsettled. "Mayhap we have. Yet I know not how as I have never traveled beyond this castle."

He pressed his lips together. "We should give it some consideration." He tapped his chin with a finger. "Mayhap your brother has spoken so often of ye, I feel I know ye. I assume he must have spoken of me."

Cormac had spoken to Muirie of him, so mayhap that was it. She tossed aside the thoughts. "I suppose."

He bowed. "Shall ye break your fast with the others?" His gaze dropped to the bannock in her grip.

She chuckled. "I shall." Her goal had been to avoid the meal, not wanting to see Elizabeth. There was something about the girl that did not sit well. Yet Gavin was a different tale altogether.

CAROLE LEHR JOHNSON

50

Chapter Six

1603

Sorcha jerked to sit upright when a hand pressed over her mouth.

"'Tis Evan, Sorcha."

Heart pounding in fear, she gasped as their breath mingled. He moved to place his mouth near her ear.

"The man was of nae danger to us. He was a lone traveler moving by night for safety's sake. I encountered him as if by chance, and he told me much. There were Campbells who questioned him, and because he held papers of his reason for the journey, they released him. He is Robert Glendinning, an itinerant man of God. He showed me the document entrusted by John Welch of Ayr."

Sorcha listened to the sincerity in his voice and relaxed at his words of encouragement. He obviously believed the man he encountered, and she had to trust his judgment. *Trust Evan.* The words returned to her. *Trust Me.*

A peace seized her, and she allowed him to help her rise. Over his shoulder golden slices of light slashed through a break in the trees, a rosy hue their backdrop.

His expression softened as he looked into her eyes, the morning light washing over his strong features. With a gentle hand, he pushed away an errant curl off her forehead. "We must return afore the others discover us missing."

She dipped her chin, his touch moving her in ways she did not want to face, so she clasped his arm instead, and they made a quick pace through the awakening forest, arousing birds to warble among the soothing ripples of the burn.

The blush of Clara's cheeks returned to her thoughts. "Evan, what kind of man is Kester?"

His head snapped toward Sorcha, sending her an unsettled expression. "Why do ye ask?"

She peered ahead to see the others stirring, knowing she had little time to share what she suspected. "Clara . . ."

"What of Clara?"

"'Tis just that I have seen her watching Kester, yet until tonight I have not seen him pay her much mind."

Evan's face softened, and his arm relaxed. "Aye. Kester is a good man."

The silence deepened, and Sorcha watched as they grew closer to their assembly. She slowed her steps, forcing him to match her pace. "I ask for I fear Clara's heart has finally opened to another."

Evan frowned. "And this is wrong?"

"Nae." She tried to form the proper answer. "I do not desire her to be hurt."

His lips twitched with unspoken humor. "I ken."

"*Well?*"

"Ye can trust Kester. Though he has not been among us overlong, I ken he and his family."

She waited for further elaboration. None was forthcoming as they approached the bustle of a camp ready to depart.

Evan shared the reason for their delay regarding the traveler, and they soon took their places to continue the arduous journey to the Highlands.

Their ascent into the mountains left Sorcha's legs aching. She struggled to keep up. Clara's support aided her. Sorcha feared she drained much of her strength by being a burden.

Evan strode behind with a few fellow travelers between them.

"Clara," Sorcha slowed, "shall ye walk ahead? I would like a word with Evan."

Clara would be left to walk directly behind Kester—alone. Their slower steps drew Kester's attention, and he turned, halting until they drew closer.

"Is all well?" Kester aimed the question, his eyes on Clara, and she blushed.

"Aye. I care to have a word with my husband." Sorcha tugged her arm from Clara's and gently nudged her forward. She watched Clara tense.

"Kester, may Clara walk alongside ye until I return?"

The man's expression registered nothing, yet Sorcha saw a spark catch in his eyes. Though he did not change his expression, she felt rather than saw his pleasure. He dipped his chin and extended a bent arm to Clara without a word.

"Nicely done." Evan's soft tone spoke next to her ear.

He took her arm and resumed walking, people skirting around them, putting more distance between them and Clara.

Sorcha pinched his side, and Evan winced. "What was that for, lass?"

"I arranged nothing. I was becoming a weight upon Clara and wanted to give her ease for a time."

"Lass, ye are nae great weight. I am certain my sister was not burdened."

"She would never say as much. I am so weary and put too much upon her."

Sorcha paused before adding, "Soon ye shall feel it too."

"Perhaps, yet I have the strength to endure the great and heavy burden." His eyes glinted with mischief.

Sorcha laughed and nearly started at the sound. When had she truly desired to laugh in such a great while?

☙❧

The rugged terrain kept Sorcha's attention on taking careful steps with Evan's firm grasp upon her—one arm around her waist and the other clutching her hand. She had not returned to Clara's side the rest of the day, and their time to encamp was soon at hand.

Their first night spent at Crianlarich brought them into the foothills of the Highlands, the journey now becoming more strenuous with the steeper climb. The Highland men knew which direction led them to their sanctuary. Sorcha still doubted. Why would Clan Stewart or Clan Grant help those who put them in danger? Her exhale contained more feeling than she intended, wishing she had not done so.

"Are ye well? We may rest awhile if need be."

"Nae. We must not linger on my account."

"I ken the concern in your eyes." He pulled her closer and slanted his head near hers. "I would not have ye worry. Trust me."

Her breath held at the remark. She twisted to stare at him. "What did ye say?"

"I ask ye to trust me." He smiled. "Do ye not do so?"

She swallowed a lump in her throat and nodded. "I do." Those two tiny words echoed in her mind. To wed him was akin to saying those words. She did not love this man. She only loved John. How could she ever trust anyone again? Her tattered heart had no choice in anything. Her life was in the hands of everyone except herself—Evan for her safety as his wife, the clan because she was bound to them by her marriage to John—and now to Clan MacDonald because she was wed to Evan and they were allied to the MacGregors.

Would her life ever be her own?

Evan broke her morbid musings by pulling her to the side of the path and stopped. "Lass, I am worried about ye. Something is wrong. Why shall ye not tell me?"

The last thread of her resolve strained to the breaking point. In her mind, she could see the needle pierce the fabric as she tugged the crimson thread taut. The blood red stitches she had made to symbolize what John had spilled at Glen Fruin. When she looked into Evan's eyes, she could almost see what he had seen that day. He saw John dying as they knelt in the blood-drenched snow. Evan's arms supported John, their heads bent together, as the MacGregor men fought around them, protecting them as they said goodbye.

It must have been something warriors sensed, for Sorcha had watched this from the hilltop above the glen bordering Loch Lomond, her tears creating a blurry shield against the scene, which became stitched into her very being forever.

Strong arms encircled her, and she did not realize she was crying until the wetness of Evan's shirt against her cheek brought her head up to peer over his shoulder. Passersby glanced with sorrowful expressions. To them it was a husband comforting his wife. To her, it was a woman who felt utterly alone in the world.

Evan's hand moved to rub her back, and he whispered words of comfort meant only for her. "Sorcha, 'tis the bairn. I have heard tell of emotions brought on by the experience."

She sniffed and rubbed her nose with the back of her hand. "Aye. Like weariness?"

He chuckled. "Aye."

"I suppose ye are right. I shall give it no more thought. Please excuse me."

"'Tis nothing to be excused. As ye said—it shall pass." He drew back to look at her and gave her an endearing smile.

Sorcha thought it was the bonniest smile she had ever seen. She suddenly reprimanded herself for her wayward thinking and turned from him.

"Did I say something wrong?"

Sorcha could not look at him. His care and kindness were too much for her. She did not deserve it. Nae, she did not deserve *him*. He had given up his future for her. Now he would have no bairns, no *true* wife. She could not forgive herself for doing this to him. Why had she agreed to this? Her tears resumed.

He pulled her closer, his voice now strained. "What is wrong? It is not the bairn, is it?"

She shook her head vigorously, saying nothing.

"What have I done?" His voice grew more insistent.

A sob caught in her throat, and she shoved him away and ran into the forest.

Heavy footsteps followed, and she stumbled until a wide, rushing burn faced her. She had nowhere to go. Dropping to her knees, she buried her faced into her hands and screamed, "John, why did ye die?"

A twig snapped, and Evan placed a comforting arm across her back. "Och, lass, he died to protect ye and the bairn and his clan."

His voice dropped to a whisper. "I wish it had been me instead. He was the best of men—not I."

It was as if the entire forest had stilled. Sorcha could hear only the rare twitter of a bird and the gurgle of the burn. Nothing else existed in that moment.

She rose slowly to sit upon her heels, the tears blurring his tormented face. "Nae!" There was more vehemence in her voice than she intended, realizing she meant it.

Evan's eyes misted, and she could see the pain in them. "I wish it more than ye know."

"Why wish such a thing? Ye have your whole life ahead of ye." The meaning in those words sliced her like a dirk. He did not have a life because of her.

She fisted the front of his shirt and pulled him close. "Because of me, ye do not have a life. Ye gave it up for John—for me, and I am sorry I allowed it!"

He cradled her cheeks in his palms. "Nae. Say not such a thing!" His eyes caressed her face and then he looked toward the water as if to gather his thoughts.

"I am sorry, Evan. I was only thinking of myself when I agreed to wed ye—and my bairn."

"As it should be. John would have wanted it so."

Men's voices traveled on the breeze toward them. Unfamiliar voices. Evan gripped Sorcha's shoulder and heaved her upward and against his side. He murmured, "Come, we must hide." His gaze swung around until he found an oak tree large enough for them to crouch behind. Taking quick, careful steps, he hunched close to the ground and led her away.

Sorcha huddled against him as they crouched behind the massive oak. The voices grew closer.

"Aye, I tell ye if we see the MacGregors we may earn a crown or two to weigh our pockets."

"There be just the twa' of us. How shall we bring aught to tha' Campbells?"

"Nae, ye *eejit*, we must tell them where we seen 'em."

The voices faded as they passed the tree and strode in the

opposite direction. Sorcha breathed a sigh of relief and sagged against Evan, her energy spent.

Evan muttered, "We must go warn everyone. They could cross our path further down." He notched his head in the direction they traveled.

Horror struck Sorcha's heart, and she nodded. They stood, and an idea came to her. "Can ye not stop them now? There are but two."

Evan froze, and his expression bore consideration at her suggestion for a moment. "Nae, 'tis murder ye suggest."

She knew he was right, were not the lives of their kinsmen worth it, and she told him so.

"I ken. But 'tis not right."

Anger gripped her. "'Tis right for them to hand us over to the Campbells who shall murder all of us?" Before he could respond, something occurred to her, and she grabbed his arm. "What if ye tie them so they cannot go anywhere for a time? Time for us to escape."

"Aye, 'tis possible." He reflected on her idea. "Would ye be agreeable to becoming bait?" He waggled an eyebrow.

Her smile wavered only a little before she sprang into action and bolted toward the men before fear gave her pause.

"Sirs! Shall ye please help a lost lass?" She made certain to keep a suitable distance from the strangers as Evan skirted a wide berth around so he could surprise them from behind, sword drawn.

The smaller of the men gave her a gap-toothed grin, which sickened Sorcha. His teeth were rotten stumps. She had encountered such men before, and their breath made her stomach lurch at the mere thought of a close encounter.

"Are ye not a verra bonny lass now?" He rubbed his hands together as if ready to sit down to a sumptuous meal.

Sorcha's skin crawled. Maybe this was not a good idea.

The other man chuckled, hanging back, allowing the shorter of the two to draw closer. "Go on, Angus, ye have—"

A shout rang out, and Evan exploded from the trees striking the taller man in the back with the flat of his sword, sending him face down into the underbrush. He did not move. Angus sprang into action with the flick of his wrist bringing a long dirk to wave in Evan's direction, a beam of light slanting through the treetops glinting off the evil-looking blade.

"Aye, so we have a trap, do we? Thinkin' to rob us?" The man's gruesome smile disgusted Sorcha, and she heaved. The moment passed, and she rushed out of the way so Evan could handle the man.

They parried one another for what seemed an age, and Sorcha saw that Evan, the more fit of the two, was trying to wear him down. It appeared to be working until the man lunged at the precise moment the sun blinded Evan.

Sorcha screamed, and it echoed through the forest, sending birds flapping out a cacophony into the sky.

Evan dropped to his knees, and the man's blade sliced the air above his head, which gave Evan time to plunge the sword into his attacker.

Sorcha gasped at the sudden sight of blood, and this time, she heaved with results.

Chapter Seven

1710

Muirie's eyes burned as she struggled to open them after a restless night. When she first found her bed, the moon beyond the trees near her window shivered in the wind, sending a strip of light to dance across her coverings.

Waking from time to time, she once thought she heard horses and the low hum of men's voices in the night. Once it ceased, she assumed she dreamt and fell again into a fitful sleep.

Before the sun rose, she left her bed and hurriedly dressed in the rough fabric of a servant. She took the stone stairs quicker than appropriate and slipped into the pre-dawn garden. Though her body ached for lack of sleep, she found the misty garden comforting with the scent of roses, always stronger in the early morning. She inhaled deeply as the spicy smell mingled with the sweet and woodsy aroma of lavender—her favorite flower.

A memory emerged of Grannam telling her the flower symbolized purity and grace. There may have been other sayings, yet the meaning remained with her from childhood.

She strolled among the mist-shrouded garden, unable to see but a few feet before her. Rather than feeling the gloom most spoke of when the air was thick with the *haar*, it calmed her. The word came back in a flash of recognition as what the highlanders call the *mist*.

Though the lavender bed was near, she could not yet see it. Shards of sunlight pierced the trees and cast strange shadows among the mist that lay over the gardens, hugging the plants like a willowy blanket.

The urge to walk among such beauty was too powerful, and she quickened her pace. The haze thickened the closer she drew to the river side of the garden. She slowed and once beside the bed of lavender, she knelt and buried her nose in the purple spiked blooms and inhaled the sweet, almost medicinal scent.

After a moment of bliss, she leaned back on her heels, broke long sprigs of the flowers, and laid them aside on the pebbled footpath.

Quietly humming, her thoughts strayed to the newly arrived guests. Lord and Lady Lamont were very agreeable, and she liked them immediately. Though she remembered them little from the few times they had come when she was a child. They were most kind to her at meals.

Their son, Gavin, was . . . different.

He was certainly handsome, and she was sure other lasses found him most bonny, yet her feeling regarding him did not seem to be those of romance. Though, she could not describe what they were otherwise.

The sound of crunching footsteps brought her head up. Who would be out this early—other than her? The steps grew closer. She squinted to peer through the haze—yet saw no one. It was akin to looking through Mistress Picken's broth.

Muirie's focus still on the path, she stood, and a man's silhouette parted the mist and halted within an arm's length.

The man was not as tall as Lord Stewart. Though, he was not a short man either. His reddish-blonde hair hung below his collar, and the piercing pale grey eyes focusing on Muirie sent ripples along her spine.

He lifted an arm as if to comfort her at his abrupt presence, then let it drop to his side and took a step back. "I must beg your forgiveness. I did not intend to startle ye."

Muirie, unable to speak, dipped her chin. Propriety made her curtsy and lower her eyes.

"Allow me to introduce myself since we have none here to do so." He bowed and cleared his throat. "I am Reid Graham, a friend of Cormac."

"Good morn, sir. I am Muiriel Stewart, ward to Lord and Lady Stewart." Muirie relaxed. "'Tis a pleasure to make your acquaintance. Are ye only now arriving?"

"Nae, yet it was mere hours ago." He peered toward the castle—though the structure could not be seen through the mist hovering around them.

A deep sigh escaped him. "I could not sleep, so I walked along the river and found myself in the gardens with ye."

The word held a hint of intimacy and warmth, filling her with the urge to draw closer to him. Yet for propriety's sake, she should not be here alone with this stranger.

Silence hung between them for a long moment before he spoke. "I do hope Cormac and Gavin have shared none of our school escapades."

Muirie lifted an eyebrow, wondering if their misadventures were akin to Cormac's dallying with Beathag.

"Nae, sir. I am not privy to what my brother does whilst in school, and I do not care to know, Mr. Graham."

His hearty laugh sent her insides tumbling, not unlike the flutter of a butterfly's erratic trail from flower to flower. The smile that lit his face was like the morning sun upon her own, warmth slipping through her. She swallowed, unable to look away.

"Please call me Reid." His smile dimmed, yet the light in his eyes did not. "Please forgive me. I mean not to be so bold. Mayhap we shall break our fast together—with the others, mistress."

She nodded and barely above a whisper added, "Please call me Muirie."

He bowed, turned, and gestured with a sweeping hand toward the castle, leaving Muirie only a moment to gather her wits before the intriguing stranger escorted her inside.

⋘⋙

In the garden, Muirie huddled closer to the plant teeming

with purple blooms, willing herself to shrink into the foliage, as men's voices reached her.

"I tell ye she shall be most willing to go. My sister is of an adventurous sort."

Deep chuckles followed the declaration, and a husky voice responded, "We have met on a few occasions, yet I do not perceive what ye say to be truth."

Cormac laughed. Muirie knew the sound well. "Ye know her not at all, sir."

"Perhaps" was the man's reply.

A brief silence hung before another male voice entered the conversation. "Mayhap your maid would happily go as her chaperone."

"My maid?" Cormac sputtered. "Who might that be?"

Muirie's stomach roiled. Did his friends know of Beathag? The realization did not bode well.

"Cormac, we are not blind."

So intent on listening to their conversation, Muirie failed to consider how close they now were to her hiding place until a booted foot landed on the hem of her skirt.

She held her breath, praying for them to move on, fearful to look up and find them staring down at her.

The men chattered on about the merits of some adventure, so she dared to glance up and found the grey eyes of Reid Graham surveying her, his foot still upon her hem.

He answered a question without taking his eyes from hers. "I think it a splendid jaunt to the sea. When shall we depart?"

A fourth voice joined in—Peader. "I say, what are ye lads

plotting without me?"

Reid's gaze lifted from hers, and he stepped away with an imperceptible nod and a lopsided smile. "Let us walk by the river and complete our plans."

Their discussion faded with the distance, and Muirie collapsed in relief. Why had he not revealed her? Cormac would have thrown one of her sermons back at her without hesitation.

Muirie considered her actions as she returned to weeding, wondering why she had hidden. When the four men were together, she became overwhelmed. Lady Stewart's words about men and the Dundee Cake resurfaced.

She sighed and pulled hard on a weed, dirt flying into her face. She coughed and could not stop a laugh bubbling inside her—Dundee Cake indeed!

A sudden image of Reid with that dashing grin standing on a platter gave her pause, her heart beating faster.

"Ye look like the cat that ate the cream." Beathag stood over her with hands on hips. "What has ye so thoughtful?"

Muirie rose, brushed the dirt from her skirt, and pushed aside the unwelcomed musings. "Nothing at all."

"Do not tell me that. I just saw Cormac and his friends ambling toward the river, their mouths quicker than their thoughts."

Muirie lifted her brows. "And what did ye hear?"

Beathag shrugged as she plucked a flower from its stem. "I am not all that certain. Something about traveling to the sea mayhap."

She knew her friend too well not to notice the forestalling

in her tone.

"Beathag?"

The girl hummed as she plucked several stems and deposited them into Muirie's basket, avoiding her gaze.

"What do ye know of their plans?"

She lifted her head and sent Muirie an innocent glance. "They wish to journey to the sea and desire our company."

Muirie fought the desire to roll her eyes. "Did ye agree?"

A long silence followed.

"Ye did?"

Beathag twisted her lips into a pretty pout. "Mayhap. I see no harm in playing your chaperone. Lord and Lady Stewart shall be away with Lord and Lady Lamont for the day, and no one shall know." She shrugged. "There is no one to tell."

Muirie straightened and snatched up her basket. "'Tis no lark, Beathag. Two women in the company of four men is unseemly." She lowered her voice. "Surely ye see folly in this?"

"Nae, I do not. 'Tis a bit of amusement with friends. Who may fault us in that?" Releasing a huff, Beathag whirled and hastened down the path toward the bakehouse.

After a few steps, she halted and turned back to Muirie. "Ye need to get off your pious throne and have some merriment!" She rushed off.

The hurtful words jabbed at Muirie's heart. Was her friend right? Or was this a dangerous adventure she would do well to avoid?

CB&SO

Muirie squared her shoulders, clenching her fists at her side.

"Cormac, I—*we*—cannot consider such a journey with four men."

"Why ever not?" Cormac slanted his head toward Beathag who stooped over a bed of mint and snipped sprigs to place into a basket looped over her arm. Her wide smile met his, and he winked at her.

Muirie snatched her basket overflowing with herbs from the pebbled path. "The two of ye are mad to think such a scheme shall go unnoticed by Lord and Lady Stewart."

Cormac took two steps closer and whispered, "They shall be gone two days."

Beathag stood beside Muirie, staring at Cormac. "In truth?"

"Aye. A messenger confirmed the acceptance of their visit this morn."

Muirie saw the mutual interest in their exchanged glances. She prayed for strength, knowing she could not allow Beathag to travel without an escort—yet they looked to Beathag to be her chaperone.

Gavin approached, Reid and Peader on his heels, their boot paces crunching in rhythm. "Cormac, have ye not been able to convince these lasses to accompany us on our journey?"

When Cormac did not answer, Gavin continued, "Well, man? What say ye?"

Muirie brought her gaze to Cormac, whose face had reddened, and a pang of sympathy filled her. "No, sir. He has not achieved his goal. 'Twould be most improper for us to travel with ye."

The men stood shoulder-to-shoulder, eyes focused on the

women. Muirie studied each expression, and an unexpected revelation hit her. The four could not have been more different standing side-by-side as if for her to compare their many differences.

Peader's tall, lean form and pallid hair appeared more dissimilar than the other three. Cormac bore hair the color of the jackdaw and held a muscular, compact figure. Reid and Gavin were of a similar tall height. Gavin's brown hair showed the lightened streaks of a man who had been much in the out of doors while Reid's light hair bore a reddish tint.

All were fit and strong, so she and Beathag should be well guarded on the journey. Muirie knew Cormac mayhap be a bit of a scoundrel, yet he would protect them—to the death if need be.

"I think Muirie is wavering in her decision." Cormac chuckled. "The look she now wears is one I have grown accustomed to."

Gavin stepped from the row and faced Muirie. "Please do not fear. We shall have a care for ye both. No harm shall come to either of ye."

His amber eyes were warm, friendly with no hint of anything other than friendship in their depths. At least that was the way Muirie sensed it to be. She swallowed hard and nodded. A cough brought her around, and her eyes met Reid's. His steady gaze held something she could not determine, a solemnness within the way he studied her, the warmth now dimmed.

Muirie looked away, disappointment in herself gnawing at her. What had she just agreed to, and would she live to regret it?

70

Chapter Eight

1603

Sorcha knelt on the forest floor, her trembling hands flat upon the soft bed of leaves, moss, and pine needles, her head spinning.

She glanced up to see Evan running to her side, his bloodied sword still clutched in one hand. He fell to his knees beside her and smoothed her hair. "Are ye hurt, lass?"

Sorcha shook her head. "I am fine." Her voice and body trembled with weakness, uncertain it was because of the bairn or from what she had just witnessed. Mayhap both.

Evan untucked his shirt and tore a piece of fabric from the hem, wadding it into a fisted hand. Sorcha glanced at the man Evan had knocked out.

He followed her gaze. "Stay here." He rose and sprinted toward the burn, returning in seconds, the cloth dripping with cold water. He bathed Sorcha's face and neck until her pale face regained some of its color.

"Thank ye." She took in the unconscious man and the dead one. "What shall we do with them?"

She turned an expectant gaze upon Evan yet found his expression to hold regret. "I had nae choice, lass. It was kill or be killed. And I could not allow anything to happen to ye."

His ministrations slowed. He released the sword and brought his fingers to caress her cheek. "Do ye not see?"

"Aye. I ken. Ye had to." Sorcha's gaze roamed over his unruly hair and handsome face, eyes darkening with worry for her. Her focus shifted to his lips. What might it feel like to press her lips to his, to try and ease his pain and comfort him? She stiffened, mortified at the course of her thoughts.

His fingers still upon her cheek, their eyes held one another's. Shouts reverberated and grew closer with each cry.

Evan grabbed his sword and bolted to his feet in one fluid motion, standing guard over Sorcha in a warrior's stance. Outnumbered they may be, but she knew Evan would protect her until he could nae longer do so.

Sorcha's breath caught and held until the men came fully into view. They were all familiar faces, Kester leading them. Her shoulders slumped with relief, and the trembling eased.

Kester's gaze traveled from Sorcha to Evan. "What has happened? Clara noticed ye missing, and someone telt her the two of ye ran into the forest."

The broad-chested man cocked his head and lifted his chin,

expecting a reply.

Evan shuffled his feet, indecision on his face. "'Twas my fault. She mistook something I said, and we did argie."

Kester's features slowly relaxed. "Aye. Ye just wed." He gave them a mischievous wink. "Oniehow, we need be takin' care of them two thievers."

Sorcha was unsure if she liked or disliked Evan's explanation of why they had argued. She supposed it would have to do—or else she must tell him why she ran.

The men kept their distance as they discussed what was to be done about the intruders she and Evan encountered. She rose and stood behind Evan, listening to their talk, and soon learned they were to bury the dead man in a more thickly wooded area. They quarreled over what to do with the man.

Evan suggested they bind him and take him farther into the trees, giving them time to be out of the area.

Another man thought he had a better idea. "I say we finish him off afore he can do us more harm. He micht get away quicker than we think."

There were further murmurings before Kester held up his hand, and all fell silent. "I agree with Evan. We are not murderers, yet we micht make it a wee bit harder for the lad ta escape by tying him ta a tree."

With a brief hesitation, all the men voiced their agreement and carried out the tasks.

Sorcha approached Evan and placed a staying hand upon his forearm, stopping him from joining the others. "May we have a word?"

His grey eyes held a deep weariness, and she faltered at the sight. She was the reason they were in this difficulty, and she hated herself for it.

"I am so verra sorrow to have caused this. Please forgive me." She fought the tears so as not to shame herself more than she already had. "I shall ask forgiveness from everyone once we camp tonight."

"Evan!" Kester caught their attention. "Shall ye and Sorcha return ta the others? We have this in hand."

Evan nodded and led Sorcha to follow the men not needed to take the scoundrel into the woods. They strode in silence until they reached the path back to camp. Clara spotted them and rushed forward, wrapping her arms around them both. "I prayed and prayed for ye, and the Lord has delivered ye."

Sorcha's heart warmed at her friend's words and affection, yet she dreaded the confession to come for the true reason they found themselves in danger.

Clara crooned and fussed over them until Kester and the other men returned. Kester asked Clara if he could speak with Evan and Sorcha alone, and she left them, standing at the side of the path.

Kester blew out a breath. "I ken why ye were in the forest, but I think it not a good thought ta tell the others. I have told them it was the bairn that made ye ill, Sorcha. 'Tis a better tale so as not to make anyone angry that ye disrupted our journey."

Sorcha's tears caught in her throat, and she held them there and nodded until she could speak. "My heart is sore at doing so, Kester. Please forgive me."

"Nae, lass, dinnae fash yourself. 'Tis truly the bairn that

likely caused it." A shadow passed over his face. "I know what a bairn can do to his mither afore they are born."

He gave a slight bow, waving for the people to commence their trek.

Sorcha stilled, waiting for Clara to rejoin them, yet when Kester reached Clara, he claimed her arm and walked on. Sorcha and Evan shared a knowing look.

"It appears," Evan said, "my sister has claimed a prize."

Pleasure coursed through Sorcha. "Or perhaps Kester has." The revealing that Kester had lost those dear to him, coupled with Clara's loss, might just bond and heal two wounded people.

♥

Sorcha was at her breaking point when they stopped at midday for food, rest, and water, her body aching, and dread of the danger that lay ahead eating at her. Keeping within the forest where the River Dochart flowed, they would cross Campbell lands and arrive at day's end near the village of Lawers. The following day, a longer journey to Dalwhinnie awaited them.

The longest day—their last—pushing on to Clan Grant territory to Freuchie Castle. Evan explained that John Grant of Freuchie gave the land to his son, Patrick, who built the castle shortly afterward. He had grander plans and deserted it, moving to Rothiemurchus. Allaster sent a missive to the man and asked for his aid, and he replied that although abandoned and in disrepair Freuchie Castle was at their disposal.

A light rain commenced as they made camp for the night,

lighting no fires to signal their presence. Sorcha shivered and wrapped her cloak closer to her neck. She sheltered under an ancient yew, keeping most of the rain at bay.

Clara found her and sat, producing a cloth encasing their evening meal.

"'Tis enough to sustain us." She unwrapped the parcel and handed Sorcha hunks of bread and cheese.

"Thank ye. I am that weary. So much so I care not to eat yet know I must."

"Aye, ye must. If not for ye, for the bairn." Clara retrieved a flask. "Have a bit of ale too."

Sorcha accepted the offering—though she preferred the clean water from the burn. She exhaled and took a bite of bread, chewing thoughtfully. They sat in silence, too drained to pass a few words between them. Clara released a low sigh, and Sorcha glanced up to see Kester approaching. She watched her friend and saw a pleasing expression pass over her.

Kester focused his gaze upon Clara. "Forgive me for interrupting your meal, but I need your help with a bairn."

Clara blinked in confusion and did not rise.

He cleared his throat. "I mean to say a bairn is in distress, and his mither cannot quiet him. I fear someone may discover us."

Sorcha handed her food to Clara and made to rise, yet Clara refused the bundle.

"Nae, I shall go. Ye have your own bairn to think of."

Kester stretched his arm out to assist her, and Clara accepted. When she rose and faced him, she kept her eyes averted, allowing him to guide her.

Clara glanced over her shoulder and met Sorcha's knowing gaze. Aye, Clara was smitten beyond all measure.

As she ate and pondered her friend's situation, Evan came to her and eased himself down with a grunt to take Clara's place.

He rested his head against the tree trunk. "All appears to be in order for the night."

Sorcha watched him, his relaxed features made him appear younger. The straight nose, dark brown hair streaked by the sun, his lips . . . Her cheeks flushed, and she looked into the forest, her ears attuned to the sound of spilling water as if over rocks piled high.

She wanted to rush toward the flow and cleanse herself of their journey, wash away these unbidden thoughts that had captured her of late about Evan MacDonald.

Disgrace filled her. It had been less than three months since John died. How could she think of another man in such a way? A current of cold, damp mist cloaked her, and she shuddered at the contact. She feared for her bairn. John's bairn. Humiliation slammed against her heart, and she rose and, without hesitation, scurried toward the sound of the water.

Evan was at her side in moments. "Where are ye going?"

She could not look at him, fearful he saw the truth in her. "Leave me be, Evan. I want to be alone and wash myself in the burn."

He took her arm and made her stop. "'Tis too cold for that. The cold will chill and sicken ye and the child as well. Ye dinnae want that, do ye?"

Her gaze stayed on the brooch that held the MacDonald plaid to his shoulder. As tears surfaced, the green, blue, red, and black lines blended, losing their clarity.

They stood close together, and once composed, she looked up, his eyes holding an emotion she had not seen before. Was it longing? His eyes were on her lips, and she panicked.

"Forgive me, I must go to the water." She backed away, and before she turned, she said, "Ye may follow at a distance. I want to be alone for a while." She inhaled deeply. "Please?"

His nod was slight, and she took long strides until the waterfall came into view, a sliver of moonlight illuminating the breathtaking scene. She wanted to swim directly to the flow and let it overtake her, knowing she could not do so for many reasons. Evan was right. She could not afford to become ill. She stood at the edge of the burn and admired God's beautiful creation.

Her gaze caught the glint of light upon a series of smooth rocks crossing to the waterfall as if by design. She glanced over her shoulder, unable to see Evan—though she felt his presence close at hand.

Sorcha placed one tentative step onto the first stone at the edge of the water, testing to see if it was secure. She remained upon it for a moment and savored the scent of the forest, pine especially sweet to her senses. They bore a cleanliness about them she could not explain. The next step was surer, and she continued, carefully until she reached the fall. She drew the icy water to herself with a cupped hand and drank her fill, the taste of it like a touch of sweetness from heaven.

She breathed in the place's essence, the peace of her surroundings. If only she could stay here forever. She and her bairn. Braving a few more steps until she stood behind the fall, she watched the water flow in front of her.

The air was not as cool here, and she assumed it was because the rocks behind her and the water in front acted as walls. She turned toward the stone and discovered it to be a shallow cave. Wishing she had a candle to explore, she inched toward the blackness with outstretched arms and waited for her fingers to make contact with the rocks. Despite taking a dozen or more steps, she still could not locate the wall.

"Sorcha?"

She whirled toward the voice, heart racing until Evan's silhouette shone against the waterfall.

Sorcha clasped her stomach and heaved a sigh. "Ye near scared the life from me, Evan MacDonald!"

"Sorry, lass, I think we must go. Clara shall be worried."

She followed him from the cave, and they walked on for a time. When they neared the camp, Evan gripped her arm and pulled her behind a tree.

"What is wrong? Why do ye stop?"

Evan brought a finger to her lips and whispered, "Stay here. 'Tis too still. We should hear something by now." He crouched and made his way toward the camp, concealing himself behind underbrush and trees. He disappeared, soon returning with Kester, who greeted her with a nod. An eerie silence followed them.

Without a word, Kester led them through the trees to a secluded spot beside the burn, the women and children huddled together, the men encircling them.

Kester took them to the man who was acting as a guard. In hushed tones, the man told Evan and Sorcha of his hearing a horse's whinny some distance from camp, and he had returned to tell Kester. They immediately rounded up the entire camp and led them to this hiding spot in a thickly wooded copse.

Sorcha drew closer to the gathered men and placed a hand on Evan's arm. "Tell them about the cave. We could hide there. 'Tis close quarters but 'twill suffice."

Evan's eyes swept her face, and he nodded, then looked at the men. "'Tis truth." He pointed toward the water. "If we follow the burn south, 'tis there we cross to the waterfall, and the cave lies behind." He pursed his lips. "We must stay upon the stones so as not to leave a trail. Have the men carry the bairns and take hold of the women so they dinnae fall."

Kester cleared his throat and glanced at Clara. "What aboot the horses? I know we have few, but they are needed."

Evan drew in an audible breath, his expression awash with concern. He and Kester stared at one another for a moment. "Aye. Where should we hide them until the Campbells pass?"

A man spoke. "Shall they not fit into the cave?"

Evan shook his head. "Nae. Yet we could take them across the burn and tie them well past our hiding place on the other side. Far enough so as not to give us away."

"Aye." Kester agreed. "We must remove the belongings and loose the horses into a glen to graze, hopeful they shall stay until we retrieve them. At least they shall not reveal us."

Nods of agreement went around the group, and Kester and

the appointed guards sprang into action.

Evan clapped Kester on the shoulder. "What do ye say to having two swift-footed men creating a false trail for the thief-loon Campbells to move afar from us?"

Kester's lips broke into a grin. "Aye. I know just the men." He turned and quietly sprinted to the back of the group.

Sorcha's trust in Evan grew in that moment. He was a natural leader, and Kester saw the value in him, following his lead without question. Her pulse thrummed in her ears, echoing from within her. Yet could she open her heart again?

82

Chapter Nine

1710

"Muirie! Ye must convince Lady Euphemia to go with them." Beathag's voice took on a desperate tone.

"She is much too wise to be convinced of anything she does not want to do." Muirie sighed and tried a different path. "Ye must see the journey is unpleasant for one of her age."

Beathag puckered her lips. "If ye promise her something she desires, maybe she could be led to go."

"And that might be . . . ?" Muirie's tone suggested mockery, yet she could not help herself. The situation was hopeless.

"We must think of something. They depart early on the

morrow."

Muirie blew out a breath. "I know not."

A deep, male voice interrupted their conversation. "And who is it ye must convince?"

Muirie looked up to see Gavin, who wore a playful smile, and she warmed at his expression. "Grannam. With her still in the castle, we shall not be able to make our excursion."

"Why is that?" He strode toward the women where they rested upon a bench beneath a willow tree.

Beathag groaned. "The old woman is most clever and shall discover our plans. Make nae doubt."

"Hm. I see." Gavin paced before them, head bent, hands clasped behind his back. "There is one who may convince her."

Beathag shot from her seat. "Please share who ye speak of, sir."

A smile illuminated his face. "Did not Peader make an impression upon the dear lady at our arrival?"

Gavin was right. For some unknown reason, Peader enchanted Grannam. He had a way about him she fed upon. Mayhap her vanity?

"Aye, ye are correct."

Beathag clapped her hands. "So what shall we do to use this to our gain?"

Gavin dipped a bow. "Leave that to me, lass." He offered a brilliant smile and departed.

Beathag looked at Muirie. "What will he do?"

Muirie shrugged. "I am uncertain what he can do. How is

Peader to convince her of anything—and why?"

"Lady Euphemia is a canny woman. Mayhap Peader shall persuade her to our way." Beathag cocked her head. "If he is able, I have no fear she shall keep our secret."

"'Tis truth. Once she is on your side, she remains."

Beathag yawned. "Well, I must be off. 'Tis time to prepare the evening meal. Mistress Picken shall have my head if I am not presently in the kitchen."

"We shall soon know if our plan shall progress. I must get through the meal to discover if that shall be so." Muirie rose and yawned as well. "Grannam's behavior shall reveal all whilst we dine."

They linked arms and strode toward the castle, Beathag adding, "Find me once ye have dined."

"I shall." Muirie heaved an exhausted sigh. "Now I must dress and appear as if I know naught and regale everyone at table with my day of excitement."

Her friend chuckled. "Aye. The happenings of the garden and such."

"Indeed."

Muirie and Beathag parted ways at the entrance to the kitchen, and Muirie made her way upstairs, her mind swirling around the intrigues of their journey to the sea. Was she mad to consider it? She yawned again, the call of her bed much too strong. Her early rising caught up with her. All she desired was sleep.

Suddenly, images of Reid and Gavin flashed before her. Their presence at table in a short while enlivened her, and she thought of how to dress and arrange her hair. She paused in the corridor and brought her hand to her forehead. Was she daft? Neither of the men could be interested in her. She held no dowry, nor did she have a relational connection to a family of nobility or gentry. She was *no one*—neither a member of the family nor a servant.

Footsteps sounded behind her, and she spun around to find Gavin. He halted at the top of the stairs.

"Good eve."

"Good eve, sir." Her disordered thoughts prevented her from finding further words.

"Shall ye dine with us this eve?" Gavin drew closer, arms folded across his chest.

"I shall."

"I look forward to conversing with ye." He dipped his chin and strolled down the corridor to the landing and out of her sight.

She drew in a hard breath, her feelings colliding. Once again, she reminded herself that Muirie Stewart was a *nobody*.

The great hall's high wooden beams sent the servant's low voices echoing through the chamber as they prepared for the evening meal. Muirie aided Beathag who kept urging her to return to her chamber and dress.

"Dinnae fash yourself, Beathag. I shall have plenty of time." Muirie placed the large vessel of flowers at the center of the table holding the platters of food from which the servants removed to carry to those who dined.

Muirie's awe at the ornate dining hall never diminished. The intricate golden-etched candelabrums along the center of the table sent flickering candlelight sparkling off the crystal goblets.

"'Twould not be seemly for ye to be caught acting the . . ."

"Go on. Say it. Acting the servant." She released an irritated breath. "I know my place—that of someone who belongs nowhere."

Beathag's eyes misted, and she turned from Muirie busying herself arranging the goblets on the long table at each place setting. Her voice quivered. "Ye are much more than ye imagine."

Muirie bit her lip to staunch the surging tears and looked away. A lad passed with a tray, and the aroma of a spiced dish caused her stomach to churn. She could not bear the thought of eating and wondered how to get through the lengthy meal.

Though it was early spring, cheerful fires burned in the fireplaces that bracketed each end of the chamber to chase the evening's chill away.

"I shall do as ye say and ready myself."

Beathag nodded.

Muirie desired nothing more than to run to her chamber and hide for as long as they had guests. Thankfully, she did not see any of them on the stairs or corridors and lay on her bed for a while. The faces of Gavin and Reid kept haunting her. Why? Each treated her respectfully and acted as if they truly enjoyed her company. Is that not how friends behaved?

Were they her friends, albeit new? Cormac was her brother *and* her friend. Was he not?

The comfort of the mattress and the weariness of the day caught up with her, and her mind and body drifted toward the trance-like ecstasy before sleep arrives. She gave in to the sensation, hoping no one would miss her at table.

It seemed mere minutes passed when her door burst open and slammed shut.

"Muirie!"

Her eyes flew open, and Beathag's frantic gaze met hers. "Ye must hurry. Lady Stewart is not happy with your absence and sent me to fetch ye!"

She groaned and rolled to one side. "Shall ye tell her I am not well?"

Beathag squared her shoulders. "What?"

A deep, painful sigh left her, guilt replacing it.

"Shall ye help me dress?"

She cocked her head. "Do ye really feel unwell?"

Hesitantly, Muirie shook her head. "Not in the body."

Beathag retrieved a dress and stood beside the bed. "Tomorrow shall lift your spirits. A visit to the sea shall be a balm, what with the sea air, the bonny sand, and four braw lads to attend us."

She lifted one brow. "Does that not sound merry?"

Muirie could not suppress the smile. Her friend always saw the best in whatever may come.

"I suppose so." Muirie turned so Beathag could assist her and resigned herself to the eve ahead. A night of pasting on a smile when she felt none, speaking clever words she did not possess, and fending off questions she knew not how to answer.

Muirie arrived in the hall, and the conversation flowed as well as the food and drink. Her skin heated at her late arrival with all eyes turned to her entrance.

The men rose, waiting for her to sit before returning to their seats. Lord Stewart slanted a puzzled expression toward her.

"Muirie, are ye well?

"I am well enough, my lord. Thank ye." She took a sip of the watered wine and forced courage. "I must apologize for my absence. Weariness overtook me, and I meant to close my eyes for a brief respite and did not wake in time."

"Ye are forgiven."

"Thank ye, my lord." Muirie lowered her gaze to her plate as a servant held a platter waiting for her to take a portion.

The hum of conversation returned, and when a low voice spoke at her side, she started and looked up.

Gavin sat to her right and repeated, "*Are* ye well?"

Reid interrupted. "Did ye not hear her, *Lamont*? She told Lord Stewart she was well." To Muirie's ears, the tone in which he said the man's name held no small amount of bitterness.

Gavin's head snapped toward Reid as if he had been slapped. "What has ye so tetchy?"

"My apologies. 'Twas not meant in offense." Reid dipped his chin. "I slept ill." He returned to his food, not meeting Muirie's eyes.

Gavin whispered, "Let us hope ye are in better spirits on

the morrow."

Reid shot him a look of disdain.

Muirie ate little, picking at her food to hide her unease. She longed to return to her bed and oblivion in slumber.

"Muirie?"

She looked up to see Grannam staring at her from across the table. "What ails ye, lass? I know when ye are *unweel*." She dragged the old Scottish pronunciation out like a curse.

"No, Grannam. Truly. I am fine." Muirie took a bite to forestall another question.

Gavin chuckled, bringing a hard look from Reid.

A crash sounded from the corridor, and Grannam grunted. "Glad I am that was not one of your precious china platters, Isabel."

"Aye, Grannam, the sound of a silver tray meeting the stone floor is unmistakable." She smiled. "Elizabeth, please tell us of your recent trip to Edinburgh. Have ye attended many balls?"

Lady Stewart expressed an air of calm, yet Muirie knew the look of her. She tried to ease the tension and with polite interest focused on her guests.

Elizabeth answered, becoming the center of attention, which she seemed to enjoy, particularly when Cormac commented. For the next half hour, she spoke of nothing other than dresses, jewelry, and dancing. And the number of men she danced with. When she asked Lady Stewart about music and what instruments the castle held, Muirie knew her intention.

Muirie smiled behind her goblet. Neither Lady Stewart nor

Grannam were easily led. Biting her lip, she tilted her head and found Reid watching her. He leaned closer.

"Elizabeth has more than met her match." He glanced in Grannam's direction.

Muirie followed his gaze and noted the old woman's tight-lipped expression, her eyes dancing with mischief.

"Ye are correct. As well as Lady Stewart. They are of a like mind."

"Lady Stewart, which instrument do ye play?" Elizabeth smiled coyly and daintily placed a bite of carrot in her mouth. Muirie marveled at how she smiled so charmingly and chewed at the same time.

To halt a burst of laughter, Muirie not so daintily placed a piece of bread in her own mouth.

Gavin whispered, "How can my sister smile with a lump of carrot in her mouth?"

Muirie sputtered, her laugh shifting to a violent cough. She snatched up her serviette and covered her mouth, trying not to meet anyone's eyes.

Lady Lamont asked with concern, "Have ye choked, my dear?"

As she shook her head, Reid answered for her. "No, my lady. Gavin told her a jest at a most importune time." His impish smile focused on his friend. "*Gavin*, please share the jest so we may all join in the amusement." Reid leisurely brought a morsel of fish to his faintly twitching lips.

Gavin picked up the gauntlet, pursed his lips, and a corner of his mouth lifted. "I fear it would not be proper to interrupt my sister's seeking of musical entertainment." He slanted his gaze toward Reid, then brought it to Elizabeth. "Were ye aware my friend relishes singing at a party?"

A bad feeling swept through Muirie. Reid's cheeks reddened, and he muttered something under his breath. He paused, fork hovering above his plate, all eyes focused on him.

"Not so very much. Only if I am forced." He pierced Gavin with a stare. "Yet . . . ye usually accompany me."

Gavin's cheeks blazed, the men volleying murderous looks at one another.

Muirie said a silent prayer for God to calm the waters before they carried their jests too far. Cormac had been silent throughout the exchange and shot a glance at Peader.

"Peader, let us take the two rogues and have a game of billiards." Cormac rose, notched his head toward the door, and slid his chair into place under the table.

Peader stood, his pale hair glinting in the candlelight, and bowed. "Lord and Lady Stewart. Thank ye for a fine meal." His eyes sought Gavin and Reid, now standing, their faces still flushed.

As they reached the door, Elizabeth called after them. "I should like to hear ye sing once Lady Stewart and I arrange our musical."

Although the girl was several seats away, Muirie thought she detected a hint of rebellion in her expression.

Only Cormac responded. "We shall see." He bowed, and the four men left them in a sea of discomfort.

Muirie looked around the table.

Lord Lamont and Lord Stewart did not appear concerned, their conversation continuing as before.

However, Lady Stewart and Grannam's gazes were upon Muirie, their eyes holding curious unease. What had she done?

94

Chapter Ten

1603

The warmth of the cave welcomed them—though with so many bodies, the air lost the fresh scent of the forest. Sorcha and Clara huddled together while the men remained at the entrance with weapons in hand. They waited for the return of the two men who were leading the Campbells away.

In what seemed like hours, their success was reported, and the group determined to take a more northeasterly path. They would stay on the west side of the burn, believing the searchers made their way opposite.

As the men told of their ruse, Sorcha listened attentively, keeping her gaze on Evan, studying him. Filtered light from the cave's entrance grazed him, revealing sun-streaked locks of brown hair that had come loose from its cord.

The roar of a deer brought the group to silence, bringing all eyes to the cave's opening. She read the thoughts of the guards. They were concerned their hiding place may belong to red deer often taking shelter in such a structure during the winter months. Spring was late in coming with snow flecking the air.

A deer would be an ideal source of food if they could burn a fire. Sorcha wondered if the back of the cave offered enough depth to hide a fire and smoke. She gripped the cold stone and trailed her hand along the wall, inching her way further into their cavernous refuge. When she rounded a curve, the path widened, and she was plunged into darkness.

Sorcha halted and waited for her vision to adjust to the blackness. After a moment, a hint of light appeared through a crack in the rock high above her head. The smoke could dissipate by the time it reached such a height, which might be perfect to cook whatever they found whether deer, fish, or fowl.

"Sorcha?" Evan's voice came softly from a distance.

She turned and called out, "Evan, come look at this."

Shuffling feet neared, and his arm wrapped around her shoulders. "Aye." He drew in a loud, deep breath. "Lass, ye shave years from my life with your wanderings."

His tone held controlled exasperation, and another pang of shame arose to have caused him to worry yet again.

"Oh, Evan. I am that sorry. 'Tis a thought I had and acted upon it."

He squeezed her against his side. "Ye are resourceful, lass.

Ye must also learn to care for your safety." His hand rested upon her stomach, and she stiffened.

He jerked back, removing his hand. "Forgive me. I was going to say for the bairn's safety as well."

She swallowed so hard she could hear it and heaved a long breath. "I am sorry—again. Ye startled me."

"It was not my place to do so—I mean, to touch ye so." He moved away from her. "I shall not do so again."

Before he could turn and leave, she held out a hand to him. "Do not go. I want to show ye something." She pointed toward the light as if he could see her hand. "Look up. See the light?"

His voice came closer once more "Aye. 'Tis a long distance from us."

"If we find food, we may cook it here, and no one shall see us."

"'Tis truth. Fish from the burn or deer." A smile lit his voice. "Or rabbits and birds."

Wishing she could see his charming smile, she asked, "Could ye start a fire?"

His chuckle warmed her. "Aye, lass." The sound of rocks scuttling across the cavern floor echoed softly off the walls. A rip of fabric split the silence, and then rocks grating against one another brought sparks flying.

Within minutes, a burst of light flashed, and she saw his face as he knelt before the flame. He rose quickly. "Stay and I shall return soon." He sprinted and before long returned with a few branches, dried leaves clinging to them.

Once the leaves ignited, he carefully held a few to the flame and added pieces of the branch. Footsteps sounded behind them, and a line of people, all carrying dried branches, arrived placing their offerings upon the growing blaze.

Kester and Clara stood shoulder-to-shoulder, smiling, and Kester said, "Now we need something ta put upon the fire."

Sorcha looked around and discovered the cave was much larger than she had imagined—large enough to accommodate their people.

One man who had helped with the two strangers said quietly, "I think we should bring the horses in. The night shall be cold, and we would not want to lose them."

Kester nodded. Agreement reverberated among the crowd.

A handful of men volunteered to bring the animals inside with night soon falling, and others hunted for food.

Once they had made their pallets and all had settled to wait for the hunters to return, Sorcha and Clara huddled together, whispering. She longed to sit by a fire with her tambor frame doing her needlework, resting in the peace that all was well in her world, awaiting John's arrival at day's end.

Sorcha shook off the sad musings and leaned a shoulder against Clara's. "Have ye and Kester come to an accord?"

Clara's head whipped around toward Sorcha. "What makes ye say such a thing?"

She pursed her lips to hide a smile. "Ye have formed a habit of walking together, so I—"

"Sorcha, say naught about it. We are friends." She turned and surveyed the fire with more interest than was necessary.

Sorcha nudged her. "'Tis naught to be ashamed of. He is a fine man."

Clara tucked her chin, and Sorcha could see the small smile that played upon her lips. "Aye, he is."

"And bonny too?" Sorcha teased.

Clara's smile widened. "Aye." The word held more emotion than Sorcha had ever heard her friend express.

A commotion sounded, and the hunters returned laden with meat. They had already cleaned and prepared it, burying the refuse so as not to reveal their hiding place.

Murmurings sounded among the group, but they knew to keep their voices low. Their lives depended upon it. This small reprieve was a celebration of sorts. Something long overdue.

Sorcha's heart swelled with pride and relief. This night would refresh them for the journey ahead.

⁂

Sorcha rotated to her side and found the back of Clara's head, thick auburn hair glossy in the low firelight. She rolled to her other side and found Evan's watchful eyes upon her.

He smiled. "Good morn, wife."

She bit the inside of her cheek and nodded. "Good morn."

Why was he sleeping so close to her? It made her feel— exposed. Although their marriage was one of convenience, she felt she owed him something for her protection. Also for the safety of her child. Not his child.

"Did I startle ye again, lass?" He propped upon one elbow.

"Nae." She hesitated. "Not really."

"If I make ye uneasy, I shall go." He made to rise, and she gripped his arm.

"Nae. 'Tis still early, and no one else is stirring. I would not have ye waken anyone." She laid upon her back and peered at the pinprick of light overhead.

"Ye always think of others afore yourself." He laid back and studied the ceiling.

Did she? Sorcha supposed it was true, but what did he mean by the words, especially the gentle way he had spoken. A silence settled over them until she asked, "Shall we make it to the Stewart holding this day?"

"'Tis hard to say. Should we do so, it shall be verra late. I shall speak to Kester and the others. If we break the journey into another shorter day, we shall arrive more freshened."

She tilted her head to look at him. "Why?"

His gaze met hers, and it came to rest upon her lips. Unsettling her, she looked away.

"We must arrive with as much strength as possible since we know not what awaits us."

Kester approached with careful steps and motioned for Evan to follow him. Before Evan rose, he offered her a tender expression.

When he had gone, Sorcha wondered what the look had meant along with his words. Did he hold feelings for her, or was it pity?

Clara sat up, and her gaze followed the two men, who soon joined the others near the cave entrance.

They broke their fast with food from the previous night's feast to fortify them for the long day ahead. Sorcha and Clara, along with the other women and children, followed their guide to a secluded spot by the burn to drink and wash.

After they had assembled, Kester spoke with authority.

"We care ta arrive at the castle when we are more rested as we know not what awaits us. The fresher we are, the stronger we are and should there be Campbells, or soldiers, we have more likely of a chance to defend ourselves."

His gaze roamed the group. "We must search for nearby caves and stay there—as we did here—until we have observed the castle for a day or so. To be certain nae one is about."

The idea seemed logical to Sorcha, and Clara nodded her understanding. One man rose and disagreed, and after some deliberation, they convinced him of the sensibleness in the plan. Cautiously, they made their way in their usual formation and followed the burn, men stationed at the front and back with others scattered throughout the line, battle-ready.

Again, Sorcha watched Clara and Kester walk together chatting. Why did she and Evan seem to have little to say to one another? Was it her, or him, raising the barricade between them?

A pain shot across her stomach, and she faltered, stumbling against Evan. He wrapped an arm around her back and steadied her.

"What is wrong?" He kept their pace, still supporting her.

When she looked into his eyes, she saw genuine fear. "'Tis only the bairn." She laid a palm against her side, and the pain returned—though not as strong.

They walked on, and he kept his hold on her, his gaze constantly wavering between her and the path.

Another movement rotated across her middle, and she realized the child had quickened. A slow smile formed on her lips. She could feel the bairn. This time she had carried a child much longer than any of the others. She laughed, and Evan jerked at the sound.

Sorcha took his hand and placed it on her stomach. His wide-eyed look made her chuckle again until it changed into one of awe.

"'Tis the bairn?" He grinned like a small lad, a curious look shone in his eyes. "Yet your belly is small." His cheeks reddened, forcing another laugh from her.

"Evan, do ye know what this means?" Tears of joy streamed down her cheeks.

His expression showed he did not understand.

"John and I have lost so many bairns. All afore they were this big." She softly patted her middle. "'Tis a sign. This bairn—*my* John's bairn—shall live."

His expression brightened, faded to sadness, and then brightened again. "Aye. I am happy for ye, Sorcha. John would be verra happy."

Overcome with joy and relief, she flung her arms around his waist, holding him close as others filtered around them, all smiling and nodding, sharing their joy.

She could hear his hard swallow, yet he held her close, his hands warm against her back. She closed her eyes and relished the feeling of being cared for, even if it was not John who held her.

CS✠SO

As they approached the end of the long day's journey at Rothiemurchus, the border of the vast forest on Clan Stewart holdings, a light snow fell from the night sky, white dots against the black.

Though she was deeply chilled, Sorcha tilted her head back, letting the soft flakes pepper her. She had always liked the snow. Sometimes she wondered if it was because of the quiet beauty it created by covering all the dead plants, leaving the green of the pines, spruces, and firs to stand out against the blue sky.

Evan nudged her. "Ye look like Clara when she was a small lass. Mither scolded her for running from the croft without her wrap or shoes."

Sorcha tittered and leaned into him for warmth. "Then we are kindred spirits. I feel as if she is my sister."

Evan examined her, and one corner of his mouth lifted. "Aye. 'Tis telling how well ye get on."

"Is it now?" Sorcha asked.

"Aye, lass. It does my heart guid."

A shout from the front of the procession halted their progress. "Aye, a gudelie place has been found for our night's rest."

Kester waved his hand above his head, encouraging all to follow. They wove their way through the heavily wooded area to what had once been a shelter-stell. Though the small stone ruin had once held sheep, it would at least provide a place for the elderly and youngest of their clan.

When Evan tried to take Sorcha and Clara there, they refused, saying they were fit enough to harbor under a thick fir.

With a skeptical stare, he turned on his heels and departed.

"I think we offended him," Clara said.

"Ye know your brother better than I." Sorcha wrapped her cloak tighter around her and lowered herself near the trunk of the fir, resting against the massive tree. The needles shed on the forest floor created a thick layer of protection against the damp earth, almost like a mattress. She relished no longer walking and released a long sigh.

"That sounds like relief." Clara chuckled. "I know how ye feel—well, nearly. I have no bairn to carry 'round."

"Nae ye dinnae, sister." Evan towered over them, feet planted wide, arms crossed over his chest.

Both women gazed up at him.

"Both of ye go shelter somewhere better than this." He spread his arms wide to encompass the area under the tree branches.

Sorcha released one arm from her cloak and patted the ground beside her. "Please sit, Evan. 'Tis making my neck pain to look up at ye."

His frown changed to an endearing smile, and he obeyed his wife, sitting close enough for their shoulders to touch.

Clara shot him a look of annoyance, and Sorcha tempered the moment by patting Clara's arm. "Evan wants to protect us." She turned to him. "We are well, Evan. The elderen and bairns need the shelter more than we."

He said nothing, holding her gaze so long she finally brought her palm to cup his cheek. "I promise I am well—just weary. Nothing a night's rest shall not repair."

He slowly relaxed and placed his hand over hers. "Should ye become ill, I shall have something to say."

Clara coughed and rose, looking down at them. "I shall find

food and drink for us." With a glimmer in her eyes, she strode away, leaving footprints in the new snow surrounding the tree.

Evan looped his arm around Sorcha's shoulder and rested his head against hers. "Do ye mind me doing this?"

A week before, she would not have known what to say, and now she found herself shaking her head. "Nae. I dinnae mind."

Chapter Eleven

1710

Muirie listened intently as the women walked to the parlor. Elizabeth continued pressing Lady Stewart to have a musical evening once they returned from their visit away.

Grannam's grip on Muirie's arm tightened when Elizabeth volunteered to stay with Grannam while the others traveled for the two-day journey.

The elder woman angled toward Muirie and muttered, "I would sooner have my eye put out by a hot poker than have that lass underfoot for two days."

Muirie cleared her throat, repressing a grin. "Grannam. Say no such thing."

Grannam reared back and peered at her. "Ye care to have

her with us whilst they are gone?" She lifted her eyes to the ceiling. "Daft child."

The thought came unbidden. "Why do ye not go with them? At least the presence of others mayhap buffer the closeness."

She studied Muirie for a time, deep in concentration. "Ye are a canny lass. Mayhap ye are right." The old woman chortled, and a thoughtful expression crossed her face. "I may claim an aching head and have my meals sent to my chamber with port and whatever I desire."

"And who is the canny lass now, Grannam?" Muirie smiled sweetly. A touch of guilt laced with relief deflated her. "A change of scenery would do ye well."

"Aye. Mayhap ye are right, child." She patted Muirie's arm.

They reached the parlor as Beathag was leaving, having delivered tea for the ladies after the dinner repast. Muirie met her gaze, and they gave one another a conspiratorial grin.

Elizabeth still chattered on about dancing and singing, and she swore to have a plan worked out by the time they returned to the castle. She suggested staying behind with Grannam, so she could work it out and have it ready by the time they all returned.

"Dinnae fash yourself, dear. I shall come along."

The girl's expression fell. It was obvious she planned to stay for reasons other than planning her musical evening.

Muirie thought it mayhap have something to do with Cormac. Elizabeth's gaze seemed to land upon him often. Not once had she seen her look upon Cormac's friends in the same manner.

Lady Stewart handed Grannam a cup of tea which she accepted with a grimace. "Aye. A bit of travel shall do my old soul a mite good."

She sipped the tea and sent a satisfied smile toward Elizabeth.

Elizabeth squinted, and Muirie saw something in the girl's eyes that made her shiver, a touch of malice lurking there. She must strengthen her guard.

"Grannam, 'tis wonderful ye have chosen to come." Lady Stewart beamed. "We shall have a grand time."

Grannam's expression disagreed. "Aye, my dear. We shall have a grand time." She winked at Muirie. "A grand *old* time." On this, she looked at Elizabeth and wiggled her eyebrows.

Muirie bit her lower lip and dipped her chin. The journey would be interesting indeed.

A hesitant knock sounded, and the door eased open.

To Muirie's surprise, Peader slipped in. He bowed, one hand behind his back and focused his attention on Grannam, stepping to stand in front of her.

"My lady." He bowed again and whipped his arm around to reveal a lovely bouquet tied neatly with purple ribbon.

The elder woman's face transformed into a girlish visage, and she tittered, bringing her fingers to her lips. "For me?"

"Aye, my lady. To the loveliest one in the castle."

Muirie gave the lad credit for his gallant gesture, yet she questioned the reason. What was there to gain from such a display?

Grannam tentatively reached for the flowers and sniffed,

her expression filled with pleasure. Her lips curved, and she patted the seat beside her. "Sit, my boy, and tell me why ye are so attentive."

He leaned closer, yet Muirie could not hear the exchange.

"While the others are gone, I shall look after ye." He took one of Grannam's hands and pressed a kiss to the back of it, gaze slanted to peer up at her.

She tilted her head, pursed her lips a moment, and whispered, "What are ye up to, lad? There is something afoot or else ye would not be courting me thus."

Muirie either saw a twinkle in her eyes, or the candlelight played a trick on her. Though she had to agree with Grannam, Peader was most definitely up to something, and she had a goodly idea what it was.

"Peader." Lady Stewart interrupted their tête-à-tête. "I am quite aware ye have a liking for my grandmother, but I care to know what plans ye have in mind for her entertainment whilst we are absent. I also must inform ye she has agreed to accompany us."

In the background, Elizabeth's murmurings gave Muirie pause. There was something else afoot in that quarter, and she discerned the result to be her brother, Elizabeth, and the chapel.

"Isabel, ye must learn to mind your manners." Grannam cleared her throat. "Mayhap I shall stay and allow young Peader to divert me as he sees fit." She brought her adoring gaze to Peader who now squirmed in his seat.

Before she turned to Grannam and Peader, Muirie noted the irritated flash in Elizabeth's eyes.

Muirie cleared her throat. "Peader, would ye be so kind as to take me to Cormac? I have a question for him."

The young man stood and bowed to Grannam. "I shall miss your company whilst ye are gone, my lady. Please have a pleasant journey." He kissed her hand once more and escorted Muirie from the chamber.

Muirie kept silent until they reached the landing, then glanced at her escort. "Which one of your friends put ye up to that?" She pointed toward the parlor.

Peader halted and looked over his shoulder. "'Twas not precisely a command." He waved a hand for her to precede him up the stairs to the floor where the other men played at billiards.

Muirie preceded him, and once they were again on the same level, she repeated the question.

Heaving a long-suffering sigh, he answered, "Cormac."

"And what did he mean to gain?"

He lowered his voice. "To hinder her so she would not be aware of our goings on." His chin lowered, watching his feet upon the corridor.

Muirie placed a hand on his arm. "Ye do not have to do as he bid."

"This I know. But he is my friend."

Respect or intimidation could gain friendship. How came Peader to be Cormac's friend? She studied him for a moment yet said nothing and waited for him to accompany her into the chamber where the clack of billiard balls reverberated.

The low burning fire sent a waft of smoke through the door, and Muirie stifled a sneeze. At their entrance, Cormac, Reid, and Gavin froze, their eyes on her, surprise in their gazes.

Gavin strode toward them, cue in hand. "To what do we owe the pleasure of a lovely lady to visit a man's domain?" He bowed over Muirie's hand and kissed it.

Peader opened his mouth to speak, but Muirie quickly spoke first, tugging her hand free from Gavin's grasp. "Cormac, I am stunned ye tasked Peader to play the frasier to influence Grannam so ye could have a day of merriment." Her fury rose. "Did ye suppose a bit of flattery would gain her silence should she discover our journey?"

Cormac's mouth dropped and then closed.

The silence hanging in the chamber gave Muirie time to consider why she came to confront her brother. What purpose did it serve? She shook her head and turned to leave, a staying hand on her shoulder halting her.

"Muirie, please forgive me." Cormac's voice held genuine remorse, and her heart tumbled, just as it had when they were small. Cormac as a boy always deferred to her choice in games, song, or sport. She could envisage his cherubic face gazing at her with adoration, and her heart swelled.

She suppressed the building tears and looked down, nodding before she sprinted from the chamber.

Cঙঽঝঞঠ

Muirie slammed the door to her chamber with a decided crash. Why had she allowed Cormac's apology to affect her so? Now she had embarrassed herself in front of him and his friends. The last person she saw when she turned to depart the chamber had been Reid, who wore an expression of curiosity and understanding.

A light tap on her door brought her head up. "I am unwell. Please depart."

The door opened a wide crack, and Beathag poked her head through. "What ails ye? Lady Stewart and her guests retired a while ago."

"I left them early. Please leave me be." She sank onto the side of the bed and released the tears she held since she departed Cormac and his friends. They must suppose her daft. How could she face them again?

Beathag ignored her plea, entered, and secured the door behind her. "What has happened?"

She fell backward onto the mattress, her stare focused on the wine-colored bed hangings. The pattern blurred through her tears, and she sputtered, "I have made a fool of myself. There will be no outing on the morrow."

"Nae! Say ye have not hindered the day. I was so looking forward to it." She plopped onto the bed beside Muirie. "Say 'tis not so."

Muirie rolled away, burying her head in the counterpane. "'Tis so. Sorry I am. I know ye looked forward to the day. 'Twill not happen."

Beathag sprang from the bed, sending the mattress to shift and roll Muirie onto her side. She slammed her fists onto her hips and glared at Muirie. "Cormac will answer for this."

She twirled toward the door, and Muirie stayed her. "No! Ye must not seek him out."

"And why ever not?" Beathag held the half-open door in one hand and the other waved erratically in the air.

"He is most likely angry with me." Muirie sat upright,

hands clasped in her lap.

"I shall speak with him." Beathag drew in a shaky breath and calmed. "We are to meet later."

"No. Ye must not do so. 'Tis unseemly at this late hour." Muirie slid from the bed, took a step forward, and opened her mouth to admonish her friend.

Without another word, Beathag withdrew, quietly closing the door behind her.

Drawing courage, Muirie splashed cold water on her face and made to follow the maid. She could not allow them to carry on in such a way and endanger both their reputations.

Careful not to disturb the house, she tiptoed silently down the stairs and into the dark courtyard. The rippling waters of the River Deveron sounded in the night, mingling with the occasional whinny of a horse. The ten stalls in the stable were now full, considering the number of their guests.

When Muirie stepped into the courtyard, her footsteps crunched, and she winced at the sound. The old tower house loomed over the stables as if a terrible beast ready to devour it. Keeping her regard on the stables, a flicker of candlelight barely shone through one of the small, shuttered windows. Low voices greeted her approach.

"No, Cormac, ye have it all wrong."

A brief pause in their words made Muirie stop at the stable doors and pressed herself against the wall.

They spoke their next words so quietly she could not discern their meaning.

After a soft sigh, Cormac said, "Ye know I love ye, lass."

Taken aback by the meaning in his tone, she understood

for the first time that mayhap he was not toying with Beathag's affections for no purpose, and he truly loved her.

"This I know, love." Beathag's breath caught on a sob, and she stammered, "M . . . m . . . mayhap Muirie is right. We can never be together, for I am a lowly servant."

Shuffling sounded followed by low sobs. Muirie imagined Cormac drawing Beathag into his arms, comforting her.

Hesitant to interrupt, she backed away when footfalls came from the same direction she had just traveled. In her frantic thoughts of what to do, she realized she needed to protect Cormac and Beathag from being discovered—they would be ruined.

With a loud cough, she stepped from the building and toward the approaching footsteps.

"Muirie?" a deep male voice called, growing closer. "What are ye doing out so late?"

Muirie's mind worked a plan to draw him from the stables.

"Good eve, Gavin. I could not sleep."

They met, and she pointed toward the gardens at the north corner of the castle closest to the river. "Would ye care to walk with me?"

He nodded and stood beside her, lifting his arm in an invitation to take it. She did so, and after a few paces, he turned his head and peered down at her.

"Do ye not fear reprisal at walking with a man without a chaperone?" He gave a brief smile and added, "In the dark?"

Her step faltered. Recovering, she kept walking. "I am certain Lord and Lady Stewart do view ye as a trusted friend of my brother's."

"Aye, I would do nothing to jeopardize our friendship."

They strolled in silence, the flow of the river a melody following them with wisps of mist gradually building around them. Muirie had always been fascinated by the rising, downy clouds taking shape as they rose from the earth, engulfing them in an ethereal world. A world full of peace. A scripture came to her, and she stopped walking.

But there went up a mist from the earth and watered the whole face of the ground.

Gavin placed his hand on hers. "Are ye unwell?"

She blinked back confusion, having forgotten she was not alone. "No. I . . ."

He pointed to a bench beneath a fir tree. "Let us sit a moment. 'Tis much too dark to walk further from the castle under the thick trees."

Muirie nodded and allowed him to escort her to be seated.

"Truly, I am well. The gathering mist brought a scripture to my mind, and it gave me pause."

His look was thoughtful. "Will ye share it?"

She dipped her chin and recited the verse.

Gavin did not speak, his gaze scanning the nighttime scene before them. The moon hung behind thin clouds, hindering its full orb.

His voice startled her. "Were ye searching for Cormac and the maid when I found ye?"

The question sent Muirie's senses scurrying into the forest, too afraid to answer. "Well. I . . ." His inquiry hit her with force. "What were ye doing out?"

He appeared unshaken. "Most likely for the same reason ye were."

"And what do ye judge that was?" She crossed her arms over her middle and stared at him.

He rose, held his hands behind his back, and paced in front of her. "When we are in school, Cormac speaks of little else than Beathag. The man is completely smitten and has been since we met."

Muirie opened her mouth to speak, thought better of it, and pressed her lips together.

Gavin stood above her, head bent, studying her. He pursed his lips for a moment. "Mayhap ye wanted to point out the error of their ways, just as I intended."

She bit her tongue before she poured out a sermon that should have made John Knox proud had he not been in his grave for more than one hundred years.

He chuckled. "I can see by your expression that is what ye intended, and I applaud ye."

"Ye do? I am all astonishment, sir."

He reclaimed his seat and turned to her. "Let us hatch a plan to see if there may be a solution to this dilemma."

Muirie wove her fingers together nervously. "I heartily agree. Yet . . ."

"'Tis not shameful to help someone see the error of their ways."

"Ashamed I am to say that I overheard part of their conversation." She swallowed hard. "I trust they truly love one another."

"I see." Gavin gripped his thighs and leaned back. "What shall we do? I thought it a mere infatuation."

"I did as well. Until tonight."

He rose. "Let us return. Should someone discover us, there mayhap be a wedding neither of us desires."

"Sir?"

"Though I hold ye in high regard, I do not wish to marry ye, Muirie."

A slap would have been kinder. What was he saying?

"Please do not look so downcast. 'Twas not meant as an affront." He reached for her hand and helped her rise. "Ye are a beautiful and kind lass, and any man would be most blessed to have ye as wife."

"And?"

"I do not have those kinds of feelings for ye. A man knows when he meets someone that stirs passion."

Her skin tingled, either from embarrassment or insult she could not discern. "I see." She hung her head.

"Muirie, can ye honestly say ye feel something other than friendship for me?"

A laugh escaped before she could respond. "No, sir. I feel no such stirring for ye either. Ye are easy to speak with and for that, I am grateful."

"Then we shall proceed as friends. Agreed?"

She studied him in the near darkness and read sincerity in the depth of his eyes. This man could be a true friend. Just as Beathag was.

Mayhap together they could form a way for Cormac and

Beathag to part ways with as little pain as possible—and she now had an ally to aid her. "Aye, Gavin. Friends we shall be."

❦

All in the castle rose before the sun appeared to say goodbye to the travelers. Muirie hung back as she was wont to do until Cormac dragged her forward to say farewell to his parents, the Lamonts, Elizabeth, and Grannam, who departed as the sun's rays broke the horizon, spears of light shooting through the open gate.

Until the group moved from Castle Deveron, Muirie kept her place at the gate, Cormac beside her.

"What are ye waiting for? We must begin our excursion."

Muirie turned to look at him as if he were mad. "It was my understanding we were not to go."

"Just because I made a senseless remark to ye in anger?" He grabbed her hand and tugged her from the gate. "Come along. Beathag has our victuals packed."

She jerked him to a stop. "We must wait. What if Grannam changes her mind and they bring her back? We will be caught."

Cormac tugged at her again. "No, we will not. Please come along."

"Why did ye not tell me last eve we were still going?" Muirie stumbled as he towed her behind him.

He lowered his voice. "Beathag searched for ye until late—ye were not abed."

They stopped in front of the stables so they could not be overheard by the stable boys preparing their horses. Gavin and Peader were already astride their mounts, their gazes on Cormac and Muirie.

Cormac lowered his voice, bitterness in his tone. "Most likely not able to find ye because ye were out searching for us, so ye could sermonize about our wicked ways."

Muirie's scrutiny shifted towards Cormac, who helped Beathag onto her mount, then he swung around to face Muirie. "Ye were seeking us, were ye not?" His face blazed, and she retreated a few steps.

"Leave me be, Cormac. I am worried for the both of ye."

His expression softened. "I know." When he sought Beathag with his eyes, they softened more and stayed upon her. "I know."

"Come along, Muirie," Gavin called out. "I shall help ye mount."

Reid appeared from the direction of the bakehouse, a sack in one hand. She met his gaze and his swung to Gavin, then returned to her. "Do ye need assistance, Muirie?"

Gavin interrupted, "I have offered."

Looking toward him still upon his horse, Reid said, "'Tis hard to achieve from that position."

As Reid offered Muirie his arm to escort her to her horse, she took in Gavin's sly smile. They approached, and Beathag greeted them and edged her horse closer to Muirie's.

"Are ye ready for an adventure?" The girl's exuberance deflated Muirie's doubt. Mayhap the day would not be ill spent.

Reid took a pace closer and wrapped his hands around her waist, lifting her effortlessly to sit upon the black mare.

His touch shot warmth through her, and she sucked in a breath. The nerve of him to handle her without permission. She was about to reprimand him when Gavin shouted, "To the sea!" and bolted toward the open gate, Peader on his heels.

By the time Muirie turned to speak to Reid about his brash behavior, he had mounted and dropped behind Cormac, leaving her and Beathag to ride beside one another, behind Reid and Cormac.

Beathag gave a brilliant smile, glanced over her shoulder toward Cormac, and pushed her mount to a trot.

They caught up with Gavin and Peader and settled into a comfortable canter riding in pairs.

The weather being fine, they traveled a respectful distance before resting the horses and refreshing themselves.

Cormac found an open area by a burn and spread a blanket for the women and displayed the victuals. He spoke to Muirie as she sat, a curious glint in his eyes.

"Muirie, attempt to eat little so we may have enough for our midday meal at the beach." He winked at her. "I know your voracious appetite."

She opened her mouth to reprimand him for his rudeness but stayed her tongue. Mustering a calm she did not feel, she sent him a slow smile and answered the insult instead. "Is that so? Shall I recant the treacle scone tale?" She lifted her brows, which met his hard stare.

He turned and strode to the burn.

Beathag clapped her hands like a child and asked to hear the story.

Muirie wished she had not spoken as rashly as Cormac.

"No. I merely wanted to give him a taste of his own medicine." She busied herself with a hunk of bread and cheese, glancing at the hunched form of Cormac sitting by the burn.

Beathag scooted closer to Muirie and whispered, "Why did that upset him so? What he said about ye was most unkind."

"'Twas." She chewed thoughtfully. "Come to think on it, I remember his embarrassment for being caught out and punished."

"Punished how so?" Beathag ate, listening intently.

"When Lord Stewart discovered Cormac's misconduct, he reprimanded him and assigned him to help in the bakehouse."

"That does not sound so fearsome."

"No. Had it not been in winter. 'Twas July and the hottest summer we had seen in a long while."

Muirie removed a pear from the basket, and her gaze swept back to Cormac, now in earnest conversation with the others. Her heart squeezed, and she felt remorse for revealing his discretion.

"Though he was of an age to heft the wood, he had difficulty from the oppressive heat and fainted. The servants who worked there were used to the task. He was not."

Beathag's eyes clouded. "I am sorry."

"As am I. I care not to hurt Cormac. Not intentionally."

"I know this. Yet he should not have said what he spoke. 'Twas cruel."

Muirie gave a humorless chuckle. "Mayhap not. After all, were I of a portly figure, it would have hurt far more."

Beathag guffawed. "'Tis truth." She brushed the crumbs

from her skirt and rose, peering down at Muirie, eyes twinkling. "I shall see if I may cheer him." She flounced away with a swish of her skirt.

Muirie watched her go, and the men parted as she approached, soon dispersing so she and Cormac might speak alone.

Gavin made a direct line toward her and sat where Beathag had been. "We must soon depart or else we shall have no time at our destination."

When Muirie looked past his shoulder, he turned to see Peader and Reid coming their way. "So much for a private conversation. Cormac was disrespectful in his jest with ye. It was most unkind—even for a brother."

Muirie made to rise, and he took her arm and aided her.

"So now ye play the gentleman." Reid's tone was not unkind nor was it in jest.

"Ye know me, Reid. I am a slow student."

After a brief pause, he gave a glowing smile. "I shall agree with that." He bowed and strode to collect his horse grazing nearby.

Muirie caught Beathag's eye, and the girl patted Cormac on the shoulder and came to assist Muirie in gathering the food.

"Is he well now?" Muirie asked under her breath.

"He is." Beathag refused to meet her eyes. "There is more to the scone story than ye know." She looked around to see that no one listened. "What happened to the baker and her husband?"

Muirie paused and searched her memory. "They left soon after. I know not why."

They worked in silence for a time, then Beathag whispered, "Have ye seen the scar he bears on his back?"

A chill rushed through Muirie, and she shook her head.

"When he fainted from the heat, he was alone. The table he fell against bore a sharp cleaver, which left a deep, ugly scar. When Lord Stewart discovered the baker left him alone with the blazing oven and all the wood to attend to by himself, he dismissed her and her husband without references."

Muirie's hand flew to her stomach, a churning so violent she thought she may be sick. "I never knew. Just that he was abed for many days. I assumed 'twas the heat."

"Cormac said his father was angry with the baker for leaving a lad of his size, and the heavy, heatsome work to do alone, which was more than he could stand for."

All the while Muirie thought Lord Stewart was extremely angry at Cormac for stealing all the scones, whilst it was something far worse.

Shame stabbed through her heart for the scars, seen and unseen, her brother carried with him.

Chapter Twelve

1603

Sorcha woke with her head on Evan's shoulder. His strong arms were around her, bringing much-needed warmth. The bairn nudged her, and she smiled at the interruption.

All was quiet in the still air except for a few soft snores from their shelter, the night sky shining with the brilliance of more stars than Sorcha could count. Snow flurries danced against the inky backdrop, reflecting the light of the stars.

Her breath caught, and she immediately thought of how God had spoken all of it into being. She recalled verses she had heard in kirk from the time she was small. The scripture brought her comfort then and did so now.

Sorcha looked to the east, finding there was no sign of the

rising sun. She settled against Evan, resting her head against his chest. Movement caught her attention, and she lifted her gaze to see Clara coming toward them.

Once Clara laid upon her cloak, Sorcha whispered, "Where have ye been?"

Clara twisted toward Sorcha. It was too dark to read her expression. "A trip to the burn for water."

Sorcha looked from Clara and watched a tall, shadowy figure walking from the spot she had seen Clara moments earlier. *Kester?*

She smiled, and Clara sniffed. "My whereabouts be not a quirkle for ye to solve." She huffed, rolled to her side, and heaved a deep sigh.

Sorcha's soft chuckle roused Evan.

"Is all well?" His groggy tone touched Sorcha.

She smoothed a wave of hair that had fallen over his eye. "Aye. All is well."

Evan straightened and surveyed the camp, his gaze halting on Kester leaning against the wall of the shelter-stell. He took Sorcha's hand and kissed the back of it before standing. "I would like a word with Kester. Return to sleep."

Sorcha watched him leave, noticing a slight swagger in his walk—self-assurance, not arrogance. He was a braw man. One many a lass would fawn over. Was she among them? She shook her head, and once again, she reprimanded herself for having thoughts of him so soon after John's death. Only three months had passed since the Battle of Glen Fruin, yet it seemed like years.

A lone tear trickled down Sorcha's cheek, and she swiped

it away. She watched the men, mere silhouettes shrouded by a swirl of falling snow as if the stars had come to dance among them.

Her mind traveled to what the future might hold—a group of people away from home searching for a place to live in peace and live their lives without fear of war and conflict. Was that so much to wish for?

Her eyelids grew heavy, and she gave in to the call of slumber, clinging to the thought that tomorrow would be their shortest day of travel.

After what seemed a short time, a horse's whinny drew her awake. Ethereal light now lit the eastern sky, the remnants of night hanging above it, a few glittering jewels of stars bidding farewell.

Clara sat up. "'Tis morn already?"

"It would appear so. Your night vigil kept ye from rest." Sorcha narrowed her eyes, her lips smiling teasingly at her friend.

Clara snatched up a handful of the fir needles and tossed them playfully in Sorcha's direction. "Leave me be."

"Aye. As long as ye tell me what ye and Kester spoke of." She lifted her eyebrows and tightened her lips, suppressing a smile.

Evan arrived and looked a question at the two women. "Are ye quarreling already?"

They sent him a glare, and he held up both hands in surrender. "'Tis none of my concern what the two of ye go on about."

He sat beside Sorcha and spoke low at her ear. "Shall ye tell me when we are along the path?"

Sorcha craned her neck to peer at him and grinned. "Perhaps."

He crossed his arms over his chest. "So that is the way of things, is it? Keeping secrets from your husband?"

She laughed aloud and took his hand in hers. "Nae. Naught like that."

Kester assisted Clara to her feet, keeping her hand in his. "'Tis time ta depart. The lads are passing around bannocks ta break our fast. We eat as we journey."

Clara's gaze never left his, and when they departed, Evan slanted a knowing look at Sorcha. "So 'tis like that I see."

Sorcha warmed at how he cared for his sister. "'Tis."

;);

The snow held until they reached the shores of a massive loch where they stopped for a brief rest. Sorcha took her food to sit near the edge of the water, resting under the boughs of a large pine. Her gaze skipped across the calm water to a small island in the middle of the loch. The ruins of a stone castle nestled there with the background of snow-capped mountains rising above. The place was so serene she felt the pull of remaining.

"'Tis breath-taking, is it not?"

Evan held a cup toward her. She took the offering, and he sat beside her.

"'Tis that and more." She chewed thoughtfully on the meager meal. "I could stay here forever."

"Aye. Me as well. But 'tis not to be, lass." His voice held sorrow and resignation. "We must move on if we are to be safe."

Sorcha brought her gaze to his. "Aye. Shall we be safe? The now, I feel as if there is no place in the world where 'tis so."

"I ken." He looked out over the water, a mix of sorrow and determination in his features.

"Evan?" She paused to gather her thoughts, not wanting to say anything to upset him.

"Aye. Ye have a question, I can see."

Her smile was tinged with sadness. "Why do men always want power? 'Tis not enough that they have silver or gold. They want more. They want our verra lives—to tell us what to believe, how to live, who to serve. What is to become of us? I fear for my child, Evan." She touched her cheeks and was surprised not to find tears there. She looked at Evan.

His eyes were awash with pain as he took her into his arms. The warm embrace brought comfort and life. The child kicked harder than ever, and Evan jerked back.

"Was that the bairn?" The stunned expression he wore brought a laugh from Sorcha, forcing the struggle from her mind.

"Aye. 'Tis."

"I like it when ye look like that."

"Like what?"

"Happy," Evan said with a twinkle in his eye.

Their gazes held for a long moment, and Sorcha lightly caressed his jaw with her fingertips. "Evan," she breathed.

"Aye, lass."

Her lips parted, unable to continue, powerless to share the

feelings that had grown for him in such a short time. It was too soon.

Sorcha swallowed, and before she pulled away, he cupped her face with his strong, capable hands and brought his lips to hers. Gently, warmly, their lips met, and time froze. Her breath came in tiny gasps as he kissed her. It was a reverent, tender connection with no urgency.

Snowflakes skittered about them, and Sorcha no longer felt the cold. She sank into him, gathering his strength and love.

Her eyes flew open. *Love?* How could she feel love for this man when her husband had just died? Shame and horror gripped her equally.

She pulled back. "Evan! I am so sorry. I meant not to do that."

His wounded look was painful to see—a stab to her heart. What had she done?

She gathered her skirts and made to rise. "This is wrong. John would—" She broke off, a franticness in her tone. "I loved him so, I carry his bairn, and now I kiss his dearest friend. Do ye not ken how wrong 'tis?"

Evan's confused expression brought her more discomfort. Was he not disturbed by their actions? Would God condemn them?

He gripped her wrists and pulled her down. "Sorcha! Stop this. John would want ye to be happy. To be cherished and cared for. Shall ye not allow me to do so?" He closed his eyes briefly. "God does not condemn us for love. John is with Him now, and we shall be so one day. Let us live out our lives as God intended."

Her breathing labored, and she frantically searched Evan's eyes. Was he right? It could not be so.

The image of the abandoned castle brought fresh grief to Sorcha. She felt a kinship with the ruined structure. The partial walls and tumbled stones made her heart ache.

Laughter once filled that home full of families, perhaps going back several hundred years. As she peered at it over the cold, clear waters, the reflection of the castle and the mountains behind seemed eerie and sad. *She* longed to be rebuilt and happy again, resting in John's arms each evening, the hope of bairns ever present.

Evan escorted her back to their group. They barely spoke, and he kept her hand on his arm for support, glancing at her often.

The sensation of his lips upon hers held in her mind—the care he had given. It was equally loving as John's, though different somehow. She knew not how to explain it, which troubled her.

A sudden jolt brought Evan's words. *"God does not condemn us for love."*

Was he in love with her? Nae, how could it be so? He was John's friend. Not a MacGregor, but close as a brother. Their clans held an alliance, and Evan had no close family remaining.

Her jaw ached, and she realized she clenched her teeth. She blinked back the disturbing thoughts and glanced at Evan. He watched her with interest, and she gave him a tight smile.

"Ye appear to have something on your mind. Will ye share it?"

Sorcha looked ahead and focused on Clara and Kester, walking with heads bent together in deep conversation.

She ran her tongue across her lips and shook her head, turning her gaze from him. Her flushed cheeks revealed more than she cared to speak.

A dull throb pounded in her head, and she lifted a hand to massage her temple, moaning with the pressure. "My head does hammer."

"Och, lass. Why did ye not tell me?" His tone held genuine concern.

"I will not have the progress of our journey affected by my aching head."

"Your well-being is of more concern. That of ye and the bairn."

Sorcha refused to say more, fearful to reveal her concerns. Evan was a kind, quiet man, and she dinnae want to hurt him. He had given up his entire life to care for her and John's child. She would not insult him. Yet she questioned the kiss and the comment he made at the loch. Perhaps he was merely referring to love as a general, Christ-like love. That revelation gave her peace. Aye, 'tis most likely the reason.

Ease poured through her, and the aching in her head lessened. She drew closer to Evan, and the smile she gave him was true. "Thank ye for your care. It would please John to know ye are such a devoted friend to his wife."

The crestfallen look from Evan caught her unawares. He dipped his chin and looked off into the distance. The heavily wooded forest lay before them and through it darkness waited.

Sorcha felt that darkness in her heart. She had hurt Evan—again.

They strode on in complete silence. Weary to the bone, Sorcha *chose* to remain calm. It seemed she continued to say, or *do*, the wrong thing. There was nothing else for it except stillness.

Once within the confines of the trees, their steps grew careful to keep their silence. Ambushes may await them, so they must be on guard. Kester said Freuchie Castle was a few hours away.

Evan took Sorcha's hand from his arm. "I must speak to Kester. Shall ye come with me to Clara so ye may walk together?"

Sorcha dipped her head in agreement, and they strode ahead where he left her to Clara's care. He and Kester eased their pace to walk behind them, whispering.

The forest thinned, and once they reached the edge, they gathered around for all to hear.

Kester spoke in a low voice. "Please take cover under the lower limbed trees while a few of us scour the area." He lifted an arm to point to the top of the castle, barely peeping from above the rise.

"We shall see how the land lies and search for caves, circling the boundary of the forest. Keep quiet and do nothing until we return." He assigned several men to keep watch over the group as the others carried out their mission.

Evan escorted Sorcha and Clara to a hidden space beside a large, felled trunk. "Stay here and dinnae come out until I call for ye."

"Aye, brother." Clara said, her voice holding a hint of humor. "We shall mind what ye say."

Evan placed a hand on his sister's shoulder and eased her to the ground behind what remained of the massive tree. He held Sorcha by her forearms and leaned close. "Please stay with Clara." His eyes implored her, a hesitation in his posture, and then he quickly kissed her cheek and sprinted away.

Sorcha's gaze met Clara's surprised look and pursed lips. "Is there something ye need to be sharing—*sister*?"

Sorcha ignored her and lowered herself to sit. "Och! I have seen the way ye look at Kester."

Clara reared back. "Aye. He is easy to look upon. Would ye not say?"

The chuckle came before Sorcha uttered a retort. "Aye. 'Tis truth."

"As well as my brother?"

Sorcha hung her head. "I have been a widow only a few months. 'Tis not proper for me to notice."

"Yet notice ye have." Clara reached to pull Sorcha into an embrace. "We are women, Sorcha. We have eyes, ears, and hearts. How may we survive without love?"

Her head still bent, Sorcha replied, "I ken. I must mourn my husband for the proper time."

"Ye are married to my brother. The time arrived when ye wed him."

The unmistakable tug in Sorcha's heart grew. "I would not dishonor John's memory by loving another so soon."

"So ye *do* have feelings for Evan?" Clara sighed. "He has

them for ye."

Sorcha raised her head to peer at her friend. "How do ye know this? He has never said so." Or had he? The comment at the loch came back to her with full force. *Love.*

CAROLE LEHR JOHNSON

Chapter Thirteen

1710

Muirie's horse increased its pace to climb the rise above the lazy burn spilling into the sea. A gust of wind whipped her hair, and she inhaled the salty breeze. The years melted away as they began their descent of the sloping hill toward the coursing waves of the pink sand beach.

The memory of the time she and Cormac snuck away to spend the day upon the sand tugged at her heart with sympathy for her brother. Though it was wrong of them to disobey Lord and Lady Stewart and leave the castle grounds, the outing had been a splendid and dangerous one at their age. When they were discovered, they were lectured about the danger of falling over the cliffs into the cold North Sea. The adventure had only bound her closer to Cormac.

Despite not being tied by blood, Cormac would always be dear to her heart.

A whistle brought Muirie's head around, and Cormac pointed to their left. A massive granite castle stretched along the edge of the cliffs. The surface reflected the mid-day sun, appearing similar in color to the pink sand beach below, as if it had once been connected and now stood apart.

Cormac spurred his horse onward, Reid following. Once they were at her side, she said, "I do not remember the castle afore."

"Nor I." Cormac's gaze swung from the castle to the beach. "Mayhap we traveled more southward, missing the castle altogether."

"'Tis a wondrous building." Reid's eyes swept the length of it. "I care to get a closer view."

Gavin, Peader, and Beathag joined them, and they took in the magnificent structure.

"'Tis beautiful." Beathag's voice held admiration. "I, too, care to see it. Do ye think they would mind?"

Cormac, obviously eager to please her, said, "Why not try? We must present ourselves and tell them we are from Castle Deveron."

Muirie gripped Cormac's arm. "No. We must not. What if your parents know these people? Our clandestine trip may be discovered."

He cocked his head in silent contemplation for a time, then nodded. "'Tis truth. Mayhap we do not visit." He winked. "Yet that shall not keep us from having a closer look. He urged his mount toward the castle. "Let us take a cantor along the length of it and then back and on to the beach."

"As long as we do not get too close," Muirie shouted in his wake.

They rode single file, all gazes turned to the elongated vastness of the castle until they reached the northern end. Turning south, they walked their horses to the beach. Muirie longed to stop and sketch the view with the endless sea as its backdrop. She held the image in her mind, concentrating so hard her head ached.

Leaving the castle behind they descended toward the sweeping crescent of wide pink sand before them, long grass flowing among the rolling dunes meeting the shore.

"'Tis beautiful!" Beathag's excitement fueled, urging her mount to the front of the line. Cormac raced after her.

Muirie watched them go, a lightheartedness lifting her spirits. She turned to find Gavin at her side.

"I suppose our journey has been a success." The way he lifted one corner of his mouth brought a familiar sensation to her, and she wondered who she had seen smile in such a way.

She opened her mouth to respond when Reid arrived at her other side, Peader racing past them, a wide smile on his otherwise reserved visage.

Muirie pointed toward Peader. "Gavin, I say ye may be right." Before either man responded, she nudged her horse into a gallop to follow Peader.

When she looked over her shoulder, Reid and Gavin were staring at one another, Reid appearing confused, Gavin laughing.

By the time she came to the burn that fed the sea, she slowed her mount and eased across the burbling water flowing over dark grey rocks. Varying shades of green moss clung to rocks along the edge of the water, clumps of feathery ferns shivered in the breeze, and birds chattered and darted overhead.

The place sent a shiver of joy through Muirie at the utter calmness surrounding her. The twenty-third Psalm spoke to her in that moment.

He maketh me to lie down in green pastures. He leadeth me beside the still waters.

She chuckled. Though these waters were not still, they calmed her. And the beach was most certainly not green pastures. "I thank Ye, Lord, for the beauty of your creation."

A male voice broke her solitude. "Well said, lass."

She jerked the reins, and the horse snorted, spinning toward the sound and rearing upward.

With quick reflexes, Gavin surged forward and gripped the horse's reins. "'Tis well, calm yourself." He patted, then rubbed the horse's neck, speaking in soothing tones.

"What goes on here!" A shout reverberated, hoofbeats pounding the ground.

Muirie's gaze met Reid's, and she held up a hand. "All is well. My mount startled, and Gavin has calmed her."

Reid drew closer, facing Gavin. "And what spooked the mare?" His gaze sought Gavin, and the accusing glare he shot the man could have turned the water to ice.

Muirie looked from one man to the other. What was the problem?

Cormac rode up, concern marring his features. "What is the matter? Has there been a mishap?"

"All is well. My horse shied, and Gavin came to my aid."

Cormac tilted his head back, a curious smile contorting his lips. "I see the way of it." He tugged his mount around and departed.

Muirie frowned, wondering what he meant.

Muirie and Beathag strolled along the warm beach, their bare feet sinking into the damp sand. "Have ye ever felt anything so wonderful?" Muirie regarded their footprints and marveled at the caressing sensation of the sand against her feet.

Beathag slipped her arm through Muirie's. "'Tis a great pleasure—and glad I am to be sharing it with my dearest friend."

"And I." Muirie brought her free hand to squeeze Beathag's arm. "'Tis a wonderful day."

Beathag pulled in a long breath and released it slowly. "I do not desire the journey home." She rubbed her hip. "Though I enjoy a cantor, I am not keen on an aching backside."

Muirie's laughter rang out. "Nor I. It would be grand if we were allowed more time."

"Aye."

"If the lasses desire to stay, I am certain we shall not be missed."

Beathag spun around, dragging Muirie with her to face Cormac, standing just behind them.

She released Muirie and slammed her fists onto her hips,

wincing when they made contact. "What do ye mean pouncing upon us without a warning?" She drew closer, their faces inches apart. "Are ye now a cat searching for prey?" She brought her hand to her chest, her breathing labored.

Cormac pursed his lips, eyes intent on hers. He leaned in and whispered, "Aye. Only for ye, *my* lass."

Muirie watched Beathag melt under Cormac's confession. She coughed and strolled down the beach.

Something in her path glinted in the afternoon sun. Kneeling, she gingerly touched the object half-buried in the sand. Her first thought was to call Beathag. When she glanced back, Beathag and Cormac sat on the sand, heads together in quiet companionship.

Her usual concern over the pair surfaced, yet it arrived with another sensation tangled within its midst—*jealousy*. Mayhap she could seek Gavin and ask his advice? Pushing aside the grim thoughts, she brushed the sand from what appeared to be a piece of glass about the size of her palm. The smooth, curved black object shone with hints of green as she tilted it in the sunlight.

"What have ye found?" Beathag strode to Muirie's side and cautiously raked the tip of her finger over the surface. "Feels like glass."

Cormac asked, "May I see?"

Muirie handed it to him, and they stared at the curious object.

"Are we ready to dine?"

They looked up to see Reid, Gavin, and Peader stumbling down the dune with unsteady steps in the deep sand drifts.

Reid, the first to reach them, asked, "Have ye found a treasure?"

Cormac handed it to him. "Have ye ever seen anything the like?"

Gavin approached and rubbed the bright surface.

Peader, as usual the quiet observer, peered over Gavin's shoulder, who shot him a questioning look. "What do ye think?"

"Sea glass," Peader answered. He returned to the dunes without a backward glance.

Reid nodded. "Aye. 'Tis."

Cormac shrugged and passed the find to Muirie. "Now ye have a reminder of the day."

Encouraged, Beathag said, "Let us keep looking. Mayhap I shall have one as well."

"May we eat before I starve?" Cormac grabbed Beathag's hand and sprinted toward Peader, calling after him to wait.

Beathag shouted over her shoulder, "If ye find another 'tis mine!"

"Aye." Muirie told her, then muttered to herself. "This one belongs to me alone."

After a long glance at the receding tide, the others climbed the dunes. Muirie looked at Reid, who remained by her side, and she clutched the rare find.

Reid loosely clasped his hands behind his back. "Shall we have a walk before we take our repast?"

"If ye like." Muirie caressed the glass with her fingertips as they walked.

The sea air invigorated Muirie, and she inhaled the salty scent, her head turning toward the waves from time to time. What would it be like to live so close to the sea? Though she loved strolling through the dense forest by Castle Deveron, the seaside equally calmed her.

Reid's deep voice broke into her thoughts. "And where do ye come from, Muirie? How were your parents acquainted with Lord and Lady Stewart?"

His question lingered in the briny air between them. Uncertain how to answer, she shrugged a shoulder. "A servant found me in a basket upon the doorstep."

Reid's pace halted, and he spun to look at Muirie, eyebrows drawn together. "Truly?"

"Aye. I know not where I came from. Lady Stewart said she has much to share once I become of age at the end of this year."

She studied his tall form, blonde hair lifting and twisting in the wind.

He met her eyes. "I am that sorry for ye."

"Have no sympathy for me. Though I am no one, it concerns me not." A sting of anger rose in her. "Just because your life has purpose gives ye no right to pity mine." She shifted so her back was to him and stared at the open sea. "Ye have meaning for ye are a dutiful son. I am not a servant—nor am I a member of the Stewart family."

He did not speak for a moment, yet when he spoke his low voice held tenderness. "Aye, I ken. Did they not care for ye? Do they not still?"

Muirie pondered this for a long moment. Why *did* they

take her in and care for her?

Beathag called from the dunes. "There the two of ye are. Come and eat."

They strode toward her in silence and went to join the others.

Beathag extended her hand, offering Muirie a piece of bread. "May I see the glass again?"

Muirie handed it to Beathag who studied it and muttered, "Sea glass? I dinnae ken glass could come from the sea." She passed it back to Muirie.

Reid paused from eating. "'Tis from a glass bottle that was lost at sea. Mayhap tossed overboard or by way of shipwreck."

He reached for the object and rather than taking it, cupped his hand beneath Muirie's, turning her palm this way and that to see the shimmering colors change.

The gesture unsettled her, and she asked in a quiet voice, "What makes it so smooth?"

"'Tis beat by the waves sending it over the sand and rocks." With one finger, Reid caressed the object. "This may be centuries old." He turned the glass over, his fingertip brushing her skin. "Mayhap from thousands of miles away and carrying a love letter."

Beathag smiled and looked at Cormac.

Reid was feeding Beathag's sense of romance, and Muirie warmed to him. Or mayhap it was his touch.

Beathag sighed. "Have a care with it. I would hate to see it lost."

Muirie tucked the glass away for safekeeping and bowed

her head in silent prayer. When she lifted her gaze, all eyes were upon her, some in question, others in acceptance.

"Do not mind my sister," Cormac said with a grin. "She is consistent in her devotion."

Gavin agreed. "An admirable trait indeed."

"A gentleman should not jest about one's faith." Reid aimed the barb with a raised brow.

Mimicking Grannam, Beathag looked at Reid and said, "Haud yer wheesht!"

Muirie snickered as Cormac burst into a bellow of laughter.

Reid looked a question at Muirie, and Peader answered. "'Tis the way a highlander would say to 'shut up.'"

The glare Reid gave Beathag sent Cormac to his feet. "Do not give her such a look, man. She jests."

Reid tilted his head back to peer up at Cormac. "I am quite aware of that, man, but I do not care to be told to shut up by anyone."

Gavin moved to a sitting position. "Reid, what ails ye? Since your arrival, ye have been cross."

An uncomfortable silence hung over them. Even the birds stilled their chatter. Reid bolted to his feet, sending birds flying away with screeches.

"I am well and find no issue in my behavior." He strode toward the edge of the dunes and halted to watch the sea with white-knuckled hands clenched behind his back.

Gavin rolled to his feet effortlessly and strode to Reid's side. Muirie watched their exchange, unable to overhear the conversation. Anger swept over Reid for a moment, yet something Gavin said calmed him. The instant change in Reid's stance puzzled Muirie. Gavin brought a hand to Reid's shoulder, and he smiled. Reid's relieved grin came slower.

Muirie frowned. Men were such strange creatures. One moment they were near to blows, and the next they were as brothers again.

Ω

A clash of thunder brought Muirie's eyes wide open, and she sat bolt upright. Blinking the sleep away, it took her an instant to remember where she was—and who she was with. Mere inches in front of her lay Reid, one arm bent behind his head, the other resting across his flat stomach. His relaxed features gave him the appearance of a younger man, more a lad than a man.

Lightning split the darkening sky. Beathag shrieked and jumped to her feet, her gaze sweeping the surrounding area. All had fallen asleep among the dunes after the long journey, much too relaxed, with full stomachs and weariness weighing on them.

Beathag knelt beside Cormac and shook him. "Rise! We must be gone afore the storm comes."

Cormac's head lolled to one side, half-closed eyes upon Beathag. His mouth curved into a groggy smile. "Aye." His lids shut, and he found one of Beatha's hands and pulled it to his chest, splaying it to rest on him while he held it in place. "Lie back and sleep. 'Tis much too—"

Thunder rolled closer, bringing Cormac to his senses. He sat upright and pulled her to stand.

Reid rose in tandem with Peader and Gavin, each looking

toward the sea which had grown in fury, heaving high, angry waves onto to the beach. The wind increased, releasing pins from the women's hair and whipping their skirts around their legs.

Peader tossed their belongings to the middle of the blanket and rapidly tied the four corners together to create a large bundle. He flung it over his shoulder and shouted above the wind. "Let us leave now. Mayhap we can outrun the storm."

Muirie knew little of storms, though the urgency overcame her, and she called out, "There is no time. We must seek shelter now!" She ran toward the horses, and they followed. "Mayhap we can take the horses to safety nearby."

Reid placed his hands around her waist and lifted her to the saddle.

"Aye." Gavin agreed. "We ride inland and find shelter as soon as may be."

With no further argument, the group galloped from the copse of trees toward the west. In minutes, the rain attacked in great, cold drops, soaking them. They rode on harder for some time, the storm increasing in strength.

Muirie scanned the landscape, which became increasingly harder to see. The icy pellets grew into torrents, and she wanted to scream from the onslaught.

Leaning her weight forward, clinging to the reins, she sobbed. "Oh, Lord, please give us shelter!"

The presence of someone at her side brought her gaze around. Reid held his hand out to her, motioning for her to come to him. She shook her head, not understanding. He fell back for a moment, then pitched closer and leapt onto the back of her horse, his now slackened reins still in his hands to keep their mounts together.

An arm came around her, and with one hand he claimed her reins, keeping a hold of his own as well. The immediate warmth of his back lessened the chill, and she relaxed into him.

Reid's breath brushed her cheek as he spoke into her ear. "I feared ye would tumble. Forgive my impertinence. 'Tis all I could think of to keep ye from falling."

Muirie turned her head to hear him more plainly, taking pleasure in his nearness. "I thank ye, sir." Her shoulders slumped, and his hold tightened. Relieved, she rested her head back, thanking God for His care.

A shout roused her, and Reid said, "Peader has found shelter ahead."

The rain continued, and Muirie thanked God for providing. Though Reid provided warmth for a time, she now felt his shivers as well as her own. Their pace slowed, and within moments, they approached the remains of a crofter's cottage. A ramshackle stone stable sat at the back with piles of hay against the rear wall.

Reid dismounted and reached for Muirie, gently sliding her from the horse, the rain intensifying. She trembled, her teeth chattering. "I . . . is it safe inside?"

The weight of her sodden dress encumbered her steps. Reid looped an arm around her waist, supporting and guiding her toward the cottage.

"Do not worry. We shall attend to a fire."

Her chuckle came out in a strange tremble. "I . . . I think

not. The wood shall be as soaked as we."

Reid shot her a worried glance as Gavin shoved the door, which creaked on rusty hinges. He waved them inside, and they took in the one-room dwelling with hesitation, a musty scent greeting them.

Beathag pushed ahead of the men. "I have seen worse." She pointed to the far corner where a slow drip plopped through the slate roof. "If 'tis the only leak, we are most fortunate."

"Aye." Peader agreed. "I shall scour for wood or peat in the stable." He dashed through the open door which let in the dim light.

Cormac crossed the small space, flinging open the shutters to the chamber's only window, releasing a small bit of light. A large table with two benches and stools sat by the fireplace.

A broken settle leaned against the wall on the other side of the room as if discarded. Gavin tested it and found it to be secure enough. He moved the table, benches, and stools across the chamber and dragged the settle to the fireplace.

"Should we not find dry wood or peat, we may burn the settle to give us warmth for the night."

Muirie straightened by Reid's side. "We cannot stay here the night. 'Tis unseemly." She swallowed. "Beathag . . ."

Her friend spoke with irritation. "I ken. Our reputations shall be ruined." She flounced to the door and gazed into the heavy rain. "It matters not. We shall not return until the morrow, and 'tis ruined already."

Muirie's shame mounted, and she went to her. "I will stand by ye. If ye are ruined, then so am I."

Beathag spun, face flaming. "It matters not." She repeated.

"They will turn me from the castle, and ye will proceed with a brief punishment. I did this to myself, not ye, Muirie." She ran into the rain, sobbing.

Reid stood shoulder to shoulder with Muirie. "She shall be fine. Worry not. We shall warm ourselves, dry our clothes, and be gone." He slipped his hand in hers. "If we must ride all the night, I shall get ye home before Lord and Lady Stewart return."

Her eyes lifted to meet his light grey gaze. Fierce sincerity flickered there, and in that moment, she would have trusted her very life to him.

Chapter Fourteen

Freuchie Castle
1603

As the group rounded the perimeter of the forest surrounding the castle, Sorcha surveyed the structure—a beautiful thing to behold. Though abandoned a few years prior, it was in remarkable condition. The U-shaped castle sat atop a wide hill with the forest far enough away to see any unwelcomed guests.

The soft, near-white hue of the granite held Sorcha's regard. It was a bonny sight indeed. Would this be their home, or would soldiers or Campbells send them running again?

Though no one seemed to be there, out of caution, Evan and Kester urged the group to set up camp in the nearby cave.

Around a fire, the children gathered at the back of the cave to play games, freer now than when their journey began. Sorcha's heart lightened to hear the joyful sound of their voices.

Clara laid a hand upon Sorcha's shoulder. "'Tis a pleasant sound?"

Sorcha met Clara's smile with one of her own. "Aye."

"And soon enough ye shall hear the like from your own bairn." Clara returned her attention to the fire where they cooked fish and bannocks.

Sorcha stroked her middle and wondered if she held a lass or lad, remembering John's words. "Lass, 'tis enough that we have a bairn what lives—whether it be he or she."

The two women carried on speaking of bairns, marriage, and their future. Sorcha refused to predict anything, instead focusing on the now. Evan was a kind, caring man, and it was time she settled into that fact. Theirs may not be a love match, but it mayhap be a happy one with mutual friendship.

Yet Sorcha's mind would not release what Evan had said at the loch. Was Clara right in saying he had feelings for her?

As if Clara read her mind, she asked, "Why dinnae ye answer my question about Evan?"

A rumble of thunder gave Sorcha pause before answering. She did not know how to reply. They shared secrets, yet this matter regarded her brother, and she did not want Clara to tell him anything they spoke of.

A deep voice asked from above. "What about Evan?" He stood, arms across his chest, head tilted. Firelight flickered throughout the large cave, illuminating beaming faces and warmth.

Clara paled, and Sorcha's gaze traveled to the food. She made unnecessary movements to attend to the cooking. Since Clara had voiced the question, she held her tongue and her breath.

Evan cleared his throat and stared at his sister. "*Clara.*"

She averted her gaze and reached to assist Sorcha in removing the fish from the fire. Evan took her hand and held it between his. "Look at me, sister."

It took Clara several moments before she did so, and her eyes glinted in the light. She pulled in a ragged breath. "Evan, dinnae ask me to tell ye. It would not be right. We spoke privately . . ." Her voice trailed into the space between the siblings before she continued. ". . . as women often do."

Evan's gaze skittered between the women. Uncertain, Sorcha pondered if the expression he wore was of genuine curiosity or fear.

"What question did ye ask Sorcha about me?"

Sorcha caught the emotion in his voice. "Evan, please dinnae quarrel because of me." She placed the cooked fish aside, hands trembling. "She asked if I have feelings for ye."

His hands released Clara, and she watched a swallow grip his throat. They sat without speaking for a time. His expression held the upspoken question, yet she could not voice an answer. Evan's eyes darkened. He stood and strode away.

"I am that sorry. I never meant to hurt ye or Evan. He is my dear, dear brother." Clara levered herself to stand. "I must go to him and seek forgiveness."

Sorcha lifted her gaze. "Are ye certain 'tis wise to do so? A man's pride is a fragile thing. Many times did I bruise John's over something small, yet he made too much of it."

Clara returned to her seat and dropped her head into her hands. "I meant naught of it. I wish for ye and Evan to be happily wed."

Sorcha shifted to sit closer and slung an arm around her shoulders. "We shall be happy enough, Clara. We both knew it was not for love. Evan is an honorable man and was John's closest friend. He just wants to protect me and the bairn."

Clara lifted her head, tears spilling over her long lashes. "Yet I believe—" she lowered her voice, "—he loves ye, and I would that ye love him in return."

Sorcha embraced Clara. What could she say to lessen her guilt? Evan was hurting too. Did he feel shame that his sister revealed too much about his feelings?

"Clara?" Sorcha lowered her voice. "Has Evan *told* ye he has feelings for me?"

Clara swiped the tears with the back of her wrist. "Nae. I know my brother. I see how he is with ye. And when he is not by your side, his eyes find ye often. The look he wears tells me all."

Sorcha hugged her closer and chuckled, shaking her head. "Are ye now a matchmaker? Or do ye have the sight?"

Straightening, Clara peered at Sorcha. "I thank ye for trying to make me merry, yet I see the way he looks at ye—"

"So ye have said. He is but being protective."

"He would do anything for John, even—" Clara slapped a hand over her mouth, face ashen.

Sorcha gripped Clara's shoulder. "What? What ails ye?"

Her friend blew out a long breath. "I need to keep silent." She gripped Sorcha's hand. "Please dinnae tell Evan . . ." She drew back abruptly, releasing Sorcha, and stood. "Please forgive me." She ran sobbing toward the cave's entrance.

Sorcha watched her go, confused and worried. She saw Evan as Clara passed him to run from the cave and into the night. He stared at Sorcha, then turned and followed his sister.

Evan and John were like brothers, and Evan was an honorable protector. He had been kind to her. Kind enough to marry her because she and her child needed a protector. There was nothing more to be said.

☙❧

A few days passed with Clara saying little to Sorcha and Evan keeping his distance unless needed for a task. The weight of burden pressed upon her. How were they to go on like this? Should she confront Evan? Did it really matter now that John was gone? Mayhap she should try to speak to Clara again.

Sorcha knelt beside the small trunk to search for another shawl for one of the elder women who needed extra warmth. When she tried to release the hasp, it held tight. She tried again, and it would not move. She sat back on her heels, nerves taut, and sighed.

She picked up a rock, held it overhead, and brought it down with force onto the stubborn hasp. "Ye stubborn *eejit*, why can ye not be the one thing easy in my life the now?"

As she brought the rock down again, a calloused hand came around hers.

"I dinnae think that shall do the hasp much good if ye ever have a need to lock it again."

Sorcha dared not look at Evan. The shame was too much. She knew not where Clara was, suspecting she still avoided her brother. She released the rock and glared at the trunk, hoping he would leave.

He lowered himself to sit by her. Leaning toward the trunk, he loosened the hasp with steady fingers, then sat back.

She clasped her hands against her bent knees and watched them tremble. A few moments later, his hand rested on top of hers.

"I think we should talk, lass."

With hesitance, Sorcha met his steady gaze. Would talking accomplish anything? Their lives were forever intertwined— yet could shattered feelings be mended? She believed she would not love another man for a long time without betraying John, and she could not convince Clara, nor Evan, that this was truth. Did Evan truly care for her—like a husband should?

He pulled her hands apart and took one in his, tugging her upward. "Come, lass, let us take a walk. Though there is a chill, the night is fine and clear."

Sorcha refused to meet his gaze yet allowed him to help her stand. Her knees buckled, and she fell against him. Once steadied, he reached for her shawl and wrapped it around her. They passed Clara, who averted her eyes, and Sorcha wanted to cry.

She supposed Evan was right. They must talk. The silence could not go on forever.

The evening air held the cold of winter, and she shivered.

Evan looped his arm around her shoulders and moved closer to her side.

"If ye are too chilled, we may return."

"Nae. I am fine."

They wove through the trees until they faced one side of the castle. A half-moon illuminated the tall stronghold set atop the rise, and it nearly took Sorcha's breath. This would be their home? By moonlight, it was even lovelier.

The many storied structure was more than sufficient to hold all of them, including others who scattered across the Highlands. Her prayers followed them for safety.

With Evan's warmth, she no longer shivered and turned to survey him. He stared at the moonlit castle.

She returned her gaze to it. "'Tis verra bonny."

"Aye. 'Tis." His tone held hesitation. "'Tis."

Sorcha released an unsteady breath. "Ye wanted to talk."

His arm slid from her shoulder, and he took her hand. "Let us go to the castle and see inside."

"We have no light."

He chuckled and held out the stub of a candle. "I come prepared, lass."

She nodded, and they rounded the castle walls to the front entrance where an iron gate rose high above them. Evan removed his hand from hers and gave the gate a shove. The barrier shifted only a few inches, so he put his full weight against it until it moved far enough for him to slip through.

Once on the other side, they stilled and peered up at the towering building. Sorcha counted four rows of windows from the ground to the top and noted how the two side wings and the larger main tower at the end created a U shape. This was a very impressive home indeed. She prayed this was their refuge yet held little hope it would be so.

Evan took her hand again, and they crossed the long courtyard, hemmed in on four sides. "Should the Lord our God bless us to remain here, we mayhap should grow our food in this area to keep it safe. 'Tis large enough."

Sorcha agreed with the plan, and as she waited for Evan to strike a flame to light the candle, she searched the courtyard for something to rest the candle upon. A piece of the grey slate roof lay upon the walkway, and she picked it up and brought it to him.

"Aye, 'tis perfect, lass. Thank ye." He sent her a warm smile. "It shall keep my bonny fingers from burning."

Sorcha took his hand in hers, not waiting for him to do so, and a slow smile spread across his lips. She liked the way he smiled—genuine—and bonny indeed. This time, she did not reprimand her thoughts as she moved with him to the wide entrance door.

Evan handed the candle to her and tried to open the door. It took all his effort to shove it open. The carved wood lacked attention, but it remained sturdy despite being faded and cracked.

The thought of soldiers or Campbells trying to force themselves in made her shudder, and Evan asked if she was well.

"Aye. 'Tis nothing, but a feeling that comes upon me at times. It means nothing."

He gave her a curious look and moved on without another word.

The door opened into a massive entrance hall flanked on both sides by wide, curving stairs, leading to the first floor. They craned their necks to peer upward, but the limited range of the candle did not reach so far.

"Should we try the stairs?" Sorcha moved to go toward them, yet Evan stayed her.

"Nae, lass. 'Tis best done in the day. We shall look around to see how damaged the old place is so we may tell the others."

They roamed the entire lower floor and found it to be in fair condition, their only companions a few mice skittering from the candlelight.

A cramp gripped Sorcha's side, and she immediately rubbed it, catching Evan's attention.

"Are ye ailing, lass? We may return now if ye wish it."

"Nae. 'Tis the bairn. I think he may be weary of walking."

Evan led her to a chair on its side in the corner. "Come, rest yourself for a while."

She did not argue, following him, and once he righted the chair and brushed it off, she gladly sat with a sigh of relief.

Evan's gaze circled the chamber as far as the light would allow, and he pulled another candle stub from his pocket and lit it from the one they carried. He held out the candle on the slate.

"Keep this to ward off the mice. I shall return soon."

Sorcha stiffened. "Where are ye going?"

He bent and placed a kiss on her cheek. "Not to worry, lass.

I go to survey a few things afore we leave. Rest yourself here. I shall not be gone long."

Nodding reassurance, Evan left Sorcha in her circle of light, watching him depart until he was out of her range.

Sorcha tried to relax, yet her surroundings commanded her attention. She knew the smell of mice and dust, yet there was another unidentifiable scent. After several minutes of rest, she rose and discovered a broad fireplace at one end of the great chamber. It appeared someone had laid a fire there long ago.

She knelt and leaned toward the large opening, and suddenly the scent of heather caught her. The recollection of putting heather upon the fire brought back a flood of memories of sitting before the fire with her tambour frame doing needlework, of her and John lying together in front of their fire talking, loving one another. *Her* John.

A tear slid down her cheek, and she did not brush it away. God was with her, and He would restore what was taken. The thought caught her in an instant—a promise. She struggled to remember the exact verse when Evan returned, his quick footsteps echoing in the empty chamber.

His footsteps halted. "Sorcha, are ye well? Why are ye on the floor?"

Sorcha gently wiped the tear from her cheek and rose. "I am well. There was a scent I did not ken, so I came to find it."

Evan was at her side in an instant and took her arm. "What was it?"

"Heather." She smiled up at him. "What did ye find?"

The excitement in Evan's voice drew her closer. "This is a

wondrous place. 'Tis lacking in furniture except for a few pieces in the bedchambers. It seems the verra large and heavy beds must have been too much to worry about taking. Mayhap one was the laird's as it is a thing of beauty. The bedclothes are, most certainly, soiled from dust and mice yet are easily cleaned."

His excited voice heartened Sorcha. "Aye. Tell me of it."

"I may sleep better than a bairn in that bed." He chuckled, then reddened in the candlelight's glow, and he drew his gaze from her.

Sorcha swallowed her embarrassment, quickly changing the course of the conversation. "Sounds heavenly." She took his arm and strode toward the front hall.

"Ye still have not told me what ye wished to speak of."

They walked on in silence until clear of the castle and into the forest before Evan spoke. "I would not have ye upset over what Clara said to ye. Ye have no need to share your feelings with anyone. I ken ye dinnae love me. We have been in each other's company for years, and John was my dearest friend." He swallowed hard. "Ye owe me naught."

Sorcha wanted to tell him she did not know what her heart was saying, so she settled on a truth. "Evan, I am indebted to ye, of that be certain. Yet I cannot think of another man except John. I shall grieve him for as long as is proper. There is nae way I may dishonor his memory."

He nodded without looking at her.

"Please dinnae fash yourself over Clara. She is my sweet friend, and I dinnae want to push her away. She only wants to see me—and my bairn—happy. 'Tis all."

Sorcha held back what Clara's true hope was for their future—that they would come to love one another.

Chapter Fifteen

1710

Muirie kept her vigil by the window, praying the violent storm would ease so they might return to Castle Deveron. Was this God's punishment for disobedience? She wrung her hands until a blazing slash of lightning cut the black night, and she screamed.

Beathag placed an encouraging arm around her shoulders. "'Tis unsettling, I know."

Muirie swallowed a sob, not wanting to show her frailty. She considered the reason for her feelings. Was it because of Reid? He was the only person there from whom she cared to hide her weaknesses.

Beathag pulled her from the window and forced her to sit

upon the settle beside Gavin. Reid stood staring into the fire, his hand braced against the narrow mantel. His booted foot nudged a stray log at the edge of the hearth, shoving it back into place.

The action sent sparks flying into the chamber, bringing the blended scent of smoking peat and wood.

"All shall be well, Muirie." Gavin's eyes were on Reid as he spoke.

The two men exchanged an unspoken message, and with a slap to his thigh, Gavin rose with a sigh. "I shall step out to check on the horses."

The weight of their situation crashed upon Muirie's heart, filling her with remorse. Tears returned, and she dipped her head to hide them.

The settle shifted, and she dared not see who sat beside her.

"Will ye not eat?" Reid's deep voice held no condemnation. "I know 'tis not much, yet ye must keep your strength."

A long silence stretched between them before he left her without a word.

Muirie leaned her head against the back of the settle. A sudden and complete weariness fell over her like the heavy, dark clouds surrounding them, holding them captive.

A hoarse whisper met her ears. "Ye must eat, Muirie."

Muirie turned to see Beathag holding a pewter cup and a piece of bread and cheese in a cloth.

"I hunger not."

"Ye must eat," Beathag repeated. "Or else ye will not be

able to sit your mount."

Muirie released a shuddering sigh. "Mayhap that should be the easier way to depart this world."

Beathag jumped to her feet, placed the food and drink on the settle, and scowled at Muirie. "Stop pitying yourself! Ye are not the only one who will be punished, Muirie Stewart!"

Her sudden spin from Muirie sent her crashing into Reid, who gripped her arms to steady her.

Though his calm expression held no ill will, his words did otherwise. "That was very unkind of ye to say to one who holds your best interest close to her heart. All of Muirie's concerns have been for ye and Cormac." He released her, not stepping away. "Ye mayhap consider apologizing."

Reid sidestepped the girl to face Muirie. "Please consider if ye do not eat. . ." His gaze dipped to the food next to her. ". . . ye may be a hindrance to our journey."

Muirie watched as he turned on his heel and strode out into the coursing rain.

Beathag slumped onto the settle and stared into the fire. They were alone in the cottage, the men having gradually shifted to the stables, concern for their only means of travel.

"I am that sorry. Reid spoke truth. I had no cause to speak thus."

"Truth he spoke." Muirie's hand rested on Beathag's arm. "I, too, am sorry." She embraced her, and when they released each other, both women wiped tears from their eyes.

"Muirie, please speak not of leaving this world." Beathag sniffled. "I could not carry on without my dearest friend . . ." A corner of her mouth lifted. ". . . *and* preacher."

"And a sermon I shall give ye, Beathag Scott." Muirie playfully slapped her shoulder.

Wind howled around the small dwelling, breathing icy air through the cracks around the window and door, making smoke from the fire spill into the chamber. Beathag strode to the fireplace and stabbed at the wood, sending up flames.

The cottage door opened with a crash, and Peader stomped in, slamming it closed with his booted foot. "'Tis brutal out there." He notched his chin toward the door. His arms held a pile of wood, and he promptly released it to one side of the hearth and knelt.

Beathag stood over the man, the iron poker still in hand. "Where have the others gone? Are they still in the stables?"

Peader lifted his gaze to peer at her, wet pale hair plastered to his forehead. "Aye." They stared at one another for a moment before he returned to attending the wood.

Beathag sent Muirie an amused look. "What are they about?"

The young man shrugged, and when he looked up, Muirie was certain a glint of humor flickered. "They are talking about our journey and what we must do."

More silence followed, and before Beathag questioned the lad further, Muirie asked, "And what do they think we *should* do?"

Peader leaned back on his heels, his features revealing nothing. "Since the storm grows worse, they judge we must stay where we are."

"And . . ." Beathag placed the tip of the poker inches from where Peader crouched and tapped it a few times. ". . . what else did they say?"

Peader cocked his head. "Mistress, are ye going to beat me into submission if I do not tell?"

Muirie could not repress a snicker. Beathag and Peader turned to watch her. She took the poker from Beathag. "Me thinks this would serve us better to use it for the purpose it was created." She propped the implement against the stone fireplace and spoke to Peader.

"Please tell us what they have decided is best and why it is so."

Peader warmed to the gentler request with a smile. He rose, dusted his hands on his breeches, and faced Muirie. "They have agreed 'tis no good may come of us by traveling in cold, wet rain for hours. 'Tis truth we should all be ill afore we reached the castle, and Lord and Lady Stewart would be most angry to have so many sick to attend to. And Lord Stewart will not look kindly upon anyone who mistreated his horses."

Not once had she considered the wellbeing of the horses, and it shamed her.

"We had not considered it. My punishment should not come before their welfare. Lord Stewart would be grieved to learn of their mistreatment, and I will not have it so."

Peader returned to tend the fire as Muirie went to the settle, and though she had no taste for it, she ate to keep her strength for the journey ahead.

The door swung inward with a freezing wind, and three soaked men strode in. Muirie shivered at the sight of them.

Each man wore a pleased expression while holding the results of their hunt.

Cormac lifted a rabbit high. "My ladies, please find a pot to stew us a bonny feast."

Beathag chortled. "Do we have more than meat?"

Gavin lifted a small bag. "We do. A small storage closet in the stables held a few carrots and leeks."

Muirie congratulated them. At least they would not starve. A hot meal was most appealing.

Beathag made the stew in a small iron pot they found tucked in a cupboard, which she cleaned with rainwater. Muirie rummaged through their belongings to find anything to use as dishes and utensils.

The men arranged the seating to accommodate all to share the meal around the table. While they waited for it to cook, the storm continued to erupt, enveloping the cottage and pounding it so forcefully that Muirie wondered if they would be swept away while trapped inside.

Gavin produced a deck of cards, and they passed the time, testing their patience. After a couple of hours, Reid yawned and said he would rest. He settled on a blanket in front of the fireplace with his hands clasped behind his head staring at the ceiling, booted feet crossed at the ankles.

Muirie watched his face in the flickering firelight as she handled her cards, paying little attention to what value they held. Rain wavered between pounding downpours to gentle pattering and wind sometimes howling through cracks in the shelter.

Beathag leaned toward Muirie and whispered, "Have a care for your hand, or ye will lose the game for us."

When Muirie looked at her, Beathag dipped her head

toward Reid.

"Ye pay more attention to him than to your cards."

Face heating, Muirie surveyed her hand, then looked to Reid again, who was watching her.

"Why do ye look at me, Muirie?"

Her heart skipped a beat, and she struggled to find the words. "I do wonder why ye lie about so early."

Reid slanted his head toward her, and their gazes held. Without breaking contact, he said, "I rest so I may take the first watch."

"Watch?"

"Aye. We have agreed to stand watch while others sleep. The moment the storm breaks—whatever the time—we then ride."

After a long moment, Reid rolled his head to peer at the ceiling. "I would not have ye worry longer than is necessary."

Beathag nudged Muirie's shoulder and spoke in a low voice. "I see Cormac may be right about the pair of ye."

"Ye *and* Cormac are mad." Pretending to arrange her cards, she wondered if they truly were—or if there was more to what they saw.

CB∞SO

Muirie woke with a start, a gust of icy wind enveloping her. Cormac pulled the door shut behind him, and Reid strolled to his spot near the fireplace. The men had agreed she and Beathag should rest nearest the heat while the men took their turns watching the storm.

"What is the hour?" Muirie tried to keep her voice low to

not waken Beathag.

Reid whispered, "Why do ye not sleep?"

Muirie shrugged, unable to answer him truthfully.

"Do ye still fret?"

Unable to form words, she looked down. The man made her uneasy, never knowing how to respond to his questions. His soft grey stare held something incomprehensible. He was always kind to her and most gentlemanly. Yet the closer he was, when he held her gaze, a flutter moved through her middle. The sensation was akin to hunger. 'Twas the closest explanation she knew.

Beathag's words rang in her ears. "*I see Cormac may be right about the pair of ye.*"

She was terrified at exactly what that meant, yet a still, small voice cautioned her to watch her step.

A stronger voice spoke near her ear, and she flinched and saw Reid kneeling beside her, worry etching his features.

"I thought ye had fainted, lass." He pushed a coil of hair from her cheek, his finger lingering on her skin. "Are ye unwell?"

Beathag moaned in her sleep and rolled from Muirie, who met Reid's eyes. "No. I am fine. 'Tis uncomfortable to sleep on a hard surface." She wiped the sleep away and made to stand.

Reid took her arm to aid her, and the fluttering began again. She had to stop this. The man would likely leave, and she would never see him again. And rightly so. She had no business feeling anything for him. Whatever way that was.

They rose together, inches apart, his gaze holding her in place, powerless to move from him until he brought a hand to cup her cheek. A cough broke the contact, and he quickly stepped back a pace.

Cormac handed Reid a cup of warm ale and asked Muirie if she cared for some. She shook her head and folded the blanket with precision. Still holding the ale, Cormac's gaze swung between the two, and when he released the cup to Reid, he said, "The weather is clearing." Once his back was to them, he released a low chuckle.

Muirie placed the blanket on the settle and stepped to the window to find the blackened sky filled with bright, twinkling stars. The sight took her breath. In that moment, she wished she were in the castle gardens smelling the lavender as she took in the glory of God's creation.

She sighed deeply, focusing on Him, leaving Reid in the recesses of her mind. There was no time for her to waste on something she could never have. True love would not be a part of her life. She was *no one.*

Hot stinging tears pushed their way to release, and she fought them. A foundling with no past and no future. Yet God loved her as no man ever could.

The Stewarts had been more than kind to her and would gladly give her a place among the servants for as long as she desired. Yet she knew she must go her own way eventually.

"Muirie."

The way he said her name so tenderly nearly broke her. She squeezed her lids tight. "Aye?"

"'Tis time to go." A warm hand cupped her shoulder and squeezed.

"Aye. I shall waken Beathag." She knelt by her friend, so he could not see her face. "Up, Beathag. We must be away at once."

While the men readied the horses, Muirie and Beathag divided bread and cheese among them to eat as they traveled. The horses pawed the ground in eagerness to be on their way.

Though the wind still held its chill, the night was clear, a partial moon to guide them. Muirie and Beathag carefully wrapped themselves in their cloaks, hoods up, and settled onto their mounts.

Cormac drew Beathag to ride beside him, leaving Muirie alone until Reid took his place beside her.

Muirie wished he had ridden with Gavin or Peader and left her to her thoughts. She must sort them out and pray for God to give her peace.

"If we stop only to water the horses, we should be at the castle before dawn. Mayhap we can slip to our chambers with none the wiser."

She heaved a pained sigh and looked at him. "'Twould depend upon when the others return."

"Did they not say their journey to be two days?"

"Aye."

"Their return is not until the morrow."

"True. Yet they did not say what time of day."

"I do not think them to depart before dawn. It is many hours from Castle Deveron. So they should not arrive until late."

Muirie's shoulders relaxed at his words. If only they had time to make themselves presentable and rest before the party returned. Could they keep the secret? Guilt stabbed at her again for agreeing to the venture.

Lord, forgive us.

Elizabeth Lamont's image came before her, and she gripped the reins, making the horse halt briefly. Reid's reflexes were swift, and he reached to calm her mount.

His gaze sought hers. "What bothers ye, lass?"

Without thinking before speaking, Muirie stammered, "E . . . Elizabeth."

"What about her?"

"Should she learn of our adventure, she will cause us trouble. Have no doubt."

He seemed to take this in and finally nodded. "Aye."

The blood drained from her face. "How may we keep it from her?"

He took one of her hands in his and held it briefly. "Have no fear. We shall devise a plan."

With his steadiness and confidence, she considered this man was capable of anything he set his mind to—and for it she was grateful.

⋘⋙

The sun sent shafts of light front the east to beyond the small party as they traveled west. Muirie glanced over her shoulder to watch the sunrise, a limitless array of colors melting into one another, the morning mist filtering the light into an ethereal glow. If only they had time to stop and watch the beauty unfolding behind them. She sighed and turned back homeward. Her countenance did not go unnoticed by Reid.

"I too wish to pause and watch the sunrise."

Muirie's breath caught in her throat. Could he know her mind?

"Mayhap we may watch the sunrise over the river one morn before I depart?"

Her head jerked around, her heart hammering. "Depart?"

"Aye. I must be away on an errand for my father."

She swallowed, wondering how long he would be gone, and said as much.

"I know not. The journey to the Colonies is a long one, and my father has not said how long I shall stay there."

"The Colonies?" She feared she sounded like a child with her abrupt questions. "I mean, 'tis a long way from Scotland."

"Aye. 'Tis." Reid watched Muirie, surveying her features as if to gain access to her thoughts.

Muirie opened her mouth to speak, and a shout broke the space between them. They peered ahead. Cormac rose in his stirrups, arm outstretched and pointing.

"'Tis the tower at Castle Deveron!"

Joy and dread coursed through Muirie. Their arrival as the sun crested the trees surrounding the castle lifted her spirits. Yet her time with Reid was near the end, which upset her.

Once they settled into the rhythm of hooves pounding earth, Reid asked, "Would ye care to watch the sunrise on the morrow? I feel I must be on my way the day following."

Again, she experienced joy and dread blending into an unknown feeling. She formed a smile. "Aye. That would be nice." Not knowing why, she added, "Mayhap the others may join us."

His features slackened as if she had disappointed him.

She wondered why she had spoken thus. Was it fear?

The question lingered in the air, and neither of them spoke for the rest of the journey.

Once they reached the castle, the servants were beginning to stir. Muirie was swift to take Beathag to Mistress Picken to discover if anyone knew of their whereabouts.

The cook blanched when she faced the women. "I have feared for ye, and thought ye were to return yestere'en." Her gnarled hands wrung a cloth. "And Master Reid has received an urgent missive from Edinburgh. The lad what brought it be in the kitchen eatin'."

Muirie's mouth dried. "What is it?"

"Oh, lass, I dinnae ken! The lad what brought it arrived late last eve. That poor boy has been pacing like a wild stag."

Beathag placed an arm around the woman's shoulders. "All shall be well. Dinnae fash yourself."

She faced Muirie. "Will ye find Master Reid?" She sniffed the air. "I smell something burning and will see to it."

Beathag led Mistress Picken into the bakehouse, the scent of burnt bread wafting from the door as they entered.

Muirie found Reid and the others in the stables speaking in hushed tones. They did not hear her approach, so she coughed, and they brought their gazes to her.

"I am sorry to interrupt. Mistress Picken said a missive has arrived for Reid." She tugged on the trim of her cloak to hide her trembling hands. "The lad remains in the kitchen."

Reid bowed. "Will ye walk with me?"

Muirie nodded and fell into step beside him. The morning activities of the castle were well underway, and the sun spilled its light across the tops of the trees. A dog barked just as a rooster crowed his morning greeting.

The kitchen now in sight, Muirie halted. "I shall leave ye to your missive and attend to my duties." She dipped her chin and turned.

"Must ye go now? Allow me to collect the message and see what my father requires of me."

Muirie hesitated. Why did he want her to wait? "Shall we meet after we break our fast? I must go." Not waiting for a response, she rushed toward the woods near the river.

Confused and afraid, she ran to the bench beneath the fir tree where she and Gavin had spoken. She sat and hugged her knees to her chest. What was she afraid of—Reid? Certainly not. He was a gentleman, yet he awakened feelings in her and challenged her all at once.

The excitement of the troublesome journey home dragged her into an exhausted sleep. Muirie slid to the forest floor where the fir needles had formed a cushion and leaned against the trunk. She fought the urge to lie down, willing herself to stay awake while weariness threatened. Wrapping the cloak tighter, the warmth of peace engulfed her, and she allowed oblivion to take her.

Muirie's lids flickered open, and the glow of filtered light met her. The pure scent of the forest muddled her thoughts. Where was she and why? Her name echoed through the trees, and she suddenly remembered hiding there, then recalling how fast she fell into slumber. The journey, coupled with overwrought emotions, had been too much.

"Muirie!"

She eased to a sitting position using the tree for support, blinking the sleep away. A red grouse sang his morning song high above her resting place. Morning? No, 'twas not possible. The angle of the sun was much too low in the west.

Bolting to her feet, Muirie stared at what remained of the red-orange glow of the setting sun. She had slept the day. The bird's song was not of the morning but of the evening, a nightingale perhaps.

The underbrush rustled and parted, and Beathag rushed toward her. "Oh, ye had us afeared, lass!" Her breathing heavy, Beathag rested her hands on bent knees. "When I came to your chamber and found it empty, I sought Cormac, and we searched everywhere."

"I am sorry. This was the only place I could think of to be alone for a time, and weariness seized me." She pointed to the space behind the bench close to the tree. "'Tis where I have been sleeping."

Beathag shook her head and huffed. "Well, I *never*!" In two long strides, she reached Muirie and tugged her arm. "Come. We must be away and let all know ye are safe."

Swallowing the lump in her throat, Muirie said, "*All?* The entire castle has been looking for me?"

"Aye." Beathag pulled her through the trees. "Except for Reid."

Muirie chilled. Why would he not look for her also?

"The missive his father sent was urgent. He was away to

Edinburgh without delay."

Her chills turned into trembling. His feeling anything for her must have been girlish imagining on her part. Why else would he leave without a word? Why, God, was his leaving breaking her heart?

Until that moment, she had not realized the depth of her growing feelings for Reid Graham. She glanced over her shoulder as they left the tree she slept beneath. Choking back a sob, all she wanted was to crawl under it and sleep away the pain.

Muirie felt Beathag's stare upon her, and she lifted her chin and met her gaze. "What? Do ye think me foolish for caring for him?"

"No, it gladdens my heart that ye have found someone to care for."

"I have not found someone. He cares little for me to leave without haste and not say farewell." She heard the bitterness in her own voice.

Beathag gasped and clapped a hand over her mouth. "I near forgot." She reached into her apron and tugged out a small pouch drawn tight by a cord. She shoved it toward Muirie. "Aye, he remembered ye."

Muirie's unsteady hands accepted the offering, and she opened it. A black stone attached to a strip of leather tumbled into her palm. It reflected the red sun's glow, shards of green shining through it.

"He said to tell ye he found it upon the ground before the storm. The cord is so ye will not easily lose it again."

"He said that?" Muirie cupped the necklace in her hand as

if it were a fragile thing. "It must have taken him a great while to make the hole and not break the glass."

"Aye. 'Tis why we could not find him. He worked on it the day, knowing he was to depart soon."

Hot tears pricked, and she heard the whinny of horses. "The stables! He may still be here." She slipped the necklace over her head and ran as hard as her legs would obey, Beathag on her heels calling after her.

Arriving at the castle entrance at the edge of the old Roman road, she turned to see him and the lad who brought the missive already far down the lane. Her painful swallow halted the threatening tears. That she had come so close to saying farewell near brought her to her knees when she saw him turn in his saddle.

Muirie lifted the necklace. The last of the sun's light caught it. He nodded and waved with a beguiling smile before he slipped into the evening mist.

182

Chapter Sixteen

1603

Sorcha stood upon the parapets relieved that the castle was large enough for them to settle inside the protective walls. She watched as the men were assigned duties. Some broke the soil for planting, others stood guard—one upon the parapets, others posted on each side of the house at ground level.

Kester remained at the gates, and as he paced slowly from side to side, his gaze found Clara's form each time. Her friend planted seeds they had gathered from the MacGregor stores before their departure.

Sorcha peered down at the activity. Evan and Clara had forbidden her to take part in the strenuous tasks, so she resigned herself to the kitchen and stillroom, performing the duties she could easily achieve. The women clucked over her like protective hens. They were determined that John's bairn would live and prosper. It warmed her heart yet also made her feel a cripple.

Leaving the heat of the kitchen for fresh air, she came to take in the view. Pulling her gaze from the garden's progress and Kester's attention for Clara, she returned to her survey of rolling hills and mountains surrounding them. The vibrant yellow gorse grew in widespread areas, and she imagined the purple heather that would soon flow across the landscape. The sweet floral scent always calmed her.

A shrill whistle drew her attention, and she looked down once more into the courtyard. Clara flailed both arms in the air. Sorcha waved back in delight at the indelicate way Clara sometimes whistled like a lad.

A caressing breeze washed over her as the guard made another turn around the tower, now humming a tune. He dipped his chin when making another pass.

Sorcha whispered a prayer, "Father God, thank Ye for bringing us safely here. Please, if 'tis in Your will, allow us to stay and live in peace." The guard's humming grew closer, and she said, "Amen," then slowly descended to the stillroom.

The light and hearty atmosphere lifted her spirits as she made her way through the castle, each floor teaming with activity. Everyone smiled and greeted her amiably. Amid the sounds of hammers, laughter, and children running about, Sorcha felt complete. If only this feeling could continue.

In the kitchen, she found Clara sitting at a small table, an assortment of seeds before her. She looked up and smiled.

"How was your wee walk up top?"

Sorcha strode to stand over Clara. "'Tis a fine day, to be sure. What have ye here?"

Clara lifted her brow and sent Sorcha a playful look.

"I know what they are. What are ye doing with them?"

"Oh, aye, sorting them." She averted her gaze and returned to her chore.

"Why do they need sorting?" Sorcha perched on the stool across from Clara and rested her elbows on the table.

The woman's skin turned a pretty shade of pink.

"Clara?"

She muttered under her breath, "I took a tiny tumble and dropped them."

"So Kester's attentions caught your notice . . . hmm?"

Clara continued sorting the seeds, and Sorcha placed a staying hand upon her arm. "'Tis no sin, Clara. He admires ye, and ye admire him. Let God lead ye."

Sorcha watched as a lone tear splashed upon the wooden surface of the table.

"I am afeard." Clara placed a hand over Sorcha's. "I am afeard," she repeated, "that something shall happen to Kester if I return his regard." The woman sniffed. "Just as—"

"I know, dear. Just because ye lost your first love does not mean ye shall lose Kester."

"Ye speak truth, Sorcha. Yet I fear if something happened to Kester, my heart shall never heal."

The declaration brought clarity to Sorcha, choking her. Was that why she could not acknowledge her growing feelings for Evan? Was she afraid as well?

The sudden scent of baked bread brought a growl from her stomach, and Clara sniggered. "Is it ye or your bairn?"

The comment broke the sadness, and Sorcha hugged her friend—now her sister. Sorcha snickered. "Mayhap both."

Clara rose and pulled Sorcha up. "Let us have a bite, then ye can help me sort the seeds."

They looped arms and strode to the kitchen worktable. "Mayhap Kester would care to help ye."

Clara nudged Sorcha in the side, making the baby kick, and Sorcha jerked. The fierceness of the kick puzzled Sorcha.

Clara paled. "I am that sorry. I dinnae mean—"

"Och, dinnae fash yourself. It was not ye, 'twas the bairn fighting back." She laughed, and the other women in the chamber joined them.

Mistress Gibbs, a widow Sorcha aided in the cave, chortled. "Aye, lass. Bairns what kick so hard are bound to be warriors."

Sorcha halted and placed a protective hand upon her stomach, fear washing over her.

"Aye, mayhap. Or he may be a man of God." Clara words lightened the moment.

The widow's gaze alighted on Sorcha, her knowing eyes misting, and she readily agreed. "Aye, pray 'tis so. A godly man is what we need more of, lass."

Sorcha's heart calmed. Aye, she desired her child to be just that—a man or woman of peace, not of war.

✠

Mistress Gibbs' words haunted Sorcha. God must be praised

for aiding them. She sought Evan before the evening meal and found him in the courtyard sitting upon a crude bench, a comely lass by his side. She recognized Maidie, a lass of no more than six and ten—very bonny to be sure.

The rise of something unknown coursed through her, and without considering her actions, she bolted toward them. Before she arrived, the flame-haired lass placed a kiss on Evan's cheek, and Sorcha snatched the girl's arm and yanked her to her feet.

"Maidie, what do ye mean by kissing my husband?" The blazes igniting her ire grew into an inferno, and she shoved aside any sense, surging on, a warrior fighting for her own.

Evan bolted to his feet and pulled Sorcha from the lass. "'Tis aricht. Maidie was thanking me for aiding her father in a task."

Sorcha looked into Maidie's eyes and saw a glint of satisfaction.

The girl lifted her chin in a sign of rebellion and glared at Sorcha. "Aye, Evan does tell truth."

Sorcha's blood boiled, seeing from the corner of her eye Evan's gaze upon her and not the lass. "I dinnae believe ye. Ye are old enough to know better. Ye may have the years of a *lass-bairn*," she spat the words as a curse, "but ye have the body and mind of a woman."

The lass's scrutiny glowed with hatred. "Ye are a mean-spirited old hag. Evan wed ye to honor his friend, not because he loved ye, so why would he not seek a more comely lass?" She spun on her heels and ran toward the stables on the other side of the yard.

Sorcha's body quaked with fury. Evan's voice spoke as if from a far distance. "Sorcha, please sit and calm yourself."

She allowed him to guide her to the bench, and when she saw the place where Maidie sat, she backed away. "I shall not sit where that harlot—"

"*Sorcha.*" Evan's calm voice held a warning as his regard skittered around the courtyard. The workers had stopped, staring at them, confusion on their faces.

"Leave me be. I shall go to my chamber." She swiped her forehead with the back of her hand, then palmed her cheek. The heat against her hand caused her mind to stray to the scene she had just witnessed. She peered at Evan. "Why did ye allow that *lass* to become so familiar? Ye know what others say of her."

"Nae. Who has spoken ill of her?"

If only she had the courage to tell him what all the women knew. She drew in a sharp breath and met his eyes. There was honest confusion there. She shook her head and rushed into the castle, maneuvering the steps as carefully as possible, meeting Clara in the great hall.

The moment their gazes held Clara hurried to her side. "What ails ye?" She brought her hand to Sorcha's forehead and jerked when it made contact. "Ye are burning with fever!"

Sorcha mimicked the action and realized she was fevered. Panic streamed through her. *The bairn!*

"Clara, what am I to do?" She gripped her stomach. "Och, nae, nae. Please dinnae take my child. I am sorry, Lord. I lost my temper." She fell to her knees and let her head rest upon the floor, sobs engulfing her.

Footsteps pounded toward them, and Sorcha felt the press of muscular arms around her.

"Sorcha, what is wrong?"

Clara's quivering voice spoke to Evan. "She is burning, Evan. I know not what caused the fever. Nae one else has it."

Evan scooped Sorcha into his arms. "Aye, dinnae Mistress Gibbs have a sickness right afore we left the cave?"

Clara walked alongside Evan. Sorcha's gaze held Clara's, her eyes clouded.

"Aye, she did."

"Mayhap it has passed to Sorcha. I shall take her to the bedchamber while ye fetch the widow. She has healing skills better than anyone here."

Sorcha saw the concern he wore as he spoke to Clara. "Fetch her quickly."

Clara dashed away.

Evan kicked the door to the bedchamber open and carried her to the makeshift bed—a pallet in front of the cold fireplace. Once settled, he searched the chamber for another blanket and gently covered her and tugged it to her chin. She followed his every move and struggled to speak, unable to release anything other than an insensible word or two.

She labored to say his name. "Evan."

He spun from the fireplace where he stroked the embers to life, rose, and strode to her side, kneeling and taking her hand.

"Aye. What do ye need, lass?"

She tried to lift her head a fraction, and he eased her back. "Nae. I shall get water."

His rapid footsteps sounded on the stairs, returning with speed. The cup he brought to her lips held cool water.

Her vision dimmed, and when it cleared, she saw the widow. "Where is Evan?" She squeaked out the question, and Clara answered.

"Gone to the stillroom to get a measure of feverfew. Allow Mistress Gibbs to look ye over, lass. All shall be well."

Evan soon returned, handed the herbs to the widow, and sat on the floor on Sorcha's other side. Her regard would not stray from him. Shame for her behavior toward Maidie weakened her spirit. Mayhap God would take her and the bairn home to John.

Her eyes squeezed shut, hoping to staunch the flow, yet they escaped. Her throat flamed, and she whispered coarsely, "Evan, I am sorry." Please tell Maidie I am sorry. 'Tis time to go to John."

Evan's voice rasped, "Nae. Ye cannot leave me now. Just when we are to begin our life together."

Mistress Gibbs nestled Sorcha's head in one hand and brought a cup to her lips. "Drink this now, lassie. 'Tis a remedy that never fails."

Her head barely shook. "Nae. 'Tis time for me to go."

"Mistress Gibbs, how could she get sick so sudden like?" Evan asked. "It came upon her too fast."

"Sometimes it happens thus. The infleenzy is a frightful ailment. Let me care for her. As ye know, I have recovered from it, and I am far weaker than this lassie."

Clara drew Evan away, and Sorcha reached a quivering arm toward them. "Nae, please . . ."

"We shall return." Clara patted Sorcha's hand and pulled Evan to one side.

Unable to keep her eyes open any longer, Sorcha drifted into a fitful sleep, dreaming she stood in a cloud of mist edging Loch Lomond, her tambour in one hand and a long red thread trailing from the other.

192

Chapter Seventeen

1710

Muirie's jaw slackened at Lady Stewart's declaration. Journey to the Highlands? For what purpose? She had never traveled from the castle, as far as Lady Stewart knew. Remorse gripped Muirie's fragile emotions at the deception.

Grannam's posture straightened, and she clapped her hands like a child. "'Twill be an agreeable journey, lass." She patted Muirie's cheek. "Do ye not want to see the Highlands?"

"Aye, Grannam. Though will it not be a long and tiresome journey?"

"Nae worse than the one I just endured, and I am much older than ye, lass."

Muirie laughed. Their recent journey paled in comparison

to the far distance they would travel to the Highlands.

Lady Stewart rang for tea, and Grannam's wince did not go unnoticed by Muirie. She leaned toward the elder woman and whispered, "If ye add extra milk, ye may like it." She winked, and Grannam chuckled.

With a swish of skirts, Lady Stewart stood over them with raised eyebrows. "The two of ye do not fool me. Ye have been conspiring against me since Muirie arrived at Castle Deveron." She returned to her seat wearing an amused smile.

The subject of travel brought a sudden pain to Muirie, thinking of Reid's absence. She resigned herself that he cared not for her as she did for him—though he left the lovely necklace. She looked upon the gift as one of only friendship. Therefore, she would settle into a more withdrawn life, surrendering to the path God had chosen for her—to not marry and pass her life at Castle Deveron.

That Lord and Lady Stewart chose to journey to the Highlands to visit friends was not to be worried over. She would play the dutiful ward and travel with them, caring for Grannam's needs.

Though intent on her needlework, it was as if Lady Stewart read Muirie's thoughts. "Ye must take a companion on our journey."

"My lady?" Muirie's attention left her own tambour frame to study the woman.

"While ye keep Grannam entertained, I believe Beathag would be an ideal companion and lady's maid."

"Entertained?" The elder woman bristled. "I need nae one to entertain me. I can tend myself." Her lips pressed together, and she frowned, chin lifting. "The thought!"

Muirie smiled, keeping her gaze on her needlework. "Aye, my lady." Beathag would thrill at the chance to accompany her. The lass had traveled no further than she.

They sat in silence until the tea arrived, Beathag bearing the tray. Muirie coughed and looked at Lady Stewart who glanced up and indicated agreement.

"Beathag?"

"Aye, my lady." She curtsied and stilled obediently in front of Lady Stewart.

"Do ye not have a sister near your age?"

"I do, my lady."

"I wonder . . . may she be willing to attend to your duties here should ye be gone for a few weeks?"

Beathag paled, her mouth slackening.

Lady Stewart looked from her needlework to the girl. "Do not fear, lass. I ask because I would like for ye to play the part of companion and lady's maid to Muirie and Grannam whilst we travel to the Highlands."

Her skin paled further, lips quivering. "I . . . I shall be most happy to do so, my lady. When do we depart?"

"Mayhap a fortnight hence?" Lady Stewart directed a smile at Beathag. "Will that suit?"

Beathag swallowed hard, and she curtsied. "Aye, my lady. Aye. And thank ye . . . thank ye." Without a word, she spun and flew from the chamber, bright with excitement.

"My lady, ye have given Beathag more joy than she has received in a long while."

Lady Stewart lowered the needlework in her lap and peered at Muirie. "Not even when the two of ye traveled with four lads to the beach?"

Muirie froze, a hard lump lodged in her throat, a heavy silence permeating the chamber. Who had revealed their excursion?

The woman held up a hand. "There is no need for ye to say aught. I shall not share how I know this. Be assured Lord Stewart shall *not* be apprised of it. Better to deal with me than him."

Grannam puffed out her chest. "Indeed."

"*Y . . . ye* will not tell him?"

"No. I fear what he will do to the lads. And ye and Beathag." She notched her head. "I imagine ye have all learned a lesson."

"Aye, my lady. That I have. And I am that sorry."

A strange glint shone in her eyes, and Muirie wondered what exactly she knew of that day. Did she know of the storm—the cottage?

An uncomfortable quiet engulfed the chamber before Lady Stewart excused herself to rest before their evening meal. The moment the door closed behind her, Grannam began her discourse.

"My child, I know not how my granddaughter discovered your wee journey, yet I must warn ye to be careful Lord Stewart is none the wiser." She sipped the milk-ladened tea. "He is a just man and will ken the way of his son. Cormac needs a firm hand. A hand his father is not afraid to use if it will keep him steady."

Dread filled Muirie as she tried to decipher what Grannam

meant. "What would he do?"

The old woman shook her head and tsked. "Send him to school on the Continent or elsewhere if it would take him from the maid."

Muirie frowned. "Cormac is of an age where schooling is to end—not begin."

"Aye, yet there is military schooling."

Fear coursed along Muirie's spine. A soldier's life was not for Cormac. He would not accept it. And what of Beathag? Would Lord Stewart send her away so she may not be here when Cormac returned?

What else could be done? She formed the thought into a question for Grannam and asked it.

Grannam grunted. "'Twill not bode well for either of them. Know this. Lord Stewart will not let them come to harm. They shall be cared for, just not together. Never that."

Tears welled in Muirie's eyes. She could not tell Beathag this truth. Her friend already lived with the chasm of their differing stations.

She thought of Reid. Even knowing him for such a short time, his absence weighed heavy upon her. Yet what if she loved him as Beathag and Cormac loved one another? The pain of separation would be unbearable.

The situation with Reid was far different—although the separating was just as painful. Most likely, she would never see Reid again.

ᕫᔕᕬ

Sun shone bright on the mid-morning day, the trees alive with birdsong, a soft wind stirring the leaves. The walk on the village road lined with oaks offered a direct view of the first cottages and shops.

Walking alongside Beathag, Muirie shifted a basket laden with food and yarn upon her arm. "What does Cormac say of our journey?"

"He is unhappy." Beathag groaned. "It appears to be a plan to keep us apart while Lord and Lady Stewart are gone." She heaved a sigh. "Cormac asked why he may not accompany us."

Neither spoke until they reached the edge of the village.

Beathag sobered. "Lord Stewart is sending Cormac to school in Glasgow."

Muirie's heart stilled. Lord Stewart had made his decision. She tried to sound surprised. "Truly?"

"Aye."

The tears in her friend's voice pained Muirie. "I wish there was something I might do."

Beathag took Muirie's arm and tugged her to a stop. "I love him. Is that such an ill thing? Why must it be that we cannot love one except from our own class? Did God not create all?" She sniffled, tugged a cloth from her apron pocket, and angrily swiped her nose.

Muirie hugged her friend. "I am that sorry." She released Beathag, placing hands on her shoulders, the basket dangling from the crook of her arm.

"'Tis not fair. Life is not fair. God never said it would be." She willed the burning tears to cease and hooked one arm through Beathag's. "Let us go to your family. When we return to the castle, we shall take the long way through the woods by the river and have a good cry.”

Beathag gave a brief smile, eyes dull with grief.

Their entrance into the cottage brought many welcoming embraces. Sharp barks, the squeal of children, and the bright smile of Beathag's mother swept them into a flurry of hugs and kisses.

“Rowan!” Mistress Scott yelled from across the chamber. “Leave Mistress Muirie be.”

Muirie stared at the adorable face of the puppy. “Are ye not the sweetest creature?” She tousled his thick, red fur and squinted. “Who named him Rowan?”

Beathag sat on the stool beside her and patted the pup's silky fur. “Cormac.” She chuckled. “He tripped over him in the stables, and it made his fury rise. I told him he was as red as the rowan berries.”

Hamish knelt to join in. “He be ours.” The child's wide smile tore at Muirie's heart. To be no more than five years of age and lose his father saddened her.

“Cormac gived him to us.” His tooth-gaped smile melted her heart further.

Muirie saw Beathag's eyes glisten. “He did?”

Beathag shrugged. “He visits from time to time. Since father died, he brings bits and pieces to help.”

Muirie had no words. Cormac helped them? Not once did he mention the Scott family nor his part in aiding them. Of late, it seemed she learned more and more about her brother. Sorrow overtook her at the thought of Cormac going away.

“He is a bonny pup, Hamish. Do Dorcas and Seona care for him?”

"Oh, aye. We all do. Even Mam." His gaze dropped to the dog. "She makes us *bathe* him," he whispered the dreaded word, making Muirie smile.

"I am certain he does not hate it all that much."

"Aye, he does. Mam says it rids him of the fleas." His small chest rose and fell on a deep sigh. "So he must endure."

Beathag burst into laughter, hugging her brother. "He is our braw little man. Repeats all he hears."

Muirie was reminded of how Cormac would do the same at that age. Misery clutched at her again. She would miss him terribly.

"Seona." Beathag motioned for her to join them, and the girl poured boiling water over the tea they had brought. She sat on the floor beside Hamish, ruffling his wavy locks.

The family was close knit, and Muirie longed for one of her own, a sudden vision of Reid flashing before her.

Beathag touched Seona's shoulder. "Lady Stewart has asked if ye care to work in the castle for a time while we are away. They have asked me to go with them to the Highlands."

Seona's mouth gaped. "*I?*"

"Aye, silly goose. Ye." Beathag squeezed her hand. "Are ye not up for the task?"

Seona perked. "Aye." A quick expression of doubt shone for a moment. "What will be my task?"

"The same as me, work in the kitchens alongside Mistress Picken. Though without Lady Stewart and Grannam there, ye will not have to serve anyone." Her chin dipped. "Mayhap Cormac from time to time."

Muirie cleared her throat. "I think not. He will most likely take his meals in the kitchen since he shall be alone."

Beathag groaned. "Aye."

Once they drank tea and ate a few of Mistress Scott's buttery bannocks they said farewell and strolled to the place where Muirie had slept beneath the fir tree by the river. They sat on the bench and in the forest's silence listened to the river burbling toward the sea. Muirie wondered how far it was between the end of the River Deveron and the beach where she found the sea glass.

Of its own will, her hand caressed the necklace hidden beneath her shift. The lump of glass resting upon her chest was her most precious belonging. A gift from Reid. Mayhap he cared a trifle.

A vision of the panels hanging upon Lady Stewart's walls trailed through Muirie's mind. Why, she could not say, yet it was vivid. Beside a loch a man lay upon the ground bleeding as another knelt beside him. As a child, she recalled staring at the wall hanging, asking Lady Stewart many questions. No answers appeared, only promises to share the story when she came of age.

"Ye are far from here, my friend," Beathag whispered. "What are ye thinking of—Reid?"

Muirie's gaze focused on the path before them leading to the river. "No. Well, I was, now I think of other things." Beathag would never understand her curiosity about the panels. The appeal of them was fierce.

"'Twill do me no good to think of him. He has gone, and I shall never see him again."

"Aye. Mayhap, yet as ye preach to us all, 'tis in God's hands."

Muirie jerked her gaze to Beathag, a weak smile tugging her lips. "So ye *have* been listening."

"Aye. Sometimes." A tiny smile lifted a corner of her mouth.

"That does warm my heart." If only Muirie might believe God had a place for her with Reid. Yet it was not to be. She would die a spinster at Deveron. God had placed her with a family to care for her needs. What else should she expect? God owed her nothing.

⊰⊱

The carriage lurched, and Muirie slammed into Beathag's shoulder, moaning an apology.

Beathag tittered. "As if ye had a choice."

Muirie glanced at Lady Stewart, whose pained face held an unsightly shade of green.

Grannam, napping in the corner against the brocade squab, released an unladylike snort. Nothing seemed to affect the elder woman. A low moan seeped from Lady Stewart's lips.

Muirie leaned toward her. "My lady, shall we tell the driver to stop? Mayhap a cool drink and a small rest from the jostling will help."

The woman nodded, releasing another groan. Muirie banged her fist on the ceiling of the carriage, bringing it to a rough halt. Within minutes, Lord Stewart jerked the carriage door open, breath bursting in and out. "What is amiss?"

Lady Stewart struggled to stoop toward the door, her hands frantically grabbing her husband's arm. He helped her down, and they hurried toward the side of the road where a burn trickled.

Muirie and Beathag followed, telling Lord Stewart they would gather whatever Lady Stewart had need of.

"Muirie!" Lord Stewart called over his shoulder. "Bring me a piece of bread and a cup of small ale—and a cloth."

Beathag turned and was halfway to the carriage before Muirie was able to respond. Muirie half ran and half slid down the incline toward the water where Lord Stewart now sat by his wife, rubbing her back, speaking words of comfort.

"Lord Stewart, Beathag is bringing what ye asked for. May I help?"

He lifted tired eyes to peer at her. "Thank ye, Muirie." He handed her his kerchief. "Please dampen this in the burn. 'Tis cold and will help revive her."

"Of course." She took the cloth and rushed to do as bid, hearing Lady Stewart murmur something. As she returned, Lord Stewart chortled. Muirie stood over them, the dripping cloth extended, a timid smile playing upon his wife's lips.

Lord Stewart looked up at Muirie. "No need to worry. My wife is with child." He laughed again. "Is that not splendid?"

Muirie's knees weakened, and she fell to the grassy knoll, relief flowing through her. A child? Was the lady not too old?

Lady Stewart tilted her head, her husband stroking her forehead with the wet cloth. Beathag ran to them and fell at Lady Stewart's feet. "Here 'tis, my lady. Mayhap this shall revive ye."

The woman accepted the bread and ale. "Thank ye, Beathag. Ye are a dear soul." After a small bite, her gaze held upon the maid, something strange glinting in her eyes. She took a sip of ale and handed the cup to Beathag. "Ye are most kind. I shall not forget."

Muirie thought this an odd thing to say and saw Beathag's puzzled expression. Was it fear? Lady Stewart always showed kindness to servants, treating them with care and not as lower than she.

"I am with child."

Beathag blinked, staring at the woman as if the world spun out of control. "My lady, are ye not of an age . . ."

Muirie swallowed, dread growing in the pit of her stomach.

Lady Stewart released a good-natured laugh. "Oh, my dear. I am not all that old to bear children. I was quite young when I gave birth to Cormac. We feared we would never have another child. Now this."

Lord Stewart squeezed his wife's hand. "We are much blessed."

Beathag nodded. "Aye. Most blessed indeed."

Muirie rose. "If ye have no further need of us, we shall return to the carriage and wait for ye to recover."

Lord and Lady Stewart nodded, their gazes held on one another, smiles lighting their faces.

Struggling uphill to the carriage, Muirie feared the long journey would be too much for Lady Stewart. They would most surely make more stops to aid in her comfort.

"I cannot grasp she is to have another child." Beathag marveled. "'Tis a remarkable thing at her age."

"Aye." Muirie's mind was not on the child yet on her future. Would she ever be blessed with a child? She thought not. For a husband must come first, and who wanted her?

The slap on her arm brought her thoughts to a stop. She slanted her head at Beathag and rubbed her arm. "Why did ye do that?"

"Ye forget I can read your mind." Beathag teased.

Muirie looked heavenward. "Oh, aye. Enlighten me."

Beathag tilted her head and pursed her lips, staring at Muirie. "Ye were wondering if ye would ever have a child of your own." She lifted her brows. "With Reid?"

Muirie bumped her shoulder against Beathag's. "Ye are wrong." After a few steps, she added, "About Reid."

"Ah. So ye were thinking of a child?"

"Aye." Muirie smiled at the thought. "I must admit, I wondered if I will ever have one."

Beathag looped her arm through Muirie's. "Ye shall. I am certain of it."

The carriage driver opened the door for them, and they settled into their seats. Grannam started at their presence.

"Have we arrived?" She straightened and peered out the window. "All I see are trees and birds. 'Tis pretty enough, though I hunger."

Sharing a smile, Muirie and Beathag retrieved food from the basket and settled Grannam comfortably until she ate. Lord and Lady Stewart returned, sharing their news, and Grannam huffed. "Another child. My word, Isabel. At your age!"

"Oh, Grannam. I shall be fine." She took cheese from the basket and savored a bite, her air one of supreme happiness.

Grannam rose and struggled to exit the carriage, saying she must care for her *personal business*. "Come along, Beathag. Ye are supposed to be taking care of me." She shot Lady Stewart a feigned hurt expression. "After all, ye are my lady's maid, are ye not?"

"Aye, my lady." Beathag dutifully followed her with a small grin.

When Muirie turned her gaze from Beathag's, she found Lady Stewart studying her.

"She is a sweet lass." Lady Stewart brushed the wrinkles from her gown. "'Tis sad that . . ." She lowered her voice. ". . . she and Cormac are not of a similar class."

Muirie bit her lip and nodded.

"I know ye have something to say about it. Do ye not?" She held Muirie's regard.

"If only . . ."

"Aye, my dear. If only." Shuffling footsteps brought their conversation to a close. The carriage door opened, Grannam's pinched expression meeting them. "'Tis travel that shall be the death of me, Isabel. Mark my words." She hoisted herself into the carriage without assistance and plopped onto her seat with a thud.

Beathag entered, wearing a thin-lipped smile. She brought with her the fragrance of pine and the outdoors.

Muirie's thoughts strayed to the interrupted conversation. Was Lady Stewart speaking solely of Cormac and Beathag—or also her and Reid?

Her mind whirled with possibilities. Reid's father was a wealthy merchant in Edinburgh, so that was not so great a divide between them. Or was it? Mayhap his father wanted him to make a better match than a lowly ward with nothing to her name. She would certainly not be his choice.

CAROLE LEHR JOHNSON

Chapter Eighteen

May 1603

Sorcha woke with a start and flinched at the pain. The more she blinked, the more the pain intensified. It felt as if someone had poured sand into her eyes. She moaned and struggled to sit upright.

Gentle hands grasped her shoulders, easing her onto the bed. Her mind cleared enough to seize the fact she lay upon a true bed and not a pallet. The flow of tears eased her pain, and she peeped at Clara's distorted face. She had never been so happy to see her friend.

"Och, Sorcha, 'tis good to have ye amongst the living. We thought ye were done for."

She grabbed Clara's arms and hung on, fearful should she

release her, she may slip into the blackness. "So I am to live?" The words scorched her throat, and she brought a hand to touch it, expecting to discover her skin on fire.

Clara settled her half-upright against a pillow. "Dinnae move. I have water from the burn for ye."

The cool water was akin to drinking heaven. Sorcha sighed deeply and handed the cup to Clara. "Thank ye," she croaked.

Clara slanted a look. "Ye sound like Evan when he is in a temper."

Sorcha's laugh scratched her throat, yet she was overjoyed to speak at all. She thanked God for saving her. He must have a purpose in doing so, though she had been ready to be with Him—and John.

Her hands went to her belly, the feel of the child calming her. Fear that she had lost the bairn while ill took her breath.

Clara sat on a stool by the bed and bathed Sorcha's face with a damp cloth. "Ye have a bit of color to your cheeks again."

Mistress Gibbs entered the chamber holding a bowl. "Ye are awake, lass! 'Tis a good thing for these old eyes to behold."

Clara rose, took the bowl from her, and offered the woman her seat. "Shall ye feed her? I must tell Evan she is awake."

Sorcha smoothed her hair and groaned. "Clara, wait. I am haggerty-taggerty—" She cut off her words at the look Clara wore.

Clara peered at Sorcha. "Aye. I shall wait." She turned and strode to the other side of the chamber and returned with a hairbrush, sitting on the floor beside Mistress Gibb's stool.

"Feed her the broth, and then I shall brush her hair." She

waved the implement in the air and beamed. "I shall collect Evan for a wee visit."

Embarrassment surged through Sorcha, and she wished she had not been so obvious about her appearance because of Evan. Still she was uncertain why she cared.

The broth strengthened her, and speaking with Mistress Gibbs lifted her spirits. After the woman left, Clara sat on the edge of the bed and brushed Sorcha's hair, giving her a moment of luxury. The last time someone brushed her hair was when she was a girl. Her mother did so each evening, and it always put her to sleep. She did not want to sleep. She wanted to see Evan. Though, she did not reveal that to his sister. By Clara's expression, she already recognized the growing affection Sorcha had for her brother.

Sorcha had not admitted it to herself, much less to her friend.

"How do ye like the bed, lass?" She pulled a long strand of Sorcha's hair gently through the bristles.

"'Tis most comfortable. Where did ye find it?"

"We dinnae find it. Evan built it for ye." She made another stroke. "He also gathered the moss to fill it."

Sorcha stiffened. Why would Evan go to so much trouble when there was a great deal to be done to care for their people?

"He did it because he cares deeply for ye."

Sorcha hung her head, which swayed with each swipe of the brush. "He is only being kind to an ailing woman with child."

Clara puffed out an irritated breath. "So ye say."

They spoke no more, and when Clara finished, she silently placed the brush on a table and departed.

Within minutes, Evan replaced Clara on the stool beside Sorcha's bed. "How are ye, lass? Mistress Gibbs says ye are fully on the mend."

She turned her gaze to meet his. Her throat ached to speak, yet she knew not what to say to him. The dark circles under his eyes and sallow skin pained her.

"Lass, ye had me afeard for your life." His elbows rested on his knees, and he raked fingers through disheveled hair. "I could not eat nor sleep." He kept his gaze upon the floor, not looking up.

She caressed his head and ran her fingers through his hair. His breathing slowed, and he stilled, his tender gaze meeting hers. "Please dinnae frighten me so again."

The scent of pine floated in through the window, and Sorcha breathed in the promising smell of summer. Of new beginnings? Mayhap they could build a life here—*together*.

CS80

Sorcha stroked her rounded stomach, soaking in the warm June sun and the sweet breeze which held the scent of heather. Within sight of the castle, Evan had set her upon a blanket beneath a fir tree with water and a bannock, ordering her to eat, drink, and sleep at leisure. She felt foolish, not helping with the chores. Evan, overly protective since her illness, demanded she rest every afternoon.

Without meaning to, the pull of sleep captured her into a sense of otherworldly calm. She welcomed the sensation and nestled onto the blanket.

Men's voices faded into her dreams, and she focused on them, trying to discern if they were friendly or not.

"I telt ye a storm be brewin'"

"Aye. I seen angry teeth just this morn."

Sorcha groggily shoved to one elbow and focused on the castle. Evan ran toward her. "Arise, lass. 'Tis time to get inside."

In her sleepy state, she tried to obey yet was unable to move quick enough. He was at her side in a moment, helping her to stand and quickly collecting items in the blanket. He shoved the bundle into her arms and scooped her up, their faces inches apart.

"Put your arms around my neck, and we shall make a run for the castle. The skies shall open any moment."

As soon as the words were free, the sky unleashed its stores upon them. The warm raindrops splashed her face, and Sorcha laughed. "'Tis glorious, Evan. 'Tis a fruitful rain to be sure."

Evan slowed his pace. "Aye, lass. I suppose 'tis. Winter is behind us."

"Our plants shall relish the nourishment, thanks to our God."

She stared into his soft grey eyes, the rain now pelting them with vigor. Had she not known better, she would credit he was crying with joy. The emotion of that sentiment brought her own tears, happy tears, yet she was not ready to tell him so.

Evan ran through the open gates, past the guards, and into the kirk, the closest covering available to them. He paused inside the door and turned so they could look upon the soaked courtyard where new plants lifted through the soil a few weeks before. The rain would increase their growth.

Sorcha smiled, and they stilled for a time. "Do not injure yourself by holding such a load. Ye may put me down now."

He let her legs slip from his arms, and her bundle fell to the stone floor, but he did not release her—nor did she release her arms from around his neck.

She stared up at him, his hair darkened by the rain, his expression unreadable as their gazes held. A gust of wind brought a shiver, breaking the moment. He grabbed the blanket, led her to the nearest pew, and bade her to sit.

Evan draped the blanket around her shoulders. "This should give ye warmth." He sat next to her and rested his hand upon her back, stroking it gently.

Was it the blanket or his touch that warmed her so? Sorcha chuckled, which surprised her.

"Why do ye laugh?" His brow furrowed, then relaxed. "Or are ye merely content?"

She placed a palm on Evan's shoulder and felt his warmth through the rough texture of his shirt. The peace of a chapel always calmed her like no other place—and mayhap it was also being with him. "Aye. That I am."

"Tell me why, lass."

Sorcha hesitated. No, she could not share her feelings. Instead, she notched her chin toward the doors that led inside the castle through the library. "We have only to walk through there and have a dry way through the castle."

When he twisted to peer at her again. "Aye. I must admit, I overlooked that wee fact."

They stared at one another, and Evan's head angled a fraction closer, his fingers smoothing a damp strand of hair off her cheek.

Booted footsteps splashed, growing nearer until they stopped at the kirk's door. Evan's hand dropped, and he turned toward the movement.

"Evan!" Kester called out as he burst inside with eyes wide.

Evan lurched to his feet, his hand still on Sorcha's back. "Kester, what is it? What has ye so distressed, mon?"

"From the battlement, Marcus spotted a large company coming over the brae." Kester looked at Sorcha yet spoke to Evan. "The lass needs ta get ta the others. We know not what we meet." He turned and strode from the kirk.

Evan's grip tightened around her. "Ye must go, lass. Find Clara and tell the others." He placed a quick kiss on her forehead before releasing her to sprint after Kester.

Sorcha gripped the blanket tighter around her, wishing Evan's arm remained to steady her. She braced herself with a hand against the pew and prayed for Evan, their safety, and for peace before hurrying from the kirk to pass on the troubling news.

ᏨᏋᎧ

Sorcha sat at the massive table in the great hall, amazed at the transformation. When the castle was abandoned, the table was one of few pieces of furnishings left behind. Benches were the first order of business when they first arrived, so no one lacked for a place to sit.

The large chamber filled with the sounds of laughter as everyone joined in to feast on roasted venison, fish, pheasant, and the winter's stored root vegetables brought with them. The area was rich with wildlife, and nuts grew on various trees in the nearby forest. Their gardens seemed to grow well, and that bounty with the area's resources would see them through the next winter.

Kester stood, lifting his cup. "Ta our kinsmen, the Grants!"

Everyone shouted and lifted cups of water. There was no ale or wine to be had, and Sorcha was glad for it. Some men were unable to hold their drink, and she could think of no better way to toast to the men sent by God to aid them.

There was much fear upon their arrival as Marcus shouted the alarm, believing the worst, that they were a company of Campbells. Indeed, it was better to be on their guard until it was determined exactly who the men were.

Sorcha thought on the fear she felt when Kester and Evan had ridden out to speak with the men, holding her breath as she watched from the ramparts. As the large company of men followed them to the castle, her fear grew, and she hurried down the winding staircase until she entered the great hall upon their arrival.

Evan's expression was unreadable as he left them for a time and returned with an opened scroll. He passed it to the leader of the group, who read it carefully, rolled it, and returned it to Evan.

The man slapped Evan on the back. "We must have a feast!" He turned to his men and issued orders Sorcha could not hear from her position by the side entry.

Evan's gaze found her. He smiled and waved her toward him.

"It appears we have found allies. These men are Grants who return from a journey for their laird and pass the castle to be sure nothing is amiss."

Elation filled her with their good fortune. She tapped the rolled letter in his hand. "And this tells them all they need to know?"

"Aye." He looped his arm around her shoulder and pulled her near the man who read the Stewart's approval for them to be there.

"Douglas Grant, please allow me to introduce ye to my wife, Sorcha MacDonald." There was pride in his voice, his hold on her growing tighter.

She dipped a curtsy, keeping a hand upon her stomach. "'Tis very nice to make your acquaintance, sir."

Douglas took one of her hands and kissed it. "Aye, 'tis my honor to meet such a lovely lady."

Evan shot him a scowl. "And where did ye learn to kiss a married woman's hand, sir?"

Sorcha whispered, "Evan, he is just being kind. 'Tis done in many places."

"Och, aye, mayhap for the unwed," he grumbled.

Douglas let out a bellowing laugh, making Sorcha jump. He bowed. "I am that sorry, madam. I meant no ill."

"None was taken." Sorcha turned sideways toward Evan and laid her palm against his chest. "My husband and I are happy to have your company. As well as your men."

"Aye. I have sent them on a hunt to supply your people with a feast."

He turned his gaze to Evan. "And ye, sir, have our future protection should ye need it. Our laird shall be most glad to hear of your safe arrival."

Evan's expression softened. "Thank ye. Ye shall stay with us a few days?"

"Aye, we shall." Douglas's gaze lifted, eyes brightening.

Sorcha moved to see what caught his attention and discovered Maidie perched in the doorway to the kitchen.

She beckoned the young woman over. "Maidie, shall ye please come and meet our guest, Douglas Grant?"

Maidie sent her a suspicious glare yet obeyed. When she reached them, she curtsied prettily, her cheeks flushed.

Douglas immediately took her hand and kissed it in the same manner as Sorcha, releasing it with less haste.

Sorcha watched Evan and nudged him with her elbow. When he looked at her, he had the good grace to redden. She lowered her voice. "Now do ye not feel ashamed?"

"Ashamed for what, *madam*?"

She laughed, bringing Douglas and Maidie's attention to them.

"Now that is a bonny sound, Evan. None which I have heard in a long while."

Evan chuckled. "Nor I, Douglas. Nor I." He looped Sorcha's arm through his and escorted her to a seat beside the fireplace, where a lad built a fire for the cool night ahead.

June might bring welcome warmth, but the evenings held a chill. Sorcha recalled passing many happy evenings sitting with tambour in hand beside John. Could she do so now with

Evan? She had begun a piece shortly after their arrival, glad she had a goodly store of thread. This picture would be one of hope, not of a battlefield filled with snow and blood.

Returning to the reverie surrounding her, she surveyed the group. Douglas and Maidie sat, heads bent in conversation. A rush of remorse swept through her for attaching Maidie to Douglas. He did not deserve a silly willy lass such as her.

She would not worry. Douglas was able to care for himself. Evan was out of danger. Again shame filled her. Evan was an honorable man—also able to care for himself.

I am sorry, Lord, for doubting Evan. He is a good man, and I am fortunate to have him.

A response arose in her mind, mayhap from her heart. *I have joined ye with Evan. Give him a chance, my child.*

The words stung. Was it her imagination, or did God really speak to her so clearly? Was their marriage truly part of His plan?

220

Chapter Nineteen

1710

Muirie's eyelids fluttered, and she swayed toward Beathag until a sudden jolt brought her head up. A golden glow streamed through the window, and her gaze traveled to the setting sun. They were to reach their destination soon.

Beathag released a tired sigh. "I am weary."

Lady Stewart agreed, shifting in her seat, an expression of exhaustion shading her pretty face. "I must agree, Beathag. The child does weary me near as much as this carriage ride."

The carriage slanted as it made a curve, and Muirie glanced out the window. An imposing castle came into view perched on the rise above them, the sun sending rays of gold, amber, and red against its pale surface, illuminating the structure.

Freuchie Castle appeared to float in the evening sky.

Beathag leaned across Muirie, and her breath caught. "Oh, 'tis magical."

"'Tis a sight to behold," said Lady Stewart.

The carriage slowed as they made their way up the brae. Muirie craned her neck to peer at the towers looming over them. Torches flickered at each side of the entrance, and once they were through the gates the courtyard was lit as if by daylight. What must have been a dozen or more torches lined the perimeter of the enclosed area.

Lord Stewart waited for Lady Stewart and helped her from the carriage. The footman then aided Grannam, Muirie, and Beathag.

"Lady Stewart!" A girl rushed across the yard, her breath coming in small gasps. "I am so glad ye have arrived."

Elizabeth curtsied, and Muirie hoped her astonishment did not show at the girl's unexpected presence at Freuchie Castle.

"Where is Cormac?" Her voice wavered, face pinched into a perfect frown.

Lady Stewart looked at her husband, an unspoken message passing between them. "He is not with us, Elizabeth. Did ye expect him?"

"Aye, I did, my lady." The girl's nostrils flared, and she moved away abruptly and ran into her mother.

"Elizabeth! What is wrong with ye, child?" Lady Lamont glared at her daughter and strode to Lord and Lady Stewart. "I am sorry, Isabel, Eric, for her behavior. I know not what comes over her at times."

Lord Stewart placed an arm around his wife's waist and

held her arm with the other. "Ye will excuse us, Cecila. My wife is most weary, and I must see to her comfort."

"Oh, Isabel! Allow me to assist ye." She took Lady Stewart's other arm, guiding her toward the castle where they were met by Lord and Lady Grant. The low hum of greetings floated across the courtyard until all were inside.

After Lady Stewart refreshed herself, Muirie accompanied her to sit with the other lords and ladies in the cavernous great hall. Elizabeth sat near the fire, face flaming as red as the glowing embers.

Lord Stewart looked around them. "Where is Gavin?"

"He and Peader are with a hunting party." Lord Lamont glanced at his host. "With Lord Grant's son, Liam." The men chattered on about hunting while the ladies spoke of more gentle subjects.

Muirie's heart gladdened to hear Gavin was in attendance. She longed to see him as if she had known him for a long time. Yet her happiness at the news was short lived when Elizabeth sent a hard glare her way. Muirie's ire rose—even more so when she pricked her finger while making a simple stitch. She inhaled deeply and exhaled slowly, forcing calm over herself, determined not to let the girl's sullen mood sour her own.

Lady Lamont spoke about their decision to arrive earlier than planned. "I must say I am surprised Cormac did not accompany ye."

Murie wondered that herself. Lady Stewart could have as easily left Beathag and brought Cormac.

"Aye. His father wanted him to attend to things at home." Lady Stewart shifted in her seat. "The lad must learn to handle estate matters."

Lady Lamont nodded. "'Tis truth. They must learn as early as is meet."

Grannam asked Lady Lamont a question while Muirie's attention stayed on Lady Stewart, who watched Elizabeth's reaction to their mention of Cormac.

The conversations in the hall converged to rival the sound of a rushing river. Realization dawned on Muirie—Lord and Lady Stewart were trying to keep Cormac from Elizabeth, not Beathag. Well . . . in truth mayhap from both.

She smiled and returned her attention to the needlework, her amusement shifting to a small chuckle.

"What is so humorous, lass?" Grannam whispered. "Will ye not share it with me? I am in sore need of entertainment." The corners of her wrinkled lips curved up, eyes crinkling.

Muirie glanced around, making certain no one heard. "I cannot say. Please do not cause me misfortune."

Grannam cackled, and all turned in their direction.

Muirie groaned under her breath. "Oh, Grannam."

"Not to worry, lass." She patted Muirie's hand, rose, and addressed the chamber. "I shall leave ye to your evening and find my bed. A long day it has been."

Lady Grant summoned a maid to escort Grannam to her chamber where Beathag unpacked the belongings. With a swish of her skirts, Grannam left the chamber with more energy than a woman of her age should possess.

As Muirie brought her gaze to her needle again, she caught the harsh glare of Elizabeth's scrutiny. Had she guessed what Muirie reasoned about Cormac's absence? The girl was devious, of that she was certain. Would she cause trouble? Mayhap this journey to the Highlands may not be as pleasant as Muirie hoped.

Gathering her things, she placed them in the basket and rose. "My ladies." She curtsied. "If ye do not mind, I shall retire. The day has been long."

"Of course, my dear." Lady Stewart rose with care and stood beside Muirie. "I shall retire as well." She placed a hand on her still flat stomach and dipped her head. "Lady Grant."

Lady Grant sent them an understanding smile. "Rest well. Should ye require anything, ye have but to ask."

Muirie's gaze traveled to the men, now locked in earnest conversation. Lord Stewart kept his wife in his sight, and he slipped away with only a glance from his companions until he arrived at his lady's side.

"Are ye unwell?" He searched her face and smiled with affection, satisfied with what he saw. "I shall escort ye."

The way they looked at one another always caused Muirie to marvel at their mutual adoration.

"Muirie." Lord Stewart captured her attention.

"Aye, my lord."

"Come. Walk with us." His kind, fatherly expression never failed to fill her with fondness for him. They had embraced her as one of their own, yet the lingering suspicions of how she came to be in their care still plagued her.

As they climbed the stone stairs, her mind returned to her beginnings. She had pieced things together through the years, yet most were unwilling to reveal more.

Mistress Picken had found her before the sun had risen. A

bairn in a basket left at the bakehouse. The way the cook told the story, she had taken the babe into her arms and wept as she carried her to Lady Stewart. Lady Stewart had inquired why the babe's hair was wet, yet seeing Mistress Picken's tear-streaked face she understood.

Muirie smiled each time she remembered the touching story of how she as an abandoned bairn touched the woman's heart. That bond held since Mistress Picken had always looked after Muirie. She did still—for which Muirie was thankful.

Once Muirie aided Lord Stewart in settling his wife, he asked Muirie to sit with her until he returned from wishing Lord Grant a good eve.

Propped upon pillows with a book of prayer on her lap, Lady Stewart looked a question at Muirie.

"Aye, my lady." Muirie sat on a stool beside the bed.

Lady Stewart's fingers caressed the prayer book. "If ye are too weary, please retire."

"Lord Stewart bid me stay with ye."

The woman puffed out a rush of air. "I shall be asleep before he returns. I have not the strength to read."

"Would ye care for me to read to ye?" Muirie had not the strength either—though she would do anything to please her guardian.

Light brown eyes shrouded in fatigue peered at her. Muirie rose, taking the book and laying it on the small table. "Rest, my lady." She pulled the counterpane until it nestled under her chin.

Before Muirie blew out the candle, Lady Stewart's eyelids

had already closed. She left one candle burning across the chamber to aid Lord Stewart.

As she closed the door, she prayed for the safety of Lady Stewart and the bairn—and she could not help but also utter a prayer that she might be so blessed in this way one day.

☙❦☙

As the morning light slowly filled her chamber, Muirie found Beathag already gone from her bed in the alcove, apparently attending to Grannam who rose with the rooster. Muirie washed, dressed, and strode to the great hall where she hoped for food to break her fast. Weariness still claimed her, and she had laid abed far too long.

The hall was empty, voices trailing from another chamber, and she strode toward them. As they grew louder and more distinct, more than one sounded familiar. She rounded the corridor and slammed into a tall, strong figure, the impact knocking her into the wall.

"Muirie!" Strong hands gripped her upper arms and steadied her.

She looked into the concerned face. "Gavin!"

Without thinking, she flung her arms around him just as Peader and another man came up beside him. She jerked backward, her face heating, and avoided the other man's gaze. He must be Lord and Lady Grant's son, Liam.

Gavin thankfully seemed unaffected as he pulled her forward and introduced her to Liam. She could only manage a shy smile. He must think her simple minded.

"'Tis a pleasure to meet ye." Liam gave an elaborate bow.

She curtsied. "'Tis a pleasure to meet ye, sir."

"And where are ye off to, lass?"

Muirie glanced at Gavin and Peader, then back to Liam. "I fear I overslept and came to break my fast."

Liam nodded, displaying a wide grin. "A habit I fear I have long tried to end."

"Come." Liam crooked his arm. "Allow me to assist ye."

Before taking it, she glanced at Gavin and lifted her brow. He nodded and fell into step with Peader behind her and Liam.

They entered a long, wide chamber, and Muirie gasped in delight. "How magnificent. Deveron has a wonderful kitchen beyond anything I have ever beheld, but this is more so."

A massive oak worktable lay at the center of the chamber large enough to accommodate a dozen people without feeling crowded. Three maids worked at various tasks, and they looked wide-eyed at the intruders. A tall, buxom woman stood before them.

"Master Liam, we can serve ye in the hall. 'Twill take only a few moments to bring ye victuals."

"No, Matilda. We shall eat here with the lovelies of the castle."

The maids twittered, their faces flushing. Matilda scolded them and set about giving orders to prepare food for the men and Muirie.

One maid fluttered her eyelashes at Peader as she cleared one end of the vast table.

Once seated, mugs of ale in hand, the men regaled Muirie

with details of their hunt.

Gavin kept his gaze on her. When Liam described how they prepared the red deer for the feast, her stomach churned, and her discomfort must have shown on her face for Gavin held up his hand.

"Stop, Liam. 'Tis not a tale for a lady. Ye shall insult her sensibilities."

Liam's face reddened. "I am sorry, lass. Please forgive a rough Highlander."

Muirie laughed. The lean man with russet hair certainly did not resemble the legendary Highland warriors. She bit her tongue to stifle the sound when Peader guffawed.

"Aye. Ye, haggis-headed lad, look like a long stick with a hunk of red hair. Not a Highlander, my friend."

Muirie's breath caught. She expected the words to send them into a fight when Liam's boisterous laugh filled the chamber.

"'Tis an accurate account of my braw appearance." He rose and revealed the muscles of his upper arms, which Muirie had to admit were not unimpressive.

The maids tittered behind their hands, and the cook lifted her gaze to the ceiling, then returned to preparing their food.

Once served, a companionable silence surrounded them as they ate until Gavin broke the quiet. "Muirie, have ye any word from Reid?"

She froze, her mouth full, and shook her head. Keeping her gaze on the bread in her hand, she chewed slowly, gaining time to calm her churning stomach. Should she have heard from him?

"I thought he may write to ye." Gavin's eyes glinted with mischief.

She swallowed. "Why would he?"

Gavin opened his mouth to reply, then refocused on his meal. When they finished, Peader asked Liam to go to the stables, and Gavin said he would follow later, wanting a word with Muirie.

"Let us sit in the courtyard," said Gavin.

Muirie nodded, and they walked until they found a bench in the shade of an oak tree.

Gavin cleared his throat. "Please forgive me for speaking about Reid in the presence of others. I was not thinking." He palmed his knees and rocked forward.

"Why ask me?" Muirie pressed her lids shut, and the scent of lavender overtook her senses.

"That day . . ." Gavin pulled in a deep breath. ". . . at the beach, Reid was jealous of our friendship. That is why he was in a foul mood."

Muirie's mind went to that day when Reid rushed from their picnic and stood apart from them. Reid had gone to him, and she remembered the anger in his expression. Then Reid's countenance cleared, and Gavin gripped his shoulder in camaraderie.

"I told him ours was a friendship. Not . . ." He raked his hand through his hair and swallowed. "Ye know."

A laugh burbled through her. Gavin was a *friend*. She knew it from the first. He was a braw lad, but he held no attraction for her.

"Gavin, I know now why I hugged ye earlier. 'Twas like

seeing a brother."

One side of his mouth quirked upward. "Aye. 'Twas the same for me."

He placed an arm around her shoulders and squeezed. "Let us not allow anyone to divide our friendship."

"We shall not." Muirie knew a kinship she had not known for some time. Cormac would always be her brother, yet now she had the blessing of two.

☙❧

The evening meal flowed with cheerful conversation, the hall warmed by a low fire and alight with candles, the aroma of roasted meat and vegetables permeating the air.

Each time Muirie glanced across the table, Elizabeth's dark eyes were upon her. The girl seemed to always wear a scowl when looking at Muirie. What had she done to make the girl dislike her so?

Grannam caught Muirie's attention and puckered her lips in distaste. Muirie knew full well what ran through her mind and what she had to say about Elizabeth Lamont.

Liam released a hearty laugh, and Elizabeth's gaze changed course to him. Her countenance altered to one of a simpering female as she demurely asked Liam what he was about.

"'Tis not for a lady's ears to reveal what occurs on a stag hunt."

She blushed prettily and lowered her chin.

Muirie's irritation swelled.

The girl was a master of deception. 'Twas not difficult to see what she was about. She had used the same contrivances on Cormac. How had she learned this? Lady Lamont did not appear the sort to teach her daughter such behavior.

"My sister has an odd constitution for a woman." Gavin chortled. "Speaking of bloodshed and the like does not affect her overmuch."

Muirie gasped, and everyone regarded her. She gulped her drink and attempted a smile. "Forgive me."

Elizabeth shot her a wicked glare. "Are ye so weak that ye cannot withstand a measure of blood?" She lifted her chin in defiance.

Muirie's jaw hardened. "No. I am not weak. I just do not abide the slaughter of *anything* with pleasure."

The girl's skin flamed, and in that moment, Muirie knew if she hadn't before she certainly had gained an enemy now.

Liam raised a glass, his expression one of diplomacy. "Let us toast to the blessings God has given us in this feast."

All joined in, Elizabeth holding Muirie's gaze with fierce determination. Muirie did not cower.

Lord Grant stood. "Gentlemen, may we adjourn to the library? The ladies shall be much more content speaking of needlework than hunting tales."

The murmurs around the table held agreement, and the men departed, yet Muirie's heart implored them to stay— Gavin in particular. She had many things to ask him, and she could use some amiable conversation instead of facing more of Elizabeth's hostility.

Lady Grant leaned closer to Lady Stewart. "I thought they would never leave." She tittered, her mouth quirking.

Muirie aided Grannam to stand, but the woman waved her

away. "I am not so old as I cannot stand on my own, child."

"I know, Grannam. Yet we have been sitting overlong, and I am stiff and in need of assistance to stand."

An amused expression lit Grannam's face. "I will gladly help ye." She patted Muirie's arm. "I am fair weary. 'Tis time for me to be abed." She hugged Muirie close and whispered into her ear. "Dinnae trust that little tart, Elizabeth. She spells trouble."

Muirie suppressed a smile. "Aye. I know that well."

"Good. Watch your back, lass."

She observed Grannam trudge up the stairs with care, keeping a close eye on her, until she disappeared onto the next landing.

"She is an ancient woman, is she not?"

Muirie jumped at the words and breath near her ear—Elizabeth.

"Not so very old." Muirie brushed invisible wrinkles from her skirt, not wanting to meet the girl's regard.

Elizabeth lifted her brows. "Well. She does move rather well for someone of her years. I shall give her that."

"Aye. She is of a stalwart nature." Muirie made to walk away, yet Elizabeth gripped her forearm.

"Why do ye dislike me?"

Muirie willed the lump in her throat to dissolve, her mind searching for a proper response. "I . . . do not *dislike* ye." She prayed God to forgive her for the lie.

She linked her hands at her waist, eyes downcast. "Your actions speak differently."

Oh, this was a well-practiced miss. Muirie must not let on she knew her game.

"Ye misunderstand. Though I care deeply for my family and do not want them hurt, I fear ye may have designs on Cormac." She had not intended to reveal so much, yet mayhap the truth was best.

Elizabeth feigned innocence. "Me and Cormac?" She threw her head back and laughed. "Why would ye think such?"

"Women have a way of seeing when a man is being watched by another."

The girl pursed her lips. "Ye have designs on Cormac."

Muirie's chest tightened. "*Me?* He is my brother!"

"No, he is not."

Rising to his defense, Muirie said, "Not by blood but by more. We have grown up together and are bound only to one another as brother and sister."

Elizabeth's features immediately softened, her shoulders falling slightly. "Well. Mayhap I have been mistaken."

Before Muirie could fully register the girl's shift in demeanor, Elizabeth looped an arm through Muirie's and changed their direction. "Let us go to the parlor and speak with the other ladies. We have much to discuss." She smiled sweetly. "Mayhap ye will share about your needlework and explain the meaning behind your stitches."

Stunned, Muirie allowed herself to be led like a lamb to the slaughter. Was she falling into a trap? She sent a plea heavenward.

God, please deliver me from deceitful plans—and protect Cormac.

Muirie needed God's direction, for left on her own she felt with each step as if she sank farther into the mire.

235

Chapter Twenty

July 1603

The day was glorious. Sorcha knelt in the garden harvesting herbs for the stillroom, inhaling the fresh summer wind, enjoying the feel of the warm earth between her fingers. Evan passed by often, always asking if she rested enough.

She assured him she did and tossed a sprinkle of dirt in his direction. He chuckled, moving on to his tasks. Since the arrival of the Grant warriors weeks before, their relationship had deepened, which Sorcha credited to the added sense of protection. The men often made visits to ensure all was well and in return were welcomed with a companionable meal and accommodations.

Douglas and Evan had formed a friendship, yet Kester held

back, suspicion etched on his rugged features. When Sorcha confided as much to Clara, she said Kester was overly cautious after witnessing the treachery at the Battle of Glenlivet.

She prayed God would ease his suspicions and guide him into a friendship with Douglas.

A shout from the parapets brought her head up, and she peered at Marcus waving at her. She returned the greeting and pressed her hands against her stiff back, stretching like a lazy cat rising from a nap in the sun. She released a contented sigh and made her way to the kitchen.

Clara kneaded dough on the worktable that centered the long chamber. Her blue eyes greeted Sorcha, twinkling with contentment. "Take a seat. Ye look faintly."

"I dinnae feel so. Just a wee bit tired." She washed her hands and rubbed a dab of Mistress Gibbs' salve onto her skin. The concoction worked wonders. She had convinced Evan to allow her to rub some on his hands, and he now expected it each evening. She smiled, thinking about their routine, as she made her way to the table and tried a piece of the cooling bread.

"Aye, ye are well enough, stealing a bite and wearing that smile and all." She pounded more dough with a sheepish smile of her own.

Sorcha suppressed a grin. "Aye?"

"Aye. That smile belongs to my brother I think."

Sorcha dipped her head, concentrating on the bread. She missed baking for John, who praised her bannocks. The memory instantly drenched the joy of her day in sorrow, and she prayed for God to remove her sadness.

She peered at her sister-in-law and smiled. "Aye. Mayhap."

Marcus bounced into the chamber like a long-legged colt. "Did I smelt bread?"

Both women laughed. The lad could ferret out anything freshly baked from the farthest brae.

Clara broke a huge chunk of bread and held it in front of him. "Wash your hands, then ye may have anything in this kitchen."

He dipped his chin and searched the chamber. When he spotted treacle scones, he yelped. "Aye, I shall wash them till the skin comes off for those."

The laughter died as Kester burst into the room and headed straight for Clara. "The Campbells have come. Hide wherever ye can. Care for Mistress Gibbs and the childer. We afear we are outnumbered."

Before Sorcha or Clara could speak, he embraced Clara, kissed her soundly, and ran from the room. Marcus dropped the bread on the table and followed him.

Clara jerked Sorcha to stand, and her voice caught on a sob. "Come! We must help with the elderen and bairns."

Sorcha moved as fast as her body would allow, longing for Evan, the words she had not shared with him on her tongue. She halted Clara, begging to be heard. "I must find Evan."

Clara pulled her toward the door. "There is nae time. We must do as Kester says or else we put others in danger."

Sorcha blinked back tears and nodded. "Aye. I ken." She allowed Clara to lead her.

They gathered the women, elders, and children, hurrying them to the cellar with candles, blankets, water, and food.

Sorcha's mind kept turning to Evan, worried for his safety and all the men protecting them. Once she and Clara settled everyone, she slipped from the cellar as Clara attempted to entertain the children with a story. As she softly opened the door, Mistress Gibbs' gaze caught hers. The woman brought her clasped hands under her chin, her lips moving in silent prayer.

Sorcha swallowed a hard lump. She nodded and closed the door behind her. She took quiet steps along the narrow corridor leading to the stairs, her hand upon one wall to keep from falling to the rough stone floor. Men's voices echoed, coming closer, as she shuffled along.

A unrecognizable voice spoke, "Aye, we are outnumbered. Do as ye are telt and try not to wirry." The sound of a slap on the shoulder followed, one she knew well among the lads, offering encouragement. "Guard our precious ones with your life, lad. Allow nae Campbell to harm them. The way is narrow here, and ye shall have to fight one at a time."

A moment of silence followed before the man continued, "Ye are a braw lad, and I know ye can do it. Remember to stand guard here in the larger area and should ye hear someone coming along the narrow hall remember only one mon at a time can follow ye, and ye have the upper hand. Dispatch him and then any other what follows. Aye?"

She heard a cough, followed by a familiar voice. "Aye, sir. I shall do as ye say."

Marcus. Och, how Sorcha feared for the lad. He may be braw in training with the men and willing to fight, yet he was a lad, working mostly in the stables. She sent up a prayer for his safety while protecting them. Mayhap they gave him this duty to keep him safe from the most imminent danger of battle. Most likely, Kester thought of the idea since Evan was occupied with organizing the men at the gates.

Her daunting task was now to get past Marcus and find Evan. If their situation was dire, she must tell him her true feelings before something happened to either of them.

೮ℬຒ

Sorcha edged along the wall toward the corner and spotted Marcus pacing. When he pivoted away from her hiding place, she took soft, quick steps and made it to the bottom of the stairs before he saw her. She only had to move three steps up, and she was out of his line of sight.

Taking a few slow, deep breaths to calm her pounding heart, she gradually made her way to the parapets. From that vantage she located Evan with ease, having become familiar with his broad shoulders, noticeable gait, and sun-streaked hair.

Before reaching the top, she paused to see where a guard stood, recognizing him at once—Ian MacGregor, a friend to Kester and a most capable warrior. He was not over tall but stout and with a booming voice. He shouted instructions down to the men, advising them of the enemy's movements.

Sorcha made certain to show herself without surprising the man from behind. When she did so, he registered utter shock and disapproval.

"Och, what are ye doing here, lass? Evan shall not be pleased."

She rushed to him and placed a calming hand on his forearm. "Please dinnae send me away, Ian. I must assure myself that Evan is well."

The broad man heaved an exasperated sigh. "Nae, ye must see 'tis not safe for ye."

"I shall not be in the way. Please allow me to stay and watch. No harm can come to me here." She cocked her head and bit her lower lip. "I promise to do all ye say."

He shook his head. "'Tis against my better judgment." His gaze roamed the battlement and then strode to stand behind the crenulation, pointing to the taller section. "Ye must stand behind this and only look around now and again through the embrasure." He inhaled and exhaled deeply. "Lass, ye ken they have arrows?"

Sorcha clenched her teeth for a moment. "Aye," she lied. She *had* forgotten that piece of valuable information. Should she flee? *No*, the great need to be near Evan overtook her once more.

"I shall do as ye say."

He moved, and she took his place, tilting her head to peer down at the top of the brae beyond the gates. Rows of warriors, wider than the breadth of the castle and three deep, lined up in numbers well beyond theirs. How were they to survive this attack?

She squinted to see the colors of their plaid, but from this distance it was difficult to be certain. They appeared to be dark—green, black, and blue—Campbell colors. An icy shiver washed over her, and she straightened, all thoughts of her promise to Ian fled.

"*Lass!*" Ian growled a warning.

Before she obeyed him, she caught sight of Evan at the

forefront of their defenses, standing with his feet planted wide, his claymore braced with the point resting upon the ground before him.

Sorcha gasped at the sight and held her breath. None of their men would live. There were too many. A war cry rose from the Campbells as they surged forward. The MacGregors on horseback plunged toward them, shouting their battle cry with weapons high.

Evan and Kester led the footmen to follow behind the horses, waving their weapons in response.

She watched as men fought like crazed animals, and the bloody scenes of the Battle of Glen Fruin returned to her with force. Her body shook as Ian shouted warnings to a group of their warriors who were about to be set upon by Campbell horsemen. His warning saved them. They disarmed the Campbells and rejoined the others.

The bloodshed took its toll on Sorcha, and she plummeted to her knees, no longer able to witness more horrors of battle. She prayed aloud, begging God to intervene.

Ian yelled a battle cry of triumph, and Sorcha pushed to her feet, struggling for a moment to see what was happening. The guard helped her stand.

"Look, Sorcha." He lifted his muscled arm and pointed to the southwest. A large party of warriors were racing over the brae, shouting a war cry she did not recognize. "'Tis Clan Grant!"

Sorcha gripped his arm tightly, scalding tears falling. She swung her gaze to the battle and sought Evan's form. He engaged a huge Campbell, swinging his claymore wildly, deflecting each of the other man's strikes.

The Grants entered the fray, easily aiding the MacGregors, sending a few of them to retreat. She continued watching Evan.

Douglas Grant rode toward him, weapon poised to strike their enemy. Just as he swung to strike the Campbell, the man's blade connected with Evan's side, felling him with one blow. Within seconds, the Campbell fell to Douglas's attack.

Screams echoed, and moments passed before she realized they came from her own throat. Evan's fall to the ground replayed in her mind as she slid into darkness.

◌◦◌

Rough hands clasped Sorcha's shoulders and eased her body to lean against a stone wall. She shook her head to clear the fog encasing her. When her vision cleared, she saw Ian's face close to hers.

"Lass, are ye well enough for me to attend me duties?" His voice held panic, and she nodded.

He straightened to his full height and peered over the battlement, shouting directions to the men below.

Sorcha struggled for breath at the image of Evan being stuck down so viciously. She twisted and used the wall to force herself up, carefully looking to the spot where she had seen Evan fall.

One of their men tossed Evan over his shoulder while keeping his claymore at the ready. Three warriors surrounded them until he moved as fast as possible toward the gates.

Sorcha held her breath until they were safely behind the

castle walls.

The Campbells found themselves well outnumbered by the Grant warriors, and many of them hastily fled to the trees. Douglas and several of his men pursued, disappearing into the forest.

She moved as fast as her bulk would allow and made her way to the great hall. The men placed Evan on the massive table, shouting for aid.

When Sorcha reached Evan's side, his eyes were closed.

"Nae, Evan. Dinnae die!"

Hot tears burned a course down her cheeks as she watched the blood seeping through his shirt, spreading to the top of his trews. She wanted to scream, but nothing came. Her gaze swept the chamber, begging to see someone who had the gift of healing. The man who brought him skittered off, a look of regret on his tortured face. She knew he must return to the battle.

Sorcha ripped the plaid from her shoulders and placed it upon the wound. She knelt beside the table and rested her head against Evan's temple. "Och, Evan. Please dinnae leave me now. *Please.*" Her sobs rebounded in the cavernous chamber, then she felt him stir. She jerked her head up and peered into the grey eyes, now shadowed with death.

With great effort, he lifted his hand to touch her hair. "Weep not for me. I go to my heavenly home, dear Sorcha. Ye shall join me one day." He coughed, and blood trickled from the corner of his mouth.

She wiped the blood away with the sleeve of her dress. "Nae, ye are going nowhere!"

The vehemence in her voice made him flinch, and he smiled timidly. "Ye are a force to be reckoned with when vexed." He coughed again, and once composed, he said, "I admire ye for it."

Rapid footsteps approached, and Sorcha looked to see Clara bolt into the chamber and straight for Evan. Mistress Gibbs rushed behind her, trying to keep up. She moved aside to let them attend to him, praying for God to give him another chance.

☙❧

"Sorcha . . . *Sorcha*. Wake, my dear."

Her head thrummed against the hard surface she slept upon as her lids fluttered open. The glowing coals of the massive fireplace faced her, the scent of burning wood and peat combining to assault her senses. Where was she?

When she rolled to her side, Clara crouched over her, wearing a weary smile. "Your husband is asking for ye."

John? Her muddled mind tried to separate her memories. How could he have survived the battle? She had watched him fall onto the blood-drenched snow.

Clara's hand brushed a strand of hair from her forehead. "I have mulled cider to refresh ye. Please drink."

She looked at the pewter cup and, with what felt like an age, she took it and sipped. Her mind cleared, and over Clara's shoulder she saw Evan's gaze upon her.

Evan?

Sorcha sat up too fast, dizziness overcoming her, almost dropping the cup if not for Clara's quick movements.

246

Clara chuckled. "Slow, lass. Evan shall go nowhere for a great while."

She helped Sorcha to her feet, supporting her as they strode to the table.

Despite his drawn features, Evan's expression remained alert. He struggled to bring his hand to meet hers, but it fell to his side.

"I am sorry, lass. I mayhap need assistance." A grimace caused his face to tighten in pain.

Sorcha almost fell against him, and Clara braced her. "Careful, lass. He needs tender care."

She found she could not keep her scrutiny from him, caressing each feature as if she had not seen him in years. Why had she turned from him? Was John's mourning period the only reason? Or did she fear giving her heart to another to have it broken once more?

Again, he tried to lift his hand, unable to do so. "Lass, will ye take my hand?"

Sorcha did as he asked and pressed his hand between both of hers.

"Let me touch ye, Sorcha, for I am uncertain ye are real. I thought never to see your bonny face again."

The statement brought fresh tears, and she raised their joined hands and rested his palm against her cheek. His fingers twitched a moment, then caressed her face. She held him steady, allowing him to do so until he paled, and his breath quickened. His head wilted to one side, and she laid his hand on his chest.

"Rest. I shall not leave your side."

He muttered, "Nae, ye must eat and rest to stay strong for the bairn—and for me."

His breathing slowed, becoming more steady. Within a few moments, he slept.

Clara squeezed her shoulder. "'Tis good for him to rest. Ye must do the same. Come, I shall get ye food and then to your bed ye go."

"Nae. Bring food, and I shall sleep here as well. I shall not leave him." She was firm in her declaration, and Clara's expression confirmed her understanding.

"Aye, if ye insist." She departed, leaving Sorcha and Evan alone.

She slumped in the chair by the table and bowed her head. Her mind went to Clara and her words about Mistress Gibbs giving Evan a decoction to ease his pain and help him sleep. The pain lacing her friend's face caused her shame. Evan was Clara's brother. How could she forget Clara would be as upset—nae, more—than she?

Sorcha stayed as she was until Clara's gentle voice spoke against her hair. "We have food and drink. Please come away for a bit."

"Och, Clara. I am sorry. Please forgive me for thinking only of my own sorrow."

Clara knelt and wrapped understanding arms around her. "There is naught to forgive. In truth, your concern reveals how much ye have come to care for my brother, and it does my heart glad."

They remained in this embrace for a time, sisters sharing a common grief.

Clara was the first to pull away. "We must wait until he is stronger before we move him to a bedchamber."

Sorcha nodded. "Ye and Mistress Gibbs go have a rest. I shall eat soon." She motioned toward the things they had brought her on the small table by the window.

Once Sorcha and Evan were alone, she knelt beside the table, her head near his, and placed her forearms on the makeshift bed. She studied his features, knowing the curve of his cheeks, his full lips, the long lashes. He was handsome in a different way than her John, yet they were both goodly to look upon. Aye, yet was not beauty in the beholder's eye?

Her mind traveled to Clara and Kester. She prayed they would make a match. Both were such kind, loyal souls who had endured much sorrow.

Before crossing the chamber to sit and watch Evan sleep, she brushed her lips across his, and prayed he would live to return the kiss—and hear her declaration of love.

Chapter Twenty-One

1710

The shifting colors of purple and blue crowned the golden hues of first light on the horizon. Muirie leaned against the ramparts of Freuchie Castle and gaped in awe at God's creation. The night had not been a pleasant one. Images of Reid warming her heart collided with those of Elizabeth and her deceitful behavior. She tossed upon her bed until faint light invaded her chamber.

The gradual rising of the sun captured her full attention until Reid forced himself into her very thoughts, shoving aside all else. Was it only because of Gavin's revealing of his talk with Reid on their adventurous trip? Did he truly care for her?

If only she knew with certainty. Although, what did it matter? He may never return. Bitter tears burned until they spilled over her lashes.

"Oh, God. Please tell me what to do and how to feel. I am confused and know not what—"

"Muirie?" Gavin's voice called to her from the doorway. "Are ye crying?"

She avoided his gaze. "Why are ye here?"

"Sleep evaded me, and I wanted to see the sun rise over the Highlands."

She watched the sky change colors yet again. "'Tis most amazing to see."

"Aye. 'Tis." His voice held awe and emotion. Not something Muirie often found in a man.

She sighed with feeling and nodded. "'Tis a peaceful thing to behold." A verse slipped through her mind, and she recited it aloud, *"For since the beginning of the world, they have not heard nor understood with the ear, neither hath the eye seen another God beside thee, which doeth so to him that waiteth for him."*

"'Tis a beautiful verse." The statement sounded wistful. "Do ye think of Reid?"

The question shot through Muirie without warning. "What?"

Gavin rested his forearms on the embrasure and stared out at the shards of colored lights blending across the sky with a boyish grin. "I think ye to be coy at revealing your true feelings for my friend."

Muirie's ire rose, and she turned from him. "Ye are quite mad."

His laughter bellowed, suppressing her anger. "I am sorry. 'Twas unfair of me."

She hung her head. "Dinnae fash yourself."

They remained in silence until the sun's hues lightened from orange to yellow.

"Beware of my sister." He sounded more sympathetic than harsh as though it pained him to disclose such a thing.

"Why do ye say this?"

"She can be most vexing."

Muirie was stunned to hear him speak in such a way about his sister.

He faced her. "I am fully aware of her nature to get what she wants. 'Tis not a becoming quality. She is still young, and I hope she will grow beyond it." Understanding shone in his amber eyes. "She tries one's patience."

Muirie could not lie, yet she would not speak ill of his sister. "She is not so very young. Is she not of a marriageable age?"

"Most assuredly. She never allows a moment to pass without reminding me of the fact." Gavin chuckled. "I thought she may set her cap for Reid, but she surprised us all by declaring for Cormac."

"Mayhap a merchant's son, albeit a wealthy one, is not a high enough station for her."

"Aye." He inhaled deeply. "Cormac could not make her happy. His heart is engaged elsewhere."

Muirie started. "What do ye know of Cormac? Has he spoken of it to ye?"

"It only takes eyes to see where his heart lies." Gavin pushed from the wall. "And it is not with Elizabeth."

He faced her, resting his shoulder against the wall. "Muirie, I love my sister but allow me to warn ye. She will stop at nothing to get what she desires. I have noticed her new regard for ye. She has a purpose and will use ye to get it. I care not to see ye hurt."

Muirie stared at him for a long moment, digesting all he said. "Thank ye for your concern. I will be on my guard. Though I know not how she could harm me."

"Trust me. She will find a way if she imagines ye may keep her from her quarry."

Muirie had seen the change in Elizabeth's expression when Cormac and Beathag were in the same chamber. The girl knew Cormac's interest did not lie with her. Would she harm Beathag?

She straightened. "I shall not allow her to harm my friend. No matter the cost."

"I admire your courage and loyalty, Muirie. Will ye share my concerns with Beathag?"

"I am uncertain." She cleared her throat, considering the question. "Should I voice my concern, or merely watch closely and protect her?"

"Let us reflect on it for a time."

"Agreed. Yet we shall not wait over long. Elizabeth may make a move without our knowing and set things in motion that are irreversible." Fear gripped Muirie as she thought about Beathag.

Gavin nodded. "'Tis truth. Let us see what happens this day

and speak again this eve."

"Very well. Until this eve."

Gavin departed, and she continued to watch the sunrise, each moment bringing another range of colors to paint the morning sky, as her heart clenched with fear. She would not stand aside while Elizabeth brought ill to Beathag and forced Cormac into a miserable marriage. He may not have his head on straight, yet he was still her brother, and she knew he loved Beathag. Every day, she saw more evidence of his care for her friend.

Muirie would do all possible to protect them both—and she was glad to have Gavin at her side.

♔

After her visit to the ramparts, Muirie returned to her chamber and considered her discussion with Gavin. How Elizabeth vexed her. She had followed Muirie around like a puppy for two days, and Muirie was weary of playing the *friend* to someone she now knew to be a willful child in the body of a woman. Heaven help any man who fell in love with her.

When Muirie opened her chamber door, Beathag paused in making her bed. Muirie opened her mouth to speak when a noise across the chamber startled her.

"Muirie! I was just telling your *maid* what a tidy chamber she keeps." Elizabeth lounged in a chair near the fireplace, a small book in her hand.

Beathag pinked, and she looked away, continuing her duties.

The edge of the door still in her hand, Muirie widened it,

leaving it open. "Elizabeth, why are ye in my chamber?" She could not keep the contempt from her voice.

The girl rose and straightened her skirt. "To see ye, my dear. Are we not friends?" She thrust out her lower lip in a pout.

Muirie blew out a breath. "Aye. We are." She strolled toward the bed and threw her shawl onto the counterpane. "That is, if ye treat *my* friend with courtesy."

Elizabeth batted her lashes. "Whatever do ye mean?"

"I mean—Beathag may fulfill the duties of a maid, but she is my dearest friend." Muirie placed both hands on her hips. "Do ye understand me, Elizabeth?"

The girl took a step back. "Aye. Ye have made that plain, *friend.*"

"Good." Muirie brought her gaze to Beathag. "Will ye see if Grannam is in need? I can attend to this."

Beathag, obviously taken aback by the turn of events, nodded and left in haste.

Muirie would speak with her later. For now, she must deal with Elizabeth. She retrieved her shawl and folded it with more care than necessary, averting her gaze.

"Why do ye dislike me?"

Muirie jerked at the voice near her ear and whirled. Elizabeth stood at arm's length from her, an unsettling sensation snaking up her spine.

"I do not dislike ye, Elizabeth." She held her breath, trying to form honest words that did not hurt the girl's feelings. Muirie finished folding the shawl and hugged it to her chest like a shield. "Yet ye have been unkind to nearly everyone at

Castle Deveron and shown disrespect to Grannam." She swallowed hard. "And ye have made it most clear ye have regards for Cormac."

Elizabeth's expression turned stony, yet she remained quiet, returning to her seat.

Muirie studied the girl's expression. "Do ye not see what ye have done?"

She shrugged and pursed her lips for a moment. "No, honestly, I do not."

Muirie took a seat beside Elizabeth and peered into her eyes. "Imagine someone treating ye the way ye just treated Beathag. How would ye feel?"

The blunt question earned no immediate answer, yet something flickered within her icy stare. They held one another's gaze until Muirie sensed the coming tears. The girl was unaware of her behavior. What or who had taught her to be so malicious? Lord and Lady Lamont did not appear to harbor ill for others. Yet she knew of dark secrets within families that rarely came to light until it was too late.

Muirie reached out and placed a hand on the girl's arm. "Has someone hurt ye, Elizabeth?"

She jerked from her touch and rose, eyes blazing. "'Tis none of your concern!"

Her intensity caught Muirie by surprise. "I do not mean to intrude, yet should ye wish to talk about it, I will listen."

One lone tear slid down her cheek, and she angrily swept it aside. "Why should ye care? I do not need your pity." She swung around, skirts spinning around her legs, and ran for the door, slamming it behind her.

Muirie leaned back in her chair, shock gripping her at the outburst. There was something wrong with Elizabeth. How might she help her *and* aid Cormac? And, for that matter, anyone else who crossed paths with the girl.

Prayer. She must pray for Elizabeth and ask God to guide her. She needed a friend—a genuine friend—one she could not manipulate or hurt.

A soft knock sounded on the door before it opened. Beathag stuck her head in. "Are ye alone?"

Muirie waved her in and toward the vacant chair by her side.

Beathag glanced around the chamber as if expecting Elizabeth to pop up and attack her. "Has the she-devil gone?"

"For now."

"What has she done?"

Muirie's fingers played with the fringes of her shawl, struggling to tell Beathag they must be patient with the girl. "She has done nothing. Well, not precisely. I fear she has been deeply injured and knows not how to befriend others."

Beathag flapped her hand in the air. "So she has deceived ye into believing her tale?"

Sadness for Elizabeth caught her heart. How could she explain this to Beathag without sharing a secret the girl had told . . . Muirie had surmised it for herself.

"She told me nothing. When I questioned her if someone had hurt her in the past, she cried and rushed from the chamber."

Beathag's mouth hung agape. "In truth?"

"Aye."

A thick silence engulfed the chamber, both deep in thought about the girl that had stormed into their lives, leaving a wave of destruction behind. If only Muirie could protect her friends from whatever future harm she would cause—and somehow help the girl as well.

ⓈⒷ

The rain poured in torrents, the scent of it strong and fresh. Muirie relaxed in the deep window seat with a book as the sky was split by a forked bolt of lightning. A memory flashed, bringing her fingers to caress the necklace she always wore, the smooth glass warming from the contact with her skin.

She turned the page in her prayer book and read from Psalms. *Thou, O God, didst send a plentiful rain . . .*

Her heartbeat grew at the corresponding words to what lay outside her window. What was God saying? She prayed, asking for wisdom. Did she not look upon rain as a difficult thing to traverse? The mud made it difficult for travel, and if overmuch continued, it washed away new crops and affected the out-of-doors work . . . Her gloomy thoughts trailed, and new ones swept in like the rain. Even in the depth of despair, one could discover beauty if one would only seek it.

Time blurs the lines of memory.

Once again, she stroked the sea glass at her neck. Was God telling her this? Because she would never see Reid again? Instead *He* would comfort her? *He* was enough.

The embroidered panels came to her mind, and she placed her book on the cushion and crossed the chamber. The panel she worked on lay atop her belongings in the small trunk. She stared at the tiny, bright stitches. Castle Deveron rested proudly in front of the forest, a small glint of the river peeking between the trees. Hidden among the green foliage sat the bench she had slept behind the day Reid left.

The panel brought her joy and sorrow in equal measure. Her birthday was months hence. Could she wait that long to see the ones Lady Stewart kept stored? Mayhap Lady Stewart would show them to her upon their return to Castle Deveron.

A gentle knock brought her attention from the trunk. "Come."

The door creaked open bit by bit, but no one entered. Muirie stood and paused, waiting for someone to make an appearance. Impatiently, she rushed to the door and snatched it open. Elizabeth fell backward, and Muirie grabbed her arms, steadying her. Elizabeth's strong rose scent brought Muirie's impatience to a halt, soothing her dampened spirit.

"Why did ye not come in when I bade ye enter?" She turned from the girl and retook her seat at the window, picking up the abandoned book.

The girl strode across the chamber and sat across from Muirie, folding her hands on her lap. "I want to apologize." She bit her lip and gazed out at the rain. "Ye were only trying to be kind."

Muirie tented the open book on the cushion to mark her place and reclined against the wall. "Aye. I was."

Speaking softly, Elizabeth said, "Rarely is anyone kind to me."

"Pardon?" Muirie had surely not heard her correctly.

Elizabeth kept her gaze on the window. "'Tis truth. Mostly

I am ignored as if I do not exist."

"Elizabeth, I find that most hard to believe. Your parents are most attentive, and Gavin is a protective brother."

"Aye. He is. Yet is always about with his friends at school or hunting." She shuffled her feet against the stone floor. "After all, he is a *man*, always the apple of our parents' eye. The heir apparent!" She spat the words as if a bitter taste invaded her mouth.

Muirie shifted to sit beside Elizabeth, one arm draped over her shoulders. "I am sure Gavin does not feel that way. Has he not shown ye affection?"

She pressed her lips tight and nodded. "He played with me until he went away to school." A trembling smile touched her lips, and she lowered her voice. "With dolls."

Muirie chuckled. "'Tis a true brother who would do that for his sister. I do not recall Cormac ever doing so with me."

At the mention of Cormac's name, Elizabeth stiffened.

"Elizabeth? Do ye truly love Cormac?" Muirie knew she perched on thin ice, still wanting to know the girl's genuine feelings.

In the long quiet that followed, rain pattered against the window, tapping a rhythmic pace, lulling Muirie. Of a sudden she only wanted sleep. A long nap may do her well. Mayhap she might dream of Reid, and her fingers found the necklace again.

"What is that?" Elizabeth pointed at the glass.

Should she tell her? Would it be something the girl could use against her in the future? Shame coursed through her at the unkind thoughts.

"It was a gift from a friend."

Elizabeth cocked her head. "A man?"

Muirie swallowed and nodded.

"Reid?"

The sound of his name stifled Muirie's calm, and she dropped her arm from Elizabeth and squared her shoulders. "I will answer that question, if ye will answer mine."

"No. I do not love Cormac." Elizabeth stated with surety. "I want a husband to take me from my life, so I may begin another somewhere else—and I do want to be loved."

What a pitiful creature she was, Muirie's regard for her plunged deeper than the North Sea. She prayed the girl would find love, yet how might she help her understand she could not bully her way into a man's affections?

"I know he is in love with the maid. His eyes follow her wherever she goes." She shook her head. "And she loves him. 'Tis as obvious as Reid caring for ye."

Muirie's jaw slackened. Could she be right? Elizabeth was far more canny than a girl her age had the right to be.

"Do ye truly believe this?"

"Aye." She lifted her chin. "'Tis amazing what a woman can do when she goes unnoticed. The things she overhears *and* sees."

Muirie studied her features. She saw no guile there. No hidden scheme. Her gaze was clear, focused, and innocent. "I believe ye."

The surprise she expressed brought a new respect for the girl. Mayhap she just needed a guiding hand. A friend.

"Do ye truly want to be my friend?"

Elizabeth's posture straightened, and she nodded eagerly. "If ye really desire it."

Muirie looped her arm through hers. "Then we shall begin anew. I ask for respect and honesty at all costs." She pulled the girl up with her, breaking their contact, and moved to stand face to face. Muirie dipped her chin. "Good day. My name is Muirie Stewart. I am pleased to make your acquaintance."

Elizabeth tittered. "Good day. My name is Elizabeth Lamont, and I am most pleased to make your acquaintance."

A knock brought their eyes to the door, and Muirie bade them enter.

Beathag stepped inside, a bundle of laundry in her arms. She froze on the threshold, her gaze swinging from one to the other. She took a step back. "I shall return later."

Muirie rushed to her, took the bundle, and placed it on the bed. "Come in and meet my new friend. She wants to be friends with ye as well, so let me introduce ye."

Elizabeth tittered again, faced Beathag, and curtsied. "I am Elizabeth Lamont. I am pleased to make your acquaintance."

Beathag's mouth gaped, and Muirie reached up, placed a finger under her chin, and gently closed it.

"Beathag, please introduce yourself to our new friend."

She blinked several times before repeating the gesture.

Muirie prayed this was not a ruse. Could she and Beathag truly trust Elizabeth? Or would they rue this day? So many questions raged in her mind.

If Elizabeth were playing them for fools, there was no telling how much pain she would cause. For all of them.

Chapter Twenty-Two

August 1603

Sorcha stayed by Evan's side, holding his hand, and only leaving for brief periods to take nourishment or tend to her personal needs. A warm summer breeze swept through the chamber where Evan lay abed, still recovering from his wounds. For weeks, he drifted in and out of consciousness, barely recognizing anyone.

She longed to tell Evan of her growing feelings, yet she held her tongue until his strength returned enough to hear what she had to say.

Sorcha tenderly released his hand as Clara examined the bandage. They stared at the fresh blood. Why did it keep bleeding so? It had been near gone a month since the battle, but Evan was not healing as Sorcha nor Clara had hoped.

Clara straightened, hands on her hips. Her expression could have soured milk.

"I shall see Mistress Gibbs. She may have another remedy." Sorcha descended the long staircase to the great hall and on to the kitchen. Mistress Gibbs would know what poultice to use. After cleansing the wound with a decoction of yarrow and wine, the healer had directly applied an ointment made from the herb. Repeating the procedure daily, it appeared to be working—until yesterday.

Her stomach roiled when she thought of the wound. She sought Mistress Gibbs, finding her in the stillroom crushing herbs, her gaze rising to meet Sorcha.

"Good day to ye, lass." She resumed her task with vigor. "What brings ye to my side of the castle?"

"'Tis Evan. The wound on his side does not heal and yet bleeds." Sorcha sat on a small rickety chair near the woman, watching her skillful hands. "The yarrow has nae more effect."

Mistress Gibbs paused and studied Sorcha. She frowned, her expression in deep thought. "That be two we have tried. The lad loses too much bluid." She rummaged among the bottles and pouches upon the shelves above the table. "If we had pigweed. 'Tis a powerful herb to stop it."

"Where is it to be found?"

The old woman tugged on her lower lip. "In these parts, I know not." She slumped to her stool and slapped both hands upon her knees. "Yet I know someone who may."

Sorcha leaped to her feet. "Who?" Hope filled her, and she repeated, "Who?"

The woman smiled. "Douglas Grant."

Sorcha threw her arms around Mistress Gibbs. "Thank ye. I shall have someone fetch him."

She chuckled. "Nae need to do that, lass."

Her stomach sank. Was she saying it was too late to save Evan? *Oh, Lord, please let it not be so.* With unsteady legs, she returned to the chair, the chamber suddenly seeming too small, the mingling scents of herbs and remedies turning her stomach.

"Do not look so downhearted, lass. I only meant to tell ye Douglas is already here." She gathered a sprig of lavender and waved it under Sorcha's nose.

The sweet scent revived her, and her heart once again sang with joy. She took the flower and sprinted to the door. "I shall find him now."

Sorcha found Douglas and Kester in the library standing over a long table with maps strewn across the surface. They looked up at her entry.

Kester frowned. "How is Evan?" Concern laced his tone, and he placed a hand on her shoulder.

"That is why I came—to seek help from Douglas." Kester stepped back, and they faced the man.

Douglas stilled, a map slack in his hand. "What may I do?"

"Mistress Gibbs must have the herb of pigweed. She deems it shall help Evan heal." She swallowed to staunch the stinging tears. "What has been tried nae longer helps, and she said ye could get what she needs."

Douglas stared at her for some time before speaking, his hand scratching his bearded chin. "Aye. To be sure our healer shall have the herb . . ." He blew out a breath. "Yet it would take some time to fetch it. Mayhap there is some closer."

Sorcha's spirit revived. "Aye?"

Kester looked at Douglas. "Do ye know what it looks like?"

Douglas shook his head and brought his gaze to Sorcha. "Lass, take me to your healer, and she can describe it to me and telt me where it grows."

"Aye. She is in the stillroom."

Kester stepped forward. "Ye go ta your husband. I shall take Douglas. We must make fast work of it."

"Aye, lass, dinnae fash yourself. Should we not find it nearby, we shall go to my home and get it from our healer. If she has none, she shall know where to discover it."

"Bless ye both." Sorcha gave them a warm smile, saying a prayer of thanks for the two men, and leaving the library, she dared to hope.

She headed for the chapel and rushed to the altar, kneeling upon the stone floor. With clasped hands under her chin, she prayed with all her strength.

"Dear God in Heaven, Ye are our creator, our Savior, and our eternity. I know Evan belongs to Ye. His faith is strong. Yet I am unable to let him go. It seems I *do* love him." Hot tears flowed down her cheeks, splashing onto the hard floor. "Please continue your healing work, Lord. Please save Evan, and let us have another chance to be together here."

She wiped at her tears with the plaid that still bore traces of Evan's blood. "It must be Your will alone, Father. Still I beg of ye to let him live. Please dinnae take another loved one from me."

Her hand fell to her middle, and she caressed the babe as

if already born. "Please let my child have Evan as his living father, to care for and protect him—or her." She smiled. "Aye, mayhap ye shall give me a daughter. It matters not just so this bairn is hale."

Sorcha's prayers continued for her child's good health and for Evan's healing until the chamber dimmed. She lit a candle for Evan upon the altar, dried her tears, and went to the kitchen for a bite of bread and cheese.

Marcus sat at the long table centering the kitchen, a glad smile upon his ruddy cheeks as he stuffed pieces of bannock into his mouth, talking around the bread.

Maidie, his audience, wore an endearing smile as he regaled the birth of a litter of puppies in the stables. The smile fell as she caught sight of Sorcha. The girl's lips thinned, and she pinched them together in a grimace.

Sorcha heaved a sigh and forged into the kitchen, ruffling Marcus's hair as she strode past. "Ye seem happy, Marcus."

"Aye. Maidie feeds me well." He sent the girl a look of adoration.

Sorcha grinned and gazed at Maidie. "Ye have a kind heart to feed the likes of this lad." She nudged him on the shoulder good-naturedly.

The lad laughed and continued eating.

"Maidie, fatten him up so he shall grow strong and straight. He's a good lad."

The lass slanted a doubtful look at Sorcha, and Sorcha had little doubt the girl did not trust her.

An idea struck her. "Maidie, have ye seen Douglas?"

Her head snapped up, cheeks pink. "Nae. Why should I?"

"He and Kester have gone to find an herb for Mistress Gibbs. Evan needs something stronger to heal his wound. I would like to know as soon as they arrive."

Marcus rose abruptly. "I shall see if they have returned and bring him to ye."

With her eyes on Maidie, Sorcha said, "Thank ye, Marcus. Bring him to the kitchen."

"Aye. 'Tis as ye say." The lad gulped from his cup, snatched another bannock from the table, and dashed from the kitchen.

Maidie watched him go, then swung her gaze to Sorcha. "Why did ye do that?"

Sorcha did not answer at once, cocking her head to survey the girl. "Do ye want to see Douglas?"

Maidie's cheeks flamed, and she dropped her gaze to peer at the dough she kneaded. With a soft, nearly inaudible voice, she said, "Aye. I do."

"Well. There ye have it." Sorcha took a warm bannock and strode from the chamber without a backward glance.

A twinge of guilt struck her. *Lord, forgive me. Please stop my maneuvering if it is not your will for them to be together.*

Before she arrived at the stairs leading to Evan's chamber, Kester and Douglas burst through the front entrance with scratches upon their faces and hands and clothes askew, yet they sported wide grins of satisfaction.

Douglas lifted a bulging sack. "We have your pigweed, lass."

Sorcha took the offering and opened it. There had to be enough pigweed to last quite a long while. The sigh she released almost made her stagger so great was her relief.

"Thank ye both!"

She turned to go, then remembered Maidie. "I go to the stillroom. Follow me, and Maidie shall feed ye. Mistress Gibbs may attend to your wounds."

Kester chuckled. "Do ye want ta know how we received them?"

As they made their way to the kitchen, Kester regaled her with their adventure for the herb.

"Aye, 'tis an apt thing ta be sure, for the boar—" He coughed against his fist. "—pig, did have a taste for the herb and dinnae want to relent."

Douglas chuckled, saying naught.

"When we made to take the herb, the boar charged us, and we dove into a thicket of thorns." He touched his chin and scowled. "When the beast sped past, Douglas wacked him on the rump with the broadside of his claymore, and he ran squealing into the trees. We dinnae hurt the creature. Although, he would have made a welcome meal."

"Aye, yet we had nae time to fritter on that task."

They entered the kitchen to Maidie's humming over a pot of stewing venison and potatoes. She stirred the contents of the great iron pot hanging above the fire and looked up at them, her gaze traveling straight to Douglas.

"Och, what happened to ye?" She gulped, strode to the man, and lifted trembling fingers to his cheek.

Sorcha gripped Kester's arm and pulled him toward the stillroom. "Let us take the herbs to Mistress Gibbs. I dare not wait any longer for her to take her healing to Evan."

Kester allowed her to lead him, yet he nodded back toward

the kitchen. "That lass moves with speed, does she not?"

"Do ye think Douglas finds her appealing, or is she too brazen?"

Kester quirked a side of his mouth. "I ken not, lass. Yet I think my new friend knows his own mind, and if she is not the lass for him, he shall have little problem telling her so."

Sorcha breathed a sigh of relief. She would not want a kind man like Douglas to be saddled with a shrew for a wife. He deserved much better.

Once they deposited the fresh herbs with Mistress Gibbs, they left her to the work of creating the potions and such that she needed to help Evan. Sorcha prayed that this time he would truly be healed.

☙❧

The candle flickered as if almost spent. The August night would not require a fire, so Sorcha found another candle to replace the dying one.

Mistress Gibbs had administered the pigweed decoction to Evan, rubbing the gash with the salve. Sorcha watched her in case she needed to do likewise. Faintness almost overtook her when she discarded the old bandage and stared at the angry wound, which now bled freely. The area surrounding the gash flamed red, a sign of infection. She stifled a sob and brought her gaze to Evan who wore a grimace of pain, his brow damp with sweat.

When the woman finished fastening the bandage, she took a step back and faced Sorcha. "Och, lass. I pray we used the new remedy in time. We must bring the fever down. I have the meadowsweet and shall go prepare it." She paused at the door. "Bathe him with cool water, lass."

Clara entered and asked Sorcha what Mistress Gibbs said. She told her and went to the basin of water, dropping a small cloth into the vessel.

Sorcha stared at her reflection. What would she do if Evan died? She placed her hand on the cloth and squeezed until her knuckles whitened. She brought the cloth to Evan and bathed his ashen skin.

"I shall fetch more water." Clara patted Sorcha's arm before leaving, muttering under her breath words Sorcha could not understand.

With the cloth in one hand, she bathed Evan's face, her other hand caressing his cheek. "Och, Evan. Please live." She choked on a sob. "I love ye, and I need ye with me."

He stirred, shaking his head from side to side and uttering incomprehensible words. She made out *John* a few times, then "*Dinnae fight.*" Was he recalling the Battle of Glen Fruin? Did he blame himself for John's death?

Suddenly, his voice strengthened, sweat trickling from his forehead. "Nae, John, ye ask too much. She shall not understand."

He stilled, then his hands fisted, mouth twitching as if speaking, but no words escaped. What did he speak of? Had something happened on the battlefield he had not shared with her?

She continued dabbing at his skin with the damp cloth—his temples, neck, chest, arms, and hands, which appeared to bring the fever down a bit. For when she placed a palm on his forehead, it was cooler than before. She would do this all night if need be.

Clara returned carrying a tray with a pitcher of fresh water, a plate of bread, and three cups and bowls. "'Tis time we ate and try to get Evan to do so. He must stay strong if he is to heal."

"Aye. 'Tis truth." Sorcha left the cloth upon Evan's forehead, adjusted him so he was sitting more upright, and retrieved a bowl of the broth. She brought a spoonful to his tight lips, trying to part them with the spoon.

"Clara, will ye help me please?"

She came to Sorcha's side and gently opened Evan's mouth while Sorcha poured the liquid in, yet he would not swallow.

Handing the bowl to Clara, Sorcha gently massaged his throat until he swallowed. She shared a smile with Clara at the small victory and repeated the action several times until he grew agitated. They took a small respite and ate broth and bread, keeping close watch over Evan.

With the bowl still in her lap, Clara rested her head against the tall sides of the chair and closed her eyes. Sorcha set the bowl aside and covered her friend with a shawl. She needed to sleep.

Sorcha returned to Evan, sat next to the bed, and held his hand. Before long, she laid her head upon their entwined hands and became drowsy with sleep.

She awakened to a gentle hand caressing her hair. Expecting to see Clara standing over her, she lifted her head, and the hand fell away, yet the chamber was empty save for her and Evan, his tender gaze upon her.

"*Sorcha.*" Evan spoke her name on a whisper, his fingers

touching her cheek, then he swallowed hard and in a hoarse voice asked, "Ye love me?"

Sorcha blinked in confusion, staring at him. "Ye heard me?"

He shifted slightly and winced. "Aye, lass. My body may be broken, but my ears are goodly." Though his lips quivered, the hint of a smile was unmistakable.

Sorcha's mouth gaped, then closed, her thoughts racing. She looked at him perplexed. "How? Ye slept most of the time, and when ye spoke, ye said such strange words as if ye were not here."

His brows lifted. "What do ye mean?"

Sorcha recalled the muttered words spoken in distress. "Ye spoke as if to John, and ye were displeased with what he said."

Evan rolled his head to one side, looking from her for a moment, then turning to meet her eyes. "Shall ye answer my question?"

The struggle to reveal all raged inside her. Is this not what she had longed for? Telling Evan she loved him?

He lifted a shaky hand to cup her neck and drew her closer. She complied and moved near until their faces were inches apart.

His gaze roamed her face. "I love ye, Sorcha. The love I feel for ye came the day we first met. Afore ye wed John." He lifted his head to brush a kiss upon her lips before falling back onto the bed, paling with the exertion.

Sorcha stilled, her fingertips touching her lips. "I dinnae understand, Evan."

With labored breathing, he said, "John was already in love

with ye, and I had nae right to seek your affection at the same time. When he visited my family, he spoke only of ye, and my da encouraged him. Said would not be fit if he let ye slip through his fingers."

He took a few steadying breaths, his gaze not leaving her face. "He asked that I return with him to see his family and meet ye. When we met, I knew why he loved ye so. *Ye* are why I stayed. John was a brother to me, and God told me to protect him . . . *and* ye, Sorcha."

She tumbled into a chair, her mind and heart in turmoil. He had loved her all this time?

These secret things were revealed as if she untangled them as thread in her needlework, intricate scenes with hidden meanings, meanings that had alluded her until that moment.

A flash of the last panel she had stitched, no *woven*, came to mind, for it seemed as if she was weaving stories of the past for those who came after her. What happened to John still haunted her, yet she felt the need to record what happened to him—her child's father—and to Clan Gregor at Glen Fruin.

The memory of Evan crouched over John's fallen body on the battlefield, caring for him as he died, sliced through her as if it happened before her again. A sudden realization seized her. "Did John ask something of ye afore he died?"

Evan flinched as if she had struck him. His gaze left hers, and he settled deeper into the bed as the door opened to reveal Clara and Mistress Gibbs.

Clara's hand flew to her chest, and she ran across the chamber and flung her arms around Evan's neck.

"Och, sister, have a care." Evan drew in a deep breath and

released it. "I am not yet well enough for the force of such an embrace."

Mistress Gibbs laughed heartily. "Aye, he is right." She patted him gently on the shoulder. "And it seems ye appear a mite better, lad." The old woman skirted the bed and checked his bandage.

Sorcha could only sit stunned and watch. What had happened between he and John at Glen Fruin?

Mistress Gibbs straightened with both fists on her hips. "Pigweed! That be the thing. Clean as a spring wind. I'll fetch more." She grinned and departed without another word.

Clara chuckled, joy apparent in her features, yet all Sorcha could do was muster a slight smile. Evan's words hung heavy on her heart. What was he *not* telling her?

Chapter Twenty-Three

1710

Muirie reclined against the scaly bark of a pine near the castle courtyard, its sweet woodsy scent filling the air. Grannam napped in a chair under the wide boughs of the tree, and Beathag laid beside her propped on one elbow, her fingertips tracing the pattern of the blanket beneath her.

"'Tis most kind of Lady Stewart to allow me to lounge in the Highland air for the afternoon." Her head lolled, lids half closing. With a sigh, she whispered the words for Muirie's ears only. "I wish Cormac was here."

Muirie glanced around, fearful someone might have heard, yet Grannam only snored, and they both chuckled.

Beathag rose and rummaged in the basket until she found the treacle scones Clan Grant's cook had prepared for them.

Muirie declined Beathag's offer for one and reached for the small lap desk beside her. Lord and Lady Stewart had presented her with the traveling desk for Christmas. He had come upon her in the garden, struggling to write while reclining on a blanket among the flowers. It was most generous of them to give her such a gift. Once settled, she prepared the bottle of ink and quill and placed a piece of parchment on the sloped surface.

"Who are ye writing to?" Beathag took a bite of scone and smiled. "These are delicious."

Distracted, Muirie muttered, "*Mmm hmm . . .*"

Her intention had been to simply record what she had seen during their time in the Highlands, yet the more she wrote, the more she realized the words were for Reid.

A purple butterfly landed on the corner of the desk, the upper part of its gossamer wings fluttering slightly to reveal silver-grey on the underside. She paused from writing and sketched the delicate creature, attempting to memorize the colors and their placement.

Grannam snorted and jerked upright. "*What?*"

Beathag rose to attend to the elder woman. "Now, now, Grannam. All is well. Ye have had a nice sleep."

"Sleep! *Me?*" The elder woman tightened the shawl around her shoulders. "Haud yer wheesht, lass!"

Beathag stepped back with a frown.

Muirie looked at her. "Pay Grannam no mind. She still sleeps."

Beathag studied Grannam, squinting. "Aye, she does look a mite odd."

"She does that sometimes when she has slept over long." Muirie watched the butterfly on its erratic path toward a grouping of flowers.

Beathag smirked. "I shall keep my distance from now on while she is sleeping. If I told someone to shut up, I would receive a slap."

Muirie snickered and resumed her letter while Grannam returned to dozing, and Beathag ambled around picking wildflowers.

My dearest Reid . . .

"Good day, ladies." Gavin strode toward them and paused at the edge of the blanket, hands on his hips.

Muirie looked up with a smile and casually placed a new sheet of paper atop the words she had written. "Good day, Gavin. How do ye fare on this beautiful day?"

Gavin surveyed the area, then he sat beside her. "I am well." He dipped his chin toward the paper. "What are ye trying to hide?"

Her skin prickled, and she looked away.

"Are ye writing to Reid?" His tone held mirth—yet not mocking.

She blew out a breath. "Aye, and no. 'Tis only for me that I write. Not to share it."

"'Tis just as well. For Reid shall return afore he would receive a letter in Virginia."

Gavin's finger touched the edge of the desk and trailed along the carved oak side. "Although ye could send it to Edinburgh to await his return."

Muirie's mind grappled with the possibility. Did she dare write to him?

"I would be glad to send it when I return to school." He paused, watching her. "Or I may deliver it to him myself."

She blanched at the suggestion. She couldn't write to Reid. He had not asked Lord Stewart if he may correspond with her. What should she do? She knew she could trust Gavin, yet could she trust herself? Her fingers found the sea glass, and Gavin's eyes met hers. She brought both hands to touch the necklace and bowed her head. "Thank ye, but I think not." She whispered, "'Twould be improper."

His tone matched hers. "Unless I have misunderstood my friend, I believe Reid is fond of ye too."

"Even if we are both *fond* of each other, where could it lead? I would not be someone his father wishes for his son to marry. I have no dowry or connections. I am no one." She almost choked on the words, and in her heart, she knew them to be truer now than ever.

Gavin's features softened as he looked at her, the affection of friendship in his eyes bringing tears to her own. "Muirie, ye *are* someone—to us who care for ye. Your worth goes beyond a title or dowry. Lord and Lady Stewart see it, and have they not cared for ye your whole life with a glad heart?"

His kind words gave her pause. She *had* been cared for most kindly and without complaint, been loved when they did not have to give it, yet she still struggled. Could she truly come to believe what Gavin said as truth?

He rested a gentle hand on her shoulder. "And, most importantly, ye are worth most to God, which in truth is where we all must find our true worth."

She bowed her head, shame filling her. He was right. God had provided for her far more than she deserved, and despite her circumstances, she had been placed in a welcoming home where her needs were met, and she had always been met with kindness.

Forgive me, Lord, and please help me to see my worth in Ye alone.

C3&80

Firelight flickered as wind gusted down the chimney, the wavering light causing Muirie to blink at her tiny stitches. The conversation with Gavin the previous day haunted her. With an exasperated grunt, she put aside the needlework and stared out at the night sky.

Thousands of stars blinked against the ebony curtain, and she marveled at the vastness. As vast as the sea. She could not think of the sea without remembering the day she shared with Reid when she found the sea glass.

"Muirie?" Elizabeth's timid voice cut through her thoughts. "Are ye unwell?"

"I am well. Come watch the stars with me."

Elizabeth came to her side as a shooting star streaked across the sky. She gasped. "What was that?"

"A shooting star. Have ye never seen one?"

"No. 'Tis beautiful. Where did it go?"

Muirie shrugged.

Elizabeth nudged her shoulder. "Yesterday, I saw ye and Gavin speaking with your heads close."

Muirie's gaze stayed upon the night sky. "Aye."

She looped her arm through Muirie's. "I would not be upset if the two of ye have come to an accord."

Muirie thought of Gavin and his care for her, but she still only felt a brotherly love toward him. "We are but friends. No more."

"Ah." The small sound held disappointment. "Does my brother feel the same?"

"Aye, he does."

"Very well. 'Twould have been nice to have ye as a sister."

"Aye, yet we are now friends, which is most welcome too."

Elizabeth nodded with a smile and began to speak, but Beathag rushed in breathless and leaned upon the door.

The women turned and shared a startled glance.

"Whatever is the matter?" Elizabeth strode to her side and placed a hand on her shoulder.

Beathag took a deep breath and wiped her forehead with the back of her hand. "Unexpected visitors. Ye must come and welcome them."

Elizabeth clapped her hands like a child. "Oh, splendid. Who is it?"

"'Tis relations of Lord and Lady Grant." She straightened, and her gaze swept Muirie and Elizabeth from head to foot. "The both of ye must ready. 'Tis not seemly to meet the guests dressed as ye are."

Elizabeth shoved her shoulder playfully. "Are ye saying we do not measure up?"

Beathag's laugh lacked joy, and Muirie detected a spark of

disquiet in her. She still distrusted Elizabeth—and for good reason.

They rushed around in their shifts, choosing proper clothing and wondering why the guests arrived so late.

Muirie yawned as Beathag adjusted her stays. "Though I care to greet the guests, I much prefer my bed."

Elizabeth tittered. "Where is your sense of adventure? There mayhap be handsome lads to greet us." She wiggled an eyebrow, bringing a genuine smile to Beathag's face.

"Ye make that look once more, and I shall not be fit to complete my task." Beathag tied Muirie's stays and moved aside. "I may make it a bit tighter if ye wish it."

"No torture please!" Muirie grinned at her friend.

Beathag tapped Muirie on the head. "Sit, and I shall arrange your hair."

Muirie faced the beautiful gilt-framed mirror with its distinctive tortoiseshell inlay of mother-of-pearl and ivory. She had marveled at its intricate design since her first day at the castle.

Elizabeth's reflection appeared in the mirror as she watched Beathag. "Ye have such artistic talent. Where did ye learn this skill?"

Beathag stilled, the hairbrush frozen in midair. "Me? Artistic?"

"Aye." She touched the curl Beathag had just pinned in place. "'Tis so natural appearing. As if God placed it to grow as ye have arranged it."

Muirie observed Beathag's response to the praise, and it appeared all her suspicious thoughts about Elizabeth fled. The girl's compliments were most sincere.

"Thank ye, Elizabeth. 'Tis most kind of ye."

"'Tis truth."

Muirie breathed a sigh of relief as the friendly exchange continued with Beathag explaining to Elizabeth how she arranged a particular section of Muirie's hair until a soft knock sounded on the chamber door.

"I shall see who 'tis." She sent Beathag a grin. "Ye go on about your art."

A maid announced that their presence had been requested to greet the guests, so Beathag quickly finished Muirie's hair and did a simple arrangement of Elizabeth's, then they made their way to the great hall.

Soft music played from the minstrel's gallery, and Beathag wished them well and stepped into the shadows at the ready should they need her.

Lord and Lady Grant motioned them forward to greet the guests.

"Walter and Sorcha MacFarlane, allow me to introduce Lord and Lady Lamont's daughter, Lady Elizabeth Lamont, and Muirie Stewart, ward of Lord and Lady Stewart."

After offering a proper greeting and a curtsy, Muirie and Elizabeth joined everyone around the long table, which was heavily laden with food.

The moment after Lord Grant said grace, conversation simmered throughout the chamber. Muirie's gaze slid to each person in turn, and when she met Gavin's smiling eyes, she warmed, overjoyed by their growing friendship. She dipped her chin in acknowledgment.

Her focus next settled upon Sorcha MacFarlane, a lovely woman of perhaps forty years of age with hair near the color of Muirie's own. She had a genuine smile and ready wit, particularly when sparring with her husband. They laughed often and sent each other adoring glances, reminding Muirie of Lord and Lady Stewart.

A pang of loss pierced Muirie at the thought of Reid. Should they ever meet again, would they grow to have this same affection? Would they have the chance?

"Muirie?" Elizabeth whispered and kicked her under the table. "What is wrong with ye? Why do ye stare so at Sorcha MacFarlane? They will think ye daft."

"What? Oh . . ." Muirie stared at her food. "Sorry. I know not why. 'Tis something so—familiar about her."

"Truly?" Elizabeth gazed at the woman a moment. "Aye. Something does seem familiar about her, yet I cannot think what it is."

Muirie's insides tightened. Why did she have such a sense of foreboding? Was there another reason for the MacFarlanes to visit Freuchie Castle?

☙❧

Muirie watched as Beathag carefully arranged her hair for the day, and they both jumped when Elizabeth barged through the door without knocking.

"Muirie, Lady Grant requests our company in the parlor for tea! Is that not enchanting?"

She turned from the mirror, mouth gaping at the intrusion. "I see we are going to have to work on your manners, Elizabeth."

Beathag's mouth quirked at one side. "A wee bit at a time, Muirie."

Elizabeth placed both hands on her hips and cocked her head. "Most humorous, dear friend. If ye were as excited as I, ye would behave the same."

The maid chuckled. "Aye. To be sure."

Elizabeth flounced onto the bed and swung her legs off the side. "It must be a special gathering to inform us so early in the day."

"Have ye broken your fast, Elizabeth?" Beathag gave a last pat to Muirie's hair and admired her work. "Perfect."

"Elizabeth?"

Her dark head popped up. "Shall we eat now?" She slid off the bed and bounded toward them, then slapped a hand over her mouth. "I near forgot! Lady Grant said to bring our needlework. Seems she wants to discuss it."

"Oh. Of course, if that is what she wants."

"I am off to assist Grannam." Beathag bid them a good day, humming a jaunty tune.

Muirie knew she missed Cormac—as did she.

Elizabeth sighed. "I do hope the lads have eaten and moved on to their activities. It is such a strain to come up with conversation that interests them."

"*Hmm.* It seems to me that Peader is interested in whatever ye have to say."

Elizabeth huffed and tossed a long curl over her shoulder. "Honestly, Muirie. Do not think it. I have no interest in him."

Muirie had seen Elizabeth's sly glances at Peader when she

thought no one was looking as well as *his* attention to her. This was a new Elizabeth. Had she been plotting she would have made her interest clear no matter who was present.

Muirie would ask Gavin about Peader. He was quiet, yet he was always kind and wore a pleasant smile. It might do Elizabeth well to have a more reserved lad.

With a tone of mirth, Muirie asked Elizabeth, "After we dine, shall we gather our needlework?"

No answer came, and Muirie pinched her friend.

"Ow!" Elizabeth rubbed her arm. "What was that for?"

"Ye are obviously not paying attention."

"So I deserved punishment? What did ye say?"

Muirie whispered into Elizabeth's ear. "Are ye secretly meeting Peader before our tea?"

"Peader?" Elizabeth's mouth twitched. "Surely ye jest."

Muirie hugged the girl to her side. "Of a certainty. Yet, seriously, I wonder what kind of lad Peader is. He is so quiet."

Elizabeth's expression sobered. "Aye. He is." She tittered. "Can ye imagine me with a timid man?"

They entered the hall, and the tantalizing scent of roasted meat and fresh bread made Muirie's stomach growl. She studied Elizabeth. "I do not think Peader timid. Just reserved. Ye can learn a lot about another by their quiet observations when they think no one watches them."

Elizabeth pursed her lips. "Ye are wise, Muirie Stewart. I shall endeavor to do this in future."

They joined the group as Gavin, Liam, and Peader argued about the best ways to track animals. Muirie noted Elizabeth's gaze settling on Peader.

When Muirie looked at Gavin, she found him watching her, then glancing at his sister, a curious smile on his lips. Did he see it too? She would make an effort to speak to him later.

When the lads realized women were in their midst, the conversation changed to a more genteel subject. Before long, Peader and Elizabeth debated the merits of a stallion or a Highland pony, and one by one, the table's occupants departed as the discussion intensified.

Muirie smiled. Perhaps Peader was not so timid after all.

She covertly rose as Gavin did the same.

"Shall we walk in the garden?" Gavin whispered to her as they passed through the door into the courtyard.

"'Tis a good idea." The sun struggled to clear the mist hanging over the castle, yet the day was still pleasant.

Gavin clasped his hands behind his back and lifted his closed eyes to the hazy sun. "Do tell what my sister is about? Has she moved past Cormac to set her sights on Peader?"

"Ye have a lot to learn about your sister. She is a changed person. Have ye not seen it?"

His head snapped in her direction. "Truly? Do ye suppose her to be so changed?"

"Have ye not noticed?"

He hung his head. "Sorry, I have not."

Muirie pressed her lips together. "Aye. I have seen it. Not to worry. She and I—and Beathag have formed an alliance."

The startled look he sent Muirie made her laugh. "Do not seem so shocked." She looped her arm through his. "Come. I shall tell ye all."

"Would my sister take exception at that?"

She chuckled. "Ye sound auld-warld."

"Do I?" He smiled. "I suppose I do. Mayhap 'tis because I have spent too much time with Grannam."

"Aye. She says things that people likely said a hundred years ago—though she is not quite to that age."

Muirie sighed, knowing the elder woman had but few years left. She would be greatly missed when her time came, yet Muirie considered herself blessed to have known her—and she was thankful that she had been like a true grandmother to her, the only one she had never known and likely ever would.

292

Chapter Twenty-Four

1603

Sorcha flinched at the sound of hoofbeats through the open window of the bedchamber. She glanced in Evan's direction and found him thankfully still sleeping.

The remedy from Mistress Gibbs had worked well the week before. His healing had progressed since he awakened—and she avoided his question. Though, she did not understand why she had been so eager to tell him only to avoid the confession in the moment.

She peered out the window to determine the cause of the noise and sucked in a sharp breath. Rising from the early morning mist, what looked like more than a hundred horses galloped toward the castle, moving upon their stronghold, barking hounds at the front. She could not determine the color of the men's plaids or their style of clothes from this distance, the haze coloring the air about them. Were they friend or foe?

Sorcha squeezed her eyes shut, fingers pressing together. *Lord, please keep us safe and help us to find a true refuge.*

Below the window, men ran about shouting orders to barricade the entrance. She watched as everyone joined in to stack stones against the gates from the piles along the walls of the courtyard. Men, women, and lads alike lifted the heavy rocks and stacked them against the base of the entry as high as they were able, then started another row to create a double barrier. The barricade would not hold for long, yet it might delay the attack until Clan Grant hopefully came to their aid.

She rushed to Evan's side and brushed a quick kiss on his cheek. "I shall return soon."

"Sorcha!" He bellowed after her as she headed for the door, the effort likely expending most of his strength. "What is happening?"

"I will find out," she called behind her, hurrying from the chamber. Winded from the descent, she stopped at the bottom of the stairs and rested a hand on the stone wall and the other protectively on her stomach.

Clara stepped inside from the courtyard, her gaze moving over her shoulder to what Sorcha guessed was Kester's retreating form.

"Did Kester say who they are?" Sorcha braced herself for the answer.

Without looking at her, Clara said, her voice trembling, "Aye. 'Tis the Campbells."

Sorcha's shoulders sank, her heart beating fast. She put an arm around Clara's shoulders. "Come. We must gather those most frail as we did the last time."

"Aye. Kester telt me." Clara shuddered. "Mistress Gibbs is seeing to it now. We shall join them soon. I wanted to say goodbye to Kester, for I know not if we shall see one another again." She broke into sobs, and Sorcha comforted her as best she could, wondering how they could survive such an attack. She thought of Evan.

"Clara, we must find a way to move your brother. He is not yet strong enough to rise."

Clara straightened as she looked at Sorcha. "Evan . . . aye, we must attend to him." She gripped Sorcha's hand and led her up the stairs.

On the first landing, Sorcha stopped, her hand clutching her side. "Go. Gather the things we need to care for him. I shall be there as soon as I am able." Clara nodded and ran onward, Sorcha's gaze upon her. She then looked out the nearest window toward the oncoming hoard of Campbell's, their green, black, and blue tartans now clear in the vanishing mist.

Before Sorcha could resume her climb, Douglas burst into the hall, gaze skittering about until he saw Sorcha. "Ye must get below stairs."

"Aye, Clara and Mistress Gibbs are attending to it. We must get Evan down there as well. He is too weak and requires help."

"We must make haste." Douglas came to her side, and she grunted when he scooped her into his arms, carrying her up the stairs.

They reached Evan's bedchamber to find him standing at the window, one hand gripping his wound. He turned to look at Douglas. "What are ye doing here? Have ye brought men?"

"Nae." Douglas slanted a look at Sorcha, easing her to stand, and she knew from his expression why he was at the castle—Maidie.

"I was on an errand . . . and broke my journey here for a few hours."

"Evan, we must get ye below." Fear clutched at Sorcha's throat, her heart still pounding.

"Aye—and to the cave." Douglas lowered his voice. "There is a secret way from the castle, and my laird would like to keep it so."

Evan dipped his chin, and Douglas strode to his side, looping one of Evan's arms over his shoulder.

When they reached the door, Evan halted their progress. "I cannot go. I must help."

Douglas gave him a scathing look. "Ye have not the strength, mon."

Evan stiffened. "I shall not hide with the women and childer. Find my bow. It has been a while since I have used it. Mayhap the skill shall return."

"Nae." Douglas hauled him to the door.

Sorcha moved closer and placed a hand on Evan's shoulder. "Heed Douglas. Once he gets ye to safety, he may ride to gather his men and return."

"Marcus may fetch the Grants. We need Douglas here." Evan's jaw clenched as a wave of pain washed over him.

"Did I not see ye training the lad with the bow when ye first arrived?" Douglas asked.

After a moment's hesitation, Evan nodded. "Aye."

"Allow the lad to wield the bow. I can ride faster and know the path well to gather my clan."

Sorcha watched Evan register what he knew to be truth.

Hesitantly, he nodded. "Aye, I shall go to the battlements and guide him."

"Nae!" Sorcha shouted. "Ye are not strong enough. Listen to Douglas."

Evan shook his head. "'Tis the only way. I shall not hide while my . . ." His voice choked, and he let the sentence die.

It took a moment for Douglas to give in. "Sorcha, go below, and I shall take Evan to Marcus. He is on the watch as we speak." He blew out an exasperated breath. "Ye have a stubborn husband, and there is nae time to waste. I must ride soon. Once I settle him, I shall come and show ye the way to the cave."

Sorcha thanked him and turned to Evan, her head pounding along with her heart. He offered her a somber smile, which she returned. "Please take care, Evan."

"Aye. Now, please go below, lass."

The pleading in his eyes won over, and Sorcha did as she was bid, praying all the way that they would yet survive another fierce battle.

⚜

Not long after Sorcha joined Clara and the others, Douglas appeared to guide them from the cellar to the cave. When

297

building the castle, a door was secreted away behind a tall wardrobe in the corner of a chamber. Douglas moved it to reveal the hidden passageway. Once everyone entered, guided by Clara with a lantern, Maidie paused in front of Douglas, and they exchanged a grieved look before she followed the others.

Sorcha stopped and faced him. "I am not going with them. I have told Clara I shall stay and look after Evan." She gave Douglas what she hoped was a pleading look. "Ye are leaving, and Marcus is yet a lad."

"Aye, lass." He breathed out the statement as if in pain. "I shall return as soon as I am able."

Douglas moved the wardrobe in place with great effort. He sprinted from the cellar, and she followed as quickly as she could and on to the battlements.

When she arrived, Evan stood beside Marcus, still gripping his side, leaning heavily against the stone wall.

"Aye, take your stand first, knock the arrow, and pull taut." Evan's breath caught, and Sorcha forced herself not to move to him. "Mind how I told ye to aim, lad?"

Marcus nodded and bit his lip, doing as Evan instructed.

Sorcha held her breath as Marcus took the shot. She dared not look over the battlement to see if it landed true. Though they were enemies, she cared not to see anyone struck down.

Evan slapped the lad on the back. "Good, Marcus. Stay the course and thin out the enemy to aid our kinsmen." He turned slightly and fell against the wall with a groan.

Sorcha rushed to his side, and as soon as he saw her, concern flickered in his eyes. "Go below. Ye and the bairn are in danger here."

Evan grimaced as Sorcha helped him sit.

"Nae. I shall stay and tend your wound." She attempted to examine the bandage, but Evan stayed her hand.

"I am well. Just a mite weak. It shall pass."

"Evan MacDonald, ye are the most stubborn of men!"

"Aye, and well ye know it."

Sorcha caught the cocky grin before it faded. "Pig-headed man."

He chuckled. "Yet ye love me." It was not a question, and his determined look sent her insides fluttering.

The war cry of the MacGregors rang loud and clear, bolstering Sorcha's faith that God was with them. Evan struggled to stand.

"Stay yourself, Evan," Sorcha commanded through gritted teeth. She put a hand on his shoulder and pressed him down. She watched Marcus, aiming and firing again. "Marcus is doing a fine job. Save your strength."

Evan groaned and did not rise again. Sorcha noted his pale countenance and feared for him. In that moment, she saw why the war cry sounded—Clan Grant had arrived.

She knelt and held his face between her palms. "Douglas has returned. Help has come again!"

Evan smiled. "Thank our God in Heaven." His gaze found her lips. "I am too weak to do so, yet I think now would be a goodly time to kiss me."

Sorcha froze, and before her courage failed her, she leaned in and kissed the man she loved.

Chapter Twenty-Five

1710

Muirie walked the parapets slowly, taking in the magnificent views, as she circled the tower. The day was fine, but in the distance, the dark clouds hung above the mountains, and beneath, a blanket of mist rolled across the valley like sea tides approaching golden sand.

Her gaze followed the flow of a lazy burn not far from the castle. Lush grass laid as carpet over the landscape close to the water, which ran across smooth stones, rippling and gliding with flickers of light like diamonds in the sun. Upon its touch of the shaded willow, long branches of slender green leaves dipped into the stream, stirring the current.

Quick movement topping the low brae startled her, and she stilled. A horse bearing a rider dashed across the landscape and through a copse of trees where she lost sight of him. She scanned the expanse to see if there were more riders.

Muirie lifted her skirts and took swift steps toward the hall. A young man, hat in hand, spoke in low tones with a footman. She waited on the bottom step until the footman took something from the man and pointed toward the kitchen.

When the footman turned, he held a cloth-wrapped parcel. He dipped his chin in greeting and strode past her. Curiosity got the better of her, so she followed him at a discreet distance, ascending the stairs, until he reached Lady Grant's parlor.

As he stepped through the door, she walked past and paused in the window alcove a few doors along the corridor to stare out across the countryside. The dark clouds now hung closer to the castle, the grey mist rolling faster toward them.

The footman appeared. He cleared his throat, a nervous smile curving the corner of his mouth. "Mistress, Lady Stewart bids ye come to the parlor." He bowed and left.

A spy she would never be. She chuckled at her attempt of covert movements. Elizabeth would have known how to achieve such a thing. Come to think of it, she had not seen Elizabeth all day.

She knocked on the parlor door, and Lady Grant bid her to enter. Lady Grant and Lady Stewart sat near the large window where the sun bathed their needles with light. The table between them held the footman's delivery, the twine still firmly in place.

Lady Grant patted a chair beside her. Muirie dutifully sat. Lady Stewart met her gaze and motioned to the parcel. "'Tis from Cormac."

When Muirie looked closer at the item, she recognized his bold script.

"Will ye open it, dear? My son does not write to his mother or father, which leaves ye."

"*Me?*" Muirie had rarely received letters from Cormac when he was at school. Why would he send them now?

She began to say so when Lady Grant spoke. "My dear Muirie, ye and Cormac are of an age, and 'tis much easier for ye to communicate than with your elders."

Muirie offered what she hoped was a warm smile and moved to the edge of her seat, pulling the parcel toward her.

The tightly bound twine would not loosen. Lady Grant smiled and slid a small dirk across the table. The lady must use it for cutting thread, which Muirie appreciated since she usually bit her thread when sewing and hated the feel of it between her teeth. She retrieved the dirk and noted its intricately carved handle.

"Do ye admire it?" Lady Grant asked with a smile.

She fingered the design and nodded. "'Tis lovely."

"And useful." Lady Stewart chuckled. "Muirie does not like the taste of thread."

"I see. Well, me must acquire one for ye."

"Oh, Lady Grant, please do not concern yourself. The auld way is fine." She slipped the blade beneath the twine, and with little pressure it sliced through.

Muirie returned the dirk to the table. The paper wrapping crackled in the quiet chamber as she unfolded it. Of the several small, folded papers stacked inside, the uppermost held her name.

When she extended a letter to Lady Stewart, the woman's eyes moistened. "One for me?" Her hand shook as she took the missive.

"Oh, Isabel." Lady Grant's voice held awe and pride. Something passed between the two women, and Muirie wondered what had occurred to cause such a reaction.

Muirie rose. "Shall I deliver these?"

Lady Stewart swallowed and nodded, a tear spilling onto the fabric in her lap.

Muirie curtsied and left them. Once out of the parlor, she ran to her chamber, praying no one was there. She wanted to be alone while she read Cormac's letter, hoping all was well, and halted in the middle of the corridor.

What if Beathag or Elizabeth—or both women were in her chamber? She would have no privacy, and she did not want to share any news until she had first read it.

The kirk—no one would bother her there, and she could pray. A jolt of regret pierced her. Prayer was something she had failed at these past weeks. Her mind too full of . . . Reid and the goings on around her.

"I am sorry, Lord. I have not preached to anyone either." After her talk with Gavin, she realized more than ever how greatly God had blessed her with the Stewarts.

⚜

Thunder clapped, and a few large drops of rain peppered Muirie as she crossed the courtyard, the prized letter tucked under her arm.

"Muirie!" Quick, short footfalls sounded on the stone porch of the castle. "Muirie, wait."

Another voice joined, entreating her to stop. The rain increased, and a cool wind whipped her hair across her face. She looked over her shoulder to see Elizabeth and Beathag rushing toward her.

She darted inside the kirk and heaved an irritated sigh at their intrusion. Why could she not have a small respite?

Self-reproach flooded her. They were her friends, and she must have more patience. Once they arrived inside, Muirie plastered on a smile. "What have the two of ye been about this day?"

"Searching the castle for ye." Elizabeth placed both hands on her slender hips. "It seems as if ye have been hiding from us." She darted Beathag a pained look.

Beathag's expression was not as accusing as Elizabeth's, but she still appeared interested in Muirie's whereabouts.

Muirie pursed her lips, thinking of how to be rid of them for a half hour. "I have been remiss in my prayers and wanted to be alone." 'Twas not a lie. Yet there was more to be added, but she would keep it to herself.

Elizabeth's mouth gaped.

Beathag scrutinized Muirie for a moment before facing Elizabeth. "Aye. She does like to pray."

"Oh." Elizabeth blushed. "I am sorry, Muirie. We did not mean to intrude."

Muirie took her hand. "Do not apologize. Ye had no way of knowing what I was about. I shall find the two of ye when I am through. Mayhap we will take a walk."

A torrent of rain sent water crashing against the chapel door, and Muirie grinned. "A game of draughts instead?"

"Meet us in the library in an hour. Will that suit?" Elizabeth looked at Beathag. "Ye shall come, can ye not?"

"Aye. Grannam shall nap at that time."

"Until our evening meal most likely," Muirie chimed in.

They departed, and she released a sigh, removing the letter still beneath her arm. She strode to the rear of the chapel and sat behind a large stone pillar where she lit the candle on the wall. She broke the letter's seal, and a folded square of paper fell onto her lap with Beathag's name scrolled across the surface.

Her heart grieved. Cormac knew their relationship would come to no good end, yet he still pursued her friend. She placed the letter beside her on the pew and unfolded her letter.

My dear Muirie,

I trust this letter finds ye well. Please give Beathag my missive. I know it pains ye greatly, yet I cannot help my feelings for her. We love each other, and there is nothing else for it. I will find a way for us to be together.

The reason I write is not solely for ye to pass on my regards to Beathag. Mother has written to me about the babe. While I am happy for her and father, I do fear for Mother's wellbeing at her age.

Muirie chuckled. Lady Stewart was not yet old and was of a strong constitution.

I share this with none but ye, for despite your preaching, ye have a good heart, sister, and I know ye love both myself and Beathag.

Whilst Reid is in Virginia, he makes inquiry for myself and Beathag to go there, and we plan to do so in secret after I am assured Mother and my brother or sister are well. Will ye be willing to care for Beathag's mother and the children? I shall leave money for ye to meet their needs. I wish there was another way for us to be together, but I do not see it.

Muirie brought her hand to her throat and whispered into the quiet, holy place, "Oh, Cormac." Hot, stinging tears struggled to be freed. How could they do this? She wanted them to be happy, but leaving their home . . . leaving *her*?

She eased to her knees before the pew, the letter falling from her hand onto the wooden seat. She bowed her head, hands clasped under her chin.

"Oh, Lord, please help them do what Ye desire. Is this Your will for them to leave their homeland, their families?" Her shoulders shook as the tears fell from her chin onto the letter, the ink slowly blurring. She snatched it up before the words faded and finished reading the letter.

Muirie, I love ye as a sister. Please do not be angry with me nor Beathag. We but want to be together.

We have many months before Mother gives birth, so do not worry yourself. There is much to be done before that day arrives. Support Beathag and continue to be her dearest friend. Mayhap ye and Reid shall travel to Virginia one day to see us.

Your loving brother,

Cormac

She sniffled and smiled. He had perceived her liking of Reid. Mayhap Reid had spoken to him and shared the same sentiment for her. *Mayhap.*

Muirie could not let her thoughts stray much farther in that direction, but instead, she laid the letter aside, allowing it to dry while she prayed longer, promising God to not let so much time go by again without prayer. When they returned to Castle Deveron, she would also start anew reading passages from the Bible that Lord Stewart kept in the library.

Cautious footsteps echoed through the chapel, and Muirie hurriedly folded the letter, placing Beathag's inside, and tucked it into her bodice. She rose and took a step from behind the pillar, revealing Gavin's surprised gaze on her.

"Muirie, please forgive my intrusion." He took a step closer, and his face fell. "What is wrong?"

She sniffed and tried to be brave. Something in his eyes told her he could be trusted. Though it was not her story to share.

"I was praying, and my emotions took flight."

"Aye. 'Tis natural when meeting with God."

She cocked her head and took in his countenance. "You understand me like no other, Gavin. As if we have known each other a long while. How is that so?"

"I know not, yet the sentiment is mutual." He grinned down at her. "And I am glad to have your friendship."

"I am too." Muirie placed a hand on his arm. "Would ye care to play a game with three lovely women?"

"Who am I to refuse such an offer?"

"In truth, my friend." Muirie's smile matched his own

happy one as he escorted her from the kirk, yet despite the joy of friendship, she could not help but worry once more about the letters concealed within her bodice.

☙❧

A noise sounded behind Muirie, and she spun, nearly losing her balance, a hand flattened to her chest. She spied her friend at the door. "Beathag, ye gave me a fright! Where have ye been?"

"Serving tea to Grannam." She crossed the chamber and retrieved her shawl. "Do ye have need of something?"

"I have a letter for ye."

Beathag froze, eyes widening, hand already stretching toward Muirie.

"Not here. Elizabeth may interrupt us." She opened the door and glanced in each direction along the corridor, an idea coming to her. "Let us go to the kirk. There is rarely anyone there."

"No," Beathag said with firmness.

Muirie frowned. "Pardon?"

Beathag laughed. "Ye do have some of the strangest expressions. Peader and Elizabeth are there. I saw them enter not a quarter-hour ago."

"Oh, I see." Elizabeth must have gone straight there after their game with Gavin, and Muirie had come in search of Beathag.

"I think not. There is a growing attraction between them. Did ye not know?"

Muirie nodded. "Well, I do recall their behavior a few days

ago. They appeared to watch one another when they thought none paid them mind."

Beathag shrugged her shawl over her shoulders. "I know not much about Peader's situation, but if he has not enough fortune nor standing, Lord and Lady Lamont are not likely to allow the union."

Like with she and Cormac.

Muirie sobered. "We must find a place where we shall be undisturbed. Elizabeth might arrive at any moment."

"I know!" Beathag's countenance brightened. "The cave."

"Cave?" Muirie's skin grew clammy. She did not like caves. Bats lived in caves, and the walls were so . . . close.

"Oh, Muirie. Are ye still afraid of them?"

She could not deny the fact. "I am not ashamed. We all fear something."

Beathag's glance flew to the window, and she strode to the door. "Let us take a walk in the forest near the castle. Mayhap to the burn. 'Tis beautiful there."

Muirie took her friend's arm. "No, let us go to the parapet and view the landscape since ye dearly love heights." She bit her tongue to stifle a laugh.

"Poor jest." Beathag paused at the door, tilting her chin haughtily. "Very well. I shall walk the parapet if ye accompany me to the cave."

Muirie pulled Beathag into the corridor. "Now ye have given a poor jest. *Hmph!*"

"I am serious. We need to overcome our fears. Truly."

Muirie pondered the notion as they strolled under the

overcast sky. Thankfully, the grey clouds no longer looked to hold rain. The cool breeze teased their hair as they made their way to the edge of the trees, the sound of the burn growing louder. Mayhap she and Beathag could bolster each other to address their fears together.

"Here. 'Tis a pleasant spot to speak." Beathag lowered herself onto a bed of pine needles and leaned against the trunk of a massive tree.

Muirie tilted her head to peer through the branches. The tree must be older than Grannam by many years. The wind caught the piney fragrance and stirred it around them—the scent, the sound of bubbling water, bird song echoing through the forest—was idyllic.

Beathag tugged at Muirie's skirt. "Sit and give me the letter. I have waited long enough."

Muirie knelt in front of her friend and pulled the letters from her bodice.

With a raised eyebrow, Beathag stared at the offering. "What is this?"

"One is for me from Cormac. I would like for ye to read it." She extended the paper toward Beathag. "This one is for ye." She waved it in the air like a fan.

Beathag made no move to take either letter, only clutched her hands in her lap.

"Why will ye not take them?"

She slowly shook her head. "I fear 'tis ill news."

The corners of Muirie's mouth lifted in amusement. "'Tis happy news."

Beathag's expression changed to one of doubt. With slow

deliberation, she took the letter Cormac had written to Muirie and painstakingly opened it. Her gaze flew across the page, her lips gradually curving, then she fell into Muirie's arms with a sigh.

"He truly loves me!"

"Was there ever any doubt?" Muirie's joy grew alongside Beathag's, yet her heart sank for Lord and Lady Stewart. Why could there not be a way to please everyone?

Beathag sat back and snatched her letter, tossing the other onto Muirie's lap.

Muirie watched Beathag as her gaze swept across the lines, her smile rapidly growing until tears streamed down her cheeks. When she lifted her gaze to Muirie's, her face was radiant. She hugged the letter to her chest.

"I cannot imagine this is happening. We shall begin a new life before the coming spring."

"I suppose ye shall." Tears burned, and Muirie awkwardly folded her letter. She must remember to hide it where it would not find its way to Lady Stewart. It would not do for her to discover Muirie's part in the deception.

Beathag jumped to her feet, holding her arms wide and spinning in a dance. "I shall be free. Free to love the man I have longed to have a life with."

Muirie glanced around. "Beathag! Lower your voice."

The woman slapped a hand across her mouth. "I am daft with happiness and know not what I do." She cackled.

Tears slipped from Muirie's eyes without warning. She tried to keep them back, yet they did not obey.

"Oh, Muirie. I know ye delight for me, so why the tears?"

"Because I shall miss ye."

Beathag wrapped an arm around Muirie. "I shall miss ye as well. Yet Reid's father has a shipping concern, so ye may travel by one of his ships anytime ye choose."

Muirie's chuckle sputtered through the tears. "I do not know if Reid has a care for me at all. Why should I assume that he . . . we . . ."

Beathag looked to the heavens. "Ye feeble-brained lass! 'Twas written all over his handsome face every time he saw ye." She snorted. "Well, he is not as handsome as Cormac of a surety, yet he is handsome."

"Indeed." Muirie retrieved her handkerchief and wiped her tears. "We seem to have found ourselves two braw lads."

Beathag nudged her shoulder. "Aye!"

Hugging each other, they swayed as happy tears flowed, their laughter weaving through the trees.

314

Chapter Twenty-Six

September 1603

The chamber held all the warriors of Clan MacGregor as well as Kester, Evan, and Douglas. Sorcha observed from the corner along with Clara, watching quietly as they plied their needlework. The aroma of smoke filled the air—though they lacked the scent of harvest, for they had not been at Freuchie long enough to have such abundance. The odor signaled the come of winter, a time of death which would eventually bring a time of life in spring.

Sorcha glanced up often as the discussions unfolded, then returned to her needlework depicting the battle that nearly killed Evan.

Kester rose abruptly, leaving his tankard of ale on the massive table. "'Tis time for us ta leave afore the weather grows colder. The Campbells shall not give up this quest in their misguided hatred." He flattened his palms against the wood and leaned toward the other men. "Do ye understand? Afore they regroup and return, we must be away!"

Sorcha caught Evan's regard upon her and dipped her chin. She knew Kester to be correct. Their dream to find safety here was not to be, yet where would they go?

Evan stood, still unsteady upon his feet, but he grew stronger each day. "Aye, Kester is right. We must move."

Douglas's gaze scanned the chamber. Sorcha wondered who he sought. Movement from the doorway leading to the kitchen caught her notice—Maidie. The girl stood half in shadow, her gaze intent on Douglas.

"My laird, John Grant, agrees we should escort ye to another place. He will provide many men to do so."

The urge to laugh with relief rose in Sorcha's chest, yet she tamped it down. To know the powerful Grants would continue to aid them in such a way was a true blessing from God.

The chamber grew silent, and Sorcha sensed the tension of uncertainty growing. Why did they delay? What other options were there but to flee?

Still standing, Evan addressed the men. "Though I am a MacDonald, my wife is a MacGregor, and her John was close to me as a brother. I have pledged my life to protect Clan Gregor." He drew in a sharp breath, his steady gaze meeting Sorcha's for a moment as if to say *to protect her*.

Tears welled in her eyes—for he had done so at every turn, nearly going to his death.

Evan shifted his attention to those in wait of his next

words. "Returning to the cave for a time would be wise. Let us clear all evidence of our presence, so our enemy shall believe we moved on far earlier than they ken."

Nods and grunts of approval sounded around the chamber.

Since there were no men of higher status than Evan—as friend of John, brother of the Gregor—they agreed to the plan. It seemed their ragged party of mostly women, children, and elders with a handful of men would move on. Yet to where?

The evening meal was announced, and they made their way to the hall. It was a somber affair, little being said about their forthcoming departure.

After they ate, Kester, Evan, and Douglas gathered in the library. A large map covered the table before them, weighted by stones on each corner. Again, Sorcha and Clara sat close to the fire, plying their needlework.

The trace of smoke from the fireplace mingled with the first scents of autumn clinging to the men's clothing.

Sorcha pulled a long piece of green thread through the fabric on which the scene of the last skirmish against the Campbells appeared by her skilled hands, Freuchie Castle rising in the background shrouded in mist.

The fifth laird of Freuchie had granted them refuge among its walls, but it was not to be. The Campbells were relentless in their pursuit.

"'Tis best ta leave now afore the weather grows colder." Kester straightened from perusing the map and looked at Evan. "Let us return to the cave until we depart as ye said and be sure we leave no trace of our presence."

Sorcha looked at Evan, who studied the map further, then

to the other men.

Douglas slanted a look at Kester. "I will inform my laird of the plan and will report back with his instructions on how best to aid ye."

"Thank ye, Douglas. We will make preparations." Evan pressed a palm against the table and pushed to his feet.

Sorcha noticed he held his injured side with the other hand. She prayed his foray to the battlements to guide Marcus had not reopened the wound. She squinted to see any sign of fresh blood, yet from her distance she could see none.

Sorcha bolted to her feet with a yelp as pain flashed across her middle. Before she could sit again, Evan was at her side, concern etched in his features.

"What ails ye?" He looped an arm around her shoulders and helped her to sit, grunting with the effort.

She swallowed hard and cupped her stomach with both hands. "I know not."

Another pain gripped her, and a hard kick sprung against her hand. Realization struck her. "'Tis the babe. He kicks with great strength." She gasped and massaged the place.

Clara touched Sorcha's shoulder. "I shall find Mistress Gibbs. She may have an answer." She near ran from the library, Kester hard on her heels.

The child chose that moment to kick from another angle as if wanting Sorcha's attention. She chuckled. "I trust this shall be a stubborn-headed lad. Like—" She almost said *like Evan* but thankfully caught herself in time.

Evan smiled. "Aye. John was a stubborn lad—though the best of men."

Sorcha nodded, struggling to smile in agreement.

Clara and Kester returned with Mistress Gibbs, who immediately took charge.

"When did this begin, lass?"

"Just now. He has kicked afore, of course—yet not like this. 'Tis painful." Sorcha ground out the last word as the bairn kicked again.

The old woman sat back on her heels. "Aye. I ken." She slowly shook her head. "He is in distress."

Sorcha's heart recoiled. No, she could not lose another babe. Tears burned, thinking of John and all the bairns they had lost. "Nae." She groaned.

Evan tried to hold her, and she pushed away from him. "I shall not lose another bairn!"

Mistress Gibbs patted her shoulder. "Not with old Gibbs here, lass. We must start by calming ye. Nae more talk of Campbells." She glared at Evan and Kester. "Do ye hear me? Ye must tell her nothing to upset her."

With stern expressions, each man nodded.

"Now." She dipped her chin. "I shall make a tea of *special* flower petals that shall help ye."

Clara rubbed Muirie's arm. "I shall see to it—and be her guard."

Mistress Gibbs cackled. "Good thought, lass. Do that very thing." She struggled to her feet with a hand pressed against her lower back. "I shall see to the makings."

Evan took Mistress Gibbs's place and cupped Sorcha's shoulders. "Please listen to her. I would not have anything happened to ye or the bairn."

Sorcha pinched her lips together and gave him a curt nod.

"Let us get ye to bed." He helped her stand with Clara on her other side.

"Mayhap I should carry ye," Evan said with all seriousness.

Sorcha grinned. "Aye. That does lift my spirits. Ye are still injured and have nae business lifting someone of my girth."

Kester stepped closer. "I shall be glad to help ye."

Evan eyed the man with skepticism. "It should be her husband."

Kester snorted, smiled, and backed away.

Clara sent him a harsh look.

To avoid embarrassment, Sorcha said, "Evan, I shall only allow your help if Clara stays at my side as well. With both of ye, we may ascend the stairs safely. I shall not have ye injured further."

He relented, yet they slowed on the stairs with Sorcha stopping at brief intervals to rest. She prayed Evan would not catch on that she was feigning fatigue, so *he* would not be overtaxed.

By the time they reached the bedchamber, Evan was once again pale, and she saw the pain imprinted upon him. She allowed them to place her on the bed and prop her against pillows.

Once Mistress Gibbs returned and urged her to drink the potion, it did not take long for Sorcha to feel drowsy. Warmth encased her and the child. Evan remained by the bed, refusing to leave even after Clara urged him to rest too.

"Mistress Gibbs, tell my stubborn-headed brother to rest." Clara jammed both fists upon her hips and glared at Evan. "He shall not listen to reason."

"Do ye truly credit he shall listen to another woman?" The old woman chuckled. "They are akin to small lads who shall not mind their mither."

Sorcha could not suppress the joy bubbling inside. "Men are so . . ." She laughed, and her head lolled side-to-side on the pillow. ". . . I know not what." She patted the space beside her and looked at Evan. "Come, husband. Rest beside me."

Evan's mouth gaped, and he glanced at his sister.

It was Clara's turn to laugh. "Aye, brother. Do as your wife bids. Ye both need to sleep." She held Sorcha's gaze a moment before speaking to Mistress Gibbs. "Mayhap ye could give Evan the same potion ye gave Sorcha."

The woman cackled. "Mayhap. It appears to calm Sorcha well indeed."

Evan rose with force. "I shall not take a woman's potion!"

Mistress Gibbs's smile lit her face. "'Tis not for a *woman* alone." When Evan shot her a disbelieving expression, she shrugged. "I will bring ye another potion and mayhap a warm cup of ale?"

Evan hesitated long enough to consider the idea and finally nodded, then resumed his seat next to the bed.

"Splendid." Clara clapped a hand on his shoulder. "I shall come with ye and perhaps bring a bit of bread and cheese to go with the ale. I think Sorcha cares for a drink as well."

Sorcha tittered as she watched her friends, warming to the idea of ale and a meal. "Aye, Clara, 'tis a good thought." She patted the bed again. "Come, Evan. We shall dine in bed as if we are royalty."

Evan blinked rapidly, wearing a puzzled look.

"Why do ye appear bewildered, love? Do ye not want to do so?" Sorcha examined him, tilting her head. She felt strange, though pleasantly so.

Clara gently pushed her brother's back and edged him toward the bed. "Aye, brother, make yourself comfortable beside your ailing wife, and the two of ye may rest and heal together."

"Aye." Sorcha moaned with feeling. "We shall await our servants." She met Clara's amused expression, realizing it was not only the potion that calmed her—yet being surrounded by those who cared for her.

He finally joined her on the bed, yet he kept his distance, not touching her. He closed his eyes, and she could not help but watch him until Clara and Mistress Gibbs returned. She winced at the odor of Mistress Gibb's potion for Evan.

He opened his eyes with a grimace. "What is that foul smelling tonic?"

Sorcha's stomach churned. "'Tis strong and effective. Ye will do well to accept it."

Evan squinted at her, a twinkle of mischief shining in his eyes. "Easy to speak since your drink dinnae smell so foul." He rested his hand on her forearm. "Dinnae fash, lass. I shall take my medicine like a guid lad."

Mistress Gibbs's eyes crinkled at the corners, and the chamber resounded with her distinctive chortle akin to the yaffingale. Sorcha recalled the red-crowned bird with its green plumage *laughing* in song. Rarely, she saw one in the treetop outside the cottage where she had grown up and marveled at the colors God had painted on his creation.

Taking a horn spoon from her medicine box, Mistress Gibbs poured a measure of the thick liquid and held it before Evan's mouth. "Drink, lad."

His throat bobbed in a hard swallow, and he pinched his nose. He licked his lips and opened his mouth a narrow crack.

Mistress Gibbs sighed. "Come on, lad. Did yer mither never give ye medicine?"

Something in Evan's appearance shifted, his gaze seeking Clara's. Sorcha had never heard he and Clara speak of their mother.

He removed his fingers from holding his nose, opened his mouth wide, and leaned toward the spoon, taking the offering with a shudder. He coughed until his eyes watered.

Clara sputtered, a hand clasped against her mouth.

Evan shot her a quailing stare, one side of his mouth tilting upward.

When she caught her breath, Clara apologized. "'Twas the way ye looked. I remember the day ye were five and stole bannocks from Mam's kitchen." She sucked in a gulp of air, tears falling, the mirth fading long enough to speak. "Ye telt her they looked lonely all lined up like little soldiers. When she scolded ye, your—" Another burst of merriment sounded before she calmed herself. "—ye had that same expression of dread about ye."

Sorcha joined in the merriment, placing her hand atop Evan's, and he fixed his gaze upon hers. The moment lingered, and he turned his hand enough to entwine their fingers, and Sorcha sensed a shift between them.

Evan looked at Mistress Gibbs. "May I have the ale to wash away this vile restorative?"

Mistress Gibbs shook her head, her eyes shining, as she handed over the drink along with the tray with cheese and bread.

He released Sorcha's hand, took a long drink of ale, and ate a bite of cheese.

Sorcha, happy to have lightness encircling them, told Mistress Gibbs she would care for her drink as well. She sipped, the warmth soothing her, and settled again in the bed.

Clara looped an arm through Mistress Gibbs's. "Mayhap we leave these two to rest now."

Mistress Gibbs nodded, and they left, leaving Sorcha and Evan alone.

Sorcha stifled a yawn, not looking at Evan. The space between them on the bed seemed to shrink with only them in the room. Mayhap the way to help in the moment would be to speak without the presence of others.

"Evan?" Her heart raced, uncertain of how to proceed.

His grey eyes peered deeper into hers than she desired.

Shame filled her at the thoughts of John as she lay abed with her husband—his closest friend. Though they had not consummated the marriage, it pained her she had wed again so soon after John's murder. Aye, for that was what she called it. 'Twas murder in that field.

The MacGregors had done no more than defend what was theirs. Accusations against Clan Gregor were lies born of the

Earl of Argyle and others who wanted to line their coffers through the blood of the MacGregors. The Campbells and those who aided them *were* murderers.

"Where are ye, lass?" Evan's soothing voice pulled her from the horror of the battle.

Sorcha tilted her head to peer out the window, gathering her thoughts. "I thought of the injustice the MacGregors have suffered at the hands of the Campbells."

"Aye. 'Tis a great wrong." He blew out a breath. "Did ye have something to ask me?"

She grasped the first thought to come to mind, his reaction at the mention of his mother. "Not exactly a question. Please tell me about your family. Clara has shared little."

His thoughtful smile told Sorcha he was moving into the past, and she welcomed it. She sorely needed a respite from what lay ahead. Another journey to an unknown place to seek safety awaited them, yet she trusted Evan and the other men to lead them.

She feared for her bairn. How could she walk such a distance as had brought them to *this* place? Would her child weather the coming storm?

For now, Sorcha took a cleansing breath and settled back in comfort, eyes on her handsome husband, as his melodic voice lulled her to sleep.

Chapter Twenty-Seven

1710

Following the evening meal, the conversation around the fireplace turned toward the history of Clan Gregor. Muirie knew not who began the tale as her thoughts had drifted to the letters she and Beathag received from Cormac.

Her friend's face had lit up like a full moon on a summer night when she had read the letter and shared about Cormac's visit to her family. He had found them well, bringing supplies and treats for her siblings.

Muirie was happy for Beathag, yet she would sorely miss her when they departed for the Colonies. She had no fear Cormac would not take good care of her. They would have a happy life together.

The mention of the MacGregor name brought Muirie from

her private thoughts. She glanced up to find Sorcha watching her with a kind smile. That familiar sensation returned. What was it about this woman? She shook off the notion and listened to Grannam telling a story.

"Aye, 'twas a braw day. A light snow covered the battlefield. One man's blood seeped into the snow whilst another knelt to comfort him. Loch Lomond lay silent as it watched a good man die at Glen Fruin." A lone tear skimmed down her wrinkled cheek. Muirie rarely saw Grannam weep, yet in this moment, her eyes held deep sorrow.

Grannam reached for Muirie and squeezed her hand as if she knew the same torment. Though Muirie held sympathy for those mourning, she knew not this battle—nor the men she spoke of.

"Aye, there have been many battles where MacGregor men lost their lives. Though at Glen Fruin, Clan Gregor was victorious." Grannam held a fist in the air, her creased lips stretching with joy. "They fought with but three hundred men, their enemies numbering eight hundred." She cackled like one of the hens at Castle Deveron.

Her mirth died, and she shook her head. "Two months later, King James issued an edict proclaiming the MacGregor name be abolished. Any who bore the name must renounce it or suffer death. The following year, authorities hanged the MacGregor and eleven of his chieftains at Mercat Cross in Edinburgh." She spat out the words like a sour apple.

"Clan Gregor scattered with many taking other names." She took a deep breath, her vigor waning. "They were hunted like animals and flushed out of the heather by bloodhounds."

Grannam's expression shifted to admiration. "There were

some what flew to the highest places where no feeble dragoon had the courage to go." She lowered her voice and leaned forward as if revealing a precious secret. "The MacGregors followed an allied clan to the Hidden Valley."

The chamber held its breath—though it seemed to Muirie some present already knew the story. Why Grannam had never shared it with her, she knew not.

Muirie caught a glimpse of Gavin and realized the story had been so fascinating she had not seen nor heard him enter. He stood behind Sorcha's chair, eyes intent upon Muirie.

They shared a smile as Grannam completed her tale.

"I fear I must retire, but I may tell ye more on the morrow."

Murmurs sounded around the chamber, begging her to go on. The elder woman lit with the brilliance of one taking pleasure in being the center of attention, of which she rarely was.

"Nae, I must rest." She rose with more strength than Muirie would have thought she had in her fatigued state. Standing strong and proud, she said, "I shall leave ye something to chew on until I may continue the story."

She met the gaze of each person. "The man what died at Loch Lomond is the ancestor of some of ye here this night."

The earlier silence paled at this declaration. A chill crept up Muirie's spine. Who was she speaking of? And why?

Gavin coughed and made his way to Grannam, taking her arm. "I will escort ye to your chamber, if ye will allow me."

"That 'tis most kind of ye, lad." The old woman peered up at him and patted his arm. "Let us hope we are not the center of gossip. To think a braw, young lad escorting an old woman to her bedchamber!"

Muirie dipped her head and chuckled behind her hand. The elder woman was brash to say the least.

As the gathering broke apart, Muirie slipped from the chamber without being noticed and climbed the stairs to the parapets to watch the stars. She needed time to ponder all Grannam said. Who was one of the relations to the man dying beside Loch Lomond? Was she? Would Lady Stewart reveal so on her birthday in a few months?

Her mind went to Reid. The image of his fair hair glinting in the sun when they stood on the beach as she held the piece of sea glass captured her heart. She touched the necklace at her throat, remembering him riding away into the mist.

Would she ever see him again?

The sweet-scented night air tickled her skin, and she drew in a deep breath, homesickness overtaking her. She longed to be at Castle Deveron where her life was, where she last saw Reid, to be where he had been. Did he long to see her again as she longed to see him?

CBSO

Haze cloaked the surrounding countryside, the sun barely breaking through enough to establish it was morning.

Muirie yawned and left the window to dress for the day. Beathag's neatly made bed proved her absence, so Muirie left to break her fast.

Pulling the door closed behind her, footsteps approached, and she waited, hoping Beathag returned from caring for Grannam. The advance stopped, and she heard whispering. One voice she recognized as Elizabeth's, the other was too low to discern who it belonged to.

Muirie called out, "Elizabeth, is that ye?"

The voices stilled, and the sudden sound of retreating footfalls echoed along the stone corridor.

How odd that Elizabeth would not answer her, for she knew her voice to be loud enough. On impulse, Muirie hurried in the direction the pair had gone. She found herself at a narrow staircase and descended. Before the steps continued downward, a small landing beside a low, narrow door gave her pause. She knocked, and when no answer came, she tried the latch. The door gave way, opening onto a walled balcony.

The view overlooked a wide strip of treeless ground and beyond it lay the thick forest. She could barely see portions of the burn as it wove through the trees. Just as she turned to leave, movement caught her eye. Far below, a man and a woman holding hands rushed toward the shelter of the trees.

Her breath hitched, and the flash of Elizabeth's blue dress flowed with her motion. Where was she going, and who was the man?

Muirie rushed to find Beathag. They must fetch the girl before anyone discovered her behavior. She faltered and froze, thinking of Gavin. He would know what to do to protect his sister.

Resuming her quick pace, she turned the corner to crash into him.

"Muirie!" He gripped her shoulders in a steadying brace. "Is something amiss?"

Between quick gasps, she relayed what she had witnessed.

"The empty-headed girl!" Exasperation colored each word.

"What foolhardy thing will she do next?" He grabbed Muirie's hand and pulled her to follow him as he took long strides, boots beating the floor. "We must find her before anyone else learns of this."

Muirie's stomach growled a protest, and Gavin sobered with a laugh. "I am afraid the answer to *that* must wait."

"Aye, Elizabeth is more important than my empty belly."

By the time they reached the place Muirie had seen her enter the trees, she gasped for breath. The mist lessened—though it was still hard to see very far ahead.

Gavin slowed their progress. "Stop and listen for voices."

Grateful for the respite, Muirie nodded, and before she spoke, soft voices sounded nearby.

Gavin placed a finger to his lips and pointed toward the burn. With careful steps they drew near the unsuspecting couple and discovered a bewildering sight.

Sitting on a felled tree tossing stones into the burn perched Grannam with Elizabeth and Peader beside her.

Muirie released a shaky breath, mind reeling. "Elizabeth." She stepped toward them. "What is the meaning of this?"

Elizabeth's blue dress swung around her ankles, and she stared wide-eyed at Muirie. "*Nothing* is the meaning of this." The girl placed her hands on her slender hips. "We are entertaining Grannam. Can ye not see?"

When Muirie's gaze landed on the elder woman, the only expression she saw was one of sheer delight.

"Muirie, my dear! I am so happy to see ye. These lovely younklins have brought me on an outing." She clapped her hands together like a child, eyes sparkling with joy.

Gavin took Muirie's arm and gently squeezed. "We see that. What has brought ye here?"

"Elizabeth heard me talking about my love of burns and outings and brought me here for the day." She lifted an arm and swayed to encompass the surrounding woods. "'Tis lovely, is it not?" Her face pinched briefly. "Dinnae worry, my dear. Isabel knows of it and has given her consent."

The air left Muirie, and she tugged Gavin toward the older woman. "Aye, Grannam, 'tis lovely."

Grannam eyed them suspiciously. "And why have ye come here alone without a chaperone?" Her eyes twinkled with mischief. "Are ye Muirie's braw young lad?"

Grannam was right. She hadn't thought of needing a chaperone with Gavin. Why was it so? They looked at each other in bewilderment, then at Grannam, Muirie speaking first.

"No, Grannam. We are only friends." And she meant it. They were friends—and that was all.

The elder woman waved her arms in the air, motioning for them to come to her. They sat, and Muirie hugged her close. She had not seen Grannam so happy in a long while.

Elizabeth smiled at Muirie. "I could tell she was getting homesick and thought this a fine diversion."

Muirie smiled in return. "Ye have done a kindful thing, and I thank ye."

"Ye are most welcome. I thank ye and Beathag for your kindness. Now I know what genuine friendship is."

Gavin plied his experience of rock-skipping with Grannam, and they settled into a companionable silence as the rocks skimmed across the burn, birds singing in the boughs of the trees. The afternoon passed pleasantly, and Muirie knew it would be a day to always treasure.

The food Elizabeth had brought was another surprise. A blanket was spread beneath the low-hanging boughs of a fir tree offering the perfect place for their feasting and respite.

Gavin reclined against the tree, long legs stretched out before him. Muirie's lids fluttered as if she had no control over them. She lolled on one arm until it could no longer support her, and giving into the drowsiness, drifted off to sleep to the sound of Grannam's laughter.

During her dream of the forest and the sound of rippling water, a voice said, "Nae, let the lass sleep. Elizabeth, ye and Peader take me to my chamber for a nap afore our evening meal. Muirie's lad will keep her safe."

In Muirie's languid state, she rolled to her side, settling further into sleep.

After a time, a soft touch against her cheek awakened her, and she opened her eyes to see Gavin staring down at her, an odd smile upon his lips.

Blinking in confusion, Muirie took in the surrounding area, only to find they were alone.

Alone! She sat bolt upright. "Where are the others?"

Gavin held the long blade of grass in his hand, twirling it in the air. "They took Grannam to the castle for a nap."

Muirie swallowed nervously. "How long ago?"

"Near on an hour."

She shot from the blanket and stood over him. "Why did someone not awaken me?"

"Grannam wished us not to do so."

Muirie's gaze swung around the blanket, then her regard landed on Gavin. Had he been dozing nearby? She gulped, ashamed he had seen her sleeping. The heat in her cheeks burned like fire.

When she turned to see Gavin's expression, she knew the truth of it. "Ye snore, Muirie."

In her fatigue, she knew he spoke the truth. How would she ever look at him again? Cormac had once caught her napping in the garden and accused her of drooling. Had Gavin witnessed that too? She refused to peer at him, busying herself with straightening her skirts and brushing off any twigs and leaves, imaginary or not.

"I must get to the castle at once." She avoided his stare and sprinted through the woods, never looking back, yet she heard his laughter echoing through the trees.

Chapter Twenty-Eight

1603

Sorcha languidly rolled to her side, inhaling with pleasure from the restful night's sleep. It had been a long time in coming of late. She flung her arm wide to stretch across the other side of the bed. What met her touch was something large, firm, and warm.

Her eyes cracked open, and her gaze was upon Evan. In her bed? Beside her? His breathing was slow and steady in slumber. She searched her memory and found it to be shadowy. Her last recollection was of Clara and Mistress Gibbs leaving them on their own, saying they would bring food and drink.

She watched Evan sleep as he lay upon his back, a lock of dark brown, sun-streaked hair resting against his forehead.

He appeared much younger in rest, yet there was still a strength to him.

A sudden flash of memory entangled her. They both sat upright against the pillows with a tray of food between them. They drank warm ale and spoke for a while, him sharing about his and Clara's family. She remembered the surge of comfort she felt at that moment, the most comfort she had felt since John was alive.

Her gaze roamed the chamber, and she located the tray with the remnants of last night's repast. Whatever Mistress Gibbs had given her certainly had aided her for she felt well rested.

Sorcha peered at Evan again. He seemed to rest in much the same way. Not wanting to disturb him, she eased from the bed, slipped on her cloak, and tiptoed to the door. Her stomach growled in protest.

"Sorcha?" Evan called, his voice groggy with sleep. "Where are ye going?"

She turned to watch him unsteadily rest upon one arm. "The bairn is hungry. Would ye care to join *us*?" A small laugh rose in her throat, and his eyes sparkled.

"Aye. Yet I would have ye return to bed first."

Sorcha swallowed hard, collecting her wits, and slowly made her way to his side of the bed, then stood stiffly, watching him. She trusted Evan, but he also unnerved her. Mayhap it was what she felt toward him that unnerved her.

He took her hand and pressed it between his own. "I dinnae remember much of last eve. Yet it w—was a pleasant time I care to repeat." He cleared his throat. "Being close to ye, speaking without wariness or interruption, sharing a meal—" His voice trailed, and his gaze dropped to their hands.

The tension lessened with her exhaled breath, yet it still held within her. "Aye. 'Twas pleasant. I am uncertain what overtook us—" She abruptly withdrew her hand and strode with quick steps to the tray across the chamber.

The rustle of linens and Evan's feet on the floor brought her gaze to see his approach. "What concerns ye, lass?"

She lifted one of the pewter cups. "Is this your ale from last eve?"

He lifted his brows, then took the cup from her and brought it to his lips, taking a sip. "Aye. 'Tis."

Sorcha retrieved the other and tipped it, barely touching her tongue to the liquid before returning it to the tray and reaching for Evan's to do the same. "Those two wily women suppose they are so cunning as not to be discovered. The ale is the same."

Evan frowned. "Ye make nae sense, lass."

She lifted her cup. "This is *my* potion mixed with ale." Tapping her finger upon Evan's cup, she said, "Yours tastes the same as mine. They wanted ye to take my potion, so ye would rest easy as I did."

He pursed his lips. "They tainted my ale just as they did yours?"

"Aye." Sorcha slowly nodded. "And we were unawares why everything was so very agreeable."

Evan clasped his hands behind his back as if forming a plan. "They must be most pleased with themselves." He stared at her, and slowly the corners of his mouth eased upward, and he chuckled. "They had us where they wanted us."

Sorcha's mind whirled, and before long, she laughed with him. "They *forced* us to rest—whether we liked it or not."

"Aye. Worst of it is, we fell for it like two drunken lads."

Tears dripped down Sorcha's cheeks, and she could not remember the last time she had felt so merry.

Evan cupped her cheeks in his hands, his thumbs brushing away the tears of joy. Their amusement faded, gazes holding one another's. He brought his lips closer to hers until they shared the same breath.

Sorcha focused on his grey eyes, finding an intensity there she had never seen before.

"*Sorcha.*" Her name sounded like a plea. "I love ye, lass. Not a love out of honor or duty. I truly love ye." His gaze hardened for such a brief time she wondered if she imagined it. "Yet there is something I must tell ye."

She moved an inch closer, her lips hovering over his. "Aye, Evan. Tell me."

He dropped his hands from her face, and as if mustering courage, squared his shoulders. "Glen Fruin . . ."

The door creaked, Clara bursting in. "Well, how are my—" She halted, eyes wide. "I . . . I am that sorry. I shall leave . . ."

Sorcha stepped back. "N . . . nae. We were just coming to forage for food and drink." She turned to Evan. "Come, husband. Let us break our fast." She would remind him once they were alone again about what he wished to tell her.

When they reached the kitchen, Sorcha was surprised to find Douglas seated next to Kester at the worktable. Douglas's eyes followed Maidie's every move as she placed a platter of hot bannocks on the table, her dreamy gaze only for him.

Sorcha and Evan shared a smile as they sat across from the two men.

"Should we adjourn to the hall and break our fast with the others?" Evan's tone held a teasing lilt aimed at Douglas.

Marcus bolted in, his expression clear he did not expect to see so many gathered there. "I did wonder where ye all got to." He sat on the bench next to Kester and glanced at Sorcha. "I miss John."

Sorcha's gaze swung to Evan, and Marcus stuttered, "I . . . I dinnae mean to disrespect ye, Evan."

Evan nodded. "Dinnae fash yourself. I miss him as well."

Marcus's shoulders relaxed, and he reached for a bannock as Maidie passed him a cup of ale.

Evan's jaw tightened. Sorcha recognized their shared pain of loss. She placed a gentle hand on his arm. The comment must have stabbed at him, and her heart hurt for him. He had walked from the battlefield—without John.

As the others spoke, Evan remained silent, barely touching his food. He rose abruptly and strode from the chamber without a word. All eyes swung to him and then to Sorcha, questions lurking in their depths.

Sorcha shrugged. "Mayhap it was remembering John."

Marcus paled. "I am that sorry."

Sorcha rose, placing a comforting hand on his shoulder. "Dinnae worry. The wound is still fresh for us all."

She tried to present a convincing smile, then followed in Evan's path. The climb to the battlements was slow, and by the time she found him leaning against the stone structure, her side pained with the exertion.

Evan flinched as she put her hand on his back. "I dinnae wish to speak, Sorcha."

"Ye said ye had something to tell me . . ." Sorcha bit her lip. ". . . afore we broke our fast."

She felt his tremor, yet he did not turn to her.

The cool morning breeze revived Sorcha as she surveyed the surrounding landscape. Autumn was upon them early this year. Mayhap it was because they were far north of their home.

Evan stood straight, lips firm. "I have something to tell ye, Sorcha. I should have done so afore we wed, but I was a coward." He pulled in a long, hard breath. "As ye know, I have loved ye for a long time."

Sorcha allowed her hand to move across his back as if to comfort him, her heart pounding.

"'Tis what happened on the battlefield at Glen Fruin." He hung his head and stayed thus for so long Sorcha thought he had decided not to speak, yet then he looked in the distance and spoke, his voice low.

"John lay dying in my arms." He swallowed with difficulty and looked into her eyes, a watery sheen covering his grey gaze. "He did ask me to care for ye. To wed ye. He knew I would do so for him."

Sorcha's hand stilled upon his back, many emotions rushing her at once. She staggered from him, bracing herself on the cool stone. Hot, unshed tears burned in her eyes. He reached for her, and she jerked from his reach. "Ye tell me this—*now*? Ye wed me out of an oath—an obligation."

"Nae! I told ye. I have loved ye from the time I met ye, and it has only grown since."

A ringing filled Sorcha's ears, and she swayed. She pictured her John covered in blood, using his last breath to make Evan promise to care for her. Why had Evan concealed this?

She steadied herself, a glare meeting him. "How can I ever trust anything ye tell me again? 'Tis a lie of the deepest . . ." She choked on the words. "All has been a lie."

Sorcha spun and rushed to the stairs, moving as quickly as possible without endangering her child.

"Sorcha!" Evan called out. "Please dinnae leave."

She shouted over her shoulder, "Leave me be, Evan!"

Sobbing all the way to her chamber, she threw herself upon the bed and curled into a ball on her side, burying her wet face against the pillow. He said he loved her, yet he was only fulfilling a friend's final wish, a final arrangement sworn at John's side.

Sorcha lost track of time, and when a knock sounded on her door, the sun was fading from the window.

Clara entered, her quick footsteps slapping against the hard floor. The bed sank with her weight. "Sorcha, my dear. Evan would not tell me why the both of ye are upset." She patted Sorcha's head as if she was a small child. "Shall ye speak with me?"

Sorcha's breath shuddered, and she pushed her head deeper into the pillow.

"Lass, ye must ken your emotions are in distress, more so because of the bairn. Mistress Gibbs shall tell it is so. The both of us have seen many a lass not being herself during such a time.”

Sorcha quieted, and her mind wandered. Clara’s words were truth. Small things made her irritable, and she snapped for no reason. Yet what Evan had kept from her made her feel . . . deceived. It was as if John and Evan had determined her future. Should she not have had a say in the matter?

She voiced her thoughts to Clara in a rush of words. When she finished, her breath caught in gasps, and the tears returned.

Clara gathered Sorcha in her arms and rocked her from side to side. “Oh, my friend. I love ye, and I love my brother. He did what John wanted, and in the bargain, he got ye—a woman he already loved.”

“Bar . . . gain,” Sorcha stammered between bursts of sobs. “I . . . I am now a *bargain*?”

Clara released a sad chuckle. “Ye are much more than a bargain. Ye are a gem, and Evan knows his good fortune. Evan dinnae fully wed ye out of obligation to John.” She exhaled. “Do ye think he would have told John he was in love with his wife?”

Sorcha stilled, the revelation hitting with a wave of pain. Mayhap she had not seen things from Evan’s side—especially if he really had loved her from afar. She prayed for God to send the answer to her struggle. What was she to do?

Of a sudden, her mind filled with moments from the past— of Evan complimenting her gown the color of yellow gorse and the way the sun highlighted the red in her hair, of John bringing her sweet-smelling heather saying Evan had noticed her fondness for it. Why had she forgotten? Was it because she only had eyes for John as she should since he was her husband? She had looked upon Evan as a brother to John, not seeing his true feelings.

Sorcha placed hands on Clara's shoulders, easing her away, meeting her sisterly gaze. "Thank ye for your kind words. I know ye mean well. 'Tis a lot to consider."

"Aye, 'Tis." Clara smiled. "He loves ye, Sorcha. Give him a chance."

"I shall think on it. Though, mayhap it shall take time. I have much to consider." She drew in and released a long breath. "I must pack for the journey." She slid to the edge of the bed, halted to draw strength, then dropped her feet to the floor.

Clara assisted Sorcha to stand. She wobbled for a moment, weak with exhaustion, before attending to packing. The task did not take long, and as she stowed the last item, the door opened, and Evan entered with quick, sure steps.

His gaze landed on Clara. "Shall ye please leave us, sister? I must have a word with my wife."

Clara squared her shoulders in surprise and nodded.

Sorcha would not meet Evan's regard, fidgeting with her needlework.

Evan placed a firm hand on her shoulder. "Please dinnae shut me out. We must speak."

Sorcha nodded. "I know, yet I am not ready. The bairn does weigh upon me."

He withdrew his hand, and she felt the loss of it. Without looking over her shoulder, she heard his departing footsteps, and loneliness engulfed her.

CʒℰꙄ

The opening of October dawned with their departure, and Sorcha's heart gladdened that Evan's strength had returned. Douglas knew of a hidden valley owned by Clan Grant that lay to the west of Freuchie Castle, a three-day journey for their group. As predicted, the autumn weather had arrived early, ushering in cold and rain.

Evan came to her several times, yet she was not ready to address his concerns. The emotions the bairn stirred kept her from facing her feelings. If only they were able to settle somewhere and live life anew without threat. They remained in the cave for three days before the journey west, and by the time they departed, everyone grew more fearful of discovery and wanted to be on their way.

Sorcha avoided Evan during this time, and when unable to do so, she remained quiet and feigned sleep.

The pain he wore was akin to a cloak. His shoulders slumped, and the shadows beneath his eyes darkened with each day. It wounded her to know she was the cause. Something inside would not allow her to open her heart to Evan, though she hoped it to be so—one day.

Sorcha stumbled as her foot met with a stone on their path, lurching forward. A muscular arm encircled her waist and pulled her against a hard chest—Evan.

"Careful, lass. I would not have ye and the bairn harmed."

She avoided his gaze and swallowed.

From behind, Clara rushed to her side. "Are ye well, lass?"

"I am fine. 'Tis the path." Sorcha breathed deeply of the chill evening air, stinging her throat. As they progressed, a beam of bright moonlight shone on the path ahead, making their way easier.

Evan kept his hold on her, and she finally relaxed against him without speaking. They walked on until Douglas, at the front of the line, signaled for them to halt. Whispered words passed down to them to stop for the night. A heavily wooded area lay ahead, a brae offering some shelter from passersby. They set guards near the path within the confines of the underbrush. A burn bubbled nearby to slake their thirst.

They lay no fires for fear of revealing their presence, dining on cold meat, cheese, and bread. Sorcha tried to recline against a large stone at the base of the brae protecting them, the hardness of it making sleep unbearable. She tossed and turned until Evan whispered by her side. "'Tis not a place to find rest." He scooted closer. "Place your head upon my lap. Mayhap ye can find some sleep away from the stone."

Sorcha shook her head and turned to lie on her side, folded hands beneath her as a pillow. The anguish of Evan and John on the battlefield of Glen Fruin still haunted her—the oath between them too much for her fragile state.

Evan's sigh gripped her heart. She knew she injured him, not knowing how to reconcile her feelings. She must have more time.

"Sorcha?" Clara's clipped tone did not penetrate her need for solace. She ignored her by feigning sleep.

"Let her be, Clara. She needs rest—she and the bairn." Evan's tone begged his sister to understand.

Rustling sounded as Clara sat beside her brother.

"Sister, let it be."

Clara's heavy sigh brought anguish to Sorcha. If only her friend could do as her brother asked. Sorcha needed time to work out her own heart.

"I cannot, Evan. She does ye an injustice. I have known for a time how ye feel about her. And ye have John's blessing."

The long silence stretched, and Sorcha thought they would part without words until Evan replied in a soft tone. "Aye. I ken. He was like a brother to me, and I would never hurt Sorcha for anything. I love her—though she does not love me. That is of a truth."

"Dinnae be so sure of it."

Clara's departing footsteps made Sorcha long to cry again. She must keep the ruse of sleep, slowing her breathing and trying not to think about the future. The future for her and the bairn—John's child.

Evan's voice whispered close to her ear, and she felt the warmth of him. It unsettled her, and she fought to remain still and quiet, the sounds of night surrounding them. Low muttering sounded. Someone hummed, another released soft cries of despair.

Warm breath tickled her ear. "Good night, my love. I shall protect ye and the bairn as long as I have breath."

Evan settled beside her, a sudden feeling of comfort engulfing her, and she drifted into restful slumber.

◖◗

Sorcha woke to a dusting of snow on the trees where their

branches stretched and protected them through the night. She appreciated the beauty of it and how it hid the ugliness beneath dead leaves and dried undergrowth. In much the same way, her handwoven scenes depicting life in uniform decorative stitches when reversed revealed an unsightly tangle of thread and knots.

Sorcha slanted her head to see if Evan still slept, finding the place beside her empty, and the pine needles pressed flat to reveal his earlier presence. She stretched her palm and laid it upon the bedding, surprised to find it still warm.

Without Evan's presence, the cold seeped through her. He was a kind man, and she had shunned him. She lay still, unable to rise. If not for her babe, she thought of staying as she was and letting the cold lull her to the sleep of death to join John. Yet she must live for their child.

How easy it would be to let go. Her eyelids fluttered, and sleep claimed her.

A voice called from far away, a deep rumbling reassuring her all was well. Aye, let eternal sleep come and take her to John.

A gentle hand cupped her shoulder. "Sorcha. 'Tis time to depart."

Sorcha released a sigh. Evan's pleasant, earthy scent was unmistakable. The backdrop of scattered snowflakes beyond his dark hair gave him an ethereal appearance like something out of a dream.

She licked her lips and suddenly remembered she should not have done so in the cold. Hurriedly, she dried them with the edge of her cloak and recalled Mistress Gibbs carrying a balm for the skin. She would seek her out.

"Are ye well?" Evan tried to help her sit, and she shoved his hands away, instantly regretting the action. He flinched, rose, and peered down at her. "As ye wish. Please ready yourself to depart."

He backed away two steps, then turned to her. "I shall have Clara bring ye food and drink."

In that moment, Sorcha hated herself. Why could she not let go of the hurt brought by what she saw as betrayal?

Clara knelt beside her, laying a cloth-wrapped bannock in her lap. She held a pewter cup, and Sorcha took it with a nod of thanks.

"Evan said ye were not yourself. Does the bairn trouble ye?"

"Nae." Sorcha would not meet her friend's eyes. She nibbled on the bannock and took a sip of water.

"I hurt for ye and Evan." Clara swallowed hard and blew out a breath. "While I know the oath made between him and John does trouble ye, I deem Evan should have kept it to himself. There was nae need for ye to know because he loves ye no matter what oath was taken. *Lads* are always hard to understand."

The word conveyed a sad tone, as if it explained everything, urging Sorcha to accept it and move on.

Mayhap Clara was right. Yet she was unable to do so. She felt a fool. Akin to being treated like a babe unable to care for herself—an eejit, even. The thought made her cringe.

Clara mistook the movement for illness. "Ye are cold." She unclasped her cloak, and Sorcha stayed her hand.

"I am warm enough. Ye cannot give me your only cover."

The woman continued until she had removed her outer garment and placed it around Sorcha's shoulders.

"Clara!" Her voice rose more than she intended, bringing Kester to them.

"What goes on? Ye must not be so loud." His gaze bored into Sorcha's. "'Tis something wrong?"

"Kester, ye must tell her I shall not take her only warmth. I am well."

His gaze swung between the two women, finally settling on Clara. "My dear, leave her be. If she says she is well, keep your cloak. Ye shall need it, and I dinnae desire to see ye unwell."

Kester and Clara regarded one another—an understanding passing between them. Each nodded, and Clara refastened her cloak.

Once Kester left them, Sorcha said, "I am that sorry, Clara. It seems I am so unsettled of late and have nae control."

Clara chuckled and softly patted Sorcha's protruding stomach. "'Tis all this little lass's fault, I am certain."

Sorcha smiled. "And ye are so certain 'tis a lass?"

"To be sure." Without hesitation, Clara nodded. "I shall get the balm from Mistress Gibbs for our lips. 'Tis a long, cold day ahead of us."

Sorcha finished her bannock and water, struggled to her feet, and made her way to the burn to freshen herself before the journey began anew. Evan had warned her to go nowhere alone. She paid him no heed, shuffling through the light snow until the sound of flowing water met her ears. The burbling murmur and smell of the water brought her comfort, and she closed her eyes to take in the peace.

Leaning upon a massive pine, she tipped her head and prayed for God to give her direction about her relationship with Evan.

Forgive.

Sorcha straightened and craned her neck to peer around as if someone had spoken the word aloud.

Evan strode toward her, his expression thick with fear.

The unbidden emotion that befell her grew more forceful the closer he drew.

"Evan MacDonald! I shall only say this once. Ye should never have told me about the oath ye made with John. 'Tis a cruel thing ye did, and I am unsure I can ever forgive ye."

The thought of the word from *God* slapped her, and she fell to her knees. "I am sorry, Lord. How can Ye forgive me when I cannot forgive others?"

In seconds, Evan held her in his arms and rocked her against him. "Shh, lass. All shall be well. I am sorry I told ye of the oath as I was unable to bear the burden upon me."

She sobbed against him until his cloak soaked with her tears. "How can ye ever forgive *me*?"

"There is naught to forgive. Ye lost your beloved husband, your home, and are with child. 'Tis a very heavy load for anyone to bear. I am unsure I could do so."

Her sobs turned to a chuckle. "Aye. Ye, nor any lad, could bear the burden of carrying a child."

She peered up at him from damp lashes. His broad smile eased her worries, and she cocked her head. "Ye are no lad,

Evan."

"Nae." He stroked her cheek with his fingertips. "I am the man who loves ye, lass."

Sorcha's heart swelled, and she leaned in to press a kiss to his lips.

354

Chapter Twenty-Nine

1710

Muirie avoided Gavin for two days. When he attempted conversation, she made excuses to leave his presence. The embarrassment of him watching her sleep caused heat to rise in her cheeks.

Shame filled her every time their eyes met. He was as a brother to her—no more. She knew he felt the same, yet he teased her about what happened. Grannam's voice before she dozed returned to her, "Muirie's lad will keep her safe."

Her stomach sank with the memory. He was *not* her lad.

Reid was . . . *no*, she could not think of such things.

The scent of smoke rose to her hiding place upon the parapet, reminding her night approached and fires against the evening chill were laid. Releasing a pained sigh, she made her way toward the stairs, opened the door, and met Gavin.

"It appears by your visage, ye are not so glad to see me." Though his voice held amusement, his appearance possessed remorse.

She pinched her lips together and tried to squeeze between him and the door's opening.

Gavin's arm rose to block her way, and she ducked to move under it. With his free hand, he stopped her, spinning her around.

"Muirie, ye are much like my sister—too much so. Avoiding confrontation when in the wrong."

Muirie's ire rose as if someone had struck her. "I am not in the wrong. I have done nothing!"

Gavin had the impudence to lift his eyes to the sky in irritation. "Do ye not see we are of kindred spirits?"

She brought her gaze to the darkening sky, a few stray stars emerging against the blue-black heavens.

Had Muirie misunderstood their friendship? Did he want more from her than that?

Gavin gently took her chin between two fingers and turned her head toward him. "Muirie. Ye are as a sister to me. I tease ye, and now ye take what happened with seriousness?"

She released a shaking breath, relief deflating her of all strength.

He cocked his head, a smile reaching his eyes. "Now do ye know?"

Muirie nodded and slapped his hand. "Why did ye not say so these two days past?"

"I did not know it was such a problem for ye. Do ye not know by now to come to me if there is an issue between us?"

"I do now." She wrapped her arms around his neck and squeezed.

He returned the gesture. "Do be careful. What if someone sees us?" He pulled away and wiggled his brows.

She playfully shoved him, and he stumbled backward, closer to the stairs. She screamed as his arms flailed in the air to grasp something to steady himself.

Gavin caught himself in time, and she gripped his forearms fiercely, tugging him toward her.

Once upright, he chuckled. "Seems we are quite the pair, are we not?"

"Aye, I suppose we are." She caught her heaving breath for a moment. "How could I have so misunderstood?"

He stepped toward the stone wall encircling them and peered toward the dusk. "Propriety warns us from meeting alone, for fear of appraisal."

She joined him, shoulder to shoulder, and inhaled the crisp night air. "'Tis truth. We dare not be found here or else be forced into marriage."

He shuddered with mock horror. "Not a pleasant situation at all."

She punched him on the shoulder. "'Twas not a proper thing to say to a lass."

His warm smile met her gaze. "Pardon me. It would feel as if I were forced to marry Elizabeth." He shuddered again.

"Ye are incorrigible."

"A large word for such a small lass." He rested a hand on her shoulder, his tone low. "I pray we shall always be friends, Muirie, and I thank ye for your kindness to Elizabeth." His regard returned to the night. "She is a morsel of trouble."

Muirie's laughter echoed in the space. "Aye, yet I believe she has changed."

"Bethank to ye."

Warmth filled her heart. "Not me. Bethank to God."

He nodded. "Aye. Indeed."

Muirie linked her arm with his, and they admired the sky's shifting from blue to inky night, specks of light revealing themselves unhurriedly until the evening near exploded with brilliance.

The creak of the oak door brought their gazes around to a circle of lantern light and the shocked expressions of Lord and Lady Grant, bringing a rush of fear through Muirie like an icy dip in the burn.

⁂

Beathag aided Muirie in changing her dress for an audience with Lady Grant. "I know not why, Muirie. She telt me to bring ye to her parlor as soon as possible."

"I am afeard 'tis no welcome news, considering the look in her ladyship's eyes, and waking ye so early."

Beathag kept her attention on her task, voice shaking. She turned Muirie around to survey her handiwork. "Ye are a picture." Head tilting, she studied Muirie as if sensing the things left untold. "What has happened?"

"I . . ." Muirie needed someone to confide in, and Beathag

was her closest friend, yet she held back for some unknown reason. 'Twas an embarrassment. She hung her head and tried to step away, yet Beathag's insistent grip held her in place. She flung herself into Beathag's arms, shivering with the uncertainty of it all.

"'Tis Gavin."

"Gavin? What of him?"

Muirie drew in a heavy breath and forged on. "He and I were on the parapets talking. We agree we feel kinship with one another—yet as siblings. Nothing more." She released her friend and perched on the edge of the bed.

"Lord and Lady Grant arrived as we were . . . standing close, watching the stars. To them it appeared romantic. 'Twas not so."

Beathag's mouth fell open, eyes wide.

"Aye. 'Tis the same look of Lady Grant."

"What did they say?" Beathag joined Muirie.

"Lady Grant said nothing. Lord Grant told us to depart and prepare to dine."

Beathag frowned. "It does explain what that gossie-fain kitchen maid was on about."

A sliver of fear crawled up Muirie's spine. "What?"

"The lass is full of the goings on of the castle. Said last eve's meal was quiet as a dead fish."

Muirie swallowed. It had been the most painful meal she had ever sat through. With Lord and Lady Grant saying little, she and Gavin did likewise, Elizabeth sending her questioning looks throughout the evening.

Beathag nudged her shoulder. "What brought this on?"

A long silence hung until Muirie decided it was best to start from the beginning, so she told her friend what had transpired at the picnic with Grannam.

"Truly?"

"Aye. 'Twas totally innocent, yet Lord and Lady Grant do not see it as such."

"And what of Lord and Lady Stewart?"

Muirie shrugged. "I know not, other than their quiet nature at table being the same as Lord and Lady Grant. I fear they must know."

They sat in stillness, each pondering their own thoughts.

Suddenly, Beathag leaped from the bed. "Ye must go at once. We have spoken far too long." The girl's face reddened, and she rushed to the other side of the chamber, returning with Muirie's shoes. "Here. Make haste!"

Lady Grant's maid appeared moments later, and Muirie followed her along winding corridors until they reached an ancient door, the dark wood with iron hinges appearing as a relic of the past.

She had not been to this part of the castle. When she entered, she found herself in a small chamber with a few books scattered on a well-worn table nestled by a rather uncomfortable-looking wooden chair. The fireplace seemed to have long ago warmed the small space.

Was this a sort of dungeon? Muirie rubbed her arms and fought to gather her wits. "Are ye certain this is where I am to be?" she asked the maid.

"Aye, mistress. I was told to bring ye here." She blushed

and left Muirie alone.

Just as Muirie sat and picked up a book, the door creaked open, and Lady Grant entered.

"Ah, Muirie. I am glad to see ye." She notched her head and strode to the only wall in the chamber that held no door, window, or fireplace. She reached toward a sconce holding a stub of candle and pushed it. The wall shuddered, and to Muirie's shock, a scraping noise sounded as part of the wall slid inward.

A secret passage . . . to the dungeon?

"Come, Muirie."

Muirie swallowed hard, rising on weak legs, and followed Lady Grant through the opening and along a narrow corridor. Rather than a menacing, cobwebbed gap, there was the scent of lavender, and the floor was swept clean. A trail of lit candles lined the stone wall, casting a warm glow in the passage. Was this a secret way to her parlor? Where were they in the castle?

At long length, Lady Grant halted in a corner where the corridor made a sharp right turn. She gripped a wall sconce as she had done before and pushed it to reveal another door. They stepped through, Muirie's mouth opening in surprise.

A vast chamber held floor to ceiling shelves crammed with books, and rather than flames, an ornate fireplace possessed a large bouquet of lavender. As she stepped into the space, she realized they were not alone. Five heads turned to meet her.

ᳩᳩ

Above the rim of her cup, Muirie's gaze found Gavin's. Stilted conversation flowed around the chamber, yet she had no heart for idle talk—nor did it seem Gavin cared to join in.

Had the situation not appeared to be so *odd*, she would have laughed at the absurdity—six women and a lone man sequestered in a secret chamber, sipping tea and nibbling scones.

Gavin's gaze seemed to hold a measure of humor mixed with dread. Why was he here? Why were they all here? And why in such a secret manner?

Grannam snorted. "Come along, Isabel. Let us get on with it. We are wasting daylight."

Isabel bit her lip. "Aye, Grannam. 'Tis time."

Lady Lamont exchanged a glance with Lady Stewart and dipped her chin in agreement.

Lady Stewart rose and moved toward a long table across the chamber. With tender care she picked up a length of cloth and laid it across her outstretched hands, coming to stand in front of Muirie.

"My dear." She gently placed the object on the low table between Muirie and Gavin.

Muirie's cup quivered in her hand as she searched for a place to set it aside.

Elizabeth jumped from her seat and took it.

"What is this, my lady?"

"A part of your past." She smoothed the cloth and cleared her throat, stepping away. "*And* Gavin's."

Muirie swiveled to look at Gavin, who looked as confused as she. *Their* past?

She leaned over the panel and recognized the familiar needlework she had long admired—the scene that hung on

Lady Stewart's parlor wall depicting a battle scene with a bleeding man lying in the snow.

Lady Stewart looked to the woman at Muirie's left.

"*Sorcha.*" The tone of her voice held a meaning that hung in the air with such emotion it startled Muirie.

Sorcha MacFarlane retrieved another panel from the table and brought it to Gavin, his expression unreadable.

"*Gavin. Muirie.*" Sorcha slanted her head, emotion in her eyes. "This is for both of ye as well. 'Tis your beginning."

Muirie stilled. *The beginning?* She couldn't see the panel Gavin cradled awkwardly in his hands. He seemed as stunned as she.

Sorcha pointed to the panel beside Muirie. "The man dying in the snow on the battlefield at Glen Fruin is your great grandfather, John MacGregor. Brother to the Gregor chieftain in 1603, Allaster MacGregor. He was the only MacGregor to die on that field."

Her eyes misted, and she swallowed before pointing to a woman standing on the brae watching the scene unfold. "This is his wife, Sorcha MacGregor."

Sorcha brought a hand to Gavin's panel, tilting it for Muirie to see. The panel featured the intricately stitched figures of two women—one older, one younger—standing at the bedside of another woman holding newborn twins.

Her fingertips brushed over the younger woman. "'Tis me." She traced a path to the twins and whispered, "'Tis ye, Gavin and Muirie." A lone tear made a slow path down her cheek. "My brother and sister."

Muirie gasped, and Gavin straightened, nearly dropping

the panel.

Sorcha caught it and stepped back, holding it dearly to her chest.

Tears welled in Muirie's eyes, not wanting to believe what had just happened. Gavin was her brother.

He found words before she did, looking to Lady Lamont. "'Tis truth, Mother?"

Lady Lamont smiled through tears and nodded. She and Lady Stewart stood together, each holding another panel, and approached Gavin and Muirie, presenting a panel to each of them.

Muirie's panel showed a sleeping babe wrapped in cloth and tucked inside a woven basket resting on the steps of a castle. One she recognized as Deveron Castle—her home.

Tears fell as she looked at Gavin, who stared at his panel with watery eyes, then he held it toward hers. The images were nearly identical except his was different castle—the home of the Lamonts.

An all-encompassing sensation settled over the chamber until gentle sobbing filled the quiet.

All peered at Grannam whose shoulders shook with sobs, yet her eyes shone with happiness not sorrow. Her breath shuddered, and she swept tears back with her hand.

"I never thought I would see the day."

Grannam rose and spryly strode toward Muirie and Gavin, halting before them. She stooped over the scene with the twins and pointed to the older woman beside Sorcha.

"'Tis me," she said proudly as she straightened with pride.

Muirie blinked at her. "Ye?"

Gavin cleared his throat, and Grannam patted his head as she would a lad. "Your mither was a dear friend to me—though I was a *wee* bit her elder." She tittered.

Gavin rose, placing the needlework gently on Muirie's lap with the other, and wrapped Grannam in his arms.

Grannam's startled look faded to one of joy. She hugged him to her, resting her grey head on his shoulder. "My dear boy," she muttered, her gaze on Muirie, as she extended an arm signaling for her to rise.

With tears, Elizabeth gathered the needlework, so Muirie could stand.

Muirie rose, and Grannam wrapped her in their embrace, Gavin looping a trembling arm around her—*his sister*.

The elder woman sniffled, her voice quivering through the tears. She notched her head toward the table. "There are more pieces of Sorcha's work to tell of your history."

Muirie and Gavin shared a look. Without question, she knew what her *twin* was thinking. The connection they felt was more than she could dream.

"'Tis much more to tell." Grannam loosened her hold on them. "We wanted to tell ye on yer next birthday, yet . . ." Her voice trailed to a whisper and halted.

Lady Stewart placed a hand on her shoulder and guided her to a seat. "Do not worry, Grannam. We will share all."

The elder woman quietly nodded and allowed herself to be seated.

Sorcha smiled at them through tears. "When I received a letter from Lady Stewart about her growing concerns of your relationship, I agreed 'twas time to reveal the truth." She motioned for them to sit. "The remaining scenes ye have not been privy to are now yours. They have long been kept safe by Lady Stewart for this day."

"For I live in the Highlands where we are more closely watched." She sent a warm smile to Muirie, then Gavin. "The year of your birth, the proscription against the MacGregors was reinstated, and ye were not safe." She paused and swallowed, preparing to speak again. "I would that Father had lived to see the two of ye grown, yet alas he perished at the hands of bloodthirsty Campbells when the proscription was reinstated."

Muirie had heard of the dangers of being a MacGregor—the tales passed down through all the clans. "So because Gavin and I were—*are*—MacGregors, our safety was a concern?"

"Aye. 'Tis so. Ye would have been torn apart and sent to Ireland or to another clan to raise ye as they saw fit. We could not risk that."

Muirie shuddered.

Gavin's words tumbled out in a rush. "Who would do such a thing?"

Sorcha clenched her hands into fists. "William of Orange, for I will not call him *our* king." She heaved a deep sigh.

The chamber filled with heavy silence, Grannam's snuffles echoing. Muirie feared for her. She had never displayed such distress, and with her age, the thought crippled her.

Gavin scrubbed a hand over his jaw, rose, and paced the chamber. "We learned of this in school. I did not know it would affect me—*us*—in such a way." His gaze settled on Lady

Lamont. "Ye are a loving and kind mother, and I will think of ye no less . . ."

His shoulders shook, and he regained his seat beside Muirie. She stretched her hand to grip his, and he clung to it fiercely.

Lady Lamont knelt before him, pulling him into her embrace, as she must have done when he was a small lad. Elizabeth followed, kneeling beside her mother.

Muirie shot to her feet, a mixture of confusion and anger tugging at her. "I—I need time to consider this."

Before anyone could stop her, she ran from the chamber, winding through the corridors until she stumbled upon the small chamber she had first entered and took her first steps toward her past—a past God had allowed.

Muirie's final step from the passage onto the parapets brought her face to face with Lord Stewart. His surprised expression turned to one of pleasure, his pale eyes surveying Muirie.

"How are ye, lass?"

Muirie took a step back. "Lord Stewart, I will not intrude upon your peace."

With one long stride, he reached her. "Please do not depart." He gestured toward the view surrounding them. "If 'tis not too windy for ye, may we speak?"

Lord Stewart had been a kind, generous guardian—though they rarely shared private moments.

She dipped her chin and stepped toward the wall, peering at the golden-hued hills fading toward the western Highlands.

"Muirie, I suppose ye are here because of the revealing of

your past."

She heaved a nervous sigh and brought her trembling hands to clasp the rough stone on top of the parapet wall. "I could not stay in the chamber with all their eyes upon me. 'Twas a shock."

"Aye. I ken Gavin feels the same."

Hot tears stung. She met Lord Stewart's compassionate gaze.

"Ye will always have a home with us, Muirie, if ye so wish it." He leaned in and kissed her forehead, the fatherly gesture almost undoing her. He pulled away. "I shall fetch Gavin. The two of ye need to face this truth together."

Muirie smiled despite her hazy vision, unable to speak. She watched him go, slumping against the stone, resting her temple on the embrasure. The cold nipped at her skin, and she shivered, wishing she had her cloak.

Shame coursed through her for fleeing the chamber, and she prayed for God's peace to envelop her aching heart. She would return and beg forgiveness for leaving her friends—her family.

The door behind scraped open, and she swung around.

Gavin paused on the threshold, and she rushed into his arms.

He hugged her tight, a deep chuckle rumbling in her ear. "I found ye here once again, *sister*."

"I am sorry. I know not why I ran." She sobbed against his chest. "'Twas too much."

"Rightfully so," he spoke against her hair.

Muirie pulled far enough away to look into his eyes. "Ye agree?"

"Aye. I wanted to flee as well, yet only one of us could do so. Elizabeth longed to follow ye, but Mother—" He coughed. "Aye, she will always be my *mother*. She would not allow it. She understood ye needed to be alone." He handed her his handkerchief.

"'Tis very understanding of them both."

He winked. "It runs in the family."

Muirie squeezed his arm. "So it would seem. Ye are a kind brother."

His expression grew thoughtful. "Can ye ken we are truly MacGregors?"

Muirie pointed to the hills. "*And* that our family was here and beyond those mountains."

"'Tis hard to grasp." He looped his arm over her shoulder. "I would like to see the Hidden Glen."

She drew back. "The what?"

"Oh, aye. Ye left afore Grannam and Sorcha shared the tale."

She looked at him expectantly, hoping he would share the story. "What does a hidden glen have to do with our past, brother?"

Chapter Thirty

October 1603

The snow peppered them with force, and Sorcha struggled with the needed vigor to take step after weary step. Evan held her on one side, encouraging her with tales to lift her spirits, yet his efforts lasted only so long as they had to stop for her to rest and regain enough strength to move onward. Her guilt grew each time she delayed their journey.

In what seemed many hours, they paused for a midday repast at the base of a mountain that would require a great deal of uphill climbing Sorcha did not relish. The day was young, so there was no thought of halting for the night.

Sorcha watched Douglas move down the line, surveying the group, assuring some they were drawing near the Hidden

Glen. When he reached Sorcha and Evan, he began to speak yet was interrupted when Marcus rushed forward with wide eyes. The lad served as their scout, so for him to return in such a manner meant trouble.

Sorcha braced herself against the rock she rested upon as Marcus gathered the two men close and began to speak in a low voice.

"I spied a band of Campbells traveling toward us. They are few in number yet well armed."

Evan's brow furrowed. He ushered Douglas and Marcus off the path and crouched with sticks in hand to draw out a plan in the snow. Marcus left and came back with Kester, and after a brief discussion, the men broke apart, and Evan returned to Sorcha.

She gripped his arm. "What must we do?"

"We shall leave the path and travel through the forest. Douglas says there is another way to the Hidden Glen. 'Tis better than facing the Campbells."

A shiver shot through her.

She heard Evan swallow, and he pulled her close. "All shall be well, lass."

She wanted to believe it. Her heart clenched, and the bairn gave a hard kick to her side.

Evan's gaze swung to her. "What, lass?"

Sorcha blinked. "I said nothing."

"Aye, ye jabbed me in the side."

She chuckled. "'Tis the babe. She kicked, and ye felt it!"

Evan placed a hand against her stomach, and the bairn

kicked again.

His smile ignited her heart, and the pride in his expression brought tears to her eyes. One would think the child was his.

"Ye said *she*."

Sorcha caressed her stomach. "Aye. So Clara says."

He pressed his lips together to hide a grin. "Och, does she now?"

"Is it a bad thing?"

"Nae, a fine bonny lass she will be. Just like her mither."

Marcus burst upon them, a franticness in his eyes, and in a low voice said, "Campbells. *Move!*" He pointed up the hillside where the forest thickened, then moved down the line to repeat the order.

Evan put a supporting arm around Sorcha's waist and guided her toward the hill, snatching up a long, leafy branch as they went. Progressing upward, he dragged the limb behind them in a side-to-side motion, concealing their trail.

Sorcha's gaze swung to the others and found the men doing likewise. She thanked God for giving them such shrewd warriors for protection. They topped the rise and shuffled downward. Once they reached the bottom of the hill, they resumed their journey, fear keeping them silent.

After a time, Marcus reported the Campbells were now behind them and traveling away. Evan thanked Marcus with a slap on the back. The lad beamed with pride and sprinted off to spread the news.

Douglas suggested they resume their travel by night, and all agreed, ready to reach safety. The snow increased, yet the knowledge their journey was near its end offered added vigor.

They stopped near dark and rested for a few hours.

Once darkness engulfed them, they would begin the last leg of their travels.

The night was colder than any they had experienced, and Sorcha wondered how she would make it through. She questioned if her child liked winter. The thought made her lips curl upward, and she touched her stomach, longing to hold the bairn in her arms.

Evan chuckled. "Is she rebelling again?"

"Nae. I think she mayhap not like cold weather."

He lifted his brows. "Aye?"

"When I shiver, she kicks with more force."

Evan moved to sit in front of her and placed both palms on her stomach. He leaned down and whispered, "Now, lassie, nae kicking your mither. We shall have none of it." He brought his head up, smiled at Sorcha, and she placed a hand on his cheek.

She smiled. "Ye shall make a fine father."

He tilted his head, brows lifted. "Why do ye say that?"

"Because ye corrected her with a gentle tone and warmth in your voice."

Sorcha thought she detected moisture in his eyes, but with the surrounding darkness, she was uncertain. She did not voice her other thought—that he also made a fine husband.

❈

A narrow stone bridge lay ahead, thinly concealed within a dense forest near a sloping hillside, water surging over large boulders down the brae. Sorcha took in the tranquil setting, wishing they might abide there a while. Dawn was soon to arrive, and Douglas said they would enter the Hidden Glen before full light.

The trees thickened at the far edge of the bridge as they made their descent. Sorcha peered upward, and the wooded brae rose above them, the sky barely visible. Once in the shelter of the trees, a signal from Douglas halted them. They gathered closer to form a solid group with Douglas at the center.

His voice low, he said, "We must be silent. The entry to the glen must never be discovered."

Someone whispered, "How can that be?"

Douglas's reply accompanied a soft chuckle. "Once safely there, ye shall ken."

He roused them to form a single line. "The way is narrow—and dark."

Sorcha gripped Evan's arm tight against her side, and he took her hand. "Och, lass, follow me and dinnae release my hand."

She nodded and stepped behind him.

Douglas sent Marcus ahead to explore any possible danger, then strode to the front, the rest shadowing behind.

They stumbled along in the darkness of the forest until Sorcha heard the fall of rushing water. It grew louder, and the scent of moist moss hung in the air. She knew a waterfall was near, and within a few minutes, a cold mist hovered over them.

A weak beam of light shone through a break in the trees, and a faint glint of water made itself known for a fleeting moment. They kept walking until they passed alongside the stone and earth of the hillside. A whisper passed along the line to cover their heads.

Sorcha pulled her cloak's hood over her hair and then they were beneath the cascade, sending a shower over them.

The icy contact on her skin made her shiver. As they walked, the sound of the fall faded into the distance, and all-embracing darkness consumed them.

Sorcha tried not to let fear gain control, and with her free hand, she groped the side of the wall, finding damp stone. Without thinking, she released Evan's hand and touched the other side to find the same hard, wet surface. The closeness of it almost undid her resolve, and she panted.

"Sorcha!" Evan whispered harshly against her ear. "All shall be well. Take my hand again and dinnae let go."

She swallowed bile, nodded as if he could see her, and grasped the air, searching for him.

His hand rested upon her shoulder, and he slid it down her arm until their fingers entwined. He kept her pressed against his side, guiding them forward.

After what Sorcha thought were hours of slow steps, the line stopped. Someone said in a hushed voice, "Douglas said we must abide here until Marcus returns to say all is clear."

Evan drew Sorcha to sit on the cave floor. He placed her in front of him, his arms around her shoulders, and eased her head back against his chest.

The complete blackness unnerved her. Evan's nearness was her only comfort.

His heartbeat pulsed against her cheek. The babe kicked in

protest as if to say she did not want to continue and found peace where they sat.

"I should like to sleep here for a long time." Sorcha sighed contentedly—though the hard ground gave little ease.

"Aye. We much need the rest." Evan's low, deep voice against her cheek thawed the chill surrounding them. "'Tis not long now. According to Douglas, this place is hidden from all the world." His whisper held awe with a tinge of disbelief.

Sorcha hung onto the tone. "'Tis hard to understand how nae one should know of its whereabouts except the Grants."

"Aye."

She heard the weariness in his voice, and guilt stabbed her. He was such a strong, steadfast man that it was hard to remember his own frailties, fears, and uncertainties that must plague him.

Sorcha lifted a hand toward his face, finding his cheek. "Ye must be weary almost as much as I." She felt a smile lift his whiskered face.

"Aye, lass. Weary to the bone, I am." He gently stroked her hair, then pressed a kiss to the top of her head. "What is your first desire once we arrive?"

Sorcha thought for a moment. "A warm bath and days of sleep."

Laughter rumbled in his chest, and she reveled in it. "Aye, lass. And I too."

The scrape of footsteps sounded, followed by mutterings that all ahead was well, and it was time to take the last portion of their journey.

Evan helped Sorcha rise, resuming their steps with a little

more strength, knowing their destination was within reach.

The sound of water and the scent of wet foliage drifted toward them as a weak trickle of light pin-pricked the exit of the passage.

Sorcha tugged her hood over her hair once more and made ready to feel the spray of cool water upon her. What she saw was astounding. The cascade was much larger than the other, and she questioned whether they would come away soaked.

She and Evan sidestepped the coursing downfall of the cold water, their view obscured. Alongside the steep brae, the group held their gazes on the landscape before them, and once they cleared the waterfall, they too saw what captured their attention.

Dawn shone on the overwhelming scope of the valley like none Sorcha had ever beheld. Though not large, it was more land than they would ever need. On the far side of the valley, a loch glistened in the early morning sun rising behind them. Its blue, the color of the vibrant sky, reflected white-grey clouds, the abundant forest bordering its shore, and a flock of birds gliding overhead.

Her gaze skimmed the surrounding mountains—jagged rocks and cliffs with perilous drops apparently kept this beautiful paradise secret from prying eyes, the only way in or out concealed behind the falls.

"Aye, lass. 'Tis a sight to behold." She stood transfixed as the others had done until Evan gripped her elbow. "We must depart. Be careful the now. 'Tis a narrow, treacherous path to the bottom."

Sorcha looked down, and dizziness caught her, reaching

for Evan's support. She had never much liked high places.

Evan moved to stand behind her, placing his warm hands upon her waist. "Dinnae look down. I have a hold on ye. Take one slow step at a time and train your eyes upon the lad in front of ye."

Blinking back tears, she said, "Aye." Not knowing what to do with her hands, she wrapped her arms around her stomach and felt the babe shift, encouraging and reminding her that she had much to live for.

ঔ

A freezing rain began, and once at the bottom, the group huddled beneath a projection of overhanging stone slashed deep into the side of the mountain. Sorcha's legs weakened with relief, and she huddled against Evan.

"I am that glad we have reached the end."

Evan's arm tightened around her, and he scanned the wide expanse of grassland that led to the loch in the distance. Kester and Clara stood with them, arm in arm, wide smiles lighting their faces.

Clara glowed with wonder. "Is it not lovely, Sorcha?"

"Oh, ye, sister. Aye." Sorcha watched Evan's expression, surprised to see a mixture of joy and skepticism there.

"Clara, I agree with ye, yet we must still move with caution." Kester patted her hand upon his arm. "Marcus has gone ahead to be sure there is nae one in the glen, and Douglas knows of a sheltered area amongst the trees." He pointed to their right, where Douglas and two men strode ahead.

In the distance, Sorcha saw Marcus carefully skirting the

edge of the trees, keeping out of sight. Had she not known when he set out, she would not have located him in the forest, his brown trews blending in with the underbrush.

The seasons changed the trees into a riot of color—a mixture of silver birch, oaks adorned with grey lichen, and gnarled pines. A few trees dotting the shore wore golden hues of red and orange.

Something moved against Sorcha's foot, and she took a step from Evan and lifted her skirt a few inches from the ground. A small grey frog leaped up to escape, and in its haste brushed against her leg, and she screamed, the sound bouncing off the stone enclosure.

Evan looked down at the offending creature, chuckling. "Oh, aye, lass. 'Tis a wee frog." He crouched and gently scooped it into his hand. With two strides, he strode to the side of their shelter and released it into the grass.

Sorcha shivered, embarrassment coursing through her. She sent an apologetic look to those around them.

Running footsteps drew their attention, and all turned to see Douglas sprinting toward them, claymore drawn, expression set into a fierce mask. He slid to a sudden stop, his gaze scouring the people. He settled his weapon inside its scabbard with a sliding hiss.

"What is amiss?"

"I am that sorry, Douglas. A creature startled me, and I screamed." Sorcha's eyes moistened, feeling like a fool.

"What creature would that be?" Douglas turned his regard upon Evan, who stood at her side.

Silence grew, then Douglas asked again. "What creature?"

In a lowered tone, Evan told him.

Douglas's eyebrows rose, and he pursed his lips. "A *frog*?" A corner of his mouth lifted, and he sputtered, then released a hoarse laugh.

Evan's attempt to keep his expression stoic failed, and he laughed with Douglas.

Sorcha smiled. "It does my heart good to hear that sound. Mayhap more creatures will startle me in future."

The corners of Evan's lips raised, amusement glinting in his eyes. "And I shall save ye from them, lass."

A surge of joy wove through Sorcha's chest, weight lifting from her shoulders now that they had finally arrived at their sanctuary.

Clara's happiness beamed as she and Kester linked arms, and the happiness spread throughout their party.

Marcus burst upon them, wearing a look of confusion. "What goes on here?"

Douglas slapped him on the back. "Aye, lad, we learned that frogs can be most entertaining."

He frowned and stared at Douglas as if he had lost his senses.

"Once we are settled, we will share the tale with ye. Do ye have anything to report?"

The lad shook his head, resting his palms on his bent knees as he regained his breath. "Nae. All is well. I have found nae trace of footprints except for creatures."

A few of the women tittered and shook their heads.

Sorcha went to Marcus. "Pay them nae heed, lad. I am

certain the men shall be glad to tell ye the story of my shame over a fire this eve."

"Aye, lass," Douglas said. "Let us be on our way." He turned to Marcus. "Bring up the rear and watch for followers."

Marcus nodded and ambled to the rear of the line, taking up his post.

Evan took Sorcha's arm and huddled closer. "Are ye rested enough to travel the last bit of our journey?"

"I suppose I could make it nae matter how weary I am." A brief silence hovered between them before she added, "Nothing shall keep me from finally being somewhere safe."

They walked on for a time through the autumn trees.

Sorcha appraised Evan's profile, recognizing a hint of stubbornness in the tilt of his chin. "What troubles ye?" she asked, trying to keep her tone light.

He slanted his gaze, his quiet words chilling her more than the cool air. "Say naught to anyone, yet I am unable to throw off the feel of the Campbells' presence."

Sorcha lowered her voice to match his and glanced over her shoulder. "Why? Have ye seen someone?"

"Nae, 'tis more of a sense." He brought his head close to hers. "I ken Douglas says only Clan Grant is aware of this glen, yet how can this be?"

"It is well hidden."

His eyes held hers for an instant. "Aye, 'tis truth."

"Are we to never be free of them?" Sorcha's spirit fell. What was to be done? Was Evan right to be so worried?

Evan clasped Sorcha's hand in his and brought it to his lips, placing a kiss on her fingers. "God has just given me a plan on how we may protect our new home."

Sorcha brightened. "How so?"

"Mayhap we should discuss it with Douglas and Kester when we break our journey."

Relief spread through Sorcha with the hope revealed in his words. His strong faith deepened her affection for him. Faith and hope were all they had, alongside each other, yet would it be enough?

☙❧

The sun hung high overhead when Douglas halted the group. A small clearing spread in front of them with the forest encircling three sides of the loch. The meadow would be a proper place to build a village. Sorcha imagined a stone cottage nestled near the trees to shelter them from the winter snow. A sudden flash of happy children playing in the meadow, picking flowers, and chasing butterflies crossed her mind, and she wondered if her child would be one of them?

The day faded. Men huddled over a fire at the trees' edge as the women huddled around a fire of their own, preparing the evening meal. The younger men gathered limbs for crude shelters.

Once they gathered for the meal, Douglas was among them, explaining Evan's plan for protection. A rotation of able-bodied men would take their places at the entrance to the glen at the edge of the falls. Upon the first sign of danger, the guard would signal the man stationed in the village to pass on the alert. Their plan was to build a tower among the trees at the edge of the village.

Another safeguard was a platform constructed in a tree above the fall entrance. The guard would release a stockpile of rocks held there on top of the trespassers.

The next day, Sorcha's pride in Evan grew when she heard of his plan. God had surely spoken it to him. She tugged another thread through the material, then brought her gaze up to see him hoist another stone upon the foundation he had built for their cottage.

Though the weather was cold, his shirt was wet from exertion. The way the shirt clung to his muscular arms made her blush, glad she was alone. Clara would not leave her be if she saw her expression.

The bairn moved, taking her thoughts from Evan for the moment. She smiled and patted her stomach.

Aye, the child was soon to arrive. She had made her presence known with more vigor since their arrival in the glen. John's face appeared in her mind, and sadness engulfed her. If only . . .

Her thoughts took her away, and she did not hear Evan's approach until he stood over her.

"Are ye well, lass? Ye appear flushed." Evan bent to retrieve the vessel holding his water and took a long swallow.

"'Tis only the sight of my braw husband."

Evan flushed at the praise and sat beside her. "Do ye truly mean that, Sorcha?"

She looked down at her needlework. "Aye. I do."

Her words appeared to please him, and he sighed with feeling. "I am that glad."

"And I as well, *husband.*"

They avoided one another's eyes—he fumbling with the water and she with a needle, feeling like a lass in the first blush of love.

Clara and Kester made their presence known, dropping to the soft cushion of pine needles.

Clara tittered nervously. "We have a bit of news for ye."

Kester claimed her hand and brought it to his lips. "Aye. Evan. Your sister has agreed to wed me."

Evan sent him a horrified look. "Oh, aye? Did ye nae think to ask her brother for approval?"

Clara paled and looked from Kester to Evan.

Sorcha leaned toward Clara. "He does jest, my friend." She jabbed Evan in the side with her elbow.

"Och! That does pain me, wife!"

Kester laughed and looked at Sorcha. "Do it again, lass. He does deserve it."

Sorcha gazed appreciatively at her husband. "Aye."

Evan rose and punched Kester on the shoulder. "Come and help your brother with his cottage afore I say ye cannot wed my sister."

Kester grunted. "What about *our* cottage?"

"We shall cross that burn when ye wed. For the time being, I need a cottage for my wife and bairn."

Evan and Kester strode away, speaking with brotherly camaraderie.

Sorcha shook her head. "They are like lads who caught the biggest fish or felled the largest deer."

Clara nodded. "Aye. 'Tis a good thing." She looked wistfully after Kester.

"I am happy for ye, Clara. He shall make a fine husband. And ye shall be a pleasing wife and mither."

Clara fumbled with the fabric of her skirt. "I pray it is so."

"If ye shall help me rise, I should like to hug ye, sweet sister. Fear not. Ye shall be perfect."

Once Clara helped Sorcha to stand, she said, "As are ye."

Sorcha prayed Clara was right. She longed to fulfill the role of wife and mother that God had called her to as best as she could. The longing for John was part of her past. She must now look to the future, and not think on Evan's earlier words of how he felt the Campbells were near. Her fervent prayers were for God to allow them to live in peace with His protection surrounding them. There would be no true peace unless he intervened, and all were assured they had truly reached their sanctuary.

Chapter Thirty-One

1710

The history of Muirie's ancestors captured her thoughts. She considered their journey across miles of rugged land, up and down steep slopes hindered by thistles, cold, and wolves, pursued by their enemy.

Gavin's lowered voice, tinged with compassion, pulled Muirie back to her time. "The elders and children must have had a hard way on that path. Being tracked as animals through snow-covered mountains and icy burns."

A pained silence fell between them, reminding Muirie of the mountains their great-grandmother traversed more than one hundred years in the past.

"Sorcha must have been a strong woman to have survived

the journey while with child."

"Aye, she must have. Grannam knows the story as well as *our* Sorcha does. Ye should ask her."

Muirie released a chuckle. "I shall. Though, I doubt I will have to coax her."

"She needs little encouragement to be the center of attention." Gavin touched Muirie's arm. "Shall we find her?"

Muirie studied him, marveling at how alike they were and how she had not noticed. She recalled what Elizabeth said when she caught Muirie staring at Sorcha MacFarlane during dinner. She had told Elizabeth there was something familiar about the woman, and Elizabeth had agreed.

"Ye favor Sorcha," Muirie blurted.

Gavin's brows furrowed. "In truth?"

"It appears the three of us share similarities."

He slanted his head, studying Muirie's face. "I see her in ye as well. Come. Let us find Grannam."

They linked arms and strolled the winding halls searching for Grannam, finding her dozing beside the low fire in the library, an open book on her lap. Beathag also dozed in a chair hidden in the shadows, her hands resting on an unfinished piece of needlework.

Muirie squeezed Gavin's arm and motioned toward her friend. They soundlessly approached Grannam and sat in the chairs beside her. Gavin gently shook her arm.

"'Tis nae time to be abed. Leave me be." She muttered in a sleep-dazed slur, her head lolling against the back of the chair.

Muirie sniggered. "Let us leave her be. We may question

her on the morrow."

Beathag rose with a start. "I am that sorry I slept. Grannam did not sleep well last night."

"'Tis no bother, Beathag. Ye need your rest as well."

The maid yawned and covered her mouth. "Aye. Will the two of ye be staying a bit? I should care to go to the kitchen for a cup of tea to revive me."

"Do so. We shall stay here until ye return." Gavin kept his regard on Grannam, as if willing her to waken.

Beathag took her leave, and Muirie relaxed, her spirit flagging.

"Gavin, were ye serious about going to the Hidden Glen?" She peered at him, still marveling that he was her brother.

"Aye. Would ye care to see it?"

"With all my heart."

He rose and looked down at her. "I will search for Father and determine what actions we can take to make it so."

Muirie twitched. "We were discussing the *possibilities* of such a journey, Gavin. Do ye mean to ask him to go?"

He squinted as if puzzled by her reaction. "Aye. Why should I not?"

"I . . . know not. 'Tis sudden to be sure." She swallowed. Did she truly desire to make the long, demanding journey? Surely there was no way to travel by carriage to such a remote place.

Gavin knelt before her, covering her hand in both of his. "Why should we not go? 'Tis our past we seek to discover."

She stared at him, awed by his determination. Fear and

indecision surged through her. *Did* she want to travel there?

Her smile grew, and she patted his hand. "Aye. 'Tis a wonderful thought."

Gavin kissed her cheek. "I shall seek Father." He sprinted from the chamber, and her heart warmed.

Grannam snorted. "I hope ye include me in your plans, lass."

Muirie jerked at the sound of her voice. "Grannam, ye are incorrigible."

"Aye. And dinnae forget it, lass." The old woman tilted her chin up in defiance. "I hear much when I feign sleep."

Muirie fought the urge to raise her eyes heavenward. "'Tis not seemly for ye to do so."

"Nae." Grannam pursed her lips. "'Tis nae matter. How else do ye expect me to learn of the goings on around me? Ye will not leave me out of traveling to the Hidden Glen. I have longed to see it."

Blowing out an exasperated breath, Muirie knew she must discourage her plan. "Grannam, ye know we desire your company on such a journey. Though, ye must understand it would be a perilous time by way of horseback. 'Tis not a journey for a coach."

The elder woman appeared to consider Muirie's words before she said, "Aye. I ken."

Muirie's compassion nearly crippled her. There was no way the elder woman could sit upon a horse for such a journey.

Grannam's eyes misted with the truth. "Aye, I ken. What I would not give to journey with ye." Her voice held deep regret.

Muirie fought the urge to tell her she could go.

Grannam leaned forward and took Muirie's hands in hers. "Will ye do me a favor, lass?"

Muirie sniffled. "Anything ye desire."

"Fetch a plant for me from the glen. Ye can plant it in the garden at Castle Deveron, so I may look upon it until I go to be with the Lord."

The revelation near undid Muirie, and tears dripped upon their clasped hands. "I am honored to do so, Grannam."

⋘⋙

A cool, misty morning dawned once the horses were ready for the ride to the Hidden Glen. Muirie's heart pounded at the thought of the long journey to the western Highlands.

Muirie and Beathag hung apart from the others, sharing a final farewell. "I will miss ye, Muirie." She gripped Muirie into a fierce hug and released her. "Do not forget me."

"Oh, Beathag. We will not be gone long. Mayhap seven nights." She lowered her voice. "And then we will journey home to Cormac."

Beathag cast her gaze to the ground. "Aye. Then we part forever."

"Oh, my dear. No. Though we may not see one another on this earth, we shall be together forever in our heavenly home if ye seek Him."

She planted her fisted hands on her hips and cocked her head, giving Muirie a glare. "Are ye going to preach to me now?"

Muirie cupped Beathag's shoulders, peering deep into her

eyes. "No. Ye are to wed Cormac, and bairns will follow. Promise me ye will raise them to love the Lord. That ye and Cormac will turn to Him as well and make things right for eternity."

Beathag seemed to consider Muirie's words, the air releasing with a huff. She spoke low. "Aye. Being married to Cormac will make my heart soar as we begin our lives together in the Colonies."

"Muirie!" Lord Stewart waved to her. "Come, lass. We are burning the light."

"We are sisters. Remember that." Muirie gave her a final hug and rushed to her horse.

Elizabeth eagerly mounted her stead, prepared for an adventure. Gavin assisted Muirie upon a white Eriskay Pony with Sorcha and her husband at the ready, followed by Peader, Lord Stewart, and two servants attending them.

At the end of the line, Gavin's horse neighed as he urged the steed to move between Muirie and Elizabeth. "Sisters, I shall be your protector from the fierce Redcoats." He withdrew his sword, twirling it above, his horse rising to the excitement in Gavin's voice, front hooves pawing the air.

Muirie laughed as Elizabeth reprimanded him. "Gavin! Do not be so fool-like. We would not have ye crack your brainbox and ruin our travels."

"Ye wound me, sister." He returned the sword to the sheath and brought a hand to his chest. "Ye think me unworthy to defend your honor?" He feigned hurt, and Muirie saw one side of his mouth twitch.

Lord Stewart's voice boomed over the farewells of those

watching them depart and extended his arm high, waving them onward.

Though Muirie longed to see the Hidden Glen, she would miss her family. She waved to them, including Grannam, who moved to stand beside Beathag. Her heart swelled that Cormac and Beathag would soon be together, glad he was doing the honorable thing.

Of a sudden, she realized God had more than answered her prayers for them. Mayhap He would for she and Reid as well. She pictured him as if he stood before her, hair falling across his forehead, and she longed to brush it back and share her feelings. If only he would return.

Her thoughts remained with Reid while Sorcha and Gavin passed words across her as she rode between them, the aromatic scent of pine hovering overhead. After what seemed an endless barrage of quips, they reached the edge of the village of Tomatin and the old stone inn where they would stop for the night.

Gold, violet, and blue radiated on the horizon, sending warmth through Muirie. God had granted them a safe journey thus far, though she ached from the bruising ride. Mayhap the inn would supply them with food and rest.

Lord Stewart bade them not to dismount until he sought within the inn. He returned in short order, wearing a wide smile. "'Tis well. Though they only have one chamber to let." He dipped his head toward Muirie, Sorcha, and Elizabeth. "Lasses, ye take the chamber, and the men will sleep in the stables."

Gavin helped Elizabeth down, and she groaned once her feet landed on the rocky ground. "Oh, how I ache." She rocked on her heels until Gavin steadied her. "Bath, bannocks, and bed for me."

Gavin chuckled. "Ye do have a way with words. Are ye becoming a poet?"

She slapped his arm and groaned with the effort. "Go away. I am too weary to quarrel with ye."

Muirie threw her leg over the saddle, slid to the ground, and grunted with the effort. "I feel much as Elizabeth does." She yawned, looking at the sunset, now ablaze with many colors.

"Go inside, and I shall take the horses to my bedchamber." Gavin laughed at his own joke.

Muirie leaned against the warmth of her horse's side. "At present, I would be joyful to be in the stables and fall onto a soft mattress of hay and sleep."

Elizabeth nodded. "Me as well." She stiffened briefly. "I cannot credit I said as much, 'tis truth. This is indeed a quest."

"Aye," Muirie said. "A rough one."

Gavin sighed with exaggerated impatience. "*Women.* Ye have no sense of adventure."

"I can truthfully say that adventure should not be so *painful.*" Elizabeth took slow, measured steps toward the inn, low moans escaping with each one.

The aroma of stew met Muirie's nose, and her stomach commented loud enough to elicit a chuckle from Gavin.

"Food has now taken first place in our evening plans. Do ye think not?"

Muirie smirked. "Aye, food is desired. Although, a bath

would not go remiss." Luxuriating in a tub of hot, lavender-scented water would be akin to heaven in that moment.

Sorcha walked up with a smile. "Agreed. I picture myself taking a bath with a bannock in each hand. Would that suit?"

With a laugh, Muirie threw an arm around Sorcha. "It shall. Let us see if there are any baths and bannocks to be had here." She led Sorcha toward the inn followed by Gavin, still in awe that she had a sister and a brother.

⚜

Muirie awakened and groaned, her body ached with each move. If only she could remain there for a few days to recover from their first day of travel. She had never traveled so far beyond Castle Deveron on horseback. How could she have known how arduous the journey would be?

A whimper echoed in the small chamber, and when she turned, she found Elizabeth huddled on the cot with her head beneath a pillow.

"Extinguish the sun and allow me to sleep." Elizabeth moaned pitifully. "Every part of my body pains me."

Muirie pulled in a long breath. "Yet we must press on. Mayhap we shall grow accustomed to the strain." She prayed that was so.

"Oh, Muirie. I *hurt*."

"As do I." Muirie rolled off the bed, standing on shaky legs. "I shall see if we may request a bath."

"That would be wonderful. Thank ye." Elizabeth eased the pillow away, gaze scanning the room. "Where is Sorcha?"

"I shall see, yet I assume she rose earlier to break her fast with her husband." Muirie dressed as quickly as she was able and went downstairs.

Peader sat in the narrow dining chamber, a bowl of porridge and a steaming cup before him. "Good morn, Muirie. Did ye rest well?"

"Good morn, Peader. I assume so."

His pleasant smile eased her aching for a moment.

"Where are the others?"

Peader glanced toward the door. "Lord Stewart is assisting Gavin and the servants with readying our horses. He said we have already burned too much of the day."

Muirie sighed. "Truly? Elizabeth and I hoped to bathe."

"Aye." His eyes held sympathy. "Sorry, I am."

"She will not be pleased."

His expression changed, and he returned his spoon to the bowl. "Leave it with me, lass." He bolted from the chamber.

Through the window overlooking the courtyard, Peader stood before Lord Stewart, his lips moving rapidly, arms waving.

Lord Stewart's face colored, then immediately calmed to one of concern, and he nodded.

Peader brightened and rushed toward the innkeeper, who strode across the yard toward the inn. They spoke for a few moments, and finally the innkeeper nodded, a slight smile on his lips as Peader handed him something. Peader dashed to the well and began drawing water, placing the wooden bucket aside and replacing it with an empty one.

He grabbed a full bucket in each hand and walked toward

the inn where the innkeeper waited, holding the kitchen door open.

Shuffling noises and voices brought her attention to the staircase, and she turned to see two servants carrying a small metal tub up the stairs. She followed and found they stopped at her door, Elizabeth standing wide-eyed in the opening.

Elizabeth clasped her hands under her chin. "How lovely! Thank ye." The young men blushed at the attention and took the tub into the chamber, then laid a fire.

Once they left, Muirie entered just as Peader arrived with two buckets of steaming water and poured them into the tub. He said nothing as Elizabeth watched him complete the task.

"Peader." Elizabeth rushed to him and kissed him on each cheek. "I am forever in your debt."

He swallowed hard, his cheeks flaming as he backed from the chamber. He muttered a "thank ye" before leaving.

Elizabeth sighed. "Is he not a dear?"

"He is that—and more, Elizabeth."

Muirie turned to go. "Enjoy your bath. I will return later."

"Will ye not bathe as well?" Elizabeth knelt before the tub, one hand waving through the water.

"Aye. When ye finish, I will have it emptied and bring more water. She eased the door closed behind her and said, "Bolt the door." The last thing she heard was Elizabeth's laughter.

She took the stairs carefully, still aching, the aroma of coffee meeting her. Gavin sat at a table by the window, eating a bannock and holding a steaming cup.

"Did ye save some for me, brother?"

His mouth quirked upward. "Aye." He rose, and before she could speak again, he left the room and returned with a pretty, plump girl on his heels.

"Ye may have whatever you wish."

Once she told the girl, she sat facing Gavin and surveyed the chamber. Dark beams hung overhead with a few lanterns placed throughout to lighten the grey, foggy morning. The small inn was dark, clean, and welcoming. Inns were rare in the Highlands, or so she had been told, and this resting place was unexpected and pleasant.

"Do ye ken what Peader did for Elizabeth?"

He lifted his gaze, mouth full of porridge. Shaking his head, he swallowed and took a sip of coffee. "No. Is there something I should ken about it?"

"No. Yet I judge there lies something between them. Do ye have a problem with your sister and Peader forming an understanding?"

His smile told Muirie all she needed to know. "So ye like Peader?"

"Aye. He is more than able to meet her needs."

Her eyebrows rose. "Truly. How so?"

He leaned in conspiratorially. "He is the eldest son of a duke."

Muirie reared back as if struck, mouth agape. "He is?"

"Aye." He kept eating, his eyes on Muirie. "Why are ye so shocked?"

"Well—he is—so quiet, and his manner of dress is simple."

The memory of Elizabeth and Peader hand-in-hand fleeing

into the woods to attend to Grannam reminded her of the companionship they shared that day. It genuinely appeared Elizabeth was drawn to Peader in spite of his lack of fashionable attire and aristocratic bearing.

Gavin said, "I see by that look ye now ken the reason for their attachment."

"Will your parents consent?"

"I believe so."

"'Tis good. They seem well suited."

He studied her for a moment. "As I judge ye and Reid to be so."

Her heart thudded. "Why would ye say such a thing? We barely know one another. He left so quickly, we had not a chance—"

He cut her off. "Muirie. I have eyes."

"And what did your *eyes* see, pray tell?" She held her breath, feeling fear and expectation in equal measure.

"Remember the day of our adventure? Reid was jealous of me and said, well . . ." His roguish smile toyed with her.

The exchange between Gavin and Reid returned to her. They were at the beach and Reid had grown angry over something. Later, Gavin told her about their talk. How could she have forgotten? Hope grew in her very spirit.

Mayhap Reid did care for her as she did for him.

Chapter Thirty-Two

November 1603

Sorcha warmed her hands over the small fireplace before she stirred the iron pot of root vegetables Douglas had brought. The aroma of venison mixed with his offering made her stomach growl, and the bairn shifted. Her time was nigh, and her prayers grew more frequent.

The cottage had one small chamber, Evan promising it would grow once winter's snow departed. Sorcha recalled the day he laid the last stone. The fatigue etched in his features still stabbed at her conscience. In her condition, she could not aid him, and the other men were busy with their own dwellings. Douglas helped by building a cottage for the widows and their children.

Sorcha stirred the porridge, then straightened her aching

back. She knew her time was near—a wee bit past—or else she had lost all sense of time since they left Loch Lomond. Their arrival the first of November—or was it October?

Och—what difference did it matter? They were safe.

The roughhewn door creaked a protest as it opened, and Evan strode in. He closed the door and paused, his regard intent on her.

His eyes twinkling with mischief, he asked, "Are ye well, lass?"

Her hand still on the small of her back, she half turned to stir the contents of the pot again. "Aye. Mayhap a wee bit weary, nae more." Her tone did not sound convincing to her own ears.

Evan's smile faded, and he crossed the space in three long strides, placed an arm around her waist, and guided her onto a low stool.

"Sit and rest." He went to the door and retrieved a plaid draped over one of the pegs in the wall and returned to Sorcha, wrapping the long fabric around her shoulders, allowing the extra length to drape over her lap.

"Evan, I have work to do." She made to rise, and he pressed her down with a hand upon her shoulder.

"Nae, lass. Ye must rest." Evan studied her, his gaze softening. "I have a small gift for ye. Close your eyes."

After a brief hesitation, Sorcha did as he asked, a smile tickling her lips. Several objects landed in her lap, and she lifted her lids. Hazelnuts were spread across the plaid.

Evan crouched in front of her and stirred the smooth, brown nuts with his forefinger. "I scoured the forest and chanced upon a hazel tree with branches out of reach of the deer and harvested these for ye.”

Sorcha rolled them around with the tips of her fingers, keeping her gaze on his offering. “Ye are most thoughtful.” She dragged in a breath. “I wish I had something of worth to give ye in return.”

He stilled her hands with his. “Ye give me much . . .”

“Aye, meals and such.” She chuckled. “If only I could do more for ye.”

“There is nae more ye could do . . .” His voice trailed off, his hold tightening on her hands. “Yet—I would have ye look upon me just once the way ye looked upon John.”

Sorcha’s breath hitched. She lifted her gaze to see the muscle in his throat move in a hard swallow, and in his eyes, she glimpsed regret.

Evan released her hands. “I am sorry, lass. I should not have asked it of ye.”

He made to rise, and she grabbed his hands and murmured, “I shall, Evan. While my love for ye is not the same as my love for John, I love ye just as strongly.” She sighed. “Yet it is a different love.”

Evan rose, pulling her up with him and into his embrace, hazelnuts scattering to the floor. He rested his chin gently upon her head. “I ken.”

Sorcha wrapped her arms around his waist as best she could without pressing too much against the babe.

Yet a rough kick jabbed Evan’s stomach, and he laughed. “It appears our daughter is jealous.”

Our daughter . . .

"Or she is ready to meet her family," Sorcha said, tears mingling with her words. For so long, she had thought of the child not having a father with John gone. Yet now as Evan spoke of their daughter with such affection, the thought of him as the child's father comforted her. God had brought Evan to them both.

Evan caressed her cheek with such tenderness, and she rose on her toes to bring her lips to his, trying to convey her growing feelings. He met her kiss in equal measure, and after several moments, he released her, both of them breathless.

"Lass, I—"

His words stopped as she cried out, a splitting pain ripping through her insides.

Evan's expression hardened. "Did she hurt ye?"

"Nae," Sorcha ground out between clenched teeth. "Nae," she repeated, doubling over, hands cradling her stomach. "Fetch Clara and Mistress Gibbs." She moaned. "Now!"

His hesitation, though brief, confused Sorcha until she recognized the fear in his eyes. He did not want to leave her alone—though he must to find help. He jerked the door open with force, and to their surprise, Clara entered with Kester on her heels.

"I hear ye scream, Sorcha. 'Tis time for the bairn to come?"

Sorcha nodded with a grimace, a lessened pain rolling through her. "I am certain the entire village did so."

Clara tittered. "Aye. Now everyone shall know your child is coming. 'Tis a good day." She hung her cloak on a peg by the door and approached Sorcha, easing her onto the stool. She turned to the men. "Fetch Mistress Gibbs. Both of ye bring water from the burn." They rushed out at her command.

Noticing the discarded plaid, Clara took it and wrapped it around Sorcha much the same as her brother had before. "All will be well, my friend."

"Aye." Hot, bitter tears caught Sorcha unawares. Did she truly believe it would be well?

This bairn was the only one she had kept this long. The others had not grown past a few weeks. The old, resentful emotions returned. Why could John nae have lived to see his child? 'Twas not fair.

Ye have Evan now, my child.

Sorcha startled and looked up to find Clara across the chamber, preparing the bed. "What did ye say?"

The woman twisted to stare at her, concern wrinkling her brow. "I said naught."

Sorcha's heart stilled, knowing it must be God calming her spirit.

The door burst open with Evan and Mistress Gibbs rushing inside. Sorcha met Evan's gaze, God's assurance mingling with the steadiness of this man who was now her husband, and she released her fear to God. No matter what happened all would be well because *God* was with them.

◌◌◌

The baby cooed as Sorcha put aside her needlework and leaned to rock the cradle Evan had so lovingly built for their daughter, Ursula. She was a bonny wee lass, hair the color of an early sunrise.

Sorcha ruffled the downy mass of curls and leaned closer

to kiss her beloved daughter's head.

"Now, is that not a bonny sight?"

Her head jerked up to see Evan smiling in the doorway. "Are ye now sneaking up on me, husband?"

Evan strode across the chamber and crouched beside the cradle, taking Sorcha's hand in his. "Did ye not hear the door, lass? For a time, I have been watching ye and our sweet babe."

Sorcha chuckled. "I suppose my attention was much taken by her."

"Aye." Hope flared in his gaze. "Mayhap ye shall one day be so with me."

Ursula released a cry, and Evan carefully gathered her in his arms and rested her head against his shoulder. He paced, rubbing her back in reassurance as he whispered words of comfort.

Sorcha marveled at how well Evan settled into fatherhood. Was she ready for him to truly be her husband? The thought both frightened and pleased her.

Heat warmed her cheeks, so she did not reply, busying herself with straightening the blanket in the cradle.

As Evan walked in circles around the cottage with Ursula, Sorcha occupied herself with preparing their evening meal. She did not push herself too far, her strength returning little by little each day.

Clara visited often to help, and Sorcha had to shoo her away, reassuring her sister-in-law she could now care for her bairn and husband, reminding her of the wedding soon to come for her and Kester. Though Clara's gaze had dropped to the floor, she could not hide her wide smile.

Sorcha stirred the pottage, her mind on the upcoming nuptials. She could not be more joyful for the couple. They deserved much happiness.

Evan whispered, "What has seized your thoughts?"

She turned to find him returning a slumbering Ursula to her cradle. She set the ladle aside and chuckled. "How Clara insists upon coming here each day to tend to us even though my vigor returns—though slowly. She needs to think of her wedding and new home."

He came to her side and wrapped his arms about her, tucking her head under his chin. "My sister is the kindest of lasses. She longs to feel needed."

Sorcha nestled her head against his neck. "As does her brother."

Evan took her shoulders and eased her a few inches from him. "Do ye think I be so needful?"

The hurt in his eyes tugged at her spirit.

"Nae. 'Tis . . ." The right words struggled to be found. "I meant ye need to love—just as everyone has wont."

He studied her, perhaps searching out the truth of the words.

"I dinnae mean to displease ye. Ye know I love ye, Evan." She cupped his cheek in her palm and lifted on her toes to press a kiss to his lips. "'Tis nae small thing to love—truly love."

His nod was slight, eyes shining with genuine affection. "Ye have already revealed that, my dear." He nuzzled her neck, all misunderstandings gone. "I shall nae more doubt ye."

Ursula made herself known with a whimper, and Evan

released Sorcha to go to the child, but she stayed him. "'Tis time for her feeding. I shall attend to her whilst ye go to your evening duties. We shall eat once ye return, and the rest of the night is ours."

"Glad I am the child now sleeps long and hard." He raised his eyebrows, eliciting a chuckle from his wife.

She shoved his shoulder. "Go on with your braw self."

He shot a playful grin over his shoulder as he closed the door behind him.

Sorcha fed Ursula, gazing at her precious face, so alert and inquisitive, searching her mother's.

"Aye, are ye not a bonny, bonny lass, my sweet? Your father would love ye like nae other." A stab of regret hit her, and she recanted. "Except for Evan. He is your father now, my love, and he shall always take good care of us. Ye can be sure of that."

Having taken her fill, Ursula's eyes grew heavy, and Sorcha brought the downy head to her lips before returning her daughter to the cradle. Checking their meal, she found it to be done and set it to the side of the hearth to keep warm until Evan's return.

Once she tidied the cottage, she sat by the fire and stitched upon the panels as her mother had taught her. The one she now worked was of the hidden glen where she hoped they would be safe until the outside world became a kinder place for MacGregors.

That I may come unto ye with joy by the will of God and may with ye be refreshed. The scripture came to her mind. Strengthened by the recall, she thanked God and prayed for

His protection over not only her family but the entire clan.

⁂

Sorcha looked out onto the early December morning that dawned bright, though a light snow during the night added another layer to what had fallen since late October. All those who fled after the Battle of Glen Fruin to the north were now assembled under a crude shelter built as the beginnings of their kirk. Once the winter faded into spring, they would add the walls.

She leaned against Evan, who held Ursula shielded in layers of blankets against the cold. With her arm looped through Evan's, Sorcha had never felt more loved and cared for. At this moment, as she watched Clara and Kester marry, the tapestry was complete. She hoped, believed, there would be other such happy scenes to add through her needlework. Her mind shifted to the panel of losing John on the battlefield, which seemed an age ago yet was mere months in the past.

The ceremony finished, they returned to their *village*, where all the cottages were clustered together at the edge of the forest.

Huddled around a crackling bonfire, Marcus played the fiddle, and voices rang out in song and laughter while some danced and partook of the feast. Sorcha took in the merriment, unable to smother her smile, her heart full of gratitude for God's deliverance and protection and the love that surrounded her.

As the days moved past from the wedding into Christmas tidings and then to spring, Sorcha looked upon all with more joy than she thought possible.

Ursula now sat without toppling over, and Evan was ever at her side, encouraging her, comforting her when she fell.

One warm day by the loch, Sorcha sat on a blanket and minded Ursula playing with a wooden toy Evan had formed from a carefully smoothed block of wood. The child kept bringing the block to her mouth, and Sorcha would replace it with a teething bannock.

"There ye go, my chippie-burdie." Sorcha patted Ursula's head and returned to her needlework, her gaze watchful of the child from the corner of her eye.

Men's voices drifted on the breeze, and she looked up to see Evan and Douglas striding toward them. She lowered the needlework to her lap and greeted them with a smile.

"What brings ye from your work? Is the kirk complete?"

Both men stood over her wearing a troubled expression. Evan's eyes slanted toward Ursula.

Sorcha swallowed hard, her stomach knotting with worry. "Ye have poor news to share?"

Evan knelt beside Ursula as Douglas crouched at the edge of the blanket and cleared his throat.

"News from Edinburgh." His gaze went out over the loch, a crease on his brow. "It has taken some months for the news to reach us." He swallowed. "'Twas in January, three months' gone, that Allaster and eighteen other MacGregors were sentenced to die."

Sorcha slumped forward, her needlework crumpling in her tightened fists. Disbelief gripped her, and she shook her head. "How can that be?"

With the bannock in his hand, Evan teased Ursula by

holding it barely out of her reach, and she cooed when he allowed her to retrieve it. "'Tis truth, Sorcha. The Campbells now have what they have wished for all these years." His tone held more than remorse, his shoulders sagging from the weight of grief.

"By murdering most of Clan Gregor?" Her voice held ice and grew colder with each word. "They now hold our lands and have convinced King James to ban our very name."

Douglas stood. "Aye, lass. They have. We must pray God keeps us safe."

She looked up at him, a long-held question returning to her. "Why do ye aid us?" Her gaze swung to Evan. "Neither of ye are MacGregors. Ye are not banned nor hunted."

Evan looked at her, determination and protectiveness flashing in his grey eyes. "Lass, ye ken I have been bound to the MacGregors since John and I were childer. Our clans are allied, and we grew up together." He caressed Ursula's cheek, then reached for Sorcha's hand, squeezing it, affection in his gaze upon her. "And now ye are my wife. Ye are my family, and I am more strongly bound than afore."

Douglas sucked in a breath. "And I because of Maidie. From the moment I saw her bonny face, my heart was tied to hers."

Peace filled Sorcha at their declarations. She knew they spoke truth, and she trusted them above all. Her heart broke for John, Allaster, and the others who had lost their lives at the hand of men who would see the blood spilled of fellow Scots. Those of their clan remaining had a purpose on this earth. Those who had died that belonged to Christ were now home.

Sorcha glanced down at the tapestry, her focus on the threads and colors mingling upon the cloth, the scene preserved, and knew she had a story to tell for Ursula and future generations. A true story of their people's history and their hope in the midst of fear and uncertainty—a history of faith woven in the mist.

Chapter Thirty-Three

1710

The morning of the third day of their journey marked their final ascent into the Hidden Glen. Muirie peered upward and wondered how they would scale such a height. The path ahead disappeared among underbrush and tangled vines, the earthy scent of foliage, earth, and moss strong in the crisp air. She strained to see past the men riding in front of her and discovered Lord Stewart twisted in his saddle, gazing at her.

"No need to worry, lass. I ken the way." He slowed his mount until they rode side by side.

"*Ye?* How came ye to know the way?"

Lord Stewart smiled, his eyes crinkling at the corners. "When I was a lad, my father brought me here." A calm passed over him as if remembering the time long past.

"Few know of its existence. 'Tis a secret, though many have tried to discover it. The knowledge has been well guarded, and rightly so, considering the return of the proscription the year of your birth."

Muirie brought her gaze to each person. "And all here are to be trusted?"

"All here are trustworthy." He patted her arm. "Fear not. The MacGregors will not be overcome."

A servant whistled a bird call, bringing Lord Stewart's attention ahead. "We are near the entrance. I must secure it. Stay close to the men." As he trotted past Elizabeth and Sorcha, he spoke in passing, which Muirie assumed to be the same instruction.

Muirie whispered to Gavin. "I wonder they do not have guards posted to keep others from entering."

Gavin nodded. "A splendid question to ask Lord Stewart."

The two women paused, waiting for Muirie to join them, Peader, Sorcha's husband, and a servant following.

A stone bridge appeared among the forest, the trees thickening at the far edge as they descended. Muirie's gaze traveled up the brae, small spots of sky peeping through the trees.

Lord Stewart addressed the group in a low voice, "We have arrived. Though the way is narrow and dark, we must be silent. With the current proscription, we must further keep this secret. Now, dismount and lead your horses forward. Have a care. The way is slippery."

Among the thick shade of the forest, the scent of moist moss and the resonance of a rushing waterfall brought Muirie a sense of peace, despite the possibility of danger.

A narrow shaft of sunlight sliced through the trees and glinted off the water of a wide burn. The path led them alongside the brae, soon becoming encrusted with earth and stone, the roar of the waterfall growing closer. Someone whispered a warning to cover their heads, and it echoed down the line. Muirie did as told, and a fine mist soon bathed her face. Suddenly, they passed beneath the falls.

Before long, the splash faded, and darkness cloaked them. Muirie tightened her grip on the horse's reins. She bravely fought the rising fear, aware that protection surrounded her. She stretched her arm until her hand contacted with damp stone. The low whinny of horses, their hooves reverberating against the stone beneath them, and the low mutterings of voices soon calmed her.

Rushing water returned with dim light shining on the path ahead. Muirie tugged her hood more securely to cover her as the spew of water intensified. Her horse side-stepped the pouring downfall of glistening water, the view ahead obscured. Once she and those following emerged, those ahead of them stood alongside the mouth of the tunnel, their gazes on the valley before them.

Muirie paused and stared at the overwhelming scope of the valley. Its visage like a dream. A loch glowed with sunlight reflecting on the calm water, mirroring the blue sky, birds floating above, and the green forest bordering its shore. Jagged rocks and cliffs with perilous drops kept this beautiful paradise secret from prying intruders, the only way in or out concealed behind the falls.

A horse sidled next to Muirie's. "'Tis a wondrous sight."

Gavin sighed and dipped his gaze. "The path down is a bit fearful though."

Muirie refused to look, pushing aside her distress of heights. The incredible sight of what her great-grandmother had seen so many years before, gripped her emotions. Was this what her ancestor experienced? Or was the overpowering fear of protecting her bairn uppermost in her mind above all else? The panel scenes she finally saw revealed her great-grandmother, Sorcha, heavy with child entering the valley.

Gavin took her hand in his. "I know not how to understand what our great-grandmother felt when she stood here as we are. Can ye imagine?"

"No. I cannot. The distress must have been overpowering. She knew not what the future held." Muirie blinked away tears. "It saddens me to think of it." She squeezed Gavin's hand and turned to him. "I am glad to have my brother and sister by my side whilst we share this moment."

Sorcha brought her mount to stand beside Muirie. "Aye. I wish all our brothers and sisters could be here as well."

Muirie and Gavin's questioning gazes were upon her.

Sorcha smiled. "Aye. Though they are much older than we, I am certain they look forward to greeting ye—though ye are bairns to them." Her mouth widened. "Mayhap ye may come visit and meet them all?"

Muirie's heart swelled as she shared a knowing look with Gavin. "Aye, we would love to meet them."

❧

The descent to the Hidden Glen held a touch of fear for Muirie at the sight of the steep path, yet a sensation of rising joy welled within her. What lay before them was the beautiful loch surrounded by stone cottages bordering the water, smoke rising from a handful of dwellings. Some lay in ruins while men repaired others.

Muirie moved to stand beside Lord Stewart. "Why were we not stopped by guards before entering?"

A corner of his mouth lifted. "They are well hidden. We share signals to reveal who we are."

Muirie nodded her understanding, amazed at the slyness of keeping so great a secret. She swayed with the movement of her horse, the scent of smoldering fires and baking bread thick in the mountain air. "Why are so many cottages crumbling?"

"Some left the glen, folding to the crown's demands to take on another name, so they would not be punished. They feared for their families." Lord Stewart's expression slackened. "I hold no ill will toward them. I may do the same if it meant my family could live in peace." With resignation in his tone, he said, "'Twas a sad day when King James decreed the name MacGregor banned."

"Aye." Sorcha agreed. "*And* when King William reimposed it, all feared as we tried to hide your birth, so ye would not be taken from us. Our mither died with your protection upon her lips. She asked that we take ye to safety afore the king's men discovered ye."

Soft weeping brought Muirie, Sorcha, and Lord Stewart's attention to Elizabeth. She rode beside Gavin, whose face held deep sorrow.

Once they broke clear of the trees, the sight of a cottage

standing under the shelter of a copse of Scots pine grabbed Muirie's attention. Flashing before her was the needlework panel with the woman and a bairn perched in front of a cottage, the woman waving at a man near the loch.

Muirie lifted her arm and pointed. "I would like to go to that cottage."

Gavin shot her a questioning look, peering at the place she gestured, then back at her. Understanding dawned in his eyes, and he nodded. "Aye."

Lord Stewart trotted ahead and led them to the place they sought, a tall man standing in front, chopping wood. He appeared to be older than Sorcha, and he lifted his arm in greeting. "Good day."

Gavin dipped his chin, saying nothing, allowing Lord Stewart to lead. "Good day, sir. We wish ye no ill." He gestured toward Gavin, Sorcha, Elizabeth, and Muirie. "We would care to speak to anyone who knows of Ursula MacGregor or Annot, her daughter."

The man seemed to consider whether to answer Lord Stewart's inquiry or remain silent. He studied each of their faces before answering, his gaze intent on Sorcha.

"Ye do appear much like me father, Iain MacGregor."

Sorcha stiffened. "Did he have a sister, Annot?"

He slanted his head. "Aye."

"'Twas my mither." She sniffed, her eyes clouding. "I did not know she had an elder brother."

Their gazes held one another's for a long moment, then his smile widened. He strode to the horse, reached up to take hold of Sorcha's waist, and swung her to the ground.

"'Tis a long while since I have seen any kin. Ye are welcome here." He picked her up and swung her around, hugging her close to his chest.

With a burst of energy, Muirie quickly dismounted and rushed toward them. "I am your cousin, as this is my sister. What is your name?"

"Iain Allaster MacGregor, after me great-grandda and his brother, my great-uncle, Allaster." He pulled Muirie into his grasp alongside Sorcha, his voice roaring with merriment. "What a grand day 'tis!"

Gavin joined them, watching the joy play out. Muirie stretched her arm and gripped his sleeve, pulling him close. "This is our brother, Gavin."

"'Tis too much! I have found kin I dared not imagine lived. Where came ye from?"

Muirie's eyes found Lord Stewart's. From his mount, his eyes twinkled with happiness as he took in their reunion.

The man looked up at Lord Stewart, face glowing.

The air stilled around them, Sorcha stepping back. "Ye were named after our ancestor, clan chief of the MacGregor's who died in Edinburgh so many years afore."

He paled. "Aye. I ken. 'Twas a sad day he and eleven other MacGregors' hanged for no good reason."

"Though 'twas more than a hundred years afore, it still stabs the heart." Sorcha hung her head and breathed deeply. "And to think the new king reestablished the ban only seven and ten years ago."

Iain peered at Muirie and Gavin. "The two of ye look no more than that. Be that why ye have come?"

Gavin nodded. "Aye. Muirie is my twin—we were born the year of the renewed proscription, our sister, Sorcha—" He placed a hand on her shoulder. "—secreted us into the houses of trusted guardians to keep us safe. We come of age this year and have just learned of our heritage. We wanted to come here and see where it all began."

Iain tilted his head. "I ken." He pivoted and pointed to the cottage behind them. "This is the home Evan MacDonald built for his wife, Sorcha MacGregor. She was the wife of John MacGregor who died at Glen Fruin—the brother of the Clan Gregor's chief."

The tranquility of the glen settled around them, a moment of quiet reverence permeating the air.

"We are safe for the now," Iain said. "Yet we know not how long will be afore the king's men will discover us."

Voices murmured, and Muirie noticed for the first time a crowd surrounded them, their faces strained with worry. She swallowed the hard lump in her throat and fretted over these people—her people. What would they do if discovered?

Her mind traced back one hundred years, recalling how her clan had been treated, and now it seemed history would repeat itself. How were they to endure? She prayed to God to wrap his protection around them. They only wanted to live in peace. Why were men so cruel? Why could they not leave others be and content themselves with what they had?

Oh, dear Lord, please place Your hand of protection on this place—on these people.

಼

The stay in the Hidden Glen was much too brief to suit Muirie.

She and her brother lodged in the cottage of their great-grandmother and soaked in their history—the history of her and her husband Evan living their remaining days together. Although Evan was not of their blood, from what Iain and Sorcha said of him, he was a godly father to Sorcha's first child—their grandmother, Ursula.

Muirie said her final goodbye to Iain and the others who had shown them sincere hospitality for two days. Now 'twas time to leave. They promised to return one day, though these *children of the mist*, as they were once called while being hunted down like dangerous wild animals not so very long ago, knew they could not safely leave the valley.

Word would spread throughout the remaining MacGregor clan to stay hidden or else bow to the king's demands and forfeit their heritage, never to speak of it again.

Departing on a sad note, the small party trudged up the mountain to the hidden opening that they must, at all costs, hold the secret close to their hearts.

Tied to her saddle was a small sweet-gale plant wrapped in rough sacking. A woman in the glen suggested it would be a goodly gift to take to Grannam. Something that would thrive in a part of Castle Deveron's garden close to the river.

They left just after sunset, and once their scout returned to be certain there was no one lurking about, they passed through and traveled a different path to Freuchie Castle. The silence hung in the night, with only the sounds of the owls and other creatures of the dark rustling about. No moon revealed their way. A rushing burn roaring alongside masked the sound of the horses' hooves scraping the rocky earth.

Lord Stewart knew of a sheltering wood where they rested,

watching the orange-gold glow of the sunrise greeting them. Peader and Gavin sat apart from them, their heads bent together in earnest conversation.

Sorcha looped an arm around Muirie's shoulders. "Our time together is near over. It does sadden me."

Sorcha cocked her head and pursed her lips. "Ye will come to visit me, will ye not?"

The smile she gave her sister fueled a warmth that radiated through her chest. "Ye cannot keep me away."

They hugged, and Sorcha walked toward her husband.

Elizabeth strode to them just as Gavin and Peader arrived. Gavin said, "Lord Stewart says we must ride while 'tis still early."

Elizabeth's heavy sigh was just the humor they needed to break the long, sorrowful silence. "My bones have all come undone from the jostling beast I ride. May we not sleep here for a bit?"

Peader inched his way closer to her and said something in her ear, eliciting a titter, and she nodded. The two left and led their horses from their nearby grazing to drink from the burn.

Lord Stewart and two servants ambled to them, reins in hand. They paused and one horse neighed. "We must be off." They made their way to the burn and allowed their mounts to drink with Elizabeth and Peader's.

Gavin took Muirie's hand and helped her rise from the makeshift seat on the fallen tree. He glanced over his shoulder and whispered, "Does it appear that my sister and Peader may have formed an understanding on our journey?"

Muirie smiled as they retrieved their horses and mounted,

ready for the tiring trip.

They acquiesced to Lord Stewart and his rush to return to Freuchie Castle and then to Castle Deveron. Muirie hoped he did not intend to leave the day after their arrival at Freuchie.

The remainder of their journey was thankfully uneventful, and the overly warm greeting they received at the castle shamed Muirie for her grumbling on their hurried trip. Yet the idea of another long ride—at least it would be in a carriage this time—made her temple throb.

Lady Stewart and Grannam welcomed them with hugs and kisses on the cheek. Lady Stewart looped her arm through her husband's, her glowing expression revealing the bairn must no longer trouble her fortitude.

Grannam was all smiles and twinkling eyes. "Are ye ready to go home, my dear? We leave on the morrow—or so Lord Stewart says."

Muirie pasted on a wide smile—though she felt far from glad.

Gavin approached and studied Muirie's expression. "What ails ye?"

She lifted her chin. "Nothing."

"There is *something*."

While the evening brought Muirie joy to be with more family and friends, it taxed her remaining strength. She excused herself and retired, finding Beathag coming down the corridor toward their chamber.

"I have Grannam settled. The festivities have worn her, and she wants to be well rested for the journey home."

Muirie's shoulders slumped. "Aye. I am that weary and

hoped Lord Stewart would delay our trip for one day."

Beathag took Muirie's hand, and they strode into the chamber and readied for bed.

"Mayhap the warm bath I took upon our arrival stole some of my strength." Muirie slid beneath the bed coverings and released a long, exhausted sigh.

Beathag's face lit with happiness. "Well, I am most anxious to be home."

Muirie rolled to her side and watched her friend get into bed. "Aye. I wonder why that should be so?"

Soft laughter echoed in the chamber as they drifted to sleep, Muirie pondering what awaited her at the end of their travels—when she came of age. No, when *they* came of age in just a few months would their lives alter?

Beathag's voice awakened Muirie, and she pulled the covers over her head. "Please allow me to sleep. I cannot move my legs." She moaned.

Beathag gripped the covers and slung them away from Muirie. "I have already packed your trunk and brought ye something to break your fast."

She sat bolt upright and snatched at the bed linens, Beathag unrelenting. "Ye must dress!"

"Och, leave me be." She flopped onto the bed, her gaze landing on the window. No sun shone, only blackness. "'Tis not the morn."

"Will be soon enough." She grabbed Muirie's wrists and tugged her until her feet met the cold stone floor.

Beathag practically dressed Muirie, constantly chatting about returning home, and wrapped the bannocks and cheese in a napkin to carry with them.

Between yawns and clouded eyes, Muirie said another sad farewell, this time to Sorcha, her husband, the Grants, the Lamonts, Elizabeth, and finally to Gavin. She promised to return to this lovely Highland castle.

When Gavin stood before her, she choked on tears, and he hugged her. "I will miss ye, sister. It will only be for a short time. Ye cannot be rid of me so easily."

Peader strolled by and wished Muirie a fond farewell, saying he was to go with Gavin and the Lamonts for a brief visit. Muirie held her tongue, wanting to tease him about Elizabeth.

Muirie watched the castle fade as the carriage rolled across another brae, cutting off her view, Lord Stewart riding alongside the carriage. She pulled herself from the window and met Beathag's gaze. She gave her a wan smile and laid her head against the squabs.

The gentle rocking soon sent her to a languid sleep. The carriage lurched to a stop, awakening her. She peered at a cobbled courtyard, a small inn a short distance from the carriage.

She rubbed the sleep away. "Are we to rest here?"

Grannam snorted. "Child, ye slept through two stops a'ready. We slumber here the night." The elder woman near tumbled from the carriage with energy Muirie could only hope for in that moment.

Once Lady Stewart, aided by her husband, left the carriage, Beathag took Muirie's arm and helped her to the inn. They dined and afterward, Muirie and Beathag went straight to their chamber. Grannam was the first to retire after eating and was already snoring in one of the three small beds.

"There will not be much sleep had here tonight with all that racket." Beathag's face scrunched with frustration.

Muirie hmphed. "I will have no trouble sleeping through anything."

She was true to her word and dropped into a deep slumber until Beathag woke her at sunrise.

"Why must we always depart so early?" She groaned.

Beathag shook out Muirie's dress and held it in front of her. "Lord Stewart is eager to arrive home. He said Cormac sent a missive urging us to return soon."

Muirie swallowed. "Is something amiss?"

She shrugged. "He did not say."

With little urging, Muirie hurriedly dressed, ate a few bites, and was ready for the final leg of their journey. Once again, she fell asleep immediately, and did not awaken for two of their quick stops to change horses, stretch, and eat. As soon as she settled inside the carriage, sleep overtook her again.

A bump in the road caused Muirie to wake, and she peered out the window to find they were encased in a dark grey fog. She was about to ask where they were when the main tower of Castle Deveron rose above the mist.

The carriage slowed, and in the stillness, she heard the river rushing toward the sea, bringing memories of the day they had spent there. Now alert, she realized this was the first time in two days she felt truly rested. They rolled through the eastern gate of the castle and longing surged through her to be in the garden.

As soon as the carriage stopped, one of the stable lads opened the door, and she jumped to the ground, the sweet-gale plant hugged to her chest. Tossing the words over her shoulder, she called out, "I will see ye all later. I must go to the garden."

She sucked in the pleasant scent of the nearby forest, river, and wanning flowers, embracing the freeing moment. This was home, where she belonged. It mattered not what her role was—whether ward or servant—this was *her* home. Why had it taken so long to see it?

Father, I am sorry I ever doubted Ye. I belong to Ye, first and foremost. In this journey Ye have given me my family, both by blood and by adoption. Your blessings are new every morning. Thank Ye.

Before finding the bench among the lavender she was so fond of, she chose a spot to plant Grannam's gift. With a sturdy stick, she dug in the moist earth and deposited the damp shrub, patting the earth lovingly around the base. She rinsed her hands in the burn and strolled to her bench.

Though the fog cloaked everything here in this moment, it mattered not. The birds sang to her, the scents surrounded her. This was peace.

Muirie pulled in another deep breath and tilted her head to look up at the trees shrouded in the mist, then returned to take in the cloudy landscape. A dark figure appeared from the edge of the garden, slowly moving toward her. She rose and squinted, trying to focus on the person. Mayhap it was Cormac. She brightened, happy to see her brother.

"Muirie?" A deep voice called through the haze.

Her hard swallow throbbed in her ears, and she took a tentative step toward the figure.

In one heartbreaking moment, the man strode from the mist—*Reid*.

Without a thought for propriety, she ran and flung herself into his arms.

"Muirie," he said against her hair. His rich voice pierced her with pleasure.

"Ye returned . . ."

"Aye. For ye, if ye will have me."

She brought her head back far enough to look into his welcoming eyes. "Always."

He tenderly moved a wave of hair from her temple, his warm fingers brushing her skin. "Ye have never been a nobody. From the moment we met, *I* belonged to *ye* and have been praying to discover if ye could ever belong to *me*."

Tears formed in Muirie's eyes, joy filling her. "Aye, Reid. Ye came to me through the mist and have returned the same. God brought us to one another." She drew closer to him, their lips a breath away. "Our lives were woven together then and now *and* always."

As their lips met in a tender promise, Muirie could almost see their future spread before her in brightly woven panels on the wall like those of her ancestors, woven as a testament of love and faith, one she and Reid would join with their own story, born of the mist.

THE END

Author's Note

Historical research is my addiction. I've had a love of history since elementary school, especially British history as most of my ancestry lies in the British Isles. The MacGregors are in my lineage, so I focused on them for this novel. I took a few liberties with the MacGregor persecution timeline to suit my story. While researching names, I noted Allaster MacGregor's name had different spellings, depending on the source. Various sources documented his name differently in both original public records and private collections.

The *Scots Dialect Dictionary* is a tremendous help and a lot of fun. I came across words that made me chuckle. A buttery is a butterfly—who knew?!

I was unable to locate certain details of the Battle of Glen Fruin, so I manipulated some facts and the chieftain's relatives. I have also taken liberties with the path traveled by Robert Glendinning, an itinerant Scottish Presbyterian preacher, so my characters could meet him.

The history of Freuchie Castle, later Castle Grant, is also an interesting piece of the past that may just find its way into another novel one day. I have used poetic license to tweak it to match my fictional timeline and added a few features to the castle that do not exist—one being a parapet that encircled the top of the castle for lookouts to walk the perimeter. During my research, I did not find any evidence of hidden rooms, secret compartments, or anything of this nature, so I created the private parlor belonging to Lady Grant.

As for Castle Deveron, I used Huntly Castle as my model. It is a lovely, ruined castle in Aberdeenshire, Scotland, which I have visited three times. I did change some facts about the structure.

Regarding horses, since the actual *as-the-crow-flies* distance between Huntly Castle and Slains Castle is just over 50 miles, I fudged a little and moved Huntly closer to the North Sea, so Muirie and her friends could make the round-trip trek in one day. I would not want to be accused of being cruel to the horses!

The treacle scones mentioned may be inaccurate, having come about a few years later, but they sounded so delicious I chose them to be available in my story's era. As for the green woodpecker, they are rare in Scotland and may have not been present during the time of my story. I wanted a unique laugh for Mistress Gibbs, so I gave the beautiful bird a cameo. Known by many names through the centuries, I settled on Yaffingale because it sounded more bird-like.

As for the Hidden Glen, I could not find any proof of the exact location the MacGregors hid, so I found a hidden glen and made it my own. For the journey from Freuchie Castle to the Hidden Glen, I took many liberties. There are numerous *hidden* glens in Scotland, so I chose one that possibly have been used by the MacGregors during the persecution years of the proscription.

After hours of research for the best way they would travel, I fudged a little because the information was illusive. The village of Tomatin wasn't founded until the 1800s, so I moved it back in time as it was likely they passed through there in the 1710 timeline. Also I didn't mention crossing any huge burns or lochs, so they wouldn't have to take extreme measures to go around them. The terrain being rugged in the early 1700s, I found no evidence of coaching inns, etc., so I created my own.

Being an *amateur* historian, please forgive any errors.

Thank you to all my treasured readers. I hope you have enjoyed Sorcha's and Muirie's journeys of faith.

God bless,
Carole

Enjoy *Woven in the Mist?*

Here's a preview of another novel
by Carole Lehr Johnson

The Burning Sands

Cornwall, England
September 1656

The girl's auburn hair glinted in the warm sun as she patted a handful of wet sand into a small pewter cup. A squeal of laughter brought her head up to peer at the boys running into the crashing swells. Wind caught her wild curls in a dance around her face, and at that moment, a series of waves grew in intensity. Her brother and his friend were swallowed by each pounding surge.

She held her breath until she saw her brother emerge with force, a look of fear crossing his face as he screamed, *"Nick! Nick!"*

Sebastian dove, and after a long while, resurfaced, eyes

searching for his friend. He repeated the action many times before Grace ran to the edge of the beach, the cup clutched to her chest.

Her eyes remained on the massive rock a distance from where the boys had begun their usual race. They always swam from this stretch of sand to the rock and back as a game. Nick usually won.

Time stretched with each of Sebastian's dives, always coming up with no sign of Nick. Grace screamed, tears coursing along her cheeks. "Sebastian, save him, please save Nick!"

She dropped to her knees in the damp sand as the clouds darkened like great grey beasts flying overhead, screeching a warning of the impending storm. The wind rose, and Grace's eyes stung from the salt spray. Her tears became sobs, and after a time, slender trembling arms wound around her shoulders.

Sebastian's shaking voice pleaded, "I tried, Grace—" his voice caught on gasping breaths, "—I tried," before burying his drenched head against her small shoulder.

Huge drops of stinging rain slapped them with such force they sprinted for shelter beneath the overhanging rocks by the cliffs edging their favorite beach.

Grace would never remember it as such again.

Chapter One

Louisiana
April 2022

The news hadn't come from a uniformed stranger.

Olivia Griffin opened the door to a bright spring day of blooming daffodils and the scent of lavender, a mild breeze playing with her hair. Her husband's closest friend, Sam, and his cousin, Billy, stood on her doorstep. Sam clutched the strap of a brown backpack slung over his shoulder.

The moment her eyes took in the bag and the pain on the men's faces the force of its meaning buckled her knees.

Reliving that surreal day came upon her with force like standing outside her present surroundings as a sad, unemotional bystander. She had sagged against the doorframe, Billy reaching out to steady her, his hoarse words still echoing in her mind.

"Livi, I am so sorry."

Olivia gripped the mug tightly, heat permeating her aching hands. Her sorting and packing became a welcomed frenzy of activity. Anything to occupy her mind.

The chirping phone intruded on her thoughts.

"Hello." Her mother's cheerful voice now a new irritant. What was happening to her?

Olivia steeled herself for the forthcoming speech.

She attempted to sound as light-hearted as the caller. "Good morning, Mom. How are you today?"

"Splendid, dear, just splendid." Her mother coughed. "This is the most marvelous spring day. I hope you plan on getting outside for a while. Maybe putter around in your lovely garden."

Olivia almost laughed. It had not been a *lovely* garden since Ian . . .

She pulled in a fortifying breath. "Yes, Mom . . . I . . ." A knock at the door halted the excuse she was about to give. "Sorry. Someone's here. I'll call you later. Love you." She punched the button to end the call and sprinted for the door, guilt hitting her more than she'd felt in a while.

The petite blonde bounced across the threshold, her arms filled with containers of takeaway. The scent trailing her through the air elicited a growl from Olivia's stomach. She'd not stopped for breakfast, and when she glanced at the clock on the mantle, she noticed it was well past lunch.

"Come on, you slug." Angie turned and looked at Olivia. "You haven't eaten all day, have you?"

Olivia slumped into a chair at the table, pulled a drink

toward her, and sipped. "You know me too well, Angie Timmons."

Angie huffed. "*Too well.*" She sat across from Olivia and retrieved her own drink. "How's the tea? Did they get it right this time?" She sent her longtime friend a playful smirk, then glanced around the room at the stacks of boxes.

"I know. I meant to take those to the thrift store days ago." Olivia dropped her chin to her chest. "It's just so hard."

Angie patted her hand but said nothing for several moments.

"Guess I'll have to take the bull by the horns, or in this case, the bullheaded friend by the hand."

Olivia lifted her head. "How so?"

"After we eat, we'll load it up, and I'll take it myself. That way, you don't have to witness its departure. As long as you have it in front of you, you'll continue to grieve." She lowered her voice. "It's been over a year."

Olivia's eyes stung, and she dropped her gaze to her left hand. The deep pink, Asscher-cut diamond winked at her from the midday sun glinting through the kitchen window. Again, painful memories caused her emotions to cut more deeply each time they resurfaced.

She crossed her forearms on the table and rested her head on them, her shoulders quaking. A chair scraping across the tile floor brought her head up to see Angie come to her side and kneel beside the chair.

Angie rested her hands on her thighs, not touching Olivia. With tears in her eyes, she said, "Livi, I think there are too many memories here."

She opened her mouth to speak, but Angie held a hand up, palm out. "No. Say nothing until you hear me out." She exhaled, then continued, "I'm not suggesting you forget Ian. Just try to go forward with your life. You are young." She laughed and bumped her shoulder against Olivia's. "*We're* young. After all, we've only been out of college for twenty years."

Olivia sniffled. "Twenty-two years, my friend."

Angie sneered. "Twenty sounds better." She lifted her brow. "Anyway, you need a serious change of scenery. Sell the house."

Olivia's eyes widened, and her back stiffened.

"Okay, okay. Rent it out for a while. You can put your stuff in storage and travel."

"Well . . . I don't know." The thought had not occurred to her since she now had full control of her life. Half of herself was *gone*. The love of her life no longer existed. How could she ever recover from that?

Ian had been a wonderful man—a wonderful husband— except for one thing they could never get past.

She heard Angie speaking, but it was as if from far away like the PA system in an airport paging someone who wasn't paying attention.

Olivia refocused at the mention of her great-grandmother. "Excuse me? What were you saying about my grandmother?"

"Your *great*-grandmother. Didn't you say she was from England and your great-grandfather served there during the war and that's how they met?"

Olivia's mind reeled.

"Yes, my great-grandmother was from a small fishing village in Cornwall on the east coast along the English Channel."

Angie rose, groaned, and staggered back to her seat. "Yeah, twenty-two years for sure."

They shared a laugh as Angie slid a plate toward Olivia. "Eat up while I convince you to go to Cornwall."

CB&SO

Olivia waved to her friend as she backed her brilliant blue SUV out of the driveway, loaded with the boxes of Ian's life. She swallowed back tears. She would live again and would wish the same for him.

Trudging into the house, she looked at the few remaining containers. It had taken her six months to go through his belongings, sorting them into stacks of items his family may want, items to go to charity, or what she would keep—mostly photograph albums full of memories that mere objects could not convey—except for the collection of tiny seashells.

Their first trip together was their honeymoon, which they spent in the Caribbean. They walked the beach early every morning, the sun blazing orange and yellow with slashes of a near purple backdrop, searching for shells to take home. She could almost smell the salty air, hear the gulls screeching overhead as the sun rose above the sparkling water. They walked hand-in-hand until one of them spotted a prize, kneeling in the cool, wet sand. Each time they repeated the ritual, it ended in a kiss.

Later, in a souvenir shop, Olivia found a miniature crystal box and discovered the tiny shells fit perfectly. This one item now graced her desk, so she could look at it as she sketched or painted.

Since Ian's death, she had found solace in her work, although she had given up her nine-to-five job creating art for a company that designed greeting cards and devotional covers. After the initial shock wore off, she began branching out with her creativity, knowing that she was the only one who would see it. Creating occupied her mind while taking her thoughts away from her husband.

The phone jangled, an intrusion to her thoughts. She picked it up and saw her grandmother's name.

"Hi, Grandma." She grinned, imagining the round, smiling face, always full of genuine happiness.

"Hello, love. How are you this evening?"

"I'm doing very well. And you?"

"Other than this arthritis, I'm brilliant." She giggled like a schoolgirl, and Olivia imagined she was most likely multi-tasking while they chatted. Her grandmother was a conundrum of epic proportions. One of her favorite sayings was, 'There is no logic in idleness.'

"Grandma, what are you doing right now—other than speaking with me?" She laughed.

"Well, my dear, I am baking your grandpa a batch of blueberry scones. Why?"

"No reason. I just like picturing you multi-tasking. It encourages me."

Grandma Knox tittered, "That is so sweet of you, dear. I believe God wants us to make the most of the time He gives us on this earth. Talking on the phone is not a burden, so why shouldn't I be doing something else while I chat? There aren't enough hours in the day after all."

"Yes, Grandma. You *are* right." Olivia paused, Angie's talk of her great-grandmother's life in Cornwall prompting her. "Grandma?"

The familiar sound of the oven door closing reminded Olivia of the countless sugar cookies she'd eaten in that kitchen.

"Yes, love."

She visualized her grandmother's pursed lips as she cleaned the kitchen while the scones baked.

"Would you be available for a *visitor* and go through my great-grandmother's mementos?"

Her grandmother cleared her throat. "Certainly. Give me a bit of notice and I'll make you breakfast, lunch, or dinner—or all three, if you'll stay a day or so."

The offer settled in Olivia's mind. A couple of days at her grandparents' house in the country might be what she needed. She no longer had any obligations. No job. Ian had made sure she was well taken care of. Her heart clenched, but before the tears came, she simply said, "I may just take you up on that." She switched her phone to speaker and began searching her calendar. Nothing for the next couple of weeks.

"What are your plans for the next few days?"

"Nothing of note. We have a church picnic on Saturday. You could come with us and see some old friends. How lovely!"

Olivia's gaze traveled to one of the framed photos on the bookshelf across the room. Her grandparents stood next to her and Ian while on a family vacation in the mountains about five years before. Her mother had taken the picture. It was an enjoyable week away, and Ian had promised he would do none of his extreme sports while there—no river rafting, mountain climbing, or hang gliding.

The trip had been good for her mother as well since her father died the previous winter. That getaway pulled her through. Her mother had not been as fortunate in marriage as Olivia. She refused to recall those memories. It was much too painful because it also brought back what else had been missing from her marriage—children. Fear of Ian dying and leaving her with children to care for alone was too great a risk.

"All right. I'll be there tomorrow afternoon."

They hung up with air kisses and goodbyes, and Olivia felt lighter than she had in a long time. Maybe Angie was right. Getting away, putting some distance between her memories of Ian, could help her move on.

ଓଽ

Olivia stretched lazily, awakening to a fully risen sun. She'd intended to take a turn on her treadmill before leaving, but she decided to forgo it for a light breakfast, a strong cup of tea, and Bible study.

Within two hours she settled behind the wheel of her mid-sized sedan, cruise-control set as she glided along I-55 toward the hilly, green countryside of north Louisiana. Even though she did not live in the crowded center of New Orleans, her little suburban world teemed with people, shopping, industry, and chaos.

At the mere hint of a hurricane, she and Ian shot north to

her grandparents' house. Since her mother lived a couple of hours east of them, they would make it a habit of taking the long way back for an overnight stay.

The day was so mild, the cloudless bluebird sky hovering overhead, lifting her spirits. She turned on music and listened to her favorite movie score. The series was filmed in Cornwall several years before, and the music took her to the rugged Cornish coast of her ancestry.

Angie had hit on something with her suggestion of ancestry and travel—even if Olivia wasn't yet convinced to go anywhere. She had, however, packed her passport and genealogy research just in case.

After a brief stop to grab a snack to get her by until she arrived for one of her grandmother's delicious lunches, Olivia forced her thoughts to Cornwall. Maybe she should take a trip to see where her great-grandparents met.

The closer she got to the small town, dark grey clouds gathered, and light sprinkles flecked her windshield. Slowing to turn into the long drive leading to the square white house upon a slight rise, she noticed a few daffodils peeking above the grass in a circle around the mailbox post. The yellow buds reached toward the rain, drinking in what the sun would soon dry up.

She parked behind her grandfather's dented and scratched old red truck. The front door of the house swung wide, and her short, stout grandmother sprinted down the steps. Susan Knox was a marvel at eighty-one. As she would say, "There are no flies on your old grandmother!"

No, the flies wouldn't dare. She was too quick for them.

"Livi, my girl!" Elderly but strong arms encircled her in a hug. "It's so nice to see you." She pushed Olivia back. "You are much too thin. We'll have to fatten you up in the brief time you'll be with us."

A tall, steel-grey haired man took a slower descent from the porch, holding onto the railings and making his way to repeat the solid hug. "She's right, you know? You look a tad thin."

Olivia placed a kiss on his cheek. "Oh, Grandpa. I eat just fine."

"That's not what Angie said."

She started. "You've been speaking with her?"

Grandma Knox jerked when the door squeaked open. "Oh, my. Billy, I quite forgot you were still with us. Come see Livi."

Olivia watched Ian's cousin move lithely down the steps, his shirt sleeves rolled up to reveal tan, muscular arms—much like Ian's. They had both inherited the same olive complexion of their ancestors who had lived in the south of France for generations, departing for New Orleans with the first French settlers over three hundred years ago.

Her breath caught at his resemblance to Ian.

She'd forgotten how much they looked alike. Perhaps her hasty decision to come had not been thought out enough. Billy living next door had never entered her thoughts. She pulled in a shaky breath and willed herself to remain calm.

"Hello, Billy." She extended her hand.

He took it and placed an arm around her, pulling her into a side-hug. "It's so good to see you, Livi. I haven't seen you since—well, since the funeral." He dropped her hand but kept his arm around her shoulders. "I stopped by to look at your grandfather's clunker." He pointed to the beat-up truck. "And they told me you would be here soon. I wanted to stay and tell you, again, how sorry I am about Ian."

She avoided his gaze. "Thank you. That's very kind."

Grandpa Knox glared at Billy. "That *old clunker* was built before you were born, my boy, and it'll likely still be running after you're gone." His tone was gruff, but Olivia knew the humor behind those amber eyes.

Olivia moved from Billy's hold and took her grandfather's arm, looking up into his wrinkled face. "You are an old marshmallow, Grandpa. I think you love that ancient truck more than you do any of us." She tugged his arm and pulled him to the house. "Come on. I'm starving for Grandma's massive lunch."

Her grandmother took her husband's other arm but glanced over her shoulder. "Billy, come along. You'll be eating with us, my love."

Billy shook his head. "Mrs. Knox, I don't think I'll ever get used to anyone calling me that." He laughed.

Grandpa Knox chimed in. "I won't either, Billy. She got that from her *mum*. It's meant to be an affectionate greeting for men or women, not romantic."

Billy shrugged, but even his olive skin couldn't hide the blush tinting his cheeks.

Ian would've turned it into a joke. Billy was more laidback and easygoing than Ian. Although their personalities were quite different, everyone liked them equally. She warmed toward him in that moment, her tension easing at finding him at her grandparents, allowing the connection between him and Ian to fade.

Olivia asked Billy how he and his family were doing and made small talk as they enjoyed the tender, delicious roast and vegetables her grandmother prepared. Compliments flew across the table as they consumed the mouthwatering meal.

After dessert of fresh apple pie and ice cream, they each groaned with varying degrees of fullness and stood to adjourn to the screened-in back porch overlooking the small lake surrounded by weeping willow trees.

Billy stood. "Thank you, but I really need to get back to work." He patted his flat stomach. "Although I don't know how much I'll be able to do with this load I'm now carrying on board."

Olivia's grandmother laughed. "Go on. As thin as you are and as hard as you work, you'll have that lunch worked off this very afternoon."

Billy eased his chair under the table. "I thank you, ma'am, but I'm not taking any chances. I can't do a thing about getting older, but I can avoid putting on extra pounds."

He slapped Grandpa Knox on the shoulder. "Here's a good example. Fit as can be."

The elder man returned the slap and grinned. "Kind of you to say, son. But these old bones aren't what they used to be."

"Couldn't tell it by looking, sir." Billy strode to Olivia. "Livi, it was a pleasure seeing you again. If you're staying a few days, maybe we can go get a cup of coffee or something."

It was her turn to blush at the invitation. She glanced at the floor and then met his eyes. "All right, Billy. Perhaps."

He walked toward the door with her grandfather following,

chatting about the truck.

"Come along, love. I have tea waiting on the porch." She took Olivia's arm and drew her alongside, chatting cheerfully as they walked.

Olivia picked up a cup of tea and sat facing the water. Long shadows of the drooping trees rippled across the lake, a pleasant breeze sending them into a slow dance.

She loved the soothing aura of this place. Why had she not come back after Ian—*left*? Was it the long drive alone?

Ian had always said that it was the perfect time for them to discuss plans whether about a vacation, household projects, or the latest books they'd read. One of the many wonderful things about their marriage was all the things they had in common. Reading was something they shared—not always the same genre—but they enjoyed discussing plots, characters, scenes . . .

Tears welled, and she averted her gaze so her grandmother could not see them. She sipped her tea and cleared her throat.

"Grandma, when will we dive into my great-grandmother's life? I'm eager to get started." She chuckled. "After all, I don't think I'll be wanting dinner this evening after that enormous lunch."

"I understand. Your grandfather likes it when I make roast. He'll just want a sandwich tonight. Says there's nothing better than a thick roast beef sandwich." Her gaze shifted to the lake, a wistful gleam in her eyes.

Olivia straightened. "Are you well?"

"Oh yes, love. I remembered the first time I made him a nice roast. Well, it was nice but a bit on the chewy side. He never complained. I did some cookbook research after that and have made them perfect ever since." She reached out and patted Olivia's hand.

Olivia nodded with a tender smile. She and Ian had loved to cook together. Their synergy was incredible. Everything about their marriage was incredible—except his need for danger. A slow burning sensation began in her stomach and wound upward to her heart. His love of extreme sports had taken him from her.

The tears flowed too fast and free, and she clenched her eyes tight to staunch the flow, but it didn't work.

A warm hand cupped her shoulder, her grandmother's arm draped around her. "Oh, my love. I am so very sorry."

They sat this way for some moments, Olivia's sobs shaking them both.

"Oh . . . Gr—Grandma! I'm so angry with him. If he had stopped all the insane sports, he'd be with me now. I love him. I miss him!"

Grandma Knox wrapped both arms around Olivia and rested her head on her granddaughter's. "I know . . . I know."

Olivia remained in the comforting embrace until her grandfather returned from seeing Billy off and interjected, "What the devil is going on here?"

His gruff tone snapped them to attention. Olivia wiped the tears away with the back of her hand while her grandmother stood, moved to a small table, and retrieved a box of tissues.

She snatched a tissue and dabbed at her eyes before handing the box to Olivia and facing her husband. "Ben, why are you being so surly? Can't you see the girl is broken?"

He crossed his arms over his chest and sent them both a stern look. "It's not my intention, but it's about time you move forward, Livi." He pulled in a long breath and slowly released it, his voice softer when he spoke again. "You have mourned Ian for over a year. I understand you had an exceptionally good marriage. A godly marriage. But God would not want you to give up your future. Ian is with Him. You will see him again, but you need to *live* in the present."

The tall man dropped into a chair and put his elbows on his knees, letting his hands dangle. "Livi, Ian didn't die on purpose just to leave you. He was *living*. Those sports he loved were a part of him." He leaned back, and his gaze bored into hers. "If you had made him choose, how long do you think it would've been before it divided the two of you?"

She blinked, tears blurring her grandfather's face. A sharp pang gripped her chest. An epiphany condemned her. Was she still grieving because she was blaming Ian for his absence?

Olivia wiped her eyes. "I love you both, but I need to be alone. To think." On slow, unsteady legs, she left the porch.

She heard their muffled voices as she climbed the stairs to her room. The room she and Ian had always settled in when they visited. It had been her room from the time she was born.

Her grandparents made it hers. She felt at home there—more so than her own home now. Her mind whirled at her grandfather's declaration.

Maybe he was right, but no one else had the courage to tell her so. Angie had said things that pointed in that direction but not so forcefully. She could see the pain in his amber eyes as he forced himself to be honest. But could she be honest with herself?

About the Author

Carole Lehr Johnson is a veteran travel consultant of more than 30 years and has served as head of genealogy at her local library.

Her love of tea and scones, castles and cottages, and all things British has led her to immerse her writing in the United Kingdom whether in the genre of historical or contemporary fiction.

Carole is the author of inspirational novels and novellas set in the U.K. Her novel, A Place in Time, was a Notable Book Award finalist at the Southern Christian Writers Conference (SCWC), and her short story, The Light in the Mist, won first place in the short story category of the SCWC's Writing Awards. She is a member of the American Christian Fiction Writers (ACFW) and served as her local chapter's president. She and her husband live in Louisiana with their goofy cats.

For more information, visit
www.carolelehrjohnson.com

Sign up for Carole's newsletter on her website for her next releases, reviews, U.K. travels & more.

Books by Carole Lehr Johnson

NOVELS

Permelia Cottage

A Place in Time

The Burning Sands

Of the Past and Eternity

Woven in the Mist

NOVELLAS

Christmas at Permelia Cottage

SPECIAL COLLECTIONS

Seasons of the Past